WILBUR SMITH

THE DARK OF THE SUN

PAN BOOKS

This book is for my wife
Mokhiniso
who is the best thing
that has ever happened to me.

First published in Great Britain 1965

This edition published 2007 by Pan Books
an imprint of Pan Macmillan, a division of Macmillan Publishers Limited
Pan Macmillan, 20 New Wharf Road, London N1 9RR
Basingstoke and Oxford
Associated companies throughout the world
www.panmacmillan.com

ISBN 978-0-330-45492-6

5 7 9 8 6

A CIP catalogue record for this book is available from the British Library.

Typeset by SetSystems Ltd, Saffron Walden, Essex
Printed and bound by CPI Group (UK) Ltd, Croydon, CR0 4YY

THE DARK OF THE SUN

Wilbur Smith was born in Central Africa in 1933. He was educated at Michaelhouse and Rhodes University.

He became a full-time writer in 1964 after the successful publication of *When the Lion Feeds*, and has written thirty novels, all meticulously researched on his numerous expeditions worldwide. His books are now translated into twenty-six languages.

THE NOVELS OF WILBUR SMITH

The Courtneys

When the Lion Feeds The Sound of Thunder
A Sparrow Falls Birds of Prey Monsoon
Blue Horizon The Triumph of the Sun

The Courtneys Of Africa

The Burning Shore Power of the Sword Rage
A Time to Die Golden Fox Assegai

The Ballantyne Novels

A Falcon Flies Men of Men The Angels Weep
The Leopard Hunts in Darkness

The Egyptian Novels

River God The Seventh Scroll
Warlock The Quest

Also

The Dark of the Sun Shout at the Devil
Gold Mine The Diamond Hunters
The Sunbird Eagle in the Sky
The Eye of the Tiger Cry Wolf
Hungry as the Sea Wild Justice
Elephant Song Those in Peril

– 1 –

'I don't like the idea,' announced Wally Hendry, and belched. He moved his tongue round his mouth getting the taste of it before he went on. 'I think the whole idea stinks like a ten-day corpse.' He lay sprawled on one of the beds with a glass balanced on his naked chest and he was sweating heavily in the Congo heat.

'Unfortunately your opinion doesn't alter the fact that we are going.' Bruce Curry went on laying out his shaving tackle without looking up.

'You shoulda told them to keep it, told them we were staying here in Elisabethville – why didn't you tell them that, hey?' Hendry picked up his glass and swallowed the contents.

'Because they pay me not to argue.' Bruce spoke without interest and looked at himself in the fly-spotted mirror above the washbasin. The face that looked back was sun-darkened with a cap of close-cropped black hair; soft hair that would be unruly and inclined to curl if it were longer. Black eyebrows slanting upwards at the corners, green eyes with a heavy fringe of lashes and a mouth which could smile as readily as it could sulk. Bruce regarded his good looks without pleasure. It was a long time since he had felt that emotion, a long time since his mouth had either smiled or sulked. He did not feel the old tolerant affection for his nose, the large slightly hooked nose that rescued his face from prettiness and gave him the air of a genteel pirate.

'Jesus!' growled Wally Hendry from the bed. 'I've had just about a gutsful of this nigger army. I don't mind fighting

– but I don't fancy going hundreds of miles out into the bush to play nursemaid to a bunch of bloody refugees.'

'It's a hell of a life,' agreed Bruce absently and spread shaving-soap on his face. The lather was very white against his tan. Under a skin that glowed so healthily that it appeared to have been freshly oiled, the muscles of his shoulders and chest changed shape as he moved. He was in good condition, fitter than he had been for many years, but this fact gave him no more pleasure than had his face.

'Get me another drink, André.' Wally Hendry thrust his empty glass into the hand of the man who sat on the edge of the bed.

The Belgian stood up and went across to the table obediently.

'More whisky and less beer in this one,' Wally instructed, turned once more to Bruce and belched again. 'That's what I think of the idea.'

As André poured Scotch whisky into the glass and filled it with beer Wally hitched around the pistol in its webbing holster until it hung between his legs.

'When are we leaving?' he asked.

'There'll be an engine and five coaches at the goods yard first thing tomorrow morning. We'll load up and get going as soon as possible.' Bruce started to shave, drawing the razor down from temple to chin and leaving the skin smooth and brown behind it.

'After three months of fighting a bunch of greasy little Gurkhas I was looking forward to a bit of fun – I haven't even had a pretty in all that time – now the second day after the ceasefire and they ship us out again.'

'C'est la guerre,' muttered Bruce, his face twisted in the act of shaving.

'What's that mean?' demanded Wally suspiciously.

'That's war,' Bruce translated.

'Talk English, Bucko.'

It was the measure of Wally Hendry that after six months

in the Belgian Congo he could neither speak nor understand a single word of French.

There was silence again, broken only by the scraping of Bruce's razor and the small metallic sound as the fourth man in the hotel room stripped and cleaned his FN rifle.

'Have a drink, Haig,' Wally invited him.

'No, thanks.' Michael Haig glanced up, not trying to conceal his distaste as he looked at Wally.

'You're another snotty bastard – don't want to drink with me, hey? Even the high-class Captain Curry is drinking with me. What makes you so goddam special?'

'You know that I don't drink.' Haig turned his attention back to his weapon, handling it with easy familiarity. For all of them the ugly automatic rifles had become an extension of their own bodies. Even while shaving Bruce had only to drop his hand to reach the rifle propped against the wall, and the two men on the bed had theirs on the floor beside them.

'You don't drink!' chuckled Wally. 'Then how did you get that complexion, Bucko? How come your nose looks like a ripe plum?'

Haig's mouth tightened and the hands on his rifle stilled.

'Cut it out, Wally,' said Bruce without heat.

'Haig don't drink,' crowed Wally, and dug the little Belgian in the ribs with his thumb, 'get that, André! He's a tee-bloody-total! My old man was a teetotal also; sometimes for two, three months at a time he was teetotal, and then he'd come home one night and sock the old lady in the clock so you could hear her teeth rattle from across the street.'

His laughter choked him and he had to wait for it to clear before he went on.

'My bet is that you're that kind of teetotal, Haig. One drink and you wake up ten days later; that's it, isn't it? One drink and – pow! – the old girl gets it in the chops and the kids don't eat for a couple of weeks.'

Haig laid the rifle down carefully on the bed and looked at Wally with his jaws clenched, but Wally had not noticed. He went on happily.

'André, take the whisky bottle and hold it under Old Teetotal Haig's nose. Let's watch him slobber at the mouth and his eyes stand out like a pair of dog's balls.'

Haig stood up. Twice the age of Wally – a man in his middle fifties, with grey in his hair and the refinement of his features not completely obliterated by the marks that life had left upon them. He had arms like a boxer and a powerful set to his shoulders. 'It's about time you learned a few manners, Hendry. Get on your feet.'

'You wanta dance or something? I don't waltz – ask André. He'll dance with you – won't you, André?'

Haig was balanced on the balls of his feet, his hands closed and raised slightly. Bruce Curry placed his razor on the shelf above the basin, and moved quietly round the table with soap still on his face to take up a position from which he could intervene. There he waited, watching the two men.

'Get up, you filthy guttersnipe.'

'Hey, André, get that. He talks pretty, hey? He talks real pretty.'

'I'm going to smash that ugly face of yours right into the middle of the place where your brain should have been.'

'Jokes! This boy is a natural comic.' Wally laughed, but there was something wrong with the sound of it. Bruce knew then that Wally was not going to fight. Big arms and swollen chest covered with ginger hair, belly flat and hard-looking, thick-necked below the wide flat-featured face with its little Mongolian eyes; but Wally wasn't going to fight. Bruce was puzzled: he remembered the night at the road bridge and he knew that Hendry was no coward, and yet now he was not going to take up Haig's challenge.

Mike Haig moved towards the bed.

'Leave him, Mike.' André spoke for the first time, his

voice soft as a girl's. 'He was only joking. He didn't mean it.'

'Hendry, don't think I'm too much of a gentleman to hit you because you're on your back. Don't make that mistake.'

'Big deal,' muttered Wally. 'This boy's not only a comic, he's a bloody hero also.'

Haig stood over him and lifted his right hand with the fist, bunched like a hammer, aimed at Wally's face.

'Haig!' Bruce hadn't raised his voice but its tone checked the older man.

'That's enough,' said Bruce.

'But this filthy little—'

'Yes, I know,' said Bruce. 'Leave him!' With his fist still up Mike Haig hesitated, and there was no movement in the room. Above them the corrugated iron roof popped loudly as it expanded in the heat of the Congo midday, and the only other sound was Haig's breathing. He was panting and his face was congested with blood.

'Please, Mike,' whispered André. 'He didn't mean it.'

Slowly Haig's anger changed to disgust and he dropped his hand, turned away and picked up his rifle from the other bed.

'I can't stand the smell in this room another minute. I'll wait for you in the truck downstairs, Bruce.'

'I won't be long,' agreed Bruce as Mike went to the door.

'Don't push your luck, Haig,' Wally called after him. 'Next time you won't get off so easily.'

In the doorway Mike Haig swung quickly, but, with a hand on his shoulder, Bruce turned him again.

'Forget it, Mike,' he said, and closed the door after him.

'He's just bloody lucky that he's an old man,' growled Wally. 'Otherwise I'd have fixed him good.'

'Sure,' said Bruce. 'It was decent of you to let him go.' The soap had dried on his face and he wet his brush to lather again.

'Yeah, I couldn't hit an old bloke like that, could I?'

'No.' Bruce smiled a little. 'But don't worry, you frightened the hell out of him. He won't try it again.'

'He'd better not!' warned Hendry. 'Next time I'll kill the old bugger.'

No, you won't, thought Bruce, you'll back down again as you have just done, as you've done a dozen times before. Mike and I are the only ones who can make you do it; in the same way as an animal will growl at its trainer but cringe away when he cracks the whip. He began shaving again.

The heat in the room was unpleasant to breathe; it drew the perspiration out of them and the smell of their bodies blended sourly with stale cigarette smoke and liquor fumes.

'Where are you and Mike going?' André ended the long silence.

'We're going to see if we can draw the supplies for this trip. If we have any luck we'll take them down to the goods yard and have Ruffy put an armed guard on them overnight,' Bruce answered him, leaning over the basin and splashing water up into his face.

'How long will we be away?'

Bruce shrugged. 'A week – ten days'. He sat on his bed and pulled on one of his jungle boots. 'That is, if we don't have any trouble.'

'Trouble, Bruce?' asked André.

'From Msapa Junction we'll have to go two hundred miles through country crawling with Baluba.'

'But we'll be in a train,' protested André. 'They've only got bows and arrows, they can't touch us.'

'André, there are seven rivers to cross – one big one – and bridges are easily destroyed. Rails can be torn up.' Bruce began to lace the boot. 'I don't think it's going to be a Sunday school picnic.'

'Christ. I think the whole thing stinks,' repeated Wally moodily. 'Why are we going anyway?'

'Because,' Bruce began patiently, 'for the last three

months the entire population of Port Reprieve has been cut off from the rest of the world. There are women and children with them. They are fast running out of food and the other necessities of life.' Bruce paused to light a cigarette, and then went on talking as he exhaled. 'All around them the Baluba tribe is in open revolt, burning, raping and killing indiscriminately. As yet they haven't attacked the town but it won't be very long until they do. Added to which there are rumours that rebel groups of Central Congolese troops and of our own forces have formed themselves into bands of heavily-armed *shufta*. They also are running amok through the northern part of the territory. Nobody knows for certain what is happening out there, but whatever it is you can be sure it's not very pretty. We are going to fetch those people in to safety.'

'Why don't the U.N. people send out a plane?' asked André.

'No landing field.'

'Helicopters?'

'Out of range.'

'For my money the bastards can stay there,' grunted Wally. 'If the Balubas fancy a little man steak, who are we to do them out of a meal? Every man's entitled to eat and as long as it's not me they're eating, more power to their teeth, say I.' He placed his foot against André back and straightened his leg suddenly, throwing the Belgian off the bed on to his knees.

'Go and get me a pretty.'

'There aren't any, Wally. I'll get you another drink.' André scrambled to his feet and reached for Wally's empty glass, but Wally's hand dropped on to his wrist.

'I said *pretty*, André, not *drink*.'

'I don't know where to find them, Wally.' André's voice was desperate. 'I don't know what to say to them even.'

'You're being stupid, Bucko. I might have to break your arm.' Wally twisted the wrist slowly. 'You know as well as I do that the bar downstairs is full of them. You know that, don't you?'

'But what do I say to them?' André's face was contorted with the pain of his twisted wrist.

'Oh, for Christ's sake, you stupid bloody frog-eater – just go down and flash a banknote. You don't have to say a dicky bird.'

'You're hurting me, Wally.'

'No? You're kidding!' Wally smiled at him, twisting harder, his slitty eyes smoky from the liquor, and Bruce could see he was enjoying it. 'Are you going, Bucko? Make up your mind – get me a pretty or get yourself a broken arm.'

'All right, if that's what you want. I'll go. Please leave me, I'll go,' mumbled André.

'That's what I want.' Wally released him, and he straightened up massaging his wrist.

'See that she's clean and not too old. You hear me?'

'Yes, Wally. I'll get one.' André went to the door and Bruce noticed his expression. It was stricken beyond the pain of a bruised wrist. What lovely creatures they are, thought Bruce, and I am one of them and yet apart from them. I am the watcher, stirred by them as much as I would be by a bad play. André went out.

'Another drink, Bucko?' said Wally expansively. 'I'll even pour you one.'

'Thanks,' said Bruce, and started on the other boot. Wally brought the glass to him and he tasted it. It was strong, and the mustiness of the whisky was ill-matched with the sweetness of the beer, but he drank it.

'You and I,' said Wally, 'we're the shrewd ones. We drink 'cause we want to, not 'cause we have to. We live like we want to live, not like other people think we should. You and I got a lot in common, Bruce. We should be friends, you and I. I mean us being so much alike.' The drink was working in him now, blurring his speech a little.

'Of course we are friends – I count you as one of my very dearest, Wally.' Bruce spoke solemnly, no trace of sarcasm showing.

'No kidding?' Wally asked earnestly. 'How's that, hey? Christ, I always thought you didn't like me. Christ, you never can tell, isn't that right? You just never can tell,' shaking his head in wonder, suddenly sentimental with the whisky. 'That's really true? You like me. Yeah, we could be buddies. How's that, Bruce? Every guy needs a buddy. Every guy needs a back stop.'

'Sure,' said Bruce. 'We're buddies. How's that, hey?'

'That's on, Bucko!' agreed Wally with deep feeling, *and I feel nothing*, thought Bruce, *no disgust, no pity – nothing. That way you are secure; they cannot disappoint you, they cannot disgust you, they cannot sicken you, they cannot smash you up again.*

They both looked up as André ushered the girl into the room. She had a sexy little pug face, painted lips – ruby on amber.

'Well done, André,' applauded Wally, looking at the girl's body. She wore high heels and a short pink dress that flared into a skirt from her waist but did not cover her knees.

'Come here, cookie.' Wally held out his hand to her and she crossed the room without hesitation, smiling a bright professional smile. Wally drew her down beside him on to the bed.

André went on standing in the doorway. Bruce got up and shrugged into his camouflage battle-jacket, buckled on his webbing belt and adjusted the holstered pistol until it hung comfortably on his outer thigh.

'Are you going?' Wally was feeding the girl from his glass.

'Yes.' Bruce put his slouch hat on his head; the red, green and white Katangese sideflash gave him an air of artificial gaiety.

'Stay a little – come on, Bruce.'

'Mike is waiting for me.' Bruce picked up his rifle.

'Muck him. Stay a little, we'll have some fun.'

'No, thanks.' Bruce went to the door.

'Hey, Bruce. Take a look at this.' Wally tipped the girl backwards over the bed, he pinned her with one arm across her chest while she struggled playfully and with the other hand he swept her skirt up above her waist.

'Take a good look at this and tell me you still want to go!'

The girl was naked under the skirt, her lower body shaven so that her plump little sex pouted sulkily.

'Come on, Bruce,' laughed Wally. 'You first. Don't say I'm not your buddy.'

Bruce glanced at the girl, her legs scissored and her body wriggled as she fought with Wally. She was giggling.

'Mike and I will be back before curfew. I want this woman out of here by then,' said Bruce.

There is no desire, he thought as he looked at her, *that is all finished*. He opened the door.

'Curry!' shouted Wally. 'You're a bloody nut also. Christ, I thought you were a man. Jesus Christ! You're as bad as the others. André, the doll boy. Haig, the rummy. What's with you, Bucko? It's women with you, isn't it? You're a bloody nut-case also!'

Bruce closed the door and stood alone in the passage. The taunt had gone through a chink in his armour and he clamped his mind down on the sting of it, smothering it.

It's all over. She can't hurt me any more. He thought with determination, remembering her, the woman, not the one in the room he had just left but the other one who had been his wife.

'The bitch,' he whispered, and then quickly, almost guiltily, 'I do not hate her. There is no hatred and there is no desire.'

– 2 –

The lobby of the Hotel Grand Leopold II was crowded. There were gendarmes carrying their weapons ostentatiously, talking loudly, lolling against walls and over the bar; women with them, varying in colour from black through to pastel brown, some already drunk; a few Belgians still with the stunned disbelieving eyes of the refugee, one of the women crying as she rocked her child on her lap; other white men in civilian clothes but with the alertness about them and the quick restless eyes of the adventurer, talking quietly with Africans in business suits; a group of journalists at one table in damp shirtsleeves, waiting and watching with the patience of vultures. And everybody sweated in the heat.

Two South African charter pilots hailed Bruce from across the room.

'Hi, Bruce. How about a snort?'

'Dave. Carl.' Bruce waved. 'Big hurry now – tonight perhaps.'

'We're flying out this afternoon.' Carl Engelbrecht shook his head. 'Back next week.'

'We'll make it then,' Bruce agreed, and went out of the front door into the Avenue du Kasai. As he stopped on the sidewalk the white-washed buildings bounced the glare into his face. The naked heat made him wince and he felt fresh sweat start out of his body beneath his battle-suit. He took the dark glasses from his top pocket and put them on as he crossed the street to the Chev three-tonner in which Mike Haig waited.

'I'll drive, Mike.'

'Okay.' Mike slid across the seat and Bruce stepped up into the cab. He started the truck north down the Avenue du Kasai.

'Sorry about that scene, Bruce.'

'No harm done.'

'I shouldn't have lost my temper like that.'

Bruce did not answer, he was looking at the deserted buildings on either side. Most of them had been looted and all of them were pock-marked with shrapnel from the mortar bursts. At intervals along the sidewalk were parked the burnt out bodies of automobiles looking like the carapaces of long-dead beetles.

'I shouldn't have let him get through to me, and yet the truth hurts like hell.'

Bruce was silent but he trod down harder on the accelerator and the truck picked up speed. *I don't want to hear*, he thought, *I am not your confessor – I just don't want to hear*. He turned into the Avenue l'Etoile, headed towards the zoo.

'He was right, he had me measured to the inch,' persisted Mike.

'We've all got our troubles, otherwise we wouldn't be here.' And then, to change Mike's mood, 'We few, we happy few. We band of brothers.'

Mike grinned and his face was suddenly boyish. 'At least we have the distinction of following the second oldest profession – we, the mercenaries.'

'The oldest profession is better paid and much more fun,' said Bruce and swung the truck into the driveway of a double-storeyed residence, parked outside the front door and switched off the engine.

Not long ago the house had been the home of the chief accountant of Union Minière du Haut, now it was the billet of 'D' section, Special Striker Force, commanded by Captain Bruce Curry.

Half a dozen of his black gendarmes were sitting on the low wall of the verandah, and as Bruce came up the front steps they shouted the greeting that had become traditional since the United Nations intervention.

'U.N. – Merde!'

'Ah!' Bruce grinned at them in the sense of companionship that had grown up between them in the past months. 'The cream of the Army of Katanga!'

He offered his cigarettes around and stood chatting idly for a few minutes before asking, 'Where's Sergeant Major?' One of the gendarmes jerked a thumb at the glass doors that led into the lounge and Bruce went through with Mike behind him.

Equipment was piled haphazardly on the expensive furniture, the stone fireplace was half filled with empty bottles, a gendarme lay snoring on the Persian carpet, one of the oil paintings on the wall had been ripped by a bayonet and the frame hung askew, the imbuia-wood coffee table tilted drunkenly towards its broken leg, and the whole lounge smelled of men and cheap tobacco.

'Hello, Ruffy,' said Bruce.

'Just in time, boss.' Sergeant Major Ruffararo grinned delightedly from the armchair which he was overflowing. 'These goddam Arabs have run fresh out of folding stuff.' He gestured at the gendarmes that crowded about the table in front of him. 'Arab' was Ruffy's word of censure or contempt, and bore no relation to a man's nationality.

Ruffy's accent was always a shock to Bruce. You never expected to hear pure Americanese come rumbling out of that huge black frame. But three years previously Ruffy had returned from a scholarship tour of the United States with a command of the idiom, a diploma in land husbandry, a prodigious thirst for bottled beer (preferably Schlitz, but any other was acceptable) and a raving dose of the Old Joe.

The memory of this last, which had been a farewell gift from a high yellow sophomore of U.C.L.A., returned most painfully to Ruffararo when he was in his cups; so painfully that it could be assuaged only by throwing the nearest citizen of the United States.

Fortunately, it was only on rare occasions that an American and the necessary five or six gallons of beer were assembled in the same vicinity so that Ruffy's latent race antipathy could find expression. A throwing by Ruffy was an unforgettable experience, both for the victim and the spectators. Bruce vividly recalled that night at the Hotel Lido when he had been a witness at one of Ruffy's most spectacular throwings.

The victims, three of them, were journalists representing publications of repute. As the evening wore on they talked louder; an American accent has a carry like a well-hit golf ball and Ruffy recognized it from across the terrace. He became silent, and in his silence drank the last gallon which was necessary to tip the balance. He wiped the froth from his upper lip and stood up with his eyes fastened on the party of Americans.

'Ruffy, hold it. Hey!' – Bruce might not have spoken. Ruffy started across the terrace. They saw him coming and fell into an uneasy silence.

The first was in the nature of a practice throw; besides, the man was not aerodynamically constructed and his stomach had too much wind resistance. A middling distance of twenty feet.

'Ruffy, leave them!' shouted Bruce.

On the next throw Ruffy was getting warmed up, but he put excessive loft into it. Thirty feet; the journalist cleared the terrace and landed on the lawn below with his empty glass still clutched in his hand.

'Run, you fool!' Bruce warned the third victim, but he was paralysed.

And this was Ruffy's best ever, he took a good grip – neck and seat of the pants – and put his whole weight into it. Ruffy must have known that he had executed the perfect throw, for his shout of 'Gonorrhoea!' as he launched his man had a ring of triumph to it.

Afterwards, when Bruce had soothed the three Americans, and they had recovered sufficiently to appreciate the fact that they were privileged by being party to a record throwing session, they all paced out the distances. The three journalists developed an almost proprietary affection for Ruffy and spent the rest of the evening buying him beers and boasting to every newcomer in the bar. One of them, he who had been thrown last and farthest, wanted to do an article on Ruffy – with pictures. Towards the end of the evening he was talking wildly of whipping up sufficient enthusiasm to have a man-throwing event included in the Olympic Games.

Ruffy accepted both their praise and their beer with modest gratitude; and when the third American offered to let Ruffy throw him again, he declined the offer on the grounds that he never threw the same man twice. All in all, it had been a memorable evening.

Apart from these occasional lapses, Ruffy had a more powerful body and happier mind than any man Bruce had ever known, and Bruce could not help liking him. He could not prevent himself smiling as he tried to reject Ruffy's invitation to play cards.

'We've got work to do now, Ruffy. Some other time.'

'Sit down, boss,' Ruffy repeated, and Bruce grimaced resignedly and took the chair opposite him.

'How much you going to bet?' Ruffy leaned forward.

'Un mille.' Bruce laid a thousand-franc note on the table; 'when that's gone, then we go.'

'No hurry,' Ruffy soothed him. 'We got all day.' He dealt the three cards face down. 'The old Christian monarch is in there somewhere; all you got to do is find him and it's the easiest mille you ever made.'

'In the middle,' whispered the gendarme standing beside Bruce's chair. 'That's him in the middle.'

'Take no notice of that mad Arab – he's lost five mille already this morning,' Ruffy advised.

Bruce turned over the right-hand card.

'Mis-luck,' crowed Ruffy. 'You got yourself the queen of hearts.' He picked up the banknote and stuffed it into his breast pocket. 'She'll see you wrong every time, that sweet-faced little bitch.' Grinning, he turned over the middle card to expose the jack of spades with his sly eyes and curly little moustache. 'She's been shacked up there with the jack right under the old king's nose.' He turned the king face up. 'Look you at that dozy old guy – he's not even facing in the right direction.'

Bruce stared at the three cards and he felt that sickness in his stomach again. The whole story was there; even the man's name was right, but the jack should have worn a beard and driven a red Jaguar and his queen of hearts never had such innocent eyes. Bruce spoke abruptly. 'That's it, Ruffy. I want you and ten men to come with me.'

'Where we going?'

'Down to Ordinance – we're drawing special supplies.'

Ruffy nodded and buttoned the playing cards into his top pocket while he selected the gendarmes to accompany them; then he asked Bruce, 'We might need some oil; what you think, boss?'

Bruce hesitated; they had only two cases of whisky left of the dozen they had looted in August. The purchasing power of a bottle of genuine Scotch was enormous and Bruce was loath to use them except in extraordinary circumstances. But now he realized that his chances of getting the supplies he needed were remote, unless he took along a substantial bribe for the quartermaster.

'Okay, Ruffy. Bring a case.'

Ruffy came up out of the chair and clapped his steel helmet on his head. The chin straps hung down on each side of his round black face.

'A full case?' He grinned at Bruce. 'You want to buy a battleship?'

'Almost,' agreed Bruce; 'go and get it.'

Ruffy disappeared into the back area of the house and returned almost immediately with a case of Grant's Standfast under one arm and half a dozen bottles of Simba beer held by their necks between the fingers of his other hand.

'We might get thirsty,' he explained.

The gendarmes climbed back into the back of the truck with a clatter of weapons and shouted cheerful abuse at their fellows on the verandah. Bruce, Mike and Ruffy crowded into the cab and Ruffy set the whisky on the floor and placed two large booted feet upon it.

'What's this all about, boss?' he asked as Bruce trundled the truck down the drive and turned into the Avenue l'Etoile. Bruce told him and when he had finished Ruffy grunted noncommittally and opened a bottle of beer with his big white chisel-blade teeth; the gas hissed softly and a little froth ran down the bottle and dripped onto his lap.

'My boys aren't going to like it,' he commented as he offered the open bottle to Mike Haig. Mike shook his head and Ruffy passed the bottle to Bruce.

Ruffy opened a bottle for himself and spoke again. 'They going to hate it like hell.' He shook his head. 'And there'll be even bigger trouble when we get to Port Reprieve and pick up the diamonds.'

Bruce glanced sideways at him, startled. 'What diamonds?'

'From the dredgers,' said Ruffy. 'You don't think they're sending us all that way just to bring in these other guys. They're worried about the diamonds, that's for sure!'

Suddenly, for Bruce, much which had puzzled him was explained. A half-forgotten conversation that he had held earlier in the year with an engineer from Union Minière jumped back into his memory. They had discussed the three diamond dredgers that worked the gravel from the bed of the Lufira swamps. The boats were based on Port Reprieve and clearly they would have returned there at the beginning of the emergency; they must still be there with three or four months' recovery of diamonds on board. Something like half a million sterling in uncut stones. That was the reason why the Katangese Government placed such priority on this expedition, the reason why such a powerful force was being used, the reason why no approaches had been made to the U.N. authorities to conduct the rescue.

Bruce smiled sardonically as he remembered the humanitarian arguments that had been given to him by the Minister of the Interior.

'It is our duty, Captain Curry. We cannot leave these people to the not-so-tender mercy of the tribesmen. It is our duty as civilized human beings.'

There were others cut off in remote mission stations and government outposts throughout southern Kasai and Katanga; nothing had been heard of them for months, but their welfare was secondary to that of the settlement at Port Reprieve.

Bruce lifted the bottle to his lips again, steering with one hand and squinting ahead through the windscreen as he drank. All right, we'll fetch them in and afterwards an ammunition box will be loaded on to a chartered aircraft, and later still there will be another deposit to a numbered account in Zurich. Why should I worry? They're paying me for it.

'I don't think we should mention the diamonds to my boys.' Ruffy spoke sadly. 'I don't think it would be a good idea at all.'

Bruce slowed the truck as they ran into the industrial area beyond the railway line. He watched the buildings as they passed, until he recognized the one he wanted and swung off the road to stop in front of the gate. He blew a blast on the hooter and a gendarme came out and inspected his pass minutely. Satisfied, he shouted out to someone beyond the gate and it swung open. Bruce drove the truck through into the yard and switched off the engine.

There were half a dozen other trucks parked in the yard, all emblazoned with the Katangese shield and surrounded by gendarmes in uniforms patchy with sweat. A white lieutenant leaned from the cab of one of the trucks and shouted.

'Ciao, Bruce!'

'How things, Sergio?' Bruce answered him.

'Crazy! Crazy!' Bruce smiled. For the Italian everything was crazy. Bruce remembered that in July, during the fighting at the road bridge, he had bent him over the bonnet of a Land Rover and with a bayonet dug a piece of schrapnel out of his hairy buttocks – that had also been crazy.

'See you around,' Bruce dismissed him and led Mike and Ruffy across the yard to the warehouse. There was a sign on the large double doors *Dépôt Ordinance – Armée du Katanga* and beyond them at a desk in a glass cubicle sat a major with a pair of Gandhi-type steel-rimmed spectacles perched on a face like that of a jovial black toad. He looked up at Bruce.

'Non,' he said with finality. 'Non, non.' Bruce produced his requisition form and laid it before him. The major brushed it aside contemptuously.

'We have not got these items, we are destitute. I cannot do it. No! I cannot do it. There are priorities. There are circumstances to consider. No, I am sorry.' He snatched a sheaf of papers from the side of his desk and turned his whole attention to them, ignoring Bruce.

'This requisition is signed by Monsieur le Président,' Bruce pointed out mildly, and the major laid down his papers and came round from behind the desk. He stood close to Bruce with the top of his head on a level with Bruce's chin.

'Had it been signed by the Almighty himself, it would be of no use. I am sorry, I am truly sorry.'

Bruce lifted his eyes and for a second allowed them to wander over the mountains of stores which packed the interior of the warehouse. From where he stood he could identify at least twenty items that he needed. The major noticed the gesture and his French became so excited that Bruce could only make out the repeated use of the word 'Non'. He glanced significantly at Ruffy and the sergeant major stepped forward and placed an arm soothingly about the major's shoulders; then very gently he led him, still protesting, out into the yard and across to the truck. He opened the door of the cab and the major saw the case of whisky.

A few minutes later, after Ruffy had prised open the lid with his bayonet and allowed the major to inspect the seals on the caps, they returned to the office with Ruffy carrying the case.

'Captain,' said the major as he picked up the requisition from the desk. 'I see now that I was mistaken. This is indeed signed by Monsieur le Président. It is my duty to afford you the most urgent priority.'

Bruce murmured his thanks and the major beamed at him. 'I will give you men to help you.'

'You are too kind. It would disrupt your routine. I have my own men.'

'Excellent,' agreed the major and waved a podgy hand around the warehouse. 'Take what you need.'

– 3 –

Again Bruce glanced at his wristwatch. It was still twenty minutes before the curfew ended at 06.00 hours. Until then he must fret away the time watching Wally Hendry finishing his breakfast. This was a spectacle without much appeal, for Hendry was a methodical but untidy eater.

'Why don't you keep your mouth closed?' snapped Bruce irritably, unable to stand it any longer.

'Do I ask you your business?' Hendry looked up from his plate. His jowls were covered with a ginger stubble of beard, and his eyes were inflamed and puffy from the previous evening's debauchery. Bruce looked away from him and checked his watch again.

The suicidal temptation to ignore the curfew and set off immediately for the railway station was very strong. It required an effort to resist it. The least he could expect if he followed that course was an arrest by one of the patrols and a delay of twelve hours while he cleared himself; the worst thing would be a shooting incident.

He poured himself another cup of coffee and sipped it slowly. Impatience has always been one of my weaknesses, he reflected; nearly every mistake I have ever made stems from that cause. But I have improved a little over the years – at twenty I wanted to live my whole life in a week. Now I'll settle for a year.

He finished his coffee and checked the time again. Five minutes before six, he could risk it now. It would take almost that long to get out to the truck.

'If you are ready, gentlemen.' He pushed back his chair and picked up his pack, slung it over his shoulder and led the way out.

Ruffy was waiting for them, sitting on a pile of stones in one of the corrugated iron goods sheds. His men squatted round a dozen small fires on the concrete floor cooking breakfast.

'Where's the train?'

'That's a good question, boss,' Ruffy congratulated him, and Bruce groaned.

'It should have been here long ago,' Bruce protested, and Ruffy shrugged.

'*Should have been* is a lot different from *is*.'

'Goddammit! We've still got to load up. We'll be lucky if we get away before noon,' snapped Bruce. 'I'll go up to the station master.'

'You'd better take him a present, boss. We've still got a case left.'

'No, hell!' Bruce growled. 'Come with me, Mike.'

With Mike beside him they crossed the tracks to the main platform and clambered up on to it. At the far end a group of railway officials stood chatting and Bruce fell upon them furiously.

Two hours later Bruce stood beside the coloured engine driver on the footplate and they puffed slowly down towards the goods yard.

The driver was a roly-poly little man with a skin too dark for mere sunburn and a set of teeth with bright red plastic gums.

'Monsieur, you do not wish to proceed to Port Reprieve?' he asked anxiously.

'Yes.'

'There is no way of telling the condition of the permanent way. No traffic has used it these last four months.'

'I know. You'll have to proceed with caution.'

'There is a United Nations barrier across the lines near the old aerodrome,' protested the man.

'We have a pass.' Bruce smiled to soothe him; his bad temper was abating now that he had his transport. 'Stop next to the first shed.'

With a hiss of steam brakes the train pulled up beside the concrete platform and Bruce jumped down.

'All right, Ruffy,' he shouted. 'Let's get cracking.'

Bruce had placed the three steel-sided open trucks in the van, for they were the easiest to defend. From behind the breast-high sides the Bren guns could sweep ahead and on both flanks. Then followed the two passenger coaches, to be used as store rooms and officer's quarters; also for accommodation of the refugees on the return journey. Finally, the locomotive in the rear, where it would be least vulnerable and would not spew smoke and soot back over the train.

The stores were loaded into four of the compartments, the windows shuttered and the doors locked. Then Bruce set about laying out his defences. In a low circle of sandbags on the roof of the leading coach he sited one of the Brens and made his own post. From here he could look down over the open trucks, back at the locomotive, and also command an excellent view of the surrounding country.

The other Brens he placed in the leading truck and put Hendry in command there. He had obtained from the major at Ordinance three of the new walkie-talkie sets; one he gave to the engine driver, another to Hendry up front, and the third he retained in his emplacement; and his system of communication was satisfactory.

It was almost twelve o'clock before these preparations were complete and Bruce turned to Ruffy who sat on the sandbags beside him.

'All set?'

'All set, boss.'

'How many missing?' Bruce had learned from experience never to expect his entire command to be in any one place at any one time.

'Eight, boss.'

'That's three more than yesterday; leaves us only fifty-two men. Do you think they've taken off into the bush also?' Five of his men had deserted with their weapons on the day of the ceasefire. Obviously they had gone out into the bush to join one of the bands of *shufta* that were already playing havoc along the main roads: ambushing all unprotected traffic, beating up lucky travellers and murdering those less fortunate, raping when they had the opportunity, and generally enjoying themselves.

'No, boss. I don't think so, those three are good boys. They'll be down in the cité indigène having themselves some fun; guess they just forgot the time.' Ruffy shook his head. 'Take us about half an hour to find them; all we do is go down and visit all the knock-shops. You want to try?'

'No, we haven't time to mess around if we are going to

make Msapa Junction before dark. We'll pick them up again when we get back.' Was there ever an army since the Boer War that treated desertion so lightly, Bruce wondered.

He turned to the radio set beside him and depressed the transmit button.

'Driver.'

'Oui, monsieur.'

'Proceed – very slowly until we approach the United Nations barrier. Stop well this side of it.'

'Oui, monsieur.'

They rolled out of the goods yard, clicking over the points; leaving the industrial quarter on their right with the Katangese guard posts on the Avenue du Cimetière intersection; out through the suburbs until ahead of them Bruce saw the U.N. positions and he felt the first stirring of anxiety. The pass he carried in the breast pocket of his jacket was signed by General Rhee Singh, but before in this war the orders of an Indian general had not been passed by a Sudanese captain to an Irish sergeant. The reception that awaited them could be exciting.

'I hope they know about us.' Mike Haig lit his cigarette with a show of nonchalance, but he peered over it anxiously at the piles of fresh earth on each side of the tracks that marked the position of emplacements.

'These boys have got bazookas, and they're Irish Arabs,' muttered Ruffy. 'I reckon it's the maddest kind of Arabs there is – Irish. How would you like a bazooka bomb up your throat, boss?'

'No, thanks, Ruffy,' Bruce declined, and pressed the button of the radio.

'Hendry!'

In the leading truck Wally Hendry picked up his set and, holding it against his chest, looked back at Bruce.

'Curry?'

'Tell your gunners to stand away from the Brens, and the rest of them to lay down their rifles.'

'Right.'

Bruce watched him relaying the order, pushing them back, moving among the gendarmes who crowded the forward trucks. Bruce could sense the air of tension that had fallen over the whole train, watched as his gendarmes reluctantly laid down their weapons and stood empty-handed staring sullenly ahead at the U.N. barrier.

'Driver!' Bruce spoke again into the radio. 'Slow down. Stop fifty metres this side of the barrier. But if there is any shooting open the throttle and take us straight through.'

'Oui, monsieur.'

Ahead of them there was no sign of a reception committee, only the hostile barrier of poles and petrol drums across the line.

Bruce stood upon the roof and lifted his arms above his head in a gesture of neutrality. It was a mistake; the movement changed the passive mood of the gendarmes in the trucks below him. One of them lifted his arms also, but his fists were clenched.

'U.N. – merde!' he shouted, and immediately the cry was taken up.

'U.N. – merde! U.N. – merde!' They chanted the war cry – laughing at first, but then no longer laughing, their voices rising sharply.

'Shut up, damn you,' Bruce roared and swung his open hand against the head of the gendarme beside him, but the man hardly noticed it. His eyes were glazing with the infectious hysteria to which the African is so susceptible; he had snatched up his rifle and was holding it across his chest; already his body was beginning to jerk convulsively as he chanted.

Bruce hooked his fingers under the rim of the man's steel helmet and yanked it forward over his eyes so the back of his neck was exposed; he chopped him with a judo blow and the gendarme slumped forward over the sandbags, his rifle slipping from his hands.

Bruce looked up desperately; in the trucks below him the hysteria was spreading.

'Stop them – Hendry, de Surrier! Stop them for God's sake.' But his voice was lost in the chanting.

A gendarme snatched up his rifle from where it lay at his feet; Bruce saw him elbow his way towards the side of the truck to begin firing; he was working the slide to lever a round into the breech.

'Mwembe!' Bruce shouted the gendarme's name, but his voice could not penetrate the uproar.

In two seconds the whole situation would dissolve into a pandemonium of tracer and bazooka fire.

Poised on the forward edge of the roof, Bruce checked for an instant to judge the distance, and then he jumped. He landed squarely on the gendarme's shoulders, his weight throwing the man forward so his face hit the steel edge of the truck, and they went down together on to the floor.

The gendarme's finger was resting on the trigger and the rifle fired as it spun from his hands. A complete hush followed the roar of the rifle and in it Bruce scrambled to his feet, drawing his pistol from the canvas holster on his hip.

'All right,' he panted, menacing the men around him. 'Come on, give me a chance to use this!' He picked out one of his sergeants and held his eyes. 'You! I'm waiting for you – start shooting!'

At the sight of the revolver the man relaxed slowly and the madness faded from his face. He dropped his eyes and shuffled awkwardly.

Bruce glanced up at Ruffy and Haig on the roof, and raised his voice.

'Watch them. Shoot the first one who starts it again.'

'Okay, boss.' Ruffy thrust forward the automatic rifle in his hands. 'Who's it going to be?' he asked cheerfully, looking down at them. But the mood had changed. Their attitudes of defiance gave way to sheepish embarrassment and a small buzz of conversation filled the silence.

'Mike,' Bruce yelled, urgent again. 'Call the driver, he's trying to take us through!'

The noise of their passage had risen, the driver accelerating at the sound of the shot, and now they were racing down towards the U.N. barrier.

Mike Haig grabbed the set, shouted an order into it, and immediately the brakes swooshed and the train jolted to a halt not a hundred yards short of the barrier.

Slowly Bruce clambered back on to the roof of the coach.

'Close?' asked Mike.

'My God!' Bruce shook his head, and lit a cigarette with slightly unsteady hands. 'Another fifty yards—!' Then he turned and stared coldly down at his gendarmes.

'Canaille! Next time you try to commit suicide don't take me with you.' The gendarme he had knocked down was now sitting up, fingering the ugly black swelling above his eye. 'My friend,' Bruce turned on him, 'later I will have something for your further discomfort!' Then to the other man in the emplacement beside him who was massaging his neck, 'And for you also! Take their names, Sergeant Major.'

'Sir!' growled Ruffy.

'Mike.' Bruce's voice changed, soft again. 'I'm going ahead to toss the blarney with our friends behind the bazookas. When I give you the signal bring the train through.'

'You don't want me to come with you?' asked Mike.

'No, stay here.' Bruce picked up his rifle, slung it over his shoulder, dropped down the ladder on to the path beside the tracks, and walked forward with the gravel crunching beneath his boots.

An auspicious beginning to the expedition, he decided grimly, tragedy averted by the wink of an eye before they had even passed the outskirts of the city.

At least the Mickies hadn't added a few bazooka bombs to the altercation. Bruce peered ahead, and could make out the shape of helmets behind the earthworks.

Without the breeze of the train's passage it was hot again, and Bruce felt himself starting to sweat.

'Stay where you are, Mister.' A deep brogue from the emplacement nearest the tracks; Bruce stopped, standing on the wooden crossties in the sun. Now he could see the faces of the men beneath the helmets: unfriendly, not smiling.

'What was the shooting for?' the voice questioned.

'We had an accident.'

'Don't have any more or we might have one also.'

'I'd not be wanting that, Paddy.' Bruce smiled thinly, and the Irishman's voice had an edge to it as he went on. 'What's your mission?'

'I have a pass, do you want to see it?' Bruce took the folded sheet of paper from his breast pocket.

'What's your mission?' repeated the Irishman.

'Proceed to Port Reprieve and relieve the town.'

'We know about you.' The Irishman nodded. 'Let me see the pass.'

Bruce left the tracks, climbed the earth wall and handed the pink slip to the Irishman. He wore the three pips of a captain, and he glanced briefly at the pass before speaking to the man beside him.

'Very well, Sergeant, you can be clearing the barrier now.'

'I'll call the train through?' Bruce asked, and the captain nodded again.

'But make sure there are no more accidents – we don't like hired killers.'

'Sure and begorrah now, Paddy, it's not your war you're a-fighting either,' snapped Bruce and abruptly turned his back on the man, jumped down on to the tracks and waved to Mike Haig on the roof of the coach.

The Irish sergeant and his party had cleared the tracks

and while the train rumbled slowly down to him Bruce struggled to control his irritation – the Irish captain's taunt had reached him. Hired killer, and of course that was what he was. Could a man sink any lower?

As the coach drew level with where he stood, Bruce caught the hand rail and swung himself aboard, waved an ironical farewell to the Irish captain and climbed up on to the roof.

'No trouble?' asked Mike.

'A bit of lip, delivered in music-hall brogue,' Bruce answered, 'but nothing serious.' He picked up the radio set.

'Driver.'

'Monsieur?'

'Do not forget my instructions.'

'I will not exceed forty kilometres the hour, and I shall at all times be prepared for an emergency stop.'

'Good!' Bruce switched off the set and sat down on the sandbags between Ruffy and Mike.

Well, he thought, here we go at last. Six hours run to Msapa Junction. That should be easy. And then – God knows, God alone knows.

The tracks curved, and Bruce looked back to see the last white-washed buildings of Elisabethville disappear among the trees. They were out into the open savannah forest.

Behind them the black smoke from the loco rolled sideways into the trees; beneath them the crossties clattered in strict rhythm, and ahead the line ran arrow straight for miles, dwindling with perspective until it merged into the olive-green mass of the forest.

Bruce lifted his eyes. Half the sky was clear and tropical blue, but in the north it was bruised with cloud, and beneath the cloud grey rain drifted down to meet the earth. The sunlight through the rain spun a rainbow, and the cloud shadow moved across the land as slowly and as darkly as a herd of grazing buffalo.

He loosened the chin strap of his helmet and laid his rifle on the roof beside him.

'You'd like a beer, boss?'

'Have you any?'

'Sure.' Ruffy called to one of the gendarmes and the man climbed down into the coach and came back with half a dozen bottles. Ruffy opened two with his teeth. Each time half the contents frothed out and splattered back along the wooden side of the coach.

'This beer's as wild as an angry woman,' he grunted as he passed a bottle to Bruce.

'It's wet anyway.' Bruce tasted it, warm and gassy and too sweet.

'Here's how!' said Ruffy.

Bruce looked down into the open trucks at the gendarmes who were settling in for the journey. Apart from the gunners at the Brens, they were lying or squatting in attitudes of complete relaxation and most of them had stripped down to their underwear. One skinny little fellow was already asleep on his back with his helmet as a pillow and the tropical sun beating full into his face.

Bruce finished his beer and threw the bottle overboard. Ruffy opened another and placed it in his hand without comment.

'Why we going so slowly, boss?'

'I told the driver to keep the speed down – give us a chance to stop if the tracks have been torn up.'

'Yeah. Them Balubas might have done that – they're mad Arabs all of them.'

The warm beer drunk in the sun was having a soothing effect on Bruce. He felt at peace, now, withdrawn from the need to make decisions, to participate in the life around him.

'Listen to that train-talk,' said Ruffy, and Bruce focused his hearing on the clickety-clack of the crossties.

'Yes, I know. You can make it say anything you want it to,' agreed Bruce.

'And it can sing,' Ruffy went on. 'It's got real music in it, like this.' He inflated the great barrel of his chest, lifted his head and let it come.

His voice was deep but with a resonance that caught the attention of the men in the open trucks below them. Those who had been sprawled in the amorphous shapes of sleep stirred and sat up. Another voice joined in humming the tune, hesitantly at first, then more confidently; then others took it up, the words were unimportant, it was the rhythm that they could not resist. They had sung together many times before and like a well-trained choir each voice found its place, the star performers leading, changing the pace, improvising, quickening until the original tune lost its identity and became one of the tribal chants. Bruce recognized it as a planting song. It was one of his favourites and he sat drinking his lukewarm beer and letting the singing wash round him, build up into the chorus like storm waves, then fall back into a tenor solo before rising once more. And the train ran on through the sunlight towards the rain clouds in the north.

Presently André came out of the coach below him and picked his way forward through the men in the trucks until he reached Hendry. The two of them stood together, André's face turned up towards the taller man and deadly earnest as he talked.

'Doll boy,' Hendry had called him, and it was an accurate description of the effeminately pretty face with the big toffee eyes; the steel helmet he wore seemed too large for his shoulders to carry.

I wonder how old he is; Bruce watched him laugh suddenly, his face still turned upwards to Hendry; not much over twenty and I have never seen anything less like a hired killer.

'How the hell did anyone like de Surrier get mixed up in this?' His voice echoed the thought, and beside him Mike answered.

'He was working in Elisabethville when it started, and he couldn't return to Belgium. I don't know the reason but I guess it was something personal. When it started his firm closed down. I suppose this was the only employment he could find.'

'That Irishman, the one at the barrier, he called me a hired killer.' Thinking of André's position in the scheme of things had turned Bruce's thoughts back to his own status. 'I hadn't thought about it that way before, but I suppose he's right. That is what we are.'

Mike Haig was silent for a moment, but when he spoke there was a stark quality in his voice.

'Look at these hands!' Involuntarily Bruce glanced down at them, and for the first time noticed that they were narrow with long moulded fingers, possessed of a functional beauty, the hands of an artist.

'Look at them,' Mike repeated, flexing them slightly; 'they were fashioned for a purpose, they were made to hold a scalpel, they were made to save life.' Then he relaxed them and let them drop on to the rifle across his lap, the long delicate fingers incongruous upon the blue metal. 'But look what they hold now!'

Bruce stirred irritably. He had not wanted to provoke another bout of Mike Haig's soul-searching. Damn the old fool – why must he always start this, he knew as well as anyone that in the mercenary army of Katanga there was a taboo upon the past. It did not exist.

'Ruffy,' Bruce snapped, 'aren't you going to feed your boys?'

'Right now, boss.' Ruffy opened another beer and handed it to Bruce. 'Hold that – it will keep your mind off food while I rustle it up.' He lumbered off along the roof of the coach still singing.

'Three years ago, it seems like all eternity,' Mike went on as though Bruce had not interrupted. 'Three years ago I was a surgeon and now this—' The desolation had spread to his eyes, and Bruce felt his pity for the man deep down where he kept it imprisoned with all his other emotions. 'I was good. I was one of the best. Royal College. Harley Street. Guy's.' Mike laughed without humour, with bitterness. 'Can you imagine my being driven in my Rolls to address the College on my advanced technique of cholecystectomy?'

'What happened?' The question was out before he could stop it, and Bruce realized how near to the surface he had let his pity rise. 'No, don't tell me. It's your business. I don't want to know.'

'But I'll tell you, Bruce, I want to. It helps somehow, talking about it.'

At first, thought Bruce, I wanted to talk also, to try and wash the pain away with words.

Mike was silent for a few seconds. Below them the singing rose and fell, and the train ran on through the forest.

'It had taken me ten hard years to get there, but at last I had done it. A fine practice; doing the work I loved with skill, earning the rewards I deserved. A wife that any man would have been proud of, a lovely home, many friends, too many friends perhaps; for success breeds friends the way a dirty kitchen breeds cockroaches.'

Mike pulled out a handkerchief and dried the back of his neck where the wind could not reach.

'Those sort of friends mean parties,' he went on. 'Parties when you've worked all day and you're tired; when you need the lift that you can get so easily from a bottle. You don't know if you have the weakness for the stuff until it's too late; until you have a bottle in the drawer of your desk; until suddenly your practice isn't so good any more.'

Mike twisted the handkerchief around his fingers as he

ploughed doggedly on. 'Then you know it suddenly. You know it when your hands dance in the morning and all you want for breakfast is *that*, when you can't wait until lunchtime because you have to operate and that's the only way you can keep your hands steady. But you know it finally and utterly when the knife turns in your hand and the artery starts to spurt and you watch it paralysed – you watch it hosing red over your gown and forming pools on the theatre floor.' Mike's voice dried up then and he tapped a cigarette from his pack and lit it. His shoulders were hunched forward and his eyes were full of shadows of his guilt. Then he straightened up and his voice was stronger.

'You must have read about it. I was headlines for a few days, all the papers. But my name wasn't Haig in those days. I got that name off a label on a bottle in a bar-room.

'Gladys stayed with me, of course, she was that type. We came out to Africa. I had enough saved from the wreck for a down payment on a tobacco farm in the Centenary block outside Salisbury. Two good seasons and I was off the bottle. Gladys was having our first baby, we had both wanted one so badly. It was all coming right again.'

Mike stuffed the handkerchief back in his pocket, and his voice lost its strength again, turned dry and husky.

'Then one day I took the truck into the village and on the way home I stopped at the club. I had been there often before, but this time they threw me out at closing time and when I got back to the farm I had a case of Scotch on the seat beside me.'

Bruce wanted to stop him; he knew what was coming and he didn't want to hear it.

'The first rains started that night and the rivers came down in flood. The telephone lines were knocked out and we were cut off. In the morning—' Mike stopped again and turned to Bruce.

'I suppose it was the shock of seeing me like that again, but in the morning Gladys went into labour. It was her first and she wasn't so young any more. She was still in labour the next day, but by then she was too weak to scream. I remember how peaceful it was without her screaming and pleading with me to help. You see she knew I had all the instruments I needed. She begged me to help. I can remember that; her voice through the fog of whisky. I think I hated her then. I think I remember hating her, it was all so confused, so mixed up with the screaming and the liquor. But at last she was quiet. I don't think I realized she was dead. I was simply glad she was quiet and I could have peace.'

He dropped his eyes from Bruce's face.

'I was too drunk to go to the funeral. Then I met a man in a bar-room, I can't remember how long after it was, I can't even remember where. It must have been on the Copperbelt. He was recruiting for Tshombe's army and I signed up; there didn't seem anything else to do.'

Neither of them spoke again until a gendarme brought food to them, hunks of brown bread spread with tinned butter and filled with bully beef and pickled onions. They ate in silence listening to the singing, and Bruce said at last:

'You needn't have told me.'

'I know.'

'Mike—' Bruce paused.

'Yes?'

'I'm sorry, if that's any comfort.'

'It is,' Mike said. 'It helps to have – not to be completely alone. I like you, Bruce.' He blurted out the last sentence and Bruce recoiled as though Mike had spat in his face.

You fool, he rebuked himself savagely, *you were wide open then. You nearly let one of them in again*.

Remorselessly he crushed down his sympathy, shocked at the effort it required, and when he picked up the radio the gentleness had gone from his eyes.

'Hendry,' he spoke into the set, 'don't talk so much. I put you up front to watch the tracks.'

From the leading truck Wally Hendry looked round and forked two fingers at Bruce in a casual obscenity, but he turned back and faced ahead.

'You'd better go and take over from Hendry,' Bruce told Mike. 'Send him back here.'

Mike Haig stood up and looked down at Bruce.

'What are you afraid of?' his voice softly puzzled.

'I gave you an order, Haig.'

'Yes, I'm on my way.'

– 4 –

The aircraft found them in the late afternoon. It was a Vampire jet of the Indian Air Force and it came from the north.

They heard the soft rumble of it across the sky and then saw it glint like a speck of mica in the sunlight above the storm clouds ahead of them.

'I bet you a thousand francs to a handful of dung that this Bucko don't know about us,' said Hendry with anticipation, watching the jet turn off its course towards them.

'Well, he does now,' said Bruce.

Swiftly he surveyed the rain clouds in front of them. They were close; another ten minutes' run and they would be under them, and once there they were safe from air attack for the belly of the clouds pressed close against the earth and the rain was a thick blue-grey mist that would reduce visibility to a few hundred feet. He switched on the radio.

'Driver, give us all the speed you have – get us into that rain.'

'Oui, monsieur,' came the acknowledgement and almost immediately the puffing of the loco quickened and the clatter of the crossties changed its rhythm.

'Look at him come,' growled Hendry. The jet fell fast

against the backdrop of cloud, still in sunlight, still a silver point of light, but growing.

Bruce clicked over the band selector of the radio, searching the ether for the pilot's voice. He tried four wavelengths and each time found only the crackle and drone of static, but with the fifth came the gentle sing-song of Hindustani. Bruce could not understand it, but he could hear that the tone was puzzled. There was a short silence on the radio while the pilot listened to an instruction from the Kamina base which was beyond the power of their small set to receive, then a curt affirmative.

'He's coming in for a closer look,' said Bruce, then raising his voice, 'Everybody under cover – and stay there.' He was not prepared to risk another demonstration of friendship.

The jet came cruising in towards them under half power, yet incredibly fast, leaving the sound of its engine far behind it, sharklike above the forest. Then Bruce could see the pilot's head through the canopy; now he could make out his features. His face was very brown beneath the silver crash helmet and he had a little moustache, the same as the jack of spades. He was so close that Bruce saw the exact moment that he recognized them as Katangese; his eyes showed white and his mouth puckered as he swore. Beside Bruce the radio relayed the oath with metallic harshness, and then the jet was banking away steeply, its engine howling in full throttle, rising, showing its swollen silver belly and the racks of rockets beneath its wings.

'That frightened seven years' growth out of him,' laughed Hendry. 'You should have let me blast him. He was close enough for me to hit him in the left eyeball.'

'You'll get another chance in a moment,' Bruce assured him grimly. The radio was gabbling with consternation as the jet dwindled back into the sky. Bruce switched quickly to their own channel.

'Driver, can't you get this thing moving?'

'Monsieur, never before has she moved as she does now.'

Once more he switched back to the jet's frequency and listened to the pilot's excited voice. The jet was turning in a wide circle, perhaps fifteen miles away. Bruce glanced at the piled mass of cloud and rain ahead of them; it was moving down to meet them, but with ponderous dignity.

'If he comes back,' Bruce shouted down at his gendarmes, 'we can be sure that it's not just to look at us again. Open fire as soon as he's in range. Give him everything you've got, we must try and spoil his aim.'

Their faces were turned up towards him, subdued by the awful inferiority of the earthbound to the hunter in the sky. Only André did not look at Bruce; he was staring at the aircraft with his jaws clenching nervously and his eyes too large for his face.

Again there was silence on the radio, and every head turned back to watch the jet.

'Come on, Bucko, come on!' grunted Hendry impatiently. He spat into the palm of his right hand and then wiped it down the front of his jacket. 'Come on, we want you.' With his thumb he flicked the safety catch of his rifle on and off, on and off.

Suddenly the radio spoke again. Two words, obviously acknowledging an order, and one of the words Bruce recognized. He had heard it before in circumstances that has burned it into his memory. The Hindustani word '*Attack!*'

'All right,' he said and stood up. 'He's coming!'

The wind fluttered his shirt against his chest. He settled his helmet firmly and pumped a round into the chamber of his FN.

'Get down into the truck, Hendry,' he ordered.

'I can see better from here.' Hendry was standing beside him, legs planted wide to brace himself against the violent motion of the train.

'As you like,' said Bruce. 'Ruffy, you get under cover.'

'Too damn hot down there in that box,' grinned the huge Negro.

'You're a mad Arab too,' said Bruce.

'Sure, we're all mad Arabs.'

The jet wheeled sharply and stooped towards the forest, levelling, still miles out on their flank.

'This Bucko is a real apprentice. He's going to take us from the side, so we can all shoot at him. If he was half awake he'd give it to us up the bum, hit the loco and make sure that we were all shooting over the top of each other,' gloated Hendry.

Silently, swiftly it closed with them, almost touching the tops of the trees. Then suddenly the cannon fire sparkled lemon-pale on its nose and all around them the air was filled with the sound of a thousand whips. Immediately every gun on the train opened up in reply. The tracers from the Brens chased each other out to meet the plane and the rifles joined their voices in a clamour that drowned the cannon fire.

Bruce aimed carefully, the jet unsteady in his sights from the lurching of the coach; then he pressed the trigger and the rifle juddered against his shoulder. From the corner of his eye he saw the empty cartridge cases spray from the breech in a bright bronze stream, and the stench of cordite stung his nostrils.

The aircraft slewed slightly, flinching from the torrent of fire.

'He's yellow!' howled Hendry. 'The bastard's yellow!'

'Hit him!' roared Ruffy. 'Keep hitting him.'

The jet twisted, lifted its nose so that the fire from its cannons passed harmlessly over their heads. Then its nose dropped again and it fired its rockets, two from under each wing. The gunfire from the train stopped abruptly as everybody ducked for safety; only the three of them on the roof kept shooting.

Shrieking like four demons in harness, leaving parallel lines of white smoke behind them, the rockets came from about four hundred yards out and they covered the distance in the time it takes to draw a deep breath, but the pilot had dropped his nose too sharply and fired too late. The rockets exploded in the embankment of the tracks below them.

The blast threw Bruce over backwards. He fell and rolled, clutching desperately at the smooth roof, but as he went over the edge his fingers caught in the guttering and he hung there. He was dazed with the concussion, the guttering cutting into his fingers, the shoulder strap of his rifle round his neck strangling him, and the gravel of the embankment rushing past beneath him.

Ruffy reached over, caught him by the front of his jacket and lifted him back like a child.

'You going somewhere, boss?' The great round face was coated with dust from the explosions, but he was grinning happily. Bruce had a confused conviction that it would take at least a case of dynamite to make any impression on that mountain of black flesh.

Kneeling on the roof Bruce tried to rally himself. He saw that the wooden side of the coach nearest the explosions was splintered and torn and the roof was covered with earth and pebbles. Hendry was sitting beside him, shaking his head slowly from side to side; a small trickle of blood ran down from a scratch on his cheek and dripped from his chin. In the open trucks the men stood or sat with stunned expressions on their faces, but the train still raced on towards the rain storm and the dust of the explosions hung in a dense brown cloud above the forest far behind them.

Bruce scrambled to his feet, searched frantically for the aircraft and found its tiny shape far off above the mass of cloud.

The radio was undamaged, protected by the sandbags from the blast. Bruce reached for it and pressed the transmit button.

'Driver, are you all right?'

'Monsieur, I am greatly perturbed. Is there—'

'You're not alone,' Bruce assured him. 'Keep this train going.'

'Oui, monsieur.'

Then he switched to the aircraft's frequency. Although his ears were singing shrilly from the explosions, he could hear that the voice of the pilot had changed its tone. There was a slowness in it, a breathless catch on some of the words. He's frightened or he's hurt, thought Bruce, but he still has time to make another pass at us before we reach the storm front.

His mind was clearing fast now, and he became aware of the complete lack of readiness in his men.

'Ruffy!' he shouted. 'Get them on their feet. Get them ready. That plane will be back any second now.'

Ruffy jumped down into the truck and Bruce heard his palm slap against flesh as he began to bully them into activity. Bruce followed him down, then climbed over into the second truck and began the same process there.

'Haig, give me a hand, help me get the lead out of them.'

Further removed from the shock of the explosion, the men in this truck reacted readily and crowded to the side, starting to reload, checking their weapons, swearing, faces losing the dull dazed expressions.

Bruce turned and shouted back, 'Ruffy, are any of your lot hurt?'

'Couple of scratches, nothing bad.'

On the roof of the coach Hendry was standing again, watching the aircraft, blood on his face and his rifle in his hands.

'Where's André?' Bruce asked Haig as they met in the middle of the truck.

'Up front. I think he's been hit.'

Bruce went forward and found André doubled up, crouching in a corner of the truck, his rifle lying beside him and both hands covering his face. His shoulders heaved as though he were in pain.

Eyes, thought Bruce, he's been hit in the eyes. He reached him and stooped over him, pulling his hands from his face, expecting to see blood.

André was crying, his cheeks wet with tears and his eyelashes gummed together. For a second Bruce stared at him and then he caught the front of his jacket and pulled him to his feet. He picked up André's rifle and the barrel was cold, not a single shot had been fired out of it. He dragged the Belgian to the side and thrust the rifle into his hands.

'De Surrier,' he snarled, 'I'm going to be standing beside you. If you do that again I'll shoot you. Do you understand?'

'I'm sorry, Bruce.' André's lips were swollen where he had bitten them; his face was smeared with tears and slack with fear. 'I'm sorry. I couldn't help it.'

Bruce ignored him and turned his attention back to the aircraft. It was turning in for its next run.

He's going to come from the side again, Bruce thought; this time he'll get us. He can't miss twice in a row.

In silence once more they watched the jet slide down the valley between two vast white mountains of cloud and level off above the forest. Small and dainty and deadly it raced in towards them.

One of the Bren guns opened up, rattling raucously, sending out tracers like bright beads on a string.

'Too soon,' muttered Bruce. 'Much too soon; he must be all of a mile out of range.'

But the effect was instantaneous. The jet swerved, almost hit the tree tops and then over-corrected, losing its line of approach.

A howl of derision went up from the train and was immediately lost in the roar as every gun opened fire. The jet loosed its remaining rockets, blindly, hopelessly, without a chance of a hit. Then it climbed steeply, turning away into the cloud ahead of them. The sound of its engines receded, was muted by the cloud and then was gone.

Ruffy was performing a dance of triumph, waving his rifle over his head. Hendry on the roof was shouting abuse at the clouds into which the jet had vanished, one of the Brens was still firing short ecstatic bursts, someone else was chanting the Katangese war cry and others were taking it up. And then the driver in the locomotive came in with his whistle, spurting steam with each shriek.

Bruce slung his rifle over his shoulder, pushed his helmet on to the back of his head, took out a cigarette and lit it, then stood watching them sing and laugh and chatter with the relief from danger.

Next to him André leaned out and vomited over the side; a little of it came out of his nose and dribbled down the front of his battle-jacket. He wiped his mouth with the back of his hand.

'I'm sorry, Bruce. I'm sorry, truly I'm sorry,' he whispered.

And they were under the cloud, its coolness slumped over them like air from an open refrigerator. The first heavy drops stung Bruce's cheek and then rolled down heavily washing away the smell of cordite, melting the dust from Ruffy's face until it shone again like washed coal.

Bruce felt his jacket cling wetly to his back.

'Ruffy, two men at each Bren. The rest of them can get back into the covered coaches. We'll relieve every hour.' He reversed his rifle so the muzzle pointed downwards. 'De Surrier, you can go, and you as well, Hendry.'

'I'll stay with you, Bruce.'

'All right then.'

The gendarmes clambered back into the covered coaches still laughing and chattering, and Ruffy came forward with a groundsheet and handed it to Bruce.

'The radios are all covered. If you don't need me, boss, I

got some business with one of those Arabs in the coach. He's got near twenty thousand francs on him; so I'd better go and give him a couple of tricks with the cards.'

'One of these days I'm going to explain your Christian monarchs to the boys. Show them that the odds are three to one against them,' Bruce threatened.

'I wouldn't do that, boss,' Ruffy advised seriously. 'All that money isn't good for them, just gets them into trouble.'

'Off you go then. I'll call you later,' said Bruce. 'Tell them I said "well done", I'm proud of them.'

'Yeah. I'll tell them,' promised Ruffy.

Bruce lifted the tarpaulin that covered the set.

'Driver, desist before you burst the boiler!'

The abandoned flight of the train steadied to a more sedate pace, and Bruce tilted his helmet over his eyes and pulled the groundsheet up around his mouth before he leaned out over the side of the truck to inspect the rocket damage.

'All the windows blown out on this side and the woodwork torn a little,' he muttered. 'But a lucky escape all the same.'

'What a miserable comic-opera war this is,' grunted Mike Haig. 'That pilot had the right idea: why risk your life when it's none of your business.'

'He was wounded,' Bruce guessed. 'I think we hit him on his first run.'

Then they were silent, with the rain driving into their faces, slitting their eyes to peer ahead along the tracks. The men at the Brens huddled into their brown and green camouflage groundsheets, all their jubilation of ten minutes earlier completely gone. They are like cats, thought Bruce as he noticed their dejection, they can't stand being wet.

'It's half past five already.' Mike spoke at last. 'Do you think we'll make Msapa Junction before nightfall?'

'With this weather it will be dark by six.' Bruce looked up at the low cloud that was prematurely bringing on the night. 'I'm not going to risk travelling in the dark. This is the edge of Baluba country and we can't use the headlights of the loco.'

'You going to stop then?'

Bruce nodded. What a stupid bloody question, he thought irritably. Then he recognized his irritation as reaction from the danger they had just experienced, and he spoke to make amends.

'We can't be far now – if we start again at first light we'll reach Msapa before sun-up.'

'My God, it's cold,' complained Mike and he shivered briefly.

'Either too hot or too cold,' Bruce agreed; he knew that it was also reaction that was making him garrulous. But he did not attempt to stop himself. 'That's one of the things about this happy little planet of ours: nothing is in moderation. Too hot or too cold, either you are hungry or you've overeaten, you are in love or you hate the world—'

'Like you?' asked Mike.

'Dammit, Mike, you're as bad as a woman. Can't you conduct an objective discussion without introducing personalities?' Bruce demanded. He could feel his temper rising to the surface, he was cold and edgy, and he wanted a smoke.

'Objective theories must have subjective application to prove their worth,' Mike pointed out. There was just a trace of an amused smile on his broad ravaged old face.

'Let's forget it then. I don't want to talk personalities,' snapped Bruce; then immediately went on to do so. 'Humanity sickens me if I think about it too much. De Surrier puking his heart out with fear, that animal Hendry, you trying to keep off the liquor, Joan—' He stopped himself abruptly.

'Who is Joan?'

'Do I ask you your business?' Bruce flashed the standard reply to all personal questions in the mercenary army of Katanga.

'No. But I'm asking you yours – who is Joan?'

All right. I'll tell him. If he wants to know, I'll tell him. Anger had made Bruce reckless.

'Joan was the bitch I married.'

'So, that's it then!'

'Yes – that's it! Now you know. So you can leave me alone.'

'Kids?'

'Two – a boy and a girl.' The anger was gone from Bruce's voice, and the raw naked pain was back for an instant. Then he rallied and his voice was neutral once more.

'And none of it matters a damn. As far as I'm concerned the whole human race – all of it – can go and lose itself. I don't want any part of it.'

'How old are you, Bruce?'

'Leave me alone, damn you!'

'How old are you?'

'I'm thirty.'

'You talk like a teenager.'

'And I feel like an old, old man.'

The amusement was no longer on Mike's face as he asked.

'What did you do before this?'

'I slept and breathed and ate – and got trodden on.'

'What did you do for a living?'

'Law.'

'Were you successful?'

'How do you measure success? If you mean, did I make money, the answer is yes.'

I made enough to pay off the house and the car, he thought bitterly, and to contest custody of my children, and finally to meet the divorce settlement. I had enough for that, but, of course, I had to sell my partnership.

'Then you'll be all right,' Mike told him. 'If you've

succeeded once you'll be able to do it again when you've recovered from the shock; when you've rearranged your life and taken other people into it to make you strong again.'

'I'm strong now, Haig. I'm strong *because* there is no one in my life. That's the only way you can be secure, on your own. Completely free and on your own.'

'Strong!' Anger flared in Mike's voice for the first time. 'On your own you're *nothing*, Curry. On your own you're so weak I could piss on you and wash you away!' Then the anger evaporated and Mike went on softly, 'But you'll find out – you're one of the lucky ones. You attract people to you. You don't have to be alone.'

'Well, that's the way I'm going to be from now on.'

'We'll see,' murmured Mike.

'Yes, we'll see,' Bruce agreed, and lifted the tarpaulin over the radio.

'Driver, we are going to halt for the night. It's too dark to proceed with safety.'

– 5 –

Brazzaville Radio came through weakly on the set and the static was bad, for outside the rain still fell and thunder rolled around the sky like an unsecured cargo at sea.

' – Our Elisabethville correspondent reports that elements of the Kantangese Army in the South Kasai province today violated the ceasefire agreement by firing upon a low-flying aircraft of the United Nations command. The aircraft, a Vampire jet fighter of the Indian Air Force, returned safely to its base at Kamina airfield. The pilot, however, was wounded by small arms fire. His condition is satisfactory.

'The United Nations Commander in Katanga, General

Rhee, has lodged a strong protest with the Kantangese government—' The announcer's voice was overlaid by the electric crackle of static.

'We winged him!' rejoiced Wally Hendry. The scab on his cheek had dried black, with angry red edges.

'Shut up,' snapped Bruce, 'we're trying to hear what's happening.'

'You can't hear a bloody thing now. André, there's a bottle in my pack. Get it! I'm going to drink to that coolie with a bullet up his—'

Then the radio cleared and the announcer's voice came through loudly.

' – at Senwati Mission fifty miles from the river harbour of Port Reprieve. A spokesman for the Central Congolese Government denied that the Congolese troops were operating in this area, and it is feared that a large body of armed bandits is taking advantage of the unsettled conditions to—' Again the static drowned it out.

'Damn this set,' muttered Bruce as he tried to tune it.

' – stated today that the removal of missile equipment from the Russian bases in Cuba had been confirmed by aerial reconnaissance—'

'That's all that we are interested in.' Bruce switched off the radio. 'What a shambles! Ruffy, where is Senwati Mission?'

'Top end of the swamp, near the Rhodesian border.'

'Fifty miles from Port Reprieve,' muttered Bruce, not attempting to conceal his anxiety.

'It's more than that by road, boss, more like a hundred.'

'That should take them three or four days in this weather, with time off for looting along the way,' Bruce calculated. 'It will be cutting it fairly fine. We must get through to Port Reprieve by tomorrow evening and pull out again at dawn the next day.'

'Why not keep going tonight?' Hendry removed the

bottle from his lips to ask. 'Better than sitting here being eaten by mosquitoes.'

'We'll stay,' Bruce answered. 'It won't do anybody much good to derail this lot in the dark.' He turned back to Ruffy. 'Three-hour watches tonight, Sergeant Major. Lieutenant Haig will take the first, then Lieutenant Hendry, then Lieutenant de Surrier, and I'll do the dawn spell.'

'Okay, boss. I'd better make sure my boys aren't sleeping.'

He left the compartment and the broken glass from the corridor windows crunched under his boots.

'I'll be on my way also.' Mike stood up and pulled the groundsheet over his shoulders.

'Don't waste the batteries of the searchlights, Mike. Sweep every ten minutes or so.'

'Okay, Bruce.' Mike looked across at Hendry. 'I'll call you at nine o'clock.'

'Jolly good show, old fruit.' Wally exaggerated Mike's accent. 'Good hunting, what!' and then as Mike left the compartment, 'Silly old bugger, why does he have to talk like that?'

No one answered him, and he pulled up his shirt behind.

'André, what's this on my back?'

'It's a pimple.'

'Well, squeeze it then.'

Bruce woke in the night, sweating, with the mosquitoes whining about his face. Outside it was still raining and occasionally the reflected light from the searchlight on the roof of the coach lit the interior dimly.

On one of the bottom bunks Mike Haig lay on his back. His face was shining with sweat and he rolled his head from side to side on the pillow. He was grinding his teeth – a sound to which Bruce had become accustomed, and he preferred it to Hendry's snores.

'You poor old bugger,' whispered Bruce.

From the bunk opposite, André de Surrier whimpered.

In sleep he looked like a child with dark soft hair falling over his forehead.

– 6 –

The rain petered out in the dawn and the sun was hot before it cleared the horizon. It lifted a warm mist from the dripping forest. As they ran north the forest thickened, the trees grew closer together and the undergrowth beneath them was coarser than it had been around Elisabethville.

Through the warm misty dawn Bruce saw the water tower at Msapa Junction rising like a lighthouse above the forest, its silver paint streaked with brown rust. Then they came round the last curve in the tracks and the little settlement huddled before them.

It was small, half a dozen buildings in all, and there was about it the desolate aspect of human habitation reverting to jungle.

Beside the tracks stood the water tower and the raised concrete coal bins. Then the station buildings of wood and iron, with the large sign above the verandah:

MSAPA JUNCTION. Elevation 963m.

There was an avenue of casia flora trees with very dark green foliage and orange flowers; and beyond that, on the edge of the forest, a row of cottages.

One of the cottages had been burned, its ruins were fire blackened and tumbled; and the gardens had lost all sense of discipline with three months' neglect.

'Driver, stop beside the water tower. You have fifteen minutes to fill your boiler.'

'Thank you, monsieur.'

With a heavy sigh of steam the loco pulled up beside the tower.

'Haig, take four men and go back to give the driver a hand.'

'Okay, Bruce.'

Bruce turned once more to the radio.

'Hendry.'

'Hello there.'

'Get a patrol together, six men, and search those cottages. Then take a look at the edge of the bush, we don't want any unexpected visitors.'

Wally Hendry waved an acknowledgement from the leading truck, and Bruce went on:

'Put de Surrier on.' He watched Hendry pass the set to André. 'De Surrier, you are in charge of the leading trucks in Hendry's absence. Keep Hendry covered, but watch the bush behind you also. They could come from there.'

Bruce switched off the set and turned to Ruffy. 'Stay up here on the roof, Ruffy. I'm going to chase them up with the watering. If you see anything, don't write me a postcard, start pooping off.'

Ruffy nodded. 'Have some breakfast to take with you.' He proffered an open bottle of beer.

'Better than bacon and eggs.' Bruce accepted the bottle and climbed down on to the platform. Sipping the beer he walked back along the train and looked up at Mike and the engine driver in the tower.

'Is it empty?' he called up at them.

'Half full, enough for a bath if you want one,' answered Mike.

'Don't tempt me.' The idea was suddenly very attractive, for he could smell his own stale body odour and his eyelids were itchy and swollen from mosquito bites. 'My kingdom for a bath.' He ran his fingers over his jowls and they rasped over stiff beard.

He watched them swing the canvas hose out over the loco. The chubby little engine driver clambered up and sat astride the boiler as he fitted the hose.

A shout behind him made Bruce turn quickly, and he saw Hendry's patrol coming back from the cottages. They were dragging two small prisoners with them.

'Hiding in the first cottage,' shouted Hendry. 'They tried to leg it into the bush.' He prodded one of them with his bayonet. The child cried out and twisted in the hands of the gendarme who held her.

'Enough of that.' Bruce stopped him from using the bayonet again and went to meet them. He looked at the two children.

The girl was close to puberty with breasts like insect bites just starting to show, thin-legged with enlarged knee-caps out of proportion to her thighs and calves. She wore only a dirty piece of trade cloth drawn up between her legs and secured around her waist by a length of bark string, and the tribal tattoo marks across her chest and cheeks and forehead stood proud in ridges of scar tissue.

'Ruffy.' Bruce called him down from the coach. 'Can you speak to them?'

Ruffy picked up the boy and held him on his hip. He was younger than the girl – seven, perhaps eight years old. Very dark-skinned and completely naked, as naked as the terror on his face.

Ruffy grunted sharply and the gendarme released the girl. She stood trembling, making no attempt to escape.

Then in a soothing rumble Ruffy began talking to the boy on his hip; he smiled as he spoke and stroked the child's head. Slowly a little of the fear melted and the boy answered in a piping treble that Bruce could not understand.

'What does he say?' urged Bruce.

'He thinks we're going to eat them,' laughed Ruffy. 'Not enough here for a decent breakfast.' He patted the skinny little arm, grey with crushed filth, then he gave an order to one of the gendarmes. The man disappeared into the coach and came back with a handful of chocolate bars. Still talking, Ruffy peeled one of them and placed it in the boy's mouth. The child's eyes widened appreciatively at the taste and he chewed quickly, his eyes on Ruffy's face, his answers now muffled with chocolate.

At last Ruffy turned to Bruce.

'No trouble here, boss. They come from a small village about an hour's walk away. Just five or six families, and no war party. These kids sneaked across to have a look at the houses, pinch what they could perhaps, but that's all.'

'How many men at this village?' asked Bruce, and Ruffy turned back to the boy. In reply to the question he held up the fingers of both hands, without interrupting the chewing.

'Does he know if the line is clear through to Port Reprieve? Have they burnt the bridges or torn up the tracks?' Both children were dumb to this question. The boy swallowed the last of his chocolate and looked hungrily at Ruffy, who filled his mouth again.

'Jesus,' muttered Hendry with deep disgust. 'Is this a crèche or something. Let's all play ring around the roses.'

'Shut up,' snapped Bruce, and then to Ruffy, 'Have they seen any soldiers?'

Two heads shaken in solemn unison.

'Have they seen any war parties of their own people?'

Again solemn negative.

'All right, give them the rest of the chocolate,' instructed Bruce. That was all he could get out of them, and time was wasting. He glanced back at the tower and saw that Haig and the engine driver had finished watering. For a further second he studied the boy. His own son would be about the same age now; it was twelve months since – Bruce stopped himself hurriedly. That way lay madness.

'Hendry, take them back to the edge of the bush and turn them loose. Hurry up. We've wasted long enough.'

'You're telling me!' grunted Hendry and beckoned to the

two children. With Hendry leading and a gendarme on each side they trotted away obediently and disappeared behind the station building.

'Driver, are your preparations complete?'

'Yes, monsieur, we are ready to depart.'

'Shovel all the coal in, we've gotta keep her rolling.' Bruce smiled at him, he liked the little man and their stilted exchanges gave him pleasure.

'Pardon, monsieur.'

'It was an imbecility, a joke – forgive me.'

'Ah, a joke!' The roly-poly stomach wobbled merrily.

'Okay, Mike,' Bruce shouted, 'get your men aboard. We are—'

A burst of automatic gunfire cut his voice short. It came from behind the station buildings, and it battered into the heat-muted morning with such startling violence that for an instant Bruce stood paralysed.

'Haig,' he yelled, 'get up front and take over from de Surrier.' That was the weak point, and Mike's party ran down the train.

'You men.' Bruce stopped the six gendarmes. 'Come with me.' They fell in behind him, and with a quick glance Bruce assured himself that the train was safe. All along its length rifle barrels were poking out protectively, while on the roof Ruffy was dragging the Bren round to cover the flank. A charge by even a thousand Baluba must fail before the fire power that was ready now to receive it.

'Come on,' said Bruce and ran, with the gendarmes behind him, to the sheltering wall of the station building. There had been no shot fired since that initial burst, which could mean either that it was a false alarm or that Hendry's party had been overwhelmed by the first rush.

The door of the station master's office was locked. Bruce kicked and it crashed open with the weight of his booted foot behind it.

I've always wanted to do that, he thought happily in his excitement, ever since I saw Gable do it in *San Francisco*.

'You four – inside! Cover us from the windows.' They crowded into the room with their rifles held ready. Through the open door Bruce saw the telegraph equipment on the table by the far wall; it was clattering metallically from traffic on the Elisabethville-Jadotville line. Why is it that under the stimulus of excitement my mind always registers irrelevances? Which thought is another irrelevancy, he decided.

'Come on, you two, stay with me.' He led them down the outside wall, keeping in close to its sheltering bulk, pausing at the corner to check the load of his rifle and slip the selector on to rapid fire.

A further moment he hesitated. What will I find around this corner? A hundred naked savages crowded round the mutilated bodies of Hendry and his gendarmes, or . . . ?

Crouching, ready to jump back behind the wall, rifle held at high port across his chest, every muscle and nerve of his body cocked like a hair-trigger, Bruce stepped sideways into the open.

Hendry and the two gendarmes stood in the dusty road beyond the first cottage. They were relaxed, talking together, Hendry reloading his rifle, cramming the magazine with big red hands on which the gingery hair caught the sunlight. A cigarette dangled from his lower lip and he laughed suddenly, throwing his head back as he did so and the cigarette ash dropped down his jacket front. Bruce noticed the long dark sweat stain across his shoulders.

The two children lay in the road fifty yards farther on.

Bruce was suddenly cold, it came from inside, a cramping coldness of the guts and chest. Slowly he straightened up and began to walk towards the children. His feet fell silently in the powder dust and the only sound was his own breathing, hoarse, as though a wounded beast followed close behind him. He walked past Hendry and the two gendarmes without looking at them; but they stopped talking, watching him uneasily.

He reached the girl first and went down on one knee beside her, laying his rifle aside and turning her gently on to her back.

'This isn't true,' he whispered. 'This can't be true.'

The bullet had taken half her chest out with it, a hole the size of a coffee cup, with the blood still moving in it, but slowly, oozing, welling up into it with the viscosity of new honey.

Bruce moved across to the boy; he felt an almost dreamlike sense of unreality.

'No, this isn't true.' He spoke louder, trying to undo it with words.

Three bullets had hit the boy; one had torn his arm loose at the shoulder and the sharp white end of the bone pointed accusingly out of the wound. The other bullets had severed his trunk almost in two.

It came from far away, like the rising roar of a train along a tunnel. Bruce could feel his whole being shaken by the strength of it, he shut his eyes and listened to the roaring in his head, and with his eyes tight closed his vision was filled with the colour of blood.

'Hold on!' a tiny voice screamed in his roaring head. 'Don't let go, fight it. Fight it as you've fought before.'

And he clung like a flood victim to the straw of his sanity while the great roaring was all around him. Then the roar was muted, rumbling away, gone past, a whisper, now nothing.

The coldness came back to him, a coldness more vast than the flood had been.

He opened his eyes and breathed again, stood up and walked back to where Hendry stood with the two gendarmes.

'Corporal,' Bruce addressed one of the men beside Hendry; and with a shock he heard that his own voice was calm, without any trace of the fury that had so nearly carried him away on its flood.

'Corporal, go back to the train. Tell Lieutenant Haig and Sergeant Major Ruffararo that I want them here.'

Thankfully the man went, and Bruce spoke to Wally Hendry in the same dispassionate tone.

'I told you to turn them loose,' he said.

'So they could run home and call the whole pack down on us – is that what you wanted, Bucko?' Hendry had recovered now, he was defiant, grinning.

'So instead you murdered them?'

'Murdered! You crazy or something, Bruce? They're Balubes, aren't they? Bloody man-eating Balubes!' shouted Hendry angrily, no longer grinning. 'What's wrong with you, man? This is war, Bucko, war. C'est la guerre, like the man said, c'est la guerre!' Then suddenly his voice moderated again. 'Let's forget it. I did what was right, now let's forget it; what's two more bloody Balubes after all the killing that's been going on? Let's forget it.'

Bruce did not answer, he lit a cigarette and looked beyond Hendry for the others to come.

'How's that, Bruce? You willing we just forget it?' persisted Hendry.

'On the contrary, Hendry, I make you a sacred oath, and I call upon God to witness it.' Bruce was not looking at him, he couldn't trust himself to look at Hendry without killing him. 'This is my promise to you: I will have you hanged for this, not shot, hanged on good hemp rope. I have sent for Haig and Ruffararo so we'll have plenty of witnesses. The first thing I do once we get back to Elisabethville will be to turn you over to the proper authorities.'

'You don't mean that!'

'I have never meant anything so seriously in my life.'

'Jesus, Bruce—!'

Then Haig and Ruffy came; they came running until they saw, and they stopped suddenly and stood uncertainly in the bright sun, looking from Bruce to the two frail little corpses lying in the road.

'What happened?' asked Mike.

'Hendry shot them,' answered Bruce.

'What for?'

'Only he knows.'

'You mean he – he just killed them, just shot them down?'

'Yes.'

'My God,' said Mike, and then again, his voice dull with shock, 'my God.'

'Go and look at them, Haig. I want you to look closely so you remember.'

Haig walked across to the children.

'You too, Ruffy. You'll be a witness at the trial.'

Mike Haig and Ruffy walked side by side to where the children lay, and stood staring down at them. Hendry shuffled his feet in the dust awkwardly and then went on loading the magazine of his rifle.

'Oh, for Chrissake!' he blustered. 'What's all the fuss? They're just a couple of Balubes.'

Wheeling slowly to face him Mike Haig's face was a yellowish colour with only his cheeks and his nose still flushed with the tiny burst of veins beneath the surface of the skin, but there was no colour in his lips. Each breath he drew sobbed in his throat. He started back towards Hendry, still breathing that way, and his mouth was working as he tried to force it to speak. As he came on he unslung the rifle from his shoulder.

'Haig!' said Bruce sharply.

'This time – you – you bloody – this is the last—' mouthed Haig.

'Watch it, Bucko!' Hendry warned him. He stepped

back, clumsily trying to fit the loaded magazine on to his rifle.

Mike Haig dropped the point of his bayonet to the level of Hendry's stomach.

'Haig!' shouted Bruce, and Haig charged surprisingly fast for a man of his age, leaning forward, leading with the bayonet at Hendry's stomach, the incoherent mouthings reaching their climax in a formless bellow.

'Come on, then!' Hendry answered him and stepped forward. As they came together Hendry swept the bayonet to one side with the butt of his own rifle. The point went under his armpit and they collided chest to chest, staggering as Haig's weight carried them backwards. Hendry dropped his rifle and locked both arms round Haig's neck, forcing his head back so that his face was tilted up at the right angle.

'Look out, Mike, he's going to butt!' Bruce had recognized the move, but his warning came too late. Hendry's head jerked forward and Mike gasped as the front of Hendry's steel helmet caught him across the bridge of his nose. The rifle slipped from Mike's grip and fell into the road, he lifted his hands and covered his face with spread fingers and the redness oozed out between them.

Again Hendry's head jerked forward like a hammer and again Mike gasped as the steel smashed into his face and fingers.

'Knee him, Mike!' Bruce yelled as he tried to take up a position from which to intervene, but they were staggering in a circle, turning like a wheel and Bruce could not get in.

Hendry's legs were braced apart as he drew his head back to strike again, and Mike's knee went up between them, all the way up with power into the fork of Hendry's crotch.

Breaking from the clinch, his mouth open in a silent scream of agony, Hendry doubled up with both hands holding his lower stomach, and sagged slowly on to his knees in the dust.

Dazed, with blood running into his mouth, Mike fumbled with the canvas flap of his holster.

'I'll kill you, you murdering swine.'

The pistol came out into his right hand; short-barrelled, blue and ugly.

Bruce stepped up behind him, his thumb found the nerve centre below the elbow and as he dug in the pistol dropped from Mike's paralysed hand and dangled on its lanyard against his knee.

'Ruffy, stop him,' Bruce shouted, for Hendry was clawing painfully at the rifle that lay in the dust beside him.

'Got it, boss!' Ruffy stooped quickly over the crawling body at his feet, in one swift movement opened the flap of the holster, drew the revolver and the lanyard snapped like cotton as he jerked on it.

They stood like that: Bruce holding Haig from behind, and Hendry crouched at Ruffy's feet. The only sound for several seconds was the hoarse rasping of breath.

Bruce felt Mike relaxing in his grip as the madness left him; he unclipped his pistol from his lanyard and let it drop.

'Leave me, Bruce. I'm all right now.'

'Are you sure? I don't want to shoot you.'

'No, I'm all right.'

'If you start it again, I'll have to shoot you. Do you understand?'

'Yes, I'll be all right now. I lost my senses for a moment.'

'You certainly did,' Bruce agreed, and released him.

They formed a circle round the kneeling Hendry, and Bruce spoke.

'If either you or Haig start it again you'll answer to me, do you hear me?'

Hendry looked up, his small eyes slitted with pain. He did not answer.

'Do you hear me?' Bruce repeated the question and Hendry nodded.

'Good! From now on, Hendry, you are under open arrest.

I can't spare men to guard you, and you're welcome to escape if you'd like to try. The local gentry would certainly entertain you most handsomely, they'd probably arrange a special banquet in your honour.'

Hendry's lips drew back in a snarl that exposed teeth with green slimy stains on them.

'But remember my promise, Hendry, as soon as we get back to—'

'Wally, Wally, are you hurt?' André came running from the direction of the station. He knelt beside Hendry.

'Get away, leave me alone.' Hendry struck out at him impatiently and André recoiled.

'De Surrier, who gave you permission to leave your post? Get back to the train.'

André looked up uncertainly, and then back to Hendry.

'De Surrier, you heard me. Get going. And you also, Haig.'

He watched them disappear behind the station building before he glanced once more at the two children. There was a smear of blood and melted chocolate across the boy's cheek and his eyes were wide open in an expression of surprise. Already the flies were settling, crawling delightedly over the two small corpses.

'Ruffy, get spades. Bury them under those trees.' He pointed at the avenue of casia flora. 'But do it quickly.' He spoke brusquely so that how he felt would not show in his voice.

'Okay, boss. I'll fix it.'

'Come on, Hendry,' Bruce snapped, and Wally Hendry heaved to his feet and followed him meekly back to the train.

– 7 –

Slowly from Msapa Junction they travelled northwards through the forest. Each tree seemed to have been cast from the same mould, tall and graceful in itself, but when multiplied countless million times the effect was that of numbing monotony. Above them was a lane of open sky with the clouds scattered, but slowly regrouping for the next assault, and the forest shut in the moist heat so they sweated even in the wind of the train's movement.

'How is your face?' asked Bruce and Mike Haig touched the parallel swellings across his forehead where the skin was broken and discoloured.

'It will do,' he decided; then he lifted his eyes and looked across the open trucks at Wally Hendry. 'You shouldn't have stopped me, Bruce.'

Bruce did not answer, but he also watched Hendry as he leaned uncomfortably against the side of the leading truck, obviously favouring his injuries, his face turned half away from them, talking to André.

'You should have let me kill him,' Mike went on. 'A man who can shoot down two small children in cold blood and then laugh about it afterwards—!' Mike left the rest unsaid, but his hands were opening and closing in his lap.

'It's none of your business,' said Bruce, sensitive to the implied rebuke. 'What are you? One of God's avenging angels?'

'None of my business, you say?' Mike turned quickly to face Bruce. 'My God, what kind of man are you? I hope for your sake you don't mean that!'

'I'll tell you in words of one syllable what kind of man I am, Haig,' Bruce answered flatly. 'I'm the kind that minds my own bloody business, that lets other people lead their own lives. I am ready to take reasonable measures to prevent others flouting the code which society has drawn up for us, but that's all. Hendry has committed murder; this I agree is a bad thing, and when we get back to Elisabethville I will bring it to the attention of the people whose business it is. But I am not going to wave banners and quote from the Bible and froth at the mouth.'

'That's all?'

'That's all.'

'You don't feel sorry for those two kids?'

'Yes I do. But pity doesn't heal bullet wounds; all it does is distress me. So I switch off the pity – they can't use it.'

'You don't feel anger or disgust or horror at Hendry?'

'The same thing applies,' explained Bruce, starting to lose patience again. 'I could work up a sweat about it if I let myself loose on an emotional orgy, as you are doing.'

'So instead you treat something as evil as Hendry with an indifferent tolerance?' asked Mike.

'Jesus Christ!' grated Bruce. 'What the hell do you want me to do?'

'I want you to stop playing dead. I want you to be able to recognize evil and to destroy it.' Mike was starting to lose his temper also; his nerves were taut.

'That's great! Do you know where I can buy a second-hand crusader outfit and a white horse, then singlehanded I will ride out to wage war on cruelty and ignorance, lust and greed and hatred and poverty—'

'That's not what I—' Mike tried to interrupt, but Bruce overrode him, his handsome face flushed darkly with anger and the sun. 'You want me to destroy evil wherever I find it. You old fool, don't you know that it has a hundred heads and that for each one you cut off another hundred grow in its place? Don't you know that it's in you also, so to destroy it you have to destroy yourself?'

'You're a coward, Curry! The first time you burn a finger you run away and build yourself an asbestos shelter—'

'I don't like being called names, Haig. Put a leash on your tongue.'

Mike paused and his expression changed, softening into a grin.

'I'm sorry, Bruce. I was just trying to teach you—'

'Thank you,' scoffed Bruce, his voice still harsh; he had not been placated by the apology. 'You are going to teach me, thanks very much! But what are you going to teach me, Haig? What are you qualified to teach? "How to find success and happiness" by Laughing Lad Haig who worked his way down to a lieutenancy in the black army of Katanga – how's that as a title for your lecture, or do you prefer something more technical like: "The applications of alcohol to spiritual research—"'

'All right, Bruce. Drop it, I'll shut up,' and Bruce saw how deeply he had wounded Mike. He regretted it then, he would have liked to unsay it. But that's one thing you can never do.

Beside him Mike Haig was suddenly much older and more tired looking, the pouched wrinkles below his eyes seemed to have deepened in the last few seconds, and a little more of the twinkle had gone from his eyes. His short laughter had a bitter humourless ring to it.

'When you put it that way it's really quite funny.'

'I punched a little low,' admitted Bruce, and then, 'perhaps I should let you shoot Hendry. A waste of ammunition really, but seeing that you want to so badly,' Bruce drew his pistol and offered it to Mike butt first, 'use mine.' He grinned disarmingly at Mike and his grin was almost impossible to resist; Mike started to laugh. It wasn't a very good joke, but somehow it caught fire between them and suddenly they were laughing together.

Mike Haig's battered features spread like warm butter and twenty years dropped from his face. Bruce leaned back against the sandbags with his mouth wide open, the pistol still in his hand and his long lean body throbbing uncontrollably with laughter.

There was something feverish in it, as though they were trying with laughter to gargle away the taste of blood and hatred. It was the laughter of despair.

Below them the men in the trucks turned to watch them, puzzled at first, and then beginning to chuckle in sympathy, not recognizing the sickness of that sound.

'Hey, boss,' called Ruffy. 'First time I ever seen you laugh like you meant it.'

And the epidemic spread, everyone was laughing, even André de Surrier was smiling.

Only Wally Hendry was untouched by it, silent and sullen, watching them with small expressionless eyes.

They came to the bridge over the Cheke in the middle of the afternoon. Both the road and the railway crossed it side by side, but after this brief meeting they diverged and the road twisted away to the left. The river was padded on each bank by dense dark green bush; three hundred yards thick, a matted tangle of thorn and tree fern with the big trees growing up through it and bursting into flower as they reached the sunlight.

'Good place for an ambush,' muttered Mike Haig, eyeing the solid green walls of vegetation on each side of the lines.

'Charming, isn't it,' agreed Bruce, and by the uneasy air of alertness that had settled on his gendarmes it was clear that they agreed with him.

The train nosed its way carefully into the river bush like a steel snake along a rabbit run, and they came to the river. Bruce switched on the set.

'Driver, stop this side of the bridge. I wish to inspect it before entrusting our precious cargo to it.'

'Oui, monsieur.'

The Cheke river at this point was fifty yards wide, deep, quick-flowing and angry with flood water which had almost covered the white sand beaches along each bank. Its bottle-green colour was smoked with mud and there were whirlpools round the stone columns of the bridge.

'Looks all right,' Haig gave his opinion. 'How far are we from Port Reprieve now?'

Bruce spread his field map on the roof of the coach between his legs and found the brackets that straddled the convoluted ribbon of the river.

'Here we are.' He touched it and then ran his finger along the stitched line of the railway until it reached the red circle that marked Port Reprieve. 'About thirty miles to go, another hour's run. We'll be there before dark.'

'Those are the Lufira hills.' Mike Haig pointed to the blue smudge that only just showed above the forest ahead of them.

'We'll be able to see the town from the top,' agreed Bruce. 'The river runs parallel to them on the other side, and the swamp is off to the right, the swamp is the source of the river.'

He rolled the map and passed it back to Ruffy who slid it into the plastic map case.

'Ruffy, Lieutenant Haig and I are going ahead to have a look at the bridge. Keep an eye on the bush.'

'Okay, boss. You want a beer to take with you?'

'Thanks.' Bruce was thirsty and he emptied half the bottle before climbing down to join Mike on the gravel embankment. Rifles unslung, watching the bush on each side uneasily, they hurried forward and with relief reached the bridge and went out into the centre of it.

'Seems solid enough,' commented Mike. 'No one has tampered with it.'

'It's wood.' Bruce stamped on the heavy wild mahogany timbers. They were three feet thick and stained with a dark chemical to inhibit rotting.

'So, it's wood?' enquired Mike.

'Wood burns,' explained Bruce. 'It would be easy to burn

it down.' He leaned his elbows on the guard rail, drained the beer bottle and dropped it to the surface of the river twenty feet below. There was a thoughtful expression on his face.

'Very probably there are Baluba in the bush' – he pointed at the banks – 'watching us at this moment. They might get the same idea. I wonder if I should leave a guard here?'

Mike leaned on the rail beside him and they both stared out to where the river took a bend two hundred yards downstream; in the crook of the bend grew a tree twice as tall as any of its neighbours. The trunk was straight and covered with smooth silvery bark and its foliage piled to a high green steeple against the clouds. It was the natural point of focus for their eyes as they weighed the problem.

'I wonder what kind of tree that is. I've never seen one like it before.' Bruce was momentarily diverted by the grandeur of it. 'It looks like a giant blue gum.'

'It's quite a sight,' Mike concurred. 'I'd like to go down and have a closer—'

Then suddenly he stiffened and there was an edge of alarm in his voice as he pointed.

'Bruce, there! What's that in the lower branches?'

'Where?'

'Just above the first fork, on the left—' Mike was pointing and suddenly Bruce saw it. For a second he thought it was a leopard, then he realized it was too dark and long.

'It's a man,' exclaimed Mike.

'Baluba,' snapped Bruce; he could see the shape now and the sheen of naked black flesh, the kilt of animal tails and the headdress of feathers. A long bow stood up behind the man's shoulder as he balanced on the branch and steadied himself with one hand against the trunk. He was watching them.

Bruce glanced round at the train. Hendry had noticed their agitation and, following the direction of Mike's raised arm, he had spotted the Baluba. Bruce realized what Hendry was going to do and he opened his mouth to shout, but before he could do so Hendry had snatched his rifle off his shoulder, swung it up and fired a long, rushing, hammering burst.

'The trigger-happy idiot,' snarled Bruce and looked back at the tree. Slabs of white bark were flying from the trunk and the bullets reaped leaves that fluttered down like crippled insects, but the Baluba had disappeared.

The gunfire ceased abruptly and in its place Hendry was shouting with hoarse excitement.

'I got him, I got the bastard.'

'Hendry!' Bruce's voice was also hoarse, but with anger, 'Who ordered you to fire?'

'He was a bloody Baluba, a mucking big bloody Baluba. Didn't you see him, hey? Didn't you see him, man?'

'Come here, Hendry.'

'I got the bastard,' rejoiced Hendry.

'Are you deaf? Come here!'

While Hendry climbed down from the truck and came towards them Bruce asked Haig:

'Did he hit him?'

'I'm not sure. I don't think so, I think he jumped. If he had been hit he'd have been thrown backwards, you know how it knocks them over.'

'Yes,' said Bruce, 'I know.' A .300 bullet from an FN struck with a force of well over a ton. When you hit a man there was no doubt about it. All right, so the Baluba was still in there.

Hendry came up, swaggering, laughing with excitement.

'So you killed, hey?' Bruce asked.

'Stone dead, stone bloody dead!'

'Can you see him?'

'No, he's down in the bush.'

'Do you want to go and have a look at him, Hendry? Do you want to go and get his ears?'

Ears are the best trophy you can take from a man, not as

good as the skin of a black-maned lion or the great bossed horns of a buffalo, but better than the scalp. The woolly cap of an African scalp is a drab thing, messy to take and difficult to cure. You have to salt it and stretch it inside out over a helmet; even then it smells badly. Ears are much less trouble and Hendry was an avid collector. He was not the only one in the army of Katanga; the taking of ears was common practice.

'Yeah, I want them.' Hendry detached the bayonet from the muzzle of his rifle. 'I'll nip down and get them.'

'You can't let anyone go in there, Bruce. Not even him,' protested Haig quietly.

'Why not? He deserves it, he worked hard for it.'

'Only take a minute.' Hendry ran his thumb along the bayonet to test the edge. My God! He really means it, thought Bruce; he'd go into that tangled stuff for a pair of ears – he's not brave, he's just stupendously lacking in imagination.

'Wait for me, Bruce, it won't take long.' Hendry started back.

'You're not serious, Bruce?' Mike asked.

'No,' agreed Bruce, 'I'm not serious,' and his voice was cold and hard as he caught hold of Hendry's shoulder and stopped him.

'Listen to me! You have no more chances – that was it. I'm waiting for you now, Hendry. Just once more, that's all. Just once more.'

Hendry's face turned sullen again.

'Don't push me, Bucko.'

'Get back to the train and bring it across,' said Bruce contemptuously and turned to Haig.

'Now we'll have to leave a guard here. They know we've gone across and they'll burn it for a certainty, especially after that little fiasco.'

'Who are you going to leave?'

'Ten men, say, under a sergeant. We'll be back by

nightfall or tomorrow morning at the latest. They should be safe enough. I doubt there is a big war party here, a few strays perhaps, but the main force will be closer to the town.'

'I hope you're right.'

'So do I,' said Bruce absently, his mind busy with the problem of defending the bridge. 'We'll strip all the sandbags off the coaches and build an emplacement here in the middle of the roadway, leave two of the battery-operated searchlights and a case of flares with them, one of the Brens and a couple of cases of grenades. Food and water for a week. No, they'll be all right.'

The train was rolling down slowly towards them – and a single arrow rose from the edge of the jungle. Slowly it rose, curving in flight and falling towards the train, dropping faster now, silently into the mass of men in the leading truck.

So Hendry had missed and the Baluba had come up stream through the thick bush to launch his arrow in retaliation. Bruce sprang to the guard rail and, using it as a rest for his rifle, opened up in short bursts, searching the green mass and seeing it tremble with his bullets. Haig was shooting also, hunting the area from which the arrow had come.

The train was up to them now and Bruce slung his rifle over his shoulder and scrambled up the side of the truck. He pushed his way to the radio set.

'Driver, stop the covered coaches in the middle of the bridge,' he snapped, and then he switched it off and looked for Ruffy.

'Sergeant Major, get all those sandbags off the roof into the roadway.' While they worked, the gendarmes would be protected from further arrows by the body of the train.

'Okay, boss.'

'Kanaki.' Bruce picked his most reliable sergeant. 'I am leaving you here with ten men to hold the bridge for us.

Take one of the Brens, and two of the lights—' Quickly Bruce issued his orders and then he had time to ask André:

'What happened to that arrow? Was anyone hit?'

'No, missed by a few inches. Here it is.'

'That was a bit of luck.' Bruce took the arrow from André and inspected it quickly. A light reed, crudely fletched with green leaves and with the iron head bound into it with a strip of rawhide. It looked fragile and ineffectual, but the barbs of the head were smeared thickly with a dark paste that had dried like toffee.

'Pleasant,' murmured Bruce, and then he shuddered slightly. He could imagine it embedded in his body with the poison purple-staining the flesh beneath the skin. He had heard that it was not a comfortable death, and the iron-tipped reed was suddenly malignant and repulsive. He snapped it in half and threw it out over the side of the bridge before he jumped down from the truck to supervise the building of the guard post.

'Not enough sandbags, boss.'

'Take the mattresses off all the bunks, Ruffy.' Bruce solved that quickly. The leather-covered coir pallets would stop an arrow with ease.

Fifteen minutes later the post was completed, a shoulder-high ring of sandbags and mattresses large enough to accommodate ten men and their equipment, with embrasures sited to command both ends of the bridge.

'We'll be back early tomorrow, Kanaki. Let none of your men leave this post for any purpose; the gaps between the timbers are sufficient for purposes of sanitation.'

'We shall enjoy enviable comfort, Captain. But we will lack that which soothes.' Kanaki grinned meaningly at Bruce.

'Ruffy, leave them a case of beer.'

'A whole case?' Ruffy made no attempt to hide his shocked disapproval of such a prodigal order.

'Is my credit not good?'

'You credit is okay, boss,' and then he changed to French to make his protest formal. 'My concern is the replacement of such a valuable commodity.'

'You're wasting time, Ruffy!'

– 8 –

From the bridge it was thirty miles to Port Reprieve. They met the road again six miles outside the town; it crossed under them and disappeared into the forest again to circle out round the high ground taking the easier route into Port Reprieve. But the railroad climbed up the hills in a series of traverses and came out at the top six hundred feet above the town. On the stony slopes the forest found meagre purchase and the vegetation was sparser; it did not obscure the view.

Standing on the roof Bruce looked out across the Lufira swamps to the north, a vastness of poisonous green swamp grass and open water, disappearing into the blue heat haze without any sign of ending. From its southern extremity it was drained by the Lufira river. The river was half a mile wide, deep olive-green, ruffled darker by eddies of wind across its surface, fenced into the very edge of the water by a solid barrier of dense river bush. In the angle formed by the swamp and the river was a headland which protected the natural harbour of Port Reprieve. The town was on a spit of land, the harbour on one side and a smaller swamp on the other. The road came round the right-hand side of the hills, crossed a causeway over the swamp and entered the single street of the town from the far side.

There were three large buildings in the centre of the town opposite the railway yard, their iron roofs bright beacons in the sunlight; and clustered round them were perhaps fifty smaller thatched dwellings.

Down on the edge of the harbour was a long shed,

obviously a workshop, and two jetties ran into the water. The diamond dredgers were moored alongside; three of them, ungainly black hulks with high superstructures and blunt ends.

It was a place of heat and fever and swamp smells, an ugly little village by a green reptile river.

'Nice place to retire,' Mike Haig grunted.

'Or open a health resort,' said Bruce.

Beyond the causeway, on the main headland, there was another cluster of buildings, just the tops were showing above the forest. Among them rose the copper-clad spire of a church.

'Mission station,' guessed Bruce.

'St Augustine's,' agreed Ruffy. 'My first wife's little brudder got himself educated there. He's an attaché to the ministry of something or other in Elisabethville now, doing damn good for himself.' Boasting a little.

'Bully for him,' said Bruce.

The train had started angling down the hills towards the town.

'Well, I reckon we've made it, boss.'

'I reckon also; all we have to do is get back again.'

'Yessir, I reckon that's all.'

And they ran into the town.

There were more than forty people in the crowd that lined the platform to welcome them.

We'll have a heavy load on the way home, thought Bruce as he ran his eye over them. He saw the bright spots of women's dresses in the throng. Bruce counted four of them. That's another complication; one day I hope I find something in this life that turns out exactly as expected, something that will run smoothly and evenly through to its right and logical conclusion. Some hope, he decided, some bloody hope.

The joy and relief of the men and women on the platform was pathetically apparent in their greetings. Most of the women were crying and the men ran beside the train like small boys as it slid in along the raised concrete platform. All of them were of mixed blood, Bruce noted. They varied in colour from creamy yellow to charcoal. The Belgians had certainly left much to be remembered by.

Standing back from the throng, a little aloof from the general jollification, was a half-blooded Belgian. There was an air of authority about him that was unmistakable. On one side of him stood a large bosomy woman of his own advanced age, darker skinned than he was; but Bruce saw immediately that she was his wife. At his other hand stood a figure dressed in a white open-necked shirt and blue jeans that Bruce at first thought was a boy, until the head turned and he saw the long plume of dark hair that hung down her back, and the unmanly double pressure beneath the white shirt.

The train stopped and Bruce jumped down on to the platform and laughingly pushed his way through the crowds towards the Belgian. Despite a year in the Congo, Bruce had not grown accustomed to being kissed by someone who had not shaved for two or three days and who smelled strongly of garlic and cheap tobacco. This atrocity was committed upon him a dozen times or more before he arrived before the Belgian.

'The Good Lord bless you for coming to our aid, Monsieur Captain.' The Belgian recognized the twin bars on the front of Bruce's helmet and held out his hand. Bruce had expected another kiss, so he accepted the handshake with relief.

'I am only glad that we are in time,' he answered.

'May I introduce myself – Martin Boussier, district manager of Union Miniére Corporation, and this is my wife, Madame Boussier.' He was a tall man, but unlike his wife, sparsely fleshed. His hair was completely silver and his skin folded, toughened and browned by a life under the equatorial sun. Bruce took an instant liking to him. Madame

Boussier pressed her bulk against Bruce and kissed him heartily. Her moustache was too soft to cause him discomfort and she smelled of toilet soap, which was a distinct improvement, decided Bruce.

'May I also present Madame Cartier,' and for the first time Bruce looked squarely at the girl. A number of things registered in his mind simultaneously: the paleness of her skin which was not unhealthy but had an opaque coolness which he wanted to touch, the size of her eyes which seemed to fill half her face, the unconscious provocation of her lips, and the use of the word *Madame* before her name.

'Captain Curry – of the Katanga Army,' said Bruce. She's too young to be married, can't be more than seventeen. She's still got that little girl freshness about her and I bet she smells like an unweaned puppy.

'Thank you for coming, monsieur.' She had a throatiness in her voice as though she were just about to laugh or to make love, and Bruce added three years to his estimate of her age. That was not a little girl's voice, nor were those little girl's legs in the jeans, and little girls had less under their shirt fronts.

His eyes came back to her face and he saw that there was colour in her cheeks now and sparks of annoyance in her eyes.

My God, he thought, I'm ogling her like a matelot on shore leave. He hurriedly transferred his attention back to Boussier, but his throat felt constricted as he asked:

'How many are you?'

'There are forty-two of us, of which five are women and two are children.'

Bruce nodded, it was what he had expected. The women could ride in one of the covered coaches. He turned and surveyed the railway yard.

'Is there a turntable on which we can revolve the locomotive?' he asked Boussier.

'No, Captain.'

They would have to reverse all the way back to Msapa Junction, another complication. It would be more difficult to keep a watch on the tracks ahead, and it would mean a sooty and uncomfortable journey.

'What precautions have you taken against attack, monsieur?'

'They are inadequate, Captain,' Boussier admitted. 'I have not sufficient men to defend the town – most of the population left before the emergency. Instead I have posted sentries on all the approaches and I have fortified the hotel to the best of my ability. It was there we intended to stand in the event of attack.'

Bruce nodded again and glanced up at the sun. It was already reddening as it dropped towards the horizon, perhaps another hour or two of daylight.

'Monsieur, it is too late to entrain all your people and leave before nightfall. I intend to load their possessions this evening. We will stay overnight and leave in the early morning.'

'We are all anxious to be away from this place; we have twice seen large parties of Baluba on the edge of the jungle.'

'I understand,' said Bruce. 'But the dangers of travelling by night exceed those of waiting another twelve hours.'

'The decision is yours,' Boussier agreed. 'What do you wish us to do now?'

'Please see to the embarkation of your people. I regret that only the most essential possessions may be entertained. We will be almost a hundred persons.'

'I shall see to that myself,' Boussier assured him, 'and then?'

'Is that the hotel?' Bruce pointed across the street at one of the large double-storeyed buildings. It was only two hundred yards from where they stood.

'Yes, Captain.'

'Good,' said Bruce. 'It is close enough. Your people can

spend the night there in more comfort than aboard the train.'

He looked at the girl again; she was watching him with a small smile on her face. It was a smile of almost maternal amusement, as though she were watching a little boy playing at soldiers. Now it was Bruce's turn to feel annoyed. He was suddenly embarrassed by his uniform and epaulettes, by the pistol at his hip, the automatic rifle across his shoulder and the heavy helmet on his head.

'I will require someone who is familiar with the area to accompany me, I want to inspect your defences,' he said to Boussier.

'Madame Cartier could show you,' suggested Boussier's wife artlessly. I wonder if she noticed our little exchange, thought Bruce. Of course she did. All women have a most sensitive nose for that sort of thing.

'Will you go with the captain, Shermaine?' asked Madame Boussier.

'As the captain wishes.' She was still smiling.

'That is settled then,' said Bruce gruffly. 'I will meet you at the hotel in ten minutes, after I have made arrangements here.' He turned back to Boussier. 'You may proceed with the embarkation, monsieur.' Bruce left them and went back to the train.

'Hendry,' he shouted, 'you and de Surrier will stay on board. We are not leaving until the morning but these people are going to load their stuff now. In the meantime rig the searchlights to sweep both sides of the track and make sure the Brens are properly sited.'

Hendry grunted an acknowledgement without looking at Bruce.

'Mike, take ten men with you and go to the hotel. I want you there in case of trouble during the night.'

'Okay, Bruce.'

'Ruffy.'

'Sa!'

'Take a gang and help the driver refuel.'

'Okay, boss. Hey, boss!'

'Yes.' Bruce turned to him.

'When you go to the hotel, have a look-see maybe they got some beer up there. We're just about fresh out.'

'I'll keep it in mind.'

'Thanks, boss.' Ruffy looked relieved. 'I'd hate like hell to die of thirst in this hole.'

The townsfolk were streaming back towards the hotel. The girl Shermaine walked with the Boussiers, and Bruce heard Hendry's voice above him.

'Jesus, look what that pretty has got in her pants. What ever it is, one thing is sure: it's round and it's in two pieces, and those pieces move like they don't belong to each other.'

'You haven't any work to do Hendry?' Bruce asked harshly.

'What's wrong, Curry?' Hendry jeered down at him. 'You got plans yourself? Is that it, Bucko?'

'She's married,' said Bruce, and immediately was surprised that he had said it.

'Sure,' laughed Hendry. 'All the best ones are married; that don't mean a thing, not a bloody thing.'

'Get on with your work,' snapped Bruce, and then to Haig, 'Are you ready? Come with me then.'

– 9 –

When they reached the hotel Boussier was waiting for them on the open verandah. He led Bruce aside and spoke quietly.

'Monsieur, I don't wish to be an alarmist but I have received some most disturbing news. There are brigands armed with modern weapons raiding down from the north.

The last reports state that they had sacked Senwati Mission about three hundred kilometres north of here.'

'Yes,' Bruce nodded, 'I know about them. We heard on the radio.'

'Then you will have realized that they can be expected to arrive here very soon.'

'I don't see them arriving before tomorrow afternoon; by then we should be well on our way to Msapa Junction.'

'I hope you are right, Monsieur. The atrocities committed by this General Moses at Senwati are beyond the conception of any normal mind. He appears to bear an almost pathological hatred for all people of European descent.' Boussier hesitated before going on. 'There were a dozen white nuns at Senwati. I have heard that they—'

'Yes,' Bruce interrupted him quickly; he did not want to listen to it. 'I can imagine. Try and prevent these stories circulating amongst your people. I don't want to have them panic.'

'Of course,' Boussier nodded.

'Do you know what force this General Moses commands?'

'It is not more than a hundred men but, as I have said, they are all armed with modern weapons. I have even heard that they have with them a cannon of some description, though I think this unlikely. They are travelling in a convoy of stolen vehicles and at Senwati they captured a gasoline tanker belonging to the commercial oil companies.'

'I see,' mused Bruce. 'But it doesn't alter my decision to remain here overnight. However, we must leave at first light tomorrow.'

'As you wish, Captain.'

'Now, monsieur,' Bruce changed the subject, 'I require some form of transport. Is that car in running order?' He pointed at a pale green Ford Ranchero station wagon parked beside the verandah wall.

'It is. It belongs to my company.' Boussier took a key ring

from his pocket and handed it to Bruce. 'Here are the keys. The tank is full of gasoline.'

'Good,' said Bruce. 'Now if we can find Madame Cartier—'

She was waiting in the hotel lounge and she stood up as Bruce and Boussier came in.

'Are you ready, madame?'

'I await your pleasure,' she answered, and Bruce looked at her sharply. Just a trace of a twinkle in her dark blue eyes suggested that she was aware of the double meaning.

They walked out to the Ford and Bruce opened the door for her.

'You are gracious, monsieur.' She thanked him and slid into the seat. Bruce went round to the driver's side and climbed in beside her.

'It's nearly dark,' he said.

'Turn right on to the Msapa Junction road, there is one post there.'

Bruce drove out along the dirt road through the town until they came to the last house before the causeway. 'Here,' said the girl and Bruce stopped the car. There were two men there, both armed with sporting rifles. Bruce spoke to them. They had seen no sign of Baluba, but they were both very nervous. Bruce made a decision.

'I want you to go back to the hotel. The Baluba will have seen the train arrive; they won't attack in force, we'll be safe tonight. But they may try and cut a few throats if we leave you out here.'

The two half-breeds gathered together their belongings and set off towards the centre of town, obviously with lighter hearts.

'Where are the others?' Bruce asked the girl.

'The next post is at the pumping station down by the river, there are three men there.'

Bruce followed her directions. Once or twice as he drove

he glanced surreptitiously at her. She sat in her corner of the seat with her legs drawn up sideways under her. She sat very still, Bruce noticed. I like a woman who doesn't fidget; it's soothing. Then she smiled; this one isn't soothing. She is as disturbing as hell! She turned suddenly and caught him looking again, but this time she smiled.

'You are English, aren't you, Captain?'

'No, I am a Rhodesian,' Bruce answered.

'It's the same,' said the girl. 'You speak French so very badly that you had to be English.'

Bruce laughed. 'Perhaps your English is better than my French,' he challenged her.

'It couldn't be much worse,' she answered him in his own language. 'You are different when you laugh, not so grim, not so heroic. Take the next road to your right.'

Bruce turned the Ford down towards the harbour.

'You are very frank,' he said. 'Also your English is excellent.'

'Do you smoke?' she asked, and when he nodded she lit two cigarettes and passed one to him.

'You are also very young to smoke, and very young to be married.'

She stopped smiling and swung her legs off the seat.

'Here is the pumping station,' she said.

'I beg your pardon. I shouldn't have said that.'

'It's of no importance.'

'It was an impertinence,' Bruce demurred.

'It doesn't matter.'

Bruce stopped the car and opened his door. He walked out on to the wooden jetty towards the pump house, and the boards rang dully under his boots. There was a mist coming up out of the reeds round the harbour and the frogs were piping in fifty different keys. He spoke to the men in the single room of the pump station.

'You can get back to the hotel by dark if you hurry.'

'Oui, monsieur,' they agreed. Bruce watched them set off up the road before they went to the car. He spun the starter motor and above the noise of it the girl asked:

'What is your given name, Captain Curry?'

'Bruce.'

She repeated it, pronouncing it 'Bruise', and then asked:

'Why are you a soldier?'

'For many reasons.' His tone was flippant.

'You do not look like a soldier, for all your badges and your guns, for all the grimness and the frequent giving of orders.'

'Perhaps I am not a very good soldier.' He smiled at her.

'You are very efficient and very grim except when you laugh. But I am glad you do not look like one,' she said.

'Where is the next post?'

'On the railway line. There are two men there. Turn to your right again at the top, Bruce.'

'You are also very efficient, Shermaine.' They were silent again, having used each other's names. Bruce could feel it between them, a good feeling, warm like new bread. But what of her husband, he thought, I wonder where he is, and what he is like. Why isn't he here with her?

'He is dead,' she said quietly. 'He died four months ago of malaria.'

With the shock of it, Shermaine answering his unspoken question and also the answer itself, Bruce could say nothing for the moment, then:

'I'm sorry.'

'There is the post,' she said, 'in the cottage with the thatched roof.'

Bruce stopped the car and switched off the engine. In the silence she spoke again.

'He was a good man, so very gentle. I only knew him for a few months but he was a good man.'

She looked very small sitting beside him in the gathering dark with the sadness on her, and Bruce felt a great wave of tenderness wash over him. He wanted to put his arm round her and hold her, to shield her from the sadness. He searched for the words, but before he found them, she roused herself and spoke in a matter-of-fact tone.

'We must hurry, it's dark already.'

At the hotel the lounge was filled with Boussier's employees; Haig had mounted a Bren in one of the upstairs windows to cover the main street and posted two men in the kitchens to cover the back. The civilians were in little groups, talking quietly, and their expressions of complete doglike trust as they looked at Bruce disconcerted him.

'Everything under control, Mike?' he asked brusquely.

'Yes, Bruce. We should be able to hold this building against a sneak attack. De Surrier and Hendry, down at the station yard, shouldn't have any trouble either.'

'Have these people,' Bruce pointed at the civilians, 'loaded their luggage?'

'Yes, it's all aboard. I have told Ruffy to issue them with food from our stores.'

'Good.' Bruce felt relief; no further complications so far.

'Where is old man Boussier?'

'He is across at his office.'

'I'm going to have a chat with him.'

Unbidden, Shermaine fell in beside Bruce as he walked out into the street, but he liked having her there.

Boussier looked up as Bruce and Shermaine walked into his office. The merciless glare of the petromax lamp accentuated the lines at the corners of his eyes and mouth, and showed up the streaks of pink scalp beneath his neatly combed hair.

'Martin, you are not still working!' exclaimed Shermaine, and he smiled at her, the calm smile of his years.

'Not really, my dear, just tidying up a few things. Please be seated, Captain.'

He came round and cleared a pile of heavy leatherbound

ledgers off the chair and packed them into a wooden case on the floor, went back to his own chair, opened a drawer in the desk, brought out a box of cheroots and offered one to Bruce.

'I cannot tell you how relieved I am that you are here, Captain. These last few months have been very trying. The doubt. The anxiety.' He struck a match and held it out to Bruce who leaned forward across the desk and lit his cheroot. 'But now it is all at an end; I feel as though a great weight has been lifted from my shoulders.' Then his voice sharpened. 'But you were not too soon. I have heard within the last hour that this General Moses and his column have left Senwati and are on the road south, only two hundred kilometres north of here. They will arrive tomorrow at their present rate of advance.'

'Where did you hear this?' Bruce demanded.

'From one of my men, and do not ask me how he knows. There is a system of communication in this country which even after all these years I do not understand. Perhaps it is the drums, I heard them this evening, I do not know. However, their information is usually reliable.'

'I had not placed them so close,' muttered Bruce. 'Had I known this I might have risked travelling tonight, at least as far as the bridge.'

'I think your decision to stay over the night was correct. General Moses will not travel during darkness – none of his men would risk that – and the condition of the road from Senwati after three months neglect is such that he will need ten or twelve hours to cover the distance.'

'I hope you're right.' Bruce was worried. 'I'm not sure that we shouldn't pull out now.'

'That involves a risk also, Captain,' Boussier pointed out. 'We know there are tribesmen in close proximity to the town. They have been seen. They must be aware of your arrival, and might easily have wrecked the lines to prevent our departure. I think your original decision is still good.'

'I know.' Bruce was hunched forward in his chair, frowning, sucking on the cheroot. At last he sat back and the frown evaporated. 'I can't risk it. I'll place a guard on the causeway, and if this Moses gentleman arrives we can hold him there long enough to embark your people.'

'That is probably the best course,' agreed Boussier. He paused, glanced towards the open windows and lowered his voice. 'There is another point, Captain, which I wish to bring to your attention.'

'Yes?'

'As you know, the activity of my company in Port Reprieve is centred on the recovery of diamonds from the Lufira swamps.'

Bruce nodded.

'I have in my safe' – Boussier jerked his thumb at the heavy steel door built into the wall behind his desk – 'nine and a half thousand carats of gem-quality diamonds and some twenty-six thousand carats of industrial diamonds.'

'I had expected that.' Bruce kept his tone non-committal.

'It may be as well if we could agree on the disposition and handling of these stones.'

'How are they packaged?' asked Bruce.

'A single wooden case.'

'Of what size and weight?'

'I will show you.'

Boussier went to the safe, turned his back to them and they heard the tumblers whirr and click. While he waited Bruce realized suddenly that Shermaine had not spoken since her initial greeting to Boussier. He glanced at her now and she smiled at him. I like a woman who knows when to keep her mouth shut.

Boussier swung the door of the safe open and carried a small wooden case across to the desk.

'There,' he said.

Bruce examined it. Eighteen inches long, nine deep and twelve wide. He lifted it experimentally.

'About twenty pounds weight,' he decided. 'The lid is sealed.'

'Yes,' agreed Boussier, touching the four wax imprints.

'Good,' Bruce nodded. 'I don't want to draw unnecessary attention to it by placing a guard upon it.'

'No, I agree.'

Bruce studied the case a few seconds longer and then he asked:

'What is the value of these stones?'

Boussier shrugged. 'Possibly five hundred million francs.' And Bruce was impressed; half a million sterling. Worth stealing, worth killing for.

'I suggest, monsieur, that you secrete this case in your luggage. In your blankets, say. I doubt there will be any danger of theft until we reach Msapa Junction. A thief will have no avenue of escape. Once we reach Msapa Junction I will make other arrangements for its safety.'

'Very well, Captain.'

Bruce stood up and glanced at his watch. 'Seven o'clock, as near as dammit. I will leave you and see to the guard on the causeway. Please make sure that your people are ready to entrain before dawn tomorrow morning.'

'Of course.'

Bruce looked at Shermaine and she stood up quickly. Bruce held the door open for her and was just about to follow her when a thought struck him.

'That mission station – St Augustine's, is it? I suppose it's deserted now?'

'No, it's not.' Boussier looked a little shamefaced. 'Father Ignatius is still there, and of course the patients at the hospital.'

'Thanks for telling me.' Bruce was bitter.

'I'm sorry, Captain. It slipped my mind, there are so many things to think of.'

'Do you know the road out to the mission?' he snapped at Shermaine. *She* should have told him.

'Yes, Bruce.'

'Well, perhaps you'd be good enough to direct me.'

'Of course.' She also looked guilty.

Bruce slammed the door of Boussier's office and strode off towards the hotel with Shermaine trotting to keep pace with him. You can't rely on anyone, he thought, not anybody!

And then he saw Ruffy coming up from the station, looking like a big bear in the dusk. With a few exceptions, Bruce corrected himself.

'Sergeant Major.'

'Hello, boss.'

'This General Moses is closer to us than we reckoned. He's reported two hundred kilometres north of here on the Senwati road.'

Ruffy whistled through his teeth. 'Are you going to take off now, Boss?'

'No, I want a machine-gun post on this end of the causeway. If they come we can hold them there long enough to get away. I want you to take command.'

'I'll see to it now.'

'I'm going out to the mission – there's a white priest there. Lieutenant Haig is in command while I'm away.'

'Okay, boss.'

– 10 –

'I'm sorry, Bruce. I should have told you.' Shermaine sat small and repentant at her end of the Ranchero.

'Don't worry about it,' said Bruce, not meaning it.

'We have tried to make Father Ignatius come in to town. Martin has spoken to him many times, but he refuses to move.'

Bruce did not answer. He took the car down on to the causeway, driving carefully. There were shreds of mist lifting out of the swamp and drifting across the concrete ramp. Small insects, bright as tracer in the headlights, zoomed in to squash against the windscreen. The froggy chorus from the swamp honked and clinked and boomed deafeningly.

'I have apologized,' she murmured.

'Yes, I heard you,' said Bruce. 'You don't have to do it again.'

She was silent, and then:

'Are you always so bad-tempered?' she asked in English.

'*Always*,' snapped Bruce, 'is one of the words which should be eliminated from the language.'

'Since it has not been, I will continue to use it. You haven't answered my question: are you always so bad-tempered?'

'I just don't like balls-ups.'

'What is *balls-up*, please?'

'What has just happened: a mistake, a situation precipitated by inefficiency, or by somebody not using his head.'

'You never make balls-up, Bruce?'

'It is not a polite expression, Shermaine. Young ladies of refinement do not use it.' Bruce changed into French.

'You never make mistakes?' she corrected herself. Bruce did not answer. That's quite funny, he thought – never make mistakes! Bruce Curry, the original balls-up.

Shermaine held one hand across her middle and sat up straight.

'Bonaparte,' she said. 'Cold, silent, efficient.'

'I didn't say that—' Bruce started to defend himself. Then in the glow from the dash light he saw her impish expression and he could not stop himself; he had to grin.

'All right, I'm acting like a child.'

'You would like a cigarette?' she asked.

'Yes, please.'

She lit it and passed it to him.

'You do not like—' she hesitated, 'mistakes. Is there anything you do like?'

'Many things,' said Bruce.

'Tell me some.'

They bumped off the end of the causeway and Bruce accelerated up the far bank.

'I like being on a mountain when the wind blows, and the taste of the sea. I like Sinatra, crayfish thermidor, the weight and balance of a Purdey Royal, and the sound of a little girl's laughter. I like the first draw of a cigarette lit from a wood fire, the scent of jasmine, the feel of silk; I also enjoy sleeping late in the morning, and the thrill of forking a queen with my knight. Shadows on the floor of a forest please me. And, of course, money. But especially I like women who do not ask too many questions.'

'Is that all?'

'No, but it's a start.'

'And apart from – mistakes, what are the things you do not like.'

'Women who ask too many questions,' and he saw her smile. 'Selfishness except my own, turnip soup, politics, blond pubic hairs, Scotch whisky, classical music and hangovers.'

'I'm sure that is not all.'

'No, not nearly.'

'You are very sensual. All these things are of the senses.'

'Agreed.'

'You do not mention other people. Why?'

'Is this the turn-off to the mission?'

'Yes, go slowly, the road is bad. Why do you not mention your relationship to other people?'

'Why do you ask so many questions? Perhaps I'll tell you some day.'

She was silent a while and then softly:

'And what do you want from life – just those things you have spoken of? Is that all you want?'

'No. Not even them. I want nothing, expect nothing; that way I cannot be disappointed.'

Suddenly she was angry. 'You not only act like a child, you talk like one.'

'Another thing I don't like: criticism.'

'You are young. You have brains, good looks—'

'Thank you, that's better.'

' – and you are a fool.'

'That's not so good. But don't fret about it.'

'I won't, don't worry,' she flamed at him. 'You can—' she searched for something devastating. 'You can go jump out of the lake.'

'Don't you mean into?'

'Into, out of, backwards, sideways. I don't care!'

'Good, I'm glad we've got that settled. There's the mission, I can see a light.'

She did not answer but sat in her corner, breathing heavily, drawing so hard on her cigarette that the glowing tip lit the interior of the Ford.

The church was in darkness, but beyond it and to one side was a long low building. Bruce saw a shadow move across one of the windows.

'Is that the hospital?'

'Yes.' Abruptly.

Bruce stopped the Ford beside the small front verandah and switched off the headlights and the ignition.

'Are you coming in?'

'No.'

'I'd like you to present me to Father Ignatius.'

For a moment she did not move, then she threw open her door and marched up the steps of the verandah without looking back at Bruce.

He followed her through the front office, down the passage, past the clinic and small operating theatre, into the ward.

'Ah, Madame Cartier.' Father Ignatius left the bed over which he was stooping and came towards her.

'I heard that the relief train had arrived at Port Reprieve. I thought you would have left by now.'

'Not yet, Father. Tomorrow morning.'

Ignatius was tall, six foot three or four, Bruce estimated, and thin. The sleeve of his brown cassock had been cut short as a concession to the climate and his exposed arms appeared to be all bone, hairless, with the veins blue and prominent. Big bony hands, and big bony feet in brown open sandals.

Like most tall, thin men he was round-shouldered. His face was not one that you would remember, an ordinary face with steel-rimmed spectacles perched on a rather shapeless nose, neither young nor old, nondescript hair without grey in it, but there was about him that unhurried serenity you often find in a man of God. He turned his attention to Bruce, scrutinizing him gently through his spectacles.

'Good evening, my son.'

'Good evening, Father.' Bruce felt uncomfortable; they always made him feel that way. If only, he wished with envy, I could be as certain of one thing in my life as this man is certain of everything in his.

'Father, this is Captain Curry.' Shermaine's tone was cold, and then suddenly she smiled again. 'He does not care for people, that is why he has come to take you to safety.'

Father Ignatius held out his hand and Bruce found the skin was cool and dry, making him conscious of the moistness of his own.

'That is most thoughtful of you,' he said smiling, sensing the tension between them. 'I don't want to seem ungrateful, but I regret I cannot accept your offer.'

'We have received reports that a column of armed bandits are only two hundred kilometres or so north of here. They will arrive within a day or two. You are in great danger, these people are completely merciless,' Bruce urged him.

'Yes,' Father Ignatius nodded. 'I have also heard, and I am taking the steps I consider necessary. I shall take all my staff and patients into the bush.'

'They'll follow you,' said Bruce.

'I think not.' Ignatius shook his head. 'They will not waste their time. They are after loot, not sick people.'

'They'll burn your mission.'

'If they do, then we shall have to rebuild it when they leave.'

'The bush is crawling with Baluba, you'll end up in the cooking pot.' Bruce tried another approach.

'No.' Ignatius shook his head. 'Nearly every member of the tribe has at one time or another been a patient in this hospital. I have nothing to fear there, they are my friends.'

'Look here, Father. Don't let us argue. My orders are to bring you back to Elisabethville. I must insist.'

'And my orders are to stay here. You do agree that mine come from a higher authority than yours?' Ignatius smiled mildly. Bruce opened his mouth to argue further; then, instead, he laughed.

'No, I won't dispute that. Is there anything you need that I might be able to supply?'

'Medicines?' asked Ignatius.

'Acriflavine, morphia, field dressings, not much I'm afraid.'

'They would help, and food?'

'Yes, I will let you have as much as I can spare,' promised Bruce.

One of the patients, a woman at the end of the ward, screamed so suddenly that Bruce started.

'She will be dead before morning,' Ignatius explained softly. 'There is nothing I can do.'

'What's wrong with her?'

'She has been in labour these past two days; there is some complication.'

'Can't you operate?'

'I am not a doctor, my son. We had one here before the trouble began, but he is here no longer – he has gone back to Elisabethville. No,' his voice seemed to carry helpless regret for all the suffering of mankind, 'No, she will die.'

'Haig!' said Bruce.

'Pardon?'

'Father, you have a theatre here. Is it fully equipped?'

'Yes, I believe so.'

'Anaesthetic?'

'We have chloroform and pentothal.'

'Good,' said Bruce. 'I'll get you a doctor. Come on, Shermaine.'

– 11 –

'This heat, this stinking heat!' Wally Hendry mopped at his face with a grubby handkerchief and threw himself down on the green leather bunk. 'You notice how Curry leaves me and you here on the train while he puts Haig up at the hotel and he goes off with that little French bit. It doesn't matter that me and you must cook in this box, long as he and his buddy Haig are all right. You notice that, hey?'

'Somebody's got to stay aboard, Wally,' André said.

'Yeah, but you notice who it is? Always you and me – those high society boys stick together, you've got to give them that, they look after each other.' He transferred his attention back to the open window of the compartment. 'Sun's down already, and still hot enough to boil eggs. I could use a drink.' He unlaced his jungle boots, peeled off his socks and regarded his large white feet with distaste. 'This stinking heat got my athlete's foot going again.'

He separated two of his toes and picked at the loose scaly skin between. 'You got any of that ointment left, André?'

'Yes, I'll get it for you.' André opened the flap of his pack, took out the tube and crossed to Wally's bunk.

'Put it on,' instructed Wally and lay back offering his feet. André took them in his lap as he sat down on the bunk and went to work. Wally lit a cigarette and blew smoke towards the roof, watching it disperse.

'Hell, I could use a drink. A beer with dew on the glass and a head that thick.' He held up four fingers, then he lifted himself on one elbow and studied André as he spread ointment between the long prehensile toes.

'How's it going?'

'Nearly finished, Wally.'

'Is it bad?'

'Not as bad as last time, it hasn't started weeping yet.'

'It itches like you wouldn't believe it,' said Wally.

André did not answer and Wally kicked him in the ribs with the flat of his free foot.

'Did you hear what I said?'

'Yes, you said it itches.'

'Well, answer me when I talk to you. I ain't talking to myself.'

'I'm sorry, Wally.'

Wally grunted and was silent a while, then:

'Do you like me, André?'

'You know I do, Wally.'

'We're friends, aren't we, André?'

'Of course, you know that, Wally.'

An expression of cunning had replaced Wally's boredom.

'You don't mind when I ask you to do things for me, like putting stuff on my feet?'

'I don't mind – it's a pleasure, Wally.'

'It's a pleasure, is it?' There was an edge in Wally's voice now. 'You like doing it?'

André looked up at him apprehensively. 'I don't mind it.' His molten toffee eyes clung to the narrow Mongolian ones in Wally's face.

'You like touching me, André?'

André stopped working with the ointment and nervously wiped his fingers on his towel.

'I said, do you like touching me, André? Do you sometimes wish I'd touch you?'

André tried to stand up, but Wally's right arm shot out and his hand fastened on André's neck, forcing him down on to the bunk.

'Answer me, damn you, do you like it?'

'You're hurting me, Wally,' whispered André.

'Shame, now ain't that a shame!'

Wally was grinning. He shifted his grip to the ridge of muscle above André's collar bone and dug his fingers in until they almost met through the flesh.

'Please, Wally, please,' whimpered André, wriggling face down on the bunk.

'You love it, don't you? Come on, answer me.'

'Yes, all right, yes. Please don't hurt me, Wally.'

'Now, tell me truly, doll boy, have you ever had it before? I mean for real.' Wally put his knee in the small of André's back, bearing down with all his weight.

'No!' shrieked André. 'I haven't. Please, Wally, don't hurt me.'

'You're lying to me, André. Don't do it.'

'All right. I was lying.' André tried to twist his head round, but Wally pushed his face into the bunk.

'Tell me all about it – come on, doll boy.'

'It was only once, in Brussels.'

'Who was this beef bandit?'

'My employer. I worked for him. He had an export agency.'

'Did he throw you out, doll boy? Did he throw you out when he was tired of you?'

'No, you don't understand!' André denied with sudden vehemence. 'You don't understand. He looked after me. I had my own apartment, my own car, everything. He wouldn't have abandoned me if it hadn't been for – for what happened. He couldn't help it, he was true to me. I swear to you – he loved me!'

Wally snorted with laughter, he was enjoying himself now.

'Loved you! Jesus wept!' He threw his head back, for the laughter was almost strangling him, and it was ten seconds before he could ask: 'Then what happened between you and your true blue lover? Why didn't you get married and settle down to raise a family, hey?' At the improbability of his own sense of humour Wally convulsed with laughter once more.

'There was an investigation. The police – ooh! you're hurting me, Wally.'

'Keep talking, mamselle!'

'The police – he had no alternative. He was a man of position, he couldn't afford the scandal. There was no other way out – there never is for us. It's hopeless, there is no happiness.'

'Cut the crap, doll boy. Just give me the story.'

'He arranged employment for me in Elisabethville, gave me money, paid for my air fare, everything. He did everything, he looked after me, he still writes to me.'

'That's beautiful, real true love. You make me want to cry.'

Then Wally's laughter changed its tone, harsher now. 'Well, get this, doll boy, and get it good. I don't like queers!' He dug his fingers in again and André squealed.

'I'll tell you a story. When I was in reform school there was a queer there that tried to touch me up. One day I got him in the shower rooms with a razor, just an ordinary Gillette razor. There were twenty guys singing and shouting in the other cubicles. He screamed just like they were all screaming when the cold water hit them. No one took any notice of him. He wanted to be a woman, so I helped him.' Hendry's voice went hoarse and gloating with the memory.

'Jesus!' he whispered. 'Jesus, the blood!' André was sobbing now, his whole body shaking.

'I won't – please, Wally, I can't help it. It was just that one time. Please leave me.'

'How would you like me to help you, André?'

'No,' shrieked André. And Hendry lost interest; he released him, left him lying on the bunk and reached for his socks.

'I'm going to find me a beer.' He laced on his boots and stood up.

'Just you remember,' he said darkly, standing over the boy on the bunk. 'Don't get any ideas with me, Bucko.' He picked up his rifle and went out into the corridor.

Wally found Boussier on the verandah of the hotel talking with a group of his men.

'Where's Captain Curry?' he demanded.

'He has gone out to the mission station.'

'When did he leave?'

'About ten minutes ago.'

'Good,' said Wally. 'Who's got the key to the bar?'

Boussier hesitated.

'The captain has ordered that the bar is to remain locked.'

Wally unslung his rifle.

'Don't give me a hard time, friend.'

'I regret, monsieur, that I must obey the captain's instructions.'

For a minute they stared at each other, and there was no sign of weakening in the older man.

'Have it your way, then,' said Wally and swaggered through the lounge to the bar-room door. He put his foot against the lock and the flimsy mechanism yielded to the pressure. The door flew open and Wally marched across to the counter, laid his rifle on it and reached underneath to the shelves loaded with Simba beer.

The first bottle he emptied without taking it from his

lips. He belched luxuriously and reached for the second, hooked the cap off with the opener and inspected the bubble of froth that appeared at its mouth.

'Hendry!' Wally looked up at Mike Haig in the doorway.

'Hello, Mike.' He grinned.

'What do you think you're doing?' Mike demanded.

'What does it look like?' Wally raised the bottle in salutation and then sipped delicately at the froth.

'Bruce has given strict orders that no one is allowed in here.'

'Oh, for Chrissake, Haig. Stop acting like an old woman.'

'Out you get, Hendry. I'm in charge here.'

'Mike,' Wally grinned at him, 'you want me to die of thirst or something?' He leaned his elbows on the counter. 'Give me a couple more minutes. Let me finish my drink.'

Mike Haig glanced behind him into the lounge and saw the interested group of civilians who were craning to see into the bar-room. He closed the door and walked across to stand opposite Hendry.

'Two minutes, Hendry,' he agreed in an unfriendly tone, 'then out with you.'

'You're not a bad guy, Mike. You and I rubbed each other up wrong. I tell you something, I'm sorry about us.'

'Drink up!' said Mike. Without turning Wally reached backwards and took a bottle of Remy Martin cognac off the shelf. He pulled the cork with his teeth, selected a brandy balloon with his free hand and poured a little of the oily amber fluid into it.

'Keep me company, Mike,' he said and slid the glass across the counter towards Haig. First without expression, and then with his face seeming to crumble, Mike Haig stared at the glass. He moistened his lips, again older and tired-looking. With a physical wrench he pulled his eyes away from the glass.

'Damn you, Hendry.' His voice unnaturally low. 'God

damn you to hell.' He hit out at the glass, spinning it off the counter to shatter against the far wall.

'Did I do something wrong, Mike?' asked Hendry softly. 'Just offered you a drink, that's all.'

The smell of spilt brandy arose, sharp, fruity with the warmth of the grape, and Mike moistened his lips again. The saliva jetting from under his tongue, and the deep yearning aching want in his stomach spreading outwards slowly, numbing him.

'Damn you,' he whispered. 'Oh, damn you, damn you,' pleading now as Hendry filled another glass.

'How long has it been, Mike? A year, two years? Try a little, just a mouthful. Remember the lift it gives you. Come on, boy. You're tired, you've worked hard. Just one – there you are. Just have this one with me.'

Mike wiped his mouth with the back of his hand, sweating now across the forehead and on his upper lip, tiny jewels of sweat squeezed out of the skin by the craving of his body.

'Come on, boy.' Wally's voice hoarse with excitement; teasing, wheedling, tempting.

Mike's hand closed round the tumbler, moving of its own volition, lifting it towards lips that were suddenly slack and trembling, his eyes filled with mingled loathing and desire.

'Just this one,' whispered Hendry. 'Just this one.'

Mike gulped it with a sudden savage flick of his arm, one swallow and the glass was empty. He held it with both hands, his head bowed over it.

'I hate you. My God, I hate you.' He spoke to Hendry, and to himself, and to the empty glass.

'That's my boy!' crowed Wally. 'That's the lad! Come on, let me fill you up.'

– 12 –

Bruce went in through the front door of the hotel with Shermaine trying to keep pace with him. There were a dozen or so people in the lobby, and an air of tension amongst them. Boussier was one of them and he came quickly to Bruce.

'I'm sorry, Captain, I could not stop them. That one, that one with the red hair, he was violent. He had his gun and I think he was ready to use it.'

'What are you talking about?' Bruce asked him, but before Boussier could answer there was the bellow of Hendry's laughter from behind the door at the far end of the lobby; the door to the bar-room.

'They are in there,' Boussier told him. 'They have been there for the past hour.'

'Goddam it to hell,' swore Bruce. 'Now of all times. Oh, goddam that bloody animal.'

He almost ran across the room and threw open the double doors. Hendry was standing against the far wall with a tumbler in one hand and his rifle in the other. He was holding the rifle by the pistol grip and waving vague circles in the air with it.

Mike Haig was building a pyramid of glasses on the bar counter. He was just placing the final glass on the pile.

'Hello, Bruce, old cock, old man, old fruit,' he greeted Bruce, and waved in an exaggerated manner. 'Just in time, you can have a couple of shots as well. But Wally's first, he gets first shot. Must abide by the rules, no cheating, strictly democratic affair, everyone has equal rights. Rank doesn't count. That's right, isn't it Wally?' Haig's features had blurred; it was as though he were melting, losing his shape. His lips were loose and flabby, his jowls hung pendulously as an old woman's breasts, and his eyes were moist.

He picked up a glass from beside the pyramid, but this

glass was nearly full and a bottle of Remy Martin cognac stood beside it.

'A very fine old brandy, absolutely exquisite.' The last two words didn't come out right, so he repeated them carefully. Then he grinned loosely at Bruce and his eyes weren't quite in focus.

'Get out of the way, Mike,' said Hendry, and raised the rifle one-handed, aiming at the pile of glasses.

'Every time she bucks, she bounces,' hooted Haig, 'and every time she bounces you win a coconut. Let her rip, old fruit.'

'Hendry, stop that,' snapped Bruce.

'Go and get mucked,' answered Hendry and fired. The rifle kicked back over his shoulder and he fell against the wall. The pyramid of glasses exploded in a shower of fragments and the room was filled with the roar of the rifle.

'Give the gentleman a coconut!' crowed Mike.

Bruce crossed the room with three quick strides and pulled the rifle out of Hendry's hand.

'All right, you drunken ape. That's enough.'

'Go and muck yourself,' growled Hendry. He was massaging his wrist; the rifle had twisted it.

'Captain Curry,' said Haig from behind the bar, 'you heard what my friend said. You go and muck yourself sideways to sleep.'

'Shut up, Haig.'

'This time I'll fix you, Curry,' Hendry growled. 'You've been on my back too long – now I'm going to shake you off!'

'Kindly descend from my friend's back, Captain Curry,' chimed in Mike Haig. 'He's not a howdah elephant, he's my blood brother. I will not allow you to persecute him.'

'Come on, Curry. Come on then!' said Wally.

'That's it, Wally. Muck him up.' Haig filled his glass again as he spoke. 'Don't let him ride you.'

'Come on then, Curry.'

'You're drunk,' said Bruce.

'Come on then; don't talk, man. Or do I have to start it?'

'No, you don't have to start it,' Bruce assured him, and lifted the rifle butt-first under his chin, swinging it up hard. Hendry's head jerked and he staggered back against the wall. Bruce looked at his eyes; they were glazed over. That will hold him, he decided; that's taken the fight out of him. He caught Hendry by the shoulder and threw him into one of the chairs. I must get to Haig before he absorbs any more of that liquor, he thought, I can't waste time sending for Ruffy and I can't leave this thing behind me while I work on Haig.

'Shermaine,' he called. She was standing in the doorway and she came to his side. 'Can you use a pistol?'

She nodded. Bruce unclipped his Smith & Wesson from its lanyard and handed it to her.

'Shoot this man if he tries to leave that chair. Stand here where he cannot reach you.'

'Bruce—' she started.

'He is a dangerous animal. Yesterday he murdered two small children and, if you let him, he'll do the same to you. You must keep him here while I get the other one.'

She lifted the pistol, holding it with both hands and her face was even paler than was usual.

'Can you do it?' Bruce asked.

'Now I can,' she said and cocked the action.

'Hear me, Hendry.' Bruce took a handful of his hair and twisted his face up. 'She'll kill you if you leave this chair. Do you understand? She'll shoot you.'

'Muck you and your little French whore, muck you both. I bet that's what you two have been doing all evening in that car – playing "hide the sausage" down by the riverside.'

Anger flashed through Bruce so violently that it startled him. He twisted Hendry's hair until he could feel it coming away in his hand. Hendry squirmed with pain.

'Shut that foul mouth – or I'll kill you.'

He meant it, and suddenly Hendry knew he meant it.

'Okay, for Chrissake, okay. Just leave me.'

Bruce loosened his grip and straightened up.

'I'm sorry, Shermaine,' he said.

'That's all right – go to the other one.'

Bruce went to the bar counter, and Haig watched him come.

'What do you want, Bruce? Have a drink.' He was nervous. 'Have a drink, we are all having a little drink. All good clean fun, Bruce. Don't get excited.'

'You're not having any more; in fact, just the opposite,' Bruce told him as he came round the counter. Haig backed away in front of him.

'What are you going to do?'

'I'll show you,' said Bruce and caught him by the wrist, turning him quickly and lifting his arm up between his shoulder-blades.

'Hey, Bruce. Cut it out, you've made me spill my drink.'

'Good,' said Bruce and slapped the empty glass out of his hand. Haig started to struggle. He was still a powerful man but the liquor had weakened him and Bruce lifted his wrist higher, forcing him on to his toes.

'Come along, buddy boy,' instructed Bruce and marched him towards the back door of the bar-room. He reached round Haig with his free hand, turned the key in the lock and opened the door.

'Through here,' he said and pushed Mike into the kitchens. He kicked the door shut behind him and went to the sink, dragging Haig with him.

'All right, Haig, let's have it up,' he said and changed his grip quickly, thrusting Haig's head down over the sink. There was a dishtowel hanging beside it which Bruce screwed into a ball; then he used his thumbs to open Haig's jaws and wedged the towel between his back teeth.

'Let's have all of it.' He probed his finger down into Haig's throat. It came up hot and gushing over his hand,

and he fought down his own nausea as he worked. When he had finished he turned on the cold tap and held Haig's head under it, washing his face and his own hand.

'Now, I've got a little job for you, Haig.'

'Leave me alone, damn you,' groaned Haig, his voice indistinct beneath the rushing tap. Bruce pulled him up and held him against the wall.

'There's a woman in childbirth at the mission. She's going to die, Haig. She's going to die if you don't do something about it.'

'No,' whispered Haig. 'No, not that. Not that again.'

'I'm taking you there.'

'No, please not that. I can't – don't you see that I can't.' The little red and purple veins in his nose and cheeks stood out in vivid contrast to his pallor. Bruce hit him open-handed across the face and the water flew in drops from his hair at the shock.

'No,' he mumbled, 'please Bruce, please.'

Bruce hit him twice more, hard. Watching him carefully, and at last he saw the first flickering of anger.

'Damn you, Bruce Curry, damn you to hell.'

'You'll do,' rejoiced Bruce. 'Thank God for that.'

He hustled Haig back through the bar-room. Shermaine still stood over Hendry, holding the pistol.

'Come on, Shermaine. You can leave that thing now. I'll attend to him when we get back.'

As they crossed the lobby Bruce asked Shermaine. 'Can you drive the Ford?'

'Yes.'

'Good,' said Bruce. 'Here are the keys. I'll sit with Haig in the back. Take us out to the mission.'

Haig lost his balance on the front steps of the hotel and nearly fell, but Bruce caught him and half carried him to the car. He pushed him into the back seat and climbed in beside him. Shermaine slid in behind the wheel, started the engine and U-turned neatly across the street.

'You can't force me to do this, Bruce. I can't, I just can't,' Haig pleaded.

'We'll see,' said Bruce.

'You don't know what it's like. You can't know. She'll die on the table.' He held out his hands palms down. 'Look at that, look at them. How can I do it with these?' His hands were trembling violently.

'She's going to die anyway,' said Bruce, his voice hard. 'So you might as well do it for her quickly and get it over with.'

Haig brought his hands up to his mouth and wiped his lips.

'Can I have a drink, Bruce? That'll help. I'll try then, if you give me a drink.'

'No,' said Bruce, and Haig began to swear. The filth poured from his lips and his face twisted with the effort. He cursed Bruce, he cursed himself, and God in a torrent of the most obscene language that Bruce had ever heard. Then suddenly he snatched at the door handle and tried to twist it open. Bruce had been waiting for this and he caught the back of Haig's collar, pulled him backwards across the seat and held him there. Haig's struggles ceased abruptly and he began to sob softly.

Shermaine drove fast; across the causeway, up the slope and into the side road. The headlights cut into the darkness and the wind drummed softly round the car. Haig was still sobbing on the back seat.

Then the lights of the mission were ahead of them through the trees and Shermaine slowed the car, turned in past the church and pulled up next to the hospital block.

Bruce helped Haig out of the car, and while he was doing so the side door of the building opened and Father Ignatius came out with a petromax lantern in his hand. The harsh white glare of the lantern lit them all and threw grotesque shadows behind them. It fell with special cruelty on Haig's face.

'Here's your doctor, Father,' Bruce announced.

Ignatius lifted the lantern and peered through his spectacles at Haig.

'Is he sick?'

'No, Father,' said Bruce. 'He's drunk.'

'Drunk? Then he can't operate?'

'Yes, he damn well can!'

Bruce took Haig through the door and along the passage to the little theatre. Ignatius and Shermaine followed them.

'Shermaine, go with Father and help him bring the woman,' Bruce ordered, and they went; then he turned his attention back to Haig.

'Are you so far down there in the slime that you can't understand me?'

'I can't do it, Bruce. It's no good.'

'Then she'll die. But this much is certain: you are going to make the attempt.'

'I've got to have a drink, Bruce.' Haig licked his lips. 'It's burning me up inside, you've got to give me one.'

'Finish the job and I'll give you a whole case.'

'I've got to have one now.'

'No.' Bruce spoke with finality. 'Have a look at what they've got here in the way of instruments. Can you do it with these?' Bruce crossed to the sterilizer and lifted the lid, the steam came up out of it in a cloud. Haig looked in also.

'That's all I need, but there's not enough light in here, and I need a drink.'

'I'll get you more light. Start cleaning up.'

'Bruce, please let me—'

'Shut up,' snarled Bruce. 'There's the basin. Start getting ready.'

Haig crossed to the handbasin; he was more steady on his feet and his features had firmed a little. You poor old bastard, thought Bruce, I hope you can do it. My God, how much I hope you can.

'Get a move on, Haig, we haven't got all night.'

Bruce left the room and went quickly down the passage to the ward. The windows of the theatre were fixed and Haig could escape only into the passage. Bruce knew that he could catch him if he tried to run for it.

He looked into the ward. Shermaine and Ignatius, with the help of an African orderly, had lifted the woman on to the theatre trolley.

'Father, we need more light.'

'I can get you another lantern, that's all.'

'Good, do that then. I'll take the woman through.'

Father Ignatius disappeared with the orderly and Bruce helped Shermaine manoeuvre the trolley down the length of the ward and into the passage. The woman was whimpering with pain, and her face was grey, waxy grey. They only go like that when they are very frightened, or when they are dying.

'She hasn't much longer,' he said.

'I know,' agreed Shermaine. 'We must hurry.'

The woman moved restlessly on the trolley and gabbled a few words; then she sighed so that the great blanket-covered mound of her belly rose and fell, and she started to whimper again.

Haig was still in the theatre. He had stripped off his battle-jacket and, in his vest, he stooped over the basin washing. He did not look round as they wheeled the woman in.

'Get her on the table,' he said, working the soap into suds up to his elbows.

The trolley was of a height with the table and, using the blanket to lift her, it was easy to slide the woman across.

'She's ready, Haig,' said Bruce. Haig dried his arms on a clean towel and turned. He came to the woman and stood over her. She did not know he was there; her eyes were open but unseeing. Haig drew a breath; he was sweating a little across his forehead and the stubble of beard on the lower part of his face was stippled with grey.

He pulled back the blanket. The woman wore a short white jacket, open-fronted, that did not cover her stomach. Her stomach was swollen out, hard-looking, with the navel inverted. Knees raised slightly and the thick peasant's thighs spread wide in the act of labour. As Bruce watched, her whole body arched in another contraction. He saw the stress of the muscles beneath the dark greyish skin as they struggled to expel the trapped foetus.

'Hurry, Mike!' Bruce was appalled by the anguish of birth. I didn't know it was like this; in sorrow thou shalt bring forth children – but this! Through the woman's dry grey swollen lips burst another of those moaning little cries, and Bruce swung towards Mike Haig.

'Hurry, goddam you!'

And Mike Haig began his examination, his hands very pale as they groped over the dark skin. At last he was satisfied and he stood back from the table.

Ignatius and the orderly came in with two more lanterns. Ignatius started to say something, but instantly he sensed the tension in the room and he fell silent. They all watched Mike Haig's face.

His eyes were tight closed, and his face was hard angles and harsh planes in the lantern light. His breathing was shallow and laboured.

I must not push him now, Bruce knew instinctively, I have dragged him to the lip of the precipice and now I must let him go over the edge on his own.

Mike opened his eyes again, and he spoke.

'Caesarian section,' he said, as though he had pronounced his own death sentence. Then his breathing stopped. They waited, and at last the breath came out of him in a sigh.

'I'll do it,' he said.

'Gowns and gloves?' Bruce fired the question at Ignatius.

'In the cupboard.'

'Get them!'

'You'll have to help me, Bruce. And you also Shermaine.'

'Yes, show me.'

Quickly they scrubbed and dressed. Ignatius held the pale green theatre gowns while they dived into them and flapped and struggled through.

'That tray, bring it here,' Mike ordered as he opened the sterilizer. With a pair of long-nosed forceps he lifted the instruments out of the steaming box and laid them on the tray naming each one as he did so.

'Scalpel, retractors, clamps.'

In the meantime the orderly was swabbing the woman's belly with alcohol and arranging the sheets.

Mike filled the syringe with pentothal and held it up to the light. He was an unfamiliar figure now; his face masked, the green skull cap covering his hair, and the flowing gown falling to his ankles. He pressed the plunger and a few drops of the pale fluid dribbled down the needle.

He looked at Bruce, only his haunted eyes showing above the mask.

'Ready?'

'Yes,' Bruce nodded. Mike stooped over the woman, took her arm and sent the needle searching under the soft black skin on the inside of her elbow. The fluid in the syringe was suddenly discoloured with drawn blood as Mike tested for the vein, and then the plunger slid slowly down the glass barrel.

The woman stopped whimpering, the tension went out of her body and her breathing slowed and became deep and unhurried.

'Come here.' Mike ordered Shermaine to the head of the table, and she took up the chloroform mask and soaked the gauze that filled the cone.

'Wait until I tell you.'

She nodded. Christ, what lovely eyes she has, thought Bruce, before he turned back to the job in hand.

'Scalpel,' said Mike from across the table, pointing to it on the tray, and Bruce handed it to him.

Afterwards the details were confused and lacking reality in Bruce's mind.

The wound opening behind the knife, the tight stretched skin parting and the tiny blood vessels starting to squirt.

Pink muscle laced with white; butter-yellow layers of subcutaneous fat, and then through to the massed bluish coils of the gut. Human tissue, soft and pulsing, glistening in the flat glare of the petromax.

Clamps and retractors, like silver insects crowding into the wound as though it were a flower.

Mike's hands, inhuman in yellow rubber, moving in the open pit of the belly. Swabbing, cutting, clamping, tying off.

Then the swollen purple bag of the womb, suddenly unzipped by the knife.

And at last, unbelievably, the child curled in a dark grey ball of legs and tiny arms, head too big for its size, and the fat pink snake of the placenta enfolding it.

Lifted out, the infant hung by its heels from Mike's hand like a small grey bat, still joined to its mother.

Scissors snipped and it was free. Mike worked a little longer, and the infant cried.

It cried with minute fury, indignant and alive. From the head of the table Shermaine laughed with spontaneous delight, and clapped her hands like a child at a Punch and Judy show. Suddenly Bruce was laughing also. It was a laugh from long ago, coming out from deep inside him.

'Take it,' said Haig and Shermaine cradled it, wet and feebly wriggling in her arms. She stood with it while Haig sewed up. Watching her face and the way she stood, Bruce suddenly and unaccountably felt the laughter snag his throat, and he wanted to cry.

Haig closed the womb, stitching the complicated pattern of knots like a skilled seamstress, then the external sutures laid neatly across the fat lips of the wound, and at last the white tape hiding it all. He covered the woman, jerked the mask from his face and looked up at Shermaine.

'You can help me clean it up,' he said, and his voice was strong again and proud. The two of them crossed to the basin.

Bruce threw off his gown and left the room, went down the passage and out into the night. He leaned against the bonnet of the Ford and lit a cigarette.

Tonight I laughed again, he told himself with wonder, and then I nearly cried. And all because of a woman and a child. It is finished now, the pretence. The withdrawal. The big act. There was more than one birth in there tonight. I laughed again, I had the need to laugh again, and the desire to cry. A woman and a child, the whole meaning of life. The abscess had burst, the poison drained, and he was ready to heal.

'Bruce, Bruce, where are you?' She came out through the door; he did not answer her for she had seen the glow of his cigarette and she came to him. Standing close in the darkness.

'Shermaine—' Bruce said, then he stopped himself. He wanted to hold her, just hold her tightly.

'Yes, Bruce.' Her face was a pale round in the darkness, very close to him.

'Shermaine, I want—' said Bruce and stopped again.

'Yes, me too,' she whispered and then, drawing away, 'come, let's go and see what your doctor is doing now.' She took his hand and led him back into the building. Her hand was cool and dry with long tapered fingers in his.

Mike Haig and Father Ignatius were leaning over the cradle that now stood next to the table on which lay the blanket-covered body of the Baluba woman. The woman was breathing softly, and the expression on her face was of deep peace.

'Bruce, come and have a look. It's a beauty,' called Haig.

Still holding hands Bruce and Shermaine crossed to the cradle.

'He'll go all of eight pounds,' announced Haig proudly. Bruce looked at the infant; newborn black babies are more handsome than ours – they have not got that half-boiled look.

'Pity he's not a trout,' murmured Bruce. 'That would be a national record.' Haig stared blankly at him for a second, then he threw back his head and laughed; it was a good sound. There was a different quality in Haig now, a new confidence in the way he held his head, a feeling of completeness about him.

'How about that drink I promised you, Mike?' Bruce tested him.

'You have it for me, Bruce, I'll duck this one.' He isn't just saying it either, thought Bruce, as he looked at his face; he really doesn't need it now.

'I'll make it a double as soon as we get back to town.' Bruce glanced at his watch. 'It's past ten, we'd better get going.'

'I'll have to stay until she comes out from the anaesthetic,' demurred Haig. 'You can come back for me in the morning.'

Bruce hesitated. 'All right then. Come on, Shermaine.'

They drove back to Port Reprieve, sitting close together in the intimate darkness of the car. They did not speak until after they had reached the causeway, then Shermaine said:

'He is a good man, your doctor. He is like Paul.'

'Who is Paul?'

'Paul was my husband.'

'Oh.' Bruce was embarrassed. The mention of that name snapped the silken thread of his mood. Shermaine went on, speaking softly and staring down the path of the headlights.

'Paul was of the same age. Old enough to have learned understanding – young men are so cruel.'

'You loved him.' Bruce spoke flatly, trying to keep any trace of jealousy from his voice.

'Love has many shapes,' she answered. Then, 'Yes, I had begun to love him. Very soon I would have loved him enough to—' She stopped.

'To what?' Bruce's voice had gone rough as a wood rasp. *Now it starts*, he thought, *once again I am vulnerable*.

'We were only married four months before he – before the fever.'

'So?' Still harsh, his eyes on the road ahead.

'I want you to know something. I must explain it all to you. It is very important. Will you be patient with me while I tell you?' There was a pleading in her voice that he could not resist and his expression softened.

'Shermaine, you don't have to tell me.'

'I must. I want you to know.' She hesitated a moment, and when she spoke again her voice had steadied. 'I am an orphan, Bruce. Both my Mama and Papa were killed by the Germans, in the bombing. I was only a few months old when it happened, and I do not remember them. I do not remember anything, not one little thing about them; there is not even a photograph.' For a second her voice had gone shaky but again it firmed. 'The nuns took me, and they were my family. But somehow that is different, not really your own. I have never had anything that has truly belonged to me, something of my very own.'

Bruce reached out and took her hand; it lay very still in his grasp. You have now, he thought, you have me for your very own.

'Then when the time came the nuns made the arrangements with Paul Cartier. He was an engineer with Union Minière du Haut here in the Congo, a man of position, a suitable man for one of their girls.

'He flew to Brussels and we were married. I was not unhappy, for although he was old – as old as Doctor Mike – yet he was very gentle and kind, of great understanding. He did not—' She stopped and turned suddenly to Bruce, gripping his hand with both of hers, leaning towards him with her face serious and pale in the half-darkness, the plume of dark hair falling forward over her shoulder and her voice full of appeal. 'Bruce, do you understand what I am trying to tell you?'

Bruce stopped the car in front of the hotel, deliberately he switched off the ignition and deliberately he spoke.

'Yes, I think so.'

'Thank you,' and she flung the door open and went out of it and up the steps of the hotel with her long jeaned legs flying and her hair bouncing on her back.

Bruce watched her go through the double doors. Then he pressed the lighter on the dashboard and fished a cigarette from his pack. He lit it, exhaled a jet of smoke against the windscreen, and suddenly he was happy. He wanted to laugh again.

He threw the cigarette away only a quarter finished and climbed out of the Ford. He looked at his wristwatch; it was after midnight. My God, I'm tired. Too much has happened today; rebirth is a severe emotional strain. And he laughed out loud, savouring the sensation, letting it come slowly shaking up his throat from his chest.

Boussier was waiting for him in the lounge. He wore a towelling dressing-gown, and the creases of sleep were on his face.

'Are all your preparations complete, monsieur?'

'Yes,' the old man answered. 'The women and the two children are asleep upstairs. Madame Cartier has just gone up.'

'I know,' said Bruce, and Boussier went on, 'As you see, I have all the men here.' He gestured at the sleeping bodies that covered the floor of the lounge and bar-room.

'Good,' said Bruce. 'We'll leave as soon as it's light tomorrow.' He yawned, then rubbed his eyes, massaging them with his finger tips.

'Where is my officer, the one with the red hair?'

'He has gone back to the train, very drunk. We had more trouble with him after you had left.' Boussier hesitated delicately. 'He wanted to go upstairs, to the women.'

'Damn him.' Bruce felt his anger coming again. 'What happened?'

'Your sergeant major, the big one, dissuaded him and took him away.'

'Thank God for Ruffy.'

'I have reserved a place for you to sleep.' Boussier pointed to a comfortable leather armchair. 'You must be exhausted.'

'That is kind of you,' Bruce thanked him. 'But first I must inspect our defences.'

– 13 –

Bruce woke with Shermaine leaning over the chair and tickling his nose. He was fully dressed with his helmet and rifle on the floor beside him and only his boots unlaced.

'You do not snore, Bruce,' she congratulated him, laughing her small husky laugh. 'That is a good thing.'

He struggled up, dopey with sleep.

'What time is it?'

'Nearly five o'clock. I have breakfast for you in the kitchen.'

'Where is Boussier?'

'He is dressing; then he will start moving them down to the train.'

'My mouth tastes as though a goat slept in it.' Bruce moved his tongue across his teeth, feeling the fur on them.

'Then I shall not kiss you good morning, mon capitaine.'

She straightened up with the laughter still in her eyes. 'But your toilet requisites are in the kitchen. I sent one of your gendarmes to fetch them from the train. You can wash in the sink.'

Bruce laced up his boots and followed her through into the kitchen, stepping over sleeping bodies on the way.

'There is no hot water,' Shermaine apologized.

'That is the least of my worries.' Bruce crossed to the table and opened his small personal pack, taking out his razor and soap and comb.

'I raided the chicken coop for you,' Shermaine confessed. 'There were only two eggs. How shall I cook them?'

'Soft boiled, one minute.' Bruce stripped off his jacket and shirt, went to the sink and filled it. He sluiced his face and lifted handfuls of water over his head, snorting with pleasure.

Then he propped his shaving mirror above the taps and spread soap on his face. Shermaine came to sit on the draining board beside him and watched with frank interest.

'I will be sorry to see the beard go,' she said. 'It looked like the pelt of an otter, I liked it.'

'Perhaps I will grow it for you one day.' Bruce smiled at her. 'Your eyes are blue, Shermaine.'

'It has taken you a long time to find that out,' she said and pouted dramatically. Her skin was silky and cool-looking, lips pale pink without make-up. Her dark hair, drawn back, emphasized the high cheek bones and the size of her eyes.

'In India "sher" means "tiger",' Bruce told her, watching her from the corner of his eye. Immediately she abandoned the pout and drew her lips up into a snarl. Her teeth were small and very white and only slightly uneven. Her eyes rolled wide and then crossed at an alarming angle. She growled. Taken by surprise, Bruce laughed and nearly cut himself.

'I cannot abide a woman who clowns before breakfast. It ruins my digestion,' he laughed at her.

'Breakfast!' said Shermaine and uncrossed her eyes, jumped off the draining board and ran to the stove.

'Only just in time.' She checked her watch. 'One minute and twenty seconds, will you forgive me?'

'This once only, never again.' Bruce washed the soap off his face, dried and combed his hair and came to the table. She had a chair ready for him.

'How much sugar in your coffee?'

'Three, please.' Bruce chopped the top off his egg, and she brought the mug and placed it in front of him.

'I like making breakfast for you.' Bruce didn't answer her. This was dangerous talk. She sat down opposite him, leaned forward on her elbows with her chin in her hands.

'You eat too fast,' she announced and Bruce raised an eyebrow. 'But at least you keep your mouth closed.'

Bruce started on his second egg.

'How old are you?'

'Thirty,' said Bruce.

'I'm twenty – nearly twenty-one.'

'A ripe old age.'

'What do you do?'

'I'm a soldier,' he answered.

'No, you're not.'

'All right, I'm a lawyer.'

'You must be clever,' she said solemnly.

'A genius, that's why I'm here.'

'Are you married?'

'No – I was. What is this, a formal interrogation?'

'Is she dead?'

'No.' He prevented the hurt from showing in his face, it was easier to do now.

'Oh!' said Shermaine. She picked up the teaspoon and concentrated on stirring his coffee.

'Is she pretty?'

'No – yes, I suppose so.'

'Where is she?' Then quickly, 'I'm sorry it's none of my business.'

Bruce took the coffee from her and drank it. Then he looked at his watch.

'It's nearly five fifteen. I must go out and get Mike Haig.'

Shermaine stood up quickly.

'I'm ready.'

'I know the way – you had better get down to the station.'

'I want to come with you.'

'Why?'

'Just because, that's why.' Searching for a reason. 'I want to see the baby again.'

'You win.' Bruce picked up his pack and they went through into the lounge. Boussier was there, dressed and efficient. His men were nearly ready to move.

'Madame Cartier and I are going out to the mission to fetch the doctor. We will be back in half an hour or so. I want all your people aboard by then.'

'Very well, Captain.'

Bruce called to Ruffy who was standing on the verandah. 'Did you load those supplies for the mission?'

'They're in the back of the Ford, boss.'

'Good. Bring all your sentries in and take them down to the station. Tell the engine driver to get steam up and keep his hand on the throttle. We'll shove off as soon as I get back with Lieutenant Haig.'

'Okay, boss.'

Bruce handed him his pack. 'Take this down for me, Ruffy.' Then his eyes fell on the large heap of cardboard cartons at Ruffy's feet. 'What's that?'

Ruffy looked a little embarrassed. 'Coupla bottles of beer, boss. Thought we might get thirsty going home.'

'Good for you!' grinned Bruce. 'Put them in a safe place and don't drink them all before I get back.'

'I'll save you one or two,' promised Ruffy.

'Come along, tiger girl,' and Bruce led Shermaine out to the Ford. She sat closer to him than the previous day, but with her legs curled up under her, as before. As they crossed the causeway she lit two cigarettes and passed one to him.

'I'll be glad to leave this place,' she said, looking out across the swamp with the mist lifting sluggishly off it in the dawn, hanging in grey shreds from the fluffy tops of the papyrus grass.

'I've hated it here since Paul died. I hate the swamp and the mosquitoes and the jungle all around. I'm glad we're going.'

'Where will you go?' Bruce asked.

'I haven't thought about it. Back to Belgium, I suppose. Anywhere away from the Congo. Away from this heat to a country where you can breathe. Away from the disease and the fear. Somewhere so that I know tomorrow I will not have to run. Where human life has meaning, away from the killing and the burning and the rape.' She drew on her cigarette almost fiercely, staring ahead at the green wall of the forest.

'I was born in Africa,' said Bruce. 'In the time when the judge's gavel was not the butt of an FN rifle, before you registered your vote with a burst of gunfire.' He spoke softly with regret. 'In the time before the hatred. But now I don't know. I haven't thought much about the future either.'

He was silent for a while. They reached the turn-off to the mission and he swung the Ford into it.

'It has all changed so quickly; I hadn't realized how quickly until I came here to the Congo.'

'Are you going to stay here, Bruce? I mean, stay here in the Congo?'

'No,' he said, 'I've had enough. I don't even know what I'm fighting for.'

He threw the butt of his cigarette out of the window.

Ahead of them were the mission buildings.

Bruce parked the car outside the hospital buildings and they sat together quietly.

'There must be some other land,' he whispered, 'and if there is I'll find it.'

He opened the door and stepped out. Shermaine slid across the seat under the wheel and joined him. They walked side by side to the hospital; her hand brushed his and he caught it, held it and felt the pressure of his fingers returned by hers. She was taller than his shoulder, but not much.

Mike Haig and Father Ignatius were together in the women's ward, too engrossed to hear the Ford arrive.

'Good morning, Michael,' called Bruce. 'What's the fancy dress for?'

Mike Haig looked up and grinned. 'Morning, Bruce. Hello, Shermaine.' Then he looked down at the faded brown cassock he wore.

'Borrowed it from Ignatius. A bit long in the leg and tight round the waist, but less out of place in a sick ward than the accoutrements of war.'

'It suits you, Doctor Mike,' said Shermaine.

'Nice to hear someone call me that again.' The smile spread all over Haig's face. 'I suppose you want to see your baby, Shermaine?'

'Is he well?'

'Mother and child both doing fine,' he assured her and led Shermaine down between the row of beds, each with a black woolly head on the pillow and big curious eyes following their progress.

'May I pick him up?'

'He's asleep, Shermaine.'

'Oh, please!'

'I doubt it will kill him. Very well, then.'

'Bruce, come and look. Isn't he a darling?' She held the tiny black body to her chest and the child snuffled, its mouth automatically starting to search. Bruce leaned forward to peer at it.

'Very nice,' he said and turned to Ignatius. 'I have those supplies I promised you. Will you send an orderly to get them out of the car?' Then to Mike Haig, 'You'd better get changed, Mike. We're all ready to leave.'

Not looking at Bruce, fiddling with the stethoscope round his neck, Mike shook his head. 'I don't think I'll be going with you, Bruce.'

Surprised, Bruce faced him.

'What?'

'I think I'll stay on here with Ignatius. He has offered me a job.'

'You must be mad, Mike.'

'Perhaps,' agreed Haig and took the infant from Shermaine, placed it back in the cradle beside its mother and tucked the sheet in round its tiny body, 'and then again, perhaps not.' He straightened up and waved a hand down the rows of occupied beds. 'There's plenty to do here, that you must admit.'

Bruce stared helplessly at him and then appealed to Shermaine.

'Talk him out of it. Perhaps you can make him see the futility of it.'

Shermaine shook her head. 'No, Bruce, I will not.'

'Mike, listen to reason, for God's sake. You can't stay here in this disease-ridden backwater, you can't—'

'I'll walk out to the car with you, Bruce. I know you're in a hurry—'

He led them out through the side door and stood by the driver's window of the Ford while they climbed in. Bruce extended his hand and Mike took it, gripping hard.

'Cheerio, Bruce. Thanks for everything.'

'Cheerio, Mike. I suppose you'll be taking orders and having yourself made into a fully licensed dispenser of salvation?'

'I don't know about that, Bruce. I doubt it. I just want another chance to do the only work I know. I just want a last-minute rally to reduce the formidable score that's been chalked up against me so far.'

'I'll report you "missing, believed killed" – throw your uniform in the river,' said Bruce.

'I'll do that.' Mike stepped back. 'Look after each other, you two.'

'I don't know what you mean,' Shermaine informed him primly, trying not to smile.

'I'm an old dog, not easy to fool,' said Mike. 'Go to it with a will.'

Bruce let out the clutch and the Ford slid forward.

'God speed, my children.' That smile spread all over Mike's face as he waved.

'Au revoir, Doctor Michael.'

'So long, Mike.'

Bruce watched him in the rear-view mirror, tall in his ill-fitting cassock, something proud and worthwhile in his stance. He waved once more and then turned and hurried back into the hospital.

Neither of them spoke until they had almost reached the main road. Shermaine nestled softly against Bruce, smiling to herself, looking ahead down the tree-lined passage of the road.

'He's a good man, Bruce.'

'Light me a cigarette, please, Shermaine.' He didn't want to talk about it. It was one of those things that can only be made grubby by words.

Slowing for the intersection, Bruce dropped her into second gear, automatically glancing to his left to make sure the main road was clear before turning into it.

'Oh my God!' he gasped.

'What is it, Bruce?' Shermaine looked up with alarm from the cigarette she was lighting.

'Look!'

A hundred yards up the road, parked close to the edge of the forest, was a convoy of six large vehicles. The first five were heavy canvas-canopied lorries painted dull military olive, the sixth was a gasoline tanker in bright yellow and red with the Shell Company insignia on the barrel-shaped body. Hitched behind the leading lorry was a squat, rubber-tyred 25-pounder anti-tank gun with its long barrel pointed jauntily skywards. Round the vehicles, dressed in an assortment of uniforms and different styled helmets, were at least sixty men. They were all armed, some with automatic weapons and others with obsolete bolt-action rifles. Most of them were urinating carelessly into the grass that lined the road, while the others were standing in small groups smoking and talking.

'General Moses!' said Shermaine, her voice small with the shock.

'Get down,' ordered Bruce and with his free hand thrust her on to the floor. He rammed the accelerator flat and the Ford roared out into the main road, swerving violently, the back end floating free in the loose dust as he held the wheel over. Correcting the skid, meeting it and straightening out, Bruce glanced at the rear-view mirror. Behind them the men had dissolved into a confused pattern of movement; he heard their shouts high and thin above the racing engine of the Ford. Bruce looked ahead; it was another hundred yards to the bend in the road that would hide them and take them down to the causeway across the swamp.

Shermaine was on her knees pulling herself up to look over the back of the seat.

'Keep on the floor, damn you!' shouted Bruce and pushed her head down roughly.

As he spoke the roadside next to them erupted in a rapid series of leaping dust fountains and he heard the high hysterical beat of machine-gun fire.

The bend in the road rushed towards them, just a few more seconds. Then with a succession of jarring crashes that shook the whole body of the car a burst of fire hit them from behind. The windscreen starred into a sheet of opaque diamond lacework, the dashboard clock exploded powdering Shermaine's hair with particles of glass, two bullets tore through the seat ripping out the stuffing like the entrails of a wounded animal.

'Close your eyes,' shouted Bruce and punched his fist through the windscreen. Slitting his own eyes against the chips of flying glass, he could just see through the hole his fist had made. The corner was right on top of them and he dragged the steering-wheel over, skidding into it, his off-side wheels bumping into the verge, grass and leaves brushing the side of the car.

Then they were through the corner and racing down towards the causeway.

'Are you all right, Shermaine?'

'Yes, are you?' She emerged from under the dashboard, a smear of blood across one cheek where the glass had scratched her, and her eyes bigger than ever with fright.

'I only pray that Boussier and Hendry are ready to pull out. Those bastards won't be five minutes behind us.'

They went across the causeway with the needle of the speedometer touching eighty, up the far side and into the main street of Port Reprieve. Bruce thrust his hand down on the hooter ring, blowing urgent warning blasts.

'Please God, let them be ready,' he muttered. With relief he saw that the street was empty and the hotel seemed deserted. He kept blowing the horn as they roared down towards the station, a great billowing cloud of dust rising behind them. Braking the Ford hard, he turned it in past the station buildings and on to the platform.

Most of Boussier's people were standing next to the train. Boussier himself was beside the last truck with his wife and the small group of women around him. Bruce shouted at them through the open window.

'Get those women into the train, the *shufta* are right behind us, we're leaving immediately.'

Without question or argument old Boussier gathered them together and hurried them up the steel ladder into the truck. Bruce drove down the station platform shouting as he went.

'Get in! For Chrissake, hurry up! They're coming!'

He braked to a standstill next to the cab of the locomotive and shouted up at the bald head of the driver.

'Get going. Don't waste a second. Give her everything she's got. There's a bunch of *shufta* not five minutes behind us.'

The driver's head disappeared into the cab without even the usual polite, 'Oui monsieur.'

'Come on, Shermaine.' Bruce grabbed her hand and dragged her from the car. Together they ran to one of the covered coaches and Bruce pushed her half way up the steel steps.

At that moment the train jerked forward so violently that she lost her grip on the handrails and tumbled backwards on top of Bruce. He was caught off balance and they fell together in a heap on the dusty platform. Above them the train gathered speed, pulling away. He remembered this nightmare from his childhood, running after a train and never catching it. He had to fight down his panic as he and Shermaine scrambled up, both of them panting, clinging to each other, the coaches clackety-clacking past them, the rhythm of their wheels mounting.

'Run!' he gasped, 'Run!' and with the panic weakening their legs he just managed to catch the handrail of the second coach. He clung to it, stumbling along beside the train, one arm round Shermaine's waist. Sergeant Major

Ruffararo leaned out, took Shermaine by the scruff of her neck and lifted her in like a lost kitten. Then he reached down for Bruce.

'Boss, some day we going to lose you if you go on playing around like that.'

'I'm sorry, Bruce,' she panted, leaning against him.

'No damage done.' He could grin at her. 'Now I want you to get into that compartment and stay there until I tell you to come out. Do you understand?'

'Yes, Bruce.'

'Off you go.' He turned from her to Ruffy. 'Up on to the roof, Sergeant Major! We're going to have fireworks. Those *shufta* have got a field gun with them and we'll be in full view of the town right up to the top of the hills.'

By the time they reached the roof of the train it had pulled out of Port Reprieve and was making its first angling turn up the slope of the hills. The sun was up now, well clear of the horizon, and the mist from the swamp had lifted so that they could see the whole village spread out beneath them.

General Moses's column had crossed the causeway and was into the main street. As Bruce watched, the leading truck swung sharply across the road and stopped. Men boiled out from under the canopy and swarmed over the field gun, unhitching it, manhandling it into position.

'I hope those Arabs haven't had any drill on that piece,' grunted Ruffy.

'We'll soon find out,' Bruce assured him grimly and looked back along the train. In the last truck Boussier stood protectively over the small group of four women and their children, like an old white-haired collie with its sheep. Crouched against the steel side of the truck, André de Surrier and half a dozen gendarmes were swinging and sighting the two Bren guns. In the second truck also the gendarmes were preparing to open fire.

'What are you waiting for?' roared Ruffy. 'Get me that field gun – start shooting.'

They fired a ragged volley, then the Bren guns joined in. With every burst André's helmet slipped forward over his eyes and he had to stop and push it back. Lying on the roof of the leading coach, Wally Hendry was firing short businesslike bursts.

The *shufta* round the field gun scattered, leaving one of their number lying in the road, but there were men behind the armour shield – Bruce could see the tops of their helmets.

Suddenly there was a long gush of white smoke from the barrel, and the shell rushed over the top of the train, with a noise like the wings of a giant pheasant.

'Over!' said Ruffy.

'Under!' to the next shot as it ploughed into the trees below them.

'And the third one right up the throat,' said Bruce. But it hit the rear of the train. They were using armour-piercing projectiles, not high explosive, for there was not the burst of yellow cordite fumes but only the crash and jolt as it struck.

Anxiously Bruce tried to assess the damage. The men and women in the rear trucks looked shaken but unharmed and he started a sigh of relief, which changed quickly to a gasp of horror as he realized what had happened.

'They've hit the coupling,' he said. 'They've sheared the coupling on the last truck.'

Already the gap was widening, as the rear truck started to roll back down the hill, cut off like the tail of a lizard.

'Jump,' screamed Bruce, cupping his hands round his mouth. 'Jump before you gather speed.'

Perhaps they did not hear him, perhaps they were too stunned to obey, but no one moved. The truck rolled back, faster and faster as gravity took it, down the hill towards the village and the waiting army of General Moses.

'What can we do, boss?'

'Nothing,' said Bruce.

The firing round Bruce had petered out into silence as every man, even Wally Hendry, stared down the slope at the receding truck. With a constriction of his throat Bruce saw old Boussier stoop and lift his wife to her feet, hold her close to his side and the two of them looking back at Bruce on the roof of the departing train. Boussier raised his right hand in a gesture of farewell and then he dropped it again and stood very still. Behind him, André de Surrier had left the Bren gun and removed his helmet. He also was looking back at Bruce, but he did not wave.

At intervals the field gun in the village punctuated the stillness with its deep boom and gush of smoke, but Bruce hardly heard it. He was watching the *shufta* running down towards the station yard to welcome the truck. Losing speed it ran into the platform and halted abruptly as it hit the buffers at the end of the line. The *shufta* swarmed over it like little black ants over the body of a beetle and faintly Bruce heard the pop, pop, pop of their rifles, saw the low sun glint on their bayonets. He turned away.

They had almost reached the crest of the hills; he could feel the train increasing speed under him. But he felt no relief, only the prickling at the corners of his eyes and the ache of it trapped in his throat.

'The poor bastards,' growled Ruffy beside him. 'The poor bastards.' And then there was another crashing jolt against the train, another hit from the field gun. This time up forward, on the locomotive. Shriek of escaping steam, the train checking its pace, losing power. But they were over the crest of the hills, the village was out of sight and gradually the train speeded up again as they started down the back slope. But steam spouted out of it, hissing white jets of it, and Bruce knew they had received a mortal wound. He switched on the radio.

'Driver, can you hear me? How bad is it?'

'I cannot see, Captain. There is too much steam. But the pressure on the gauge is dropping swiftly.'

'Use all you can to take us down the hill. It is imperative that we pass the level crossing before we halt. It is absolutely imperative – if we stop this side of the level crossing they will be able to reach us with their lorries.'

'I will try, Captain.'

They rocketed down the hills but as soon as they reached the level ground their speed began to fall off. Peering through the dwindling clouds of steam Bruce saw the pale brown ribbon of road ahead of them, and they were still travelling at a healthy thirty miles an hour as they passed it. When finally the train trickled to a standstill Bruce estimated that they were three or four miles beyond the level crossing, safely walled in by the forest and hidden from the road by three bends.

'I doubt they'll find us here, but if they do they'll have to come down the line from the level crossing to get at us. We'll go back a mile and lay an ambush in the forest on each side of the line,' said Bruce.

'Those Arabs won't be following us, boss. They've got themselves women and a whole barful of liquor. Be two or three days before old General Moses can sober them up enough to move them on.'

'You're probably right, Ruffy. But we'll take no chances. Get that ambush laid and then we'll try and think up some idea for getting home.'

Suddenly a thought occurred to him: Martin Boussier had the diamonds with him. They would not be too pleased about that in Elisabethville.

Almost immediately Bruce was disgusted with himself. The diamonds were by far the least important thing that they had left behind in Port Reprieve.

– 14 –

André de Surrier held his steel helmet against his chest the way a man holds his hat at a funeral, the wind blew cool and caressing through his dark sweat-damp hair. His hearing was dulled by the strike of the shell that had cut the truck loose from the rear of the train, he could hear one of the children crying and the crooning, gentling voice of its mother. He stared back up the railway line at the train, saw the great bulk of Ruffy beside Bruce Curry on the roof of the second coach.

'They can't help us now.' Boussier spoke softly. 'There's nothing they can do.' He lifted his hand stiffly in almost a military salute and then dropped it to his side. 'Be brave, ma chère,' he said to his wife. 'Please be brave,' and she clung to him.

André let the helmet drop from his hands. It clanged on to the metal floor of the truck. He wiped the sweat from his face with nervous fluttering hands and then turned slowly to look down at the village.

'I don't want to die,' he whispered. 'Not like this, not now, please not now.' One of his gendarmes laughed, a sound without mirth, and stepped across to the Bren. He pushed André away from it and started firing at the tiny running figures of the men in the station yard.

'No,' shrilled André. 'Don't do that, no, don't antagonize them. They'll kill us if you do that—'

'They'll kill us anyway,' laughed the gendarme and emptied the magazine in one long despairing burst. André started towards him, perhaps to pull him away from the gun, but his resolve did not carry him that far. His hands dropped to his sides, clenching and unclenching. His lips quivered and then opened to spill out his terror.

'No!' he screamed. 'Please, no! No! Oh, God have mercy.

Oh, save me, don't let this happen to me, please, God. Oh, my God.'

He stumbled to the side of the truck and clambered on to it. The truck was slowing as it ran into the platform. He could see men coming with rifles in their hands, shouting as they ran, black men in dirty tattered uniforms, their faces working with excitement, pink shouting mouths, baying like hounds in a pack.

André jumped and the dusty concrete of the platform grazed his cheek and knocked the wind out of him. He crawled to his knees, clutching his stomach and trying to scream. A rifle butt hit him between the shoulder-blades and he collapsed. Above him a voice shouted in French.

'He is white, keep him for the general. Don't kill him.' And again the rifle butt hit him, this time across the side of the head. He lay in the dust, dazed, with the taste of blood in his mouth and watched them drag the others from the truck.

They shot the black gendarmes on the platform, without ceremony, laughing as they competed with each other to use their bayonets on the corpses. The two children died quickly torn from their mothers, held by the feet and swung head first against the steel side of the truck.

Old Boussier tried to prevent them stripping his wife and was bayoneted from behind in anger, and then shot twice with a pistol held to his head as he lay on the platform.

All this happened in the first few minutes before the officers arrived to control them; by that time André and the four women were the only occupants of the truck left alive.

André lay where he had fallen, watching in fascinated skin-crawling horror as they tore the clothing off the women and with a man to each arm and each leg held them down on the platform as though they were calves to be branded, hooting with laughter at their struggling naked bodies, bickering for position, already unbuckling belts, pushing each other, arguing, some of them with fresh blood on their clothing.

But then two men, who by their air of authority and the red sashes across their chests were clearly officers, joined the crowd. One of them fired his pistol in the air to gain their attention and both of them started a harangue that slowly had effect. The women were dragged up and herded off towards the hotel.

One of the officers came across to where André lay, stooped over him and lifted his head by taking a handful of hair.

'Welcome, mon ami. The general will be very pleased to see you. It is a pity that your other white friends have left us, but then, one is better than nothing.'

He pulled André into a sitting position, peered into his face and then spat into his eyes with sudden violence. 'Bring him! The general will talk to him later.'

They tied André to one of the columns on the front verandah of the hotel and left him there. He could have twisted his head and looked through the large windows into the lounge at what they were doing to the women, but he did not. He could hear what was happening; by noon the screams had become groans and sobbing; by mid-afternoon the women were making no sound at all. But the queue of *shufta* was still out of the front door of the lounge. Some of them had been to the head of the line and back to the tail three or four times.

All of them were drunk now. One jovial fellow carried a bottle of Parfait Amour liqueur in one hand and a bottle of Harpers whisky in the other. Every time he came back to join the queue again he stopped in front of André.

'Will you drink with me, little white boy?' he asked. 'Certainly you will,' he answered himself, filled his mouth from one of the bottles and spat it into André's face. Each time it got a big laugh from the others waiting in the line. Occasionally one of the other *shufta* would stop in front of

André, unsling his rifle, back away a few paces, sight along the bayonet at André's face and then charge forward, at the last moment twisting the point aside so that it grazed his cheek. Each time André could not suppress his shriek of terror, and the waiting men nearly collapsed with merriment.

Towards evening they started to burn the houses on the outskirts of town. One group, sad with liquor and rape, sat together at the end of the verandah and started to sing. Their deep beautiful voices carrying all the melancholy savagery of Africa, they kept on singing while an argument between two *shufta* developed into a knife fight in the road outside the hotel.

The sweet bass lilt of singing covered the coarse breathing of the two circling, bare-chested knife fighters and the shuffle, shuffle, quick shuffle of their feet in the dust. When finally they locked together for the kill, the singing rose still deep and strong but with a triumphant note to it. One man stepped back with his rigid right arm holding the knife buried deep in the other's belly and as the loser sank down, sliding slowly off the knife, the singing sank with him, plaintive, regretful and lamenting into silence.

They came for André after dark. Four of them less drunk than the others. They led him down the street to the Union Minière offices. General Moses was there, sitting alone at the desk in the front office.

There was nothing sinister about him; he looked like an elderly clerk, a small man with the short woollen cap of hair grizzled to grey above the ears and a pair of horn-rimmed spectacles. On his chest he wore three rows of full-dress medals; each of his fingers was encased in rings to the second joint, diamonds, emeralds and the occasional red glow of a ruby; most of them had been designed for women, but the metal had been cut to enlarge them for his stubby black fingers. The face was almost kindly, except the eyes. There was a blankness of expression in them, the lifeless eyes of a madman. On the desk in front of him was a small wooden case made of unvarnished deal which bore the seal of the Union Minière Company stencilled in black upon its side. The lid was open, and as André came in through the door with his escort General Moses lifted a white canvas bag from the case, loosened the drawstring and poured a pile of dark grey industrial diamonds on to the blotter in front of him.

He prodded them thoughtfully with his finger, stirring them so they glittered dully in the harsh light of the petromax.

'Was this the only case in the truck?' he asked without looking up.

'Oui, mon général. There was only one,' answered one of André's escorts.

'You are certain?'

'Oui, mon général. I myself have searched thoroughly.'

General Moses took another of the canvas bags from the case and emptied it on to the blotter. He grunted with disappointment as he saw the drab little stones. He reached for another bag, and another, his anger mounting steadily as each yielded only dirty grey and black industrial diamonds. Soon the pile on the blotter would have filled a pint jug.

'Did you open the case?' he snarled.

'Non, mon général. It was sealed. The seal was not broken, you saw that.'

General Moses grunted again, his dark chocolate face set hard with frustration. Once more he dipped his hand into the wooden case and suddenly he smiled.

'Ah!' he said pleasantly. 'Yes! yes! what is this?' He brought out a cigar box, with the gaudy wrappers still on the cedarwood. A thumbnail prised the lid back and he beamed happily. In a nest of cotton wool, sparkling, breaking the white light of the petromax into all the rainbow colours of the spectrum, were the gem stones. General Moses picked one up and held it between thumb and forefinger.

'Pretty,' he murmured. 'Pretty, so pretty.' He swept the industrial stones to one side and laid the gem in the centre of the blotter. Then one by one he took the others from the cigar box, fondling each and laying it on the blotter, counting them, smiling, once chuckling softly, touching them, arranging them in patterns.

'Pretty,' he kept whispering. 'Bon – forty-one, forty-two. Pretty! My darlings! Forty-three.'

Then suddenly he scooped them up and poured them into one of the canvas bags, tightened the drawstring, dropped it into his breast pocket above the medals and buttoned the flap.

He laid his black, bejewelled hands on the desk in front of him and looked up at André.

His eyes were smoky yellow with black centres behind his spectacles. They had an opaque, dreamlike quality.

'Take off his clothes,' he said in a voice that was as expressionless as the eyes.

They stripped André with rough dispatch and General Moses looked at his body.

'So white,' he murmured. 'Why so white?' Suddenly his jaws began chewing nervously and there was a faint shine of sweat on his forehead. He came round from behind the desk, a small man, yet with an intensity about him that doubled his size.

'White like the maggots that feed in the living body of the elephant.' He brought his face close to André's. 'You should be fatter, my maggot, having fed so long and so well. You should be much fatter.'

He touched André's body, running his hands down his flanks in a caress.

'But now it is too late, little white maggot,' he said, and

André cringed from his touch and from his voice. 'For the elephant has shaken you from the wound, shaken you out on to the ground, shaken you out beneath his feet – and will you pop when he crushes you?'

His voice was still soft though the sweat oozed in oily lines down his cheeks and the dreaminess of his eyes had been replaced by a burning black brightness.

'We shall see,' he said and drew back. 'We shall see, my maggot,' he repeated, and brought his knee up into André's crotch with a force that jerked his whole frame and flung his shoulders back.

The agony flared through André's lower body, fierce as the touch of heated steel. It clamped in on his stomach, contracting it in a spasm like childbirth, it rippled up across the muscles of his chest into his head and burst beneath the roof of his skull in a whiteness that blinded him.

'Hold him,' commanded General Moses, his voice suddenly shrill. The two guards took André by the elbows and forced him to his knees, so that his genitals and lower belly were easily accessible to the general's boots. They had done this often.

'For the times you gaoled me!' And General Moses swung his booted foot into André's body. The pain blended with the other pain, and it was too strong for André to scream.

'This, for the insults,' and André could feel his testicles crush beneath it. Still it was too strong – he could not use his voice.

'This, for the times I have grovelled.' The pain had passed its zenith, this time he could scream with it. He opened his mouth and filled his empty lungs.

'This, for the times I have hungered.' Now he must scream. Now he must – the pain, oh, sweet Christ, I must, please let me scream.

'This, for your white man's justice.' Why can't I, please let me. Oh, no! No – please. Oh, God, oh, please.

'This, for your prisons and your Kiboko!'

The kicks so fast now, like the beat of an insane drummer, like rain on a tin roof. In his stomach he felt something tear.

'And this, and this, and this.'

The face before him filled the whole field of his vision. The voice and the sound of the boot into him filled his ears.

'This, and this, and this.' The voice high-pitched and within him the sudden warm flood of internal bleeding.

The pain was fading now as his body closed it out in defence, and he had not screamed. The leap of elation as he knew it. *This last thing I can do well, I can die now WITHOUT SCREAMING*. He tried to stand up, but they held him down and his legs were not his own, they were on the other side of the great numb warmth of his belly. He lifted his head and looked at the man who was killing him.

'This for the white filth that bore you, and this, and this—'

The blows were not a part of reality, he could feel the shock of them as though he stood close to a man who was cutting down a tree with an axe. And André smiled.

He was still smiling when they let him fall forward to the floor.

'I think he is dead,' said one of the guards. General Moses turned away and walked back to his seat at the desk. He was shaking as though he had run a long way, and his breathing was deep and fast. The jacket of his uniform was soaked with sweat. He sank into the chair and his body seemed to crumple; slowly the brightness faded from his eyes until once more they were filmed over, opaque and dreamy. The two guards squatted down quickly on each side of André's body; they knew it would be a long wait.

Through the open window there came an occasional shout of drunken laughter, and the red flicker and leap of flames.

– 15 –

Bruce stood in the centre of the tracks and searched the floor of the forest critically. At last he could make out the muzzle of the Bren protruding a few inches from the patch of elephant grass. Despite the fact that he knew exactly where to look for it, it had taken him a full two minutes to find it.

'That'll do, Ruffy,' he decided. 'We can't get it much better than that.'

'I reckon not, boss.'

Bruce raised his voice. 'Can you hear me?' There were muffled affirmatives from the bush on each side, and Bruce continued.

'If they come you must let them reach this spot before you open fire. I will mark it for you.' He went to a small shrub beside the line, broke off a branch and dropped it on the tracks.

'Can you see that?'

Again the affirmatives from the men in ambush. 'You will be relieved before darkness – until then stay where you are.'

The train was hidden beyond a bend in the line, half a mile ahead, and Bruce walked back with Ruffy.

The engine driver was waiting for them, talking with Wally Hendry beside the rear truck.

'Any luck?' Bruce asked him.

'I regret, mon capitaine, that she is irreparably damaged. The boiler is punctured in two places and there is considerable disruption of the copper tubing.'

'Thank you,' Bruce nodded. He was neither surprised nor disappointed. It was precisely what his own judgement had told him after a brief examination of the locomotive.

'Where is Madame Cartier?' he asked Wally.

'*Madame* is preparing the luncheon, *monsir*,' Wally told

him with heavy sarcasm. 'Why do you ask, Bucko? Are you feeling randy again so soon, hey? You feel like a slice of veal for lunch, is that it?'

Bruce snuffed out the quick flare of his temper and walked past him. He found Shermaine with four gendarmes in the cab of the locomotive. They had scraped the coals from the furnace into a glowing heap on the steel floor and were chopping potatoes and onions into the five gallon pots.

The gendarmes were all laughing at something Shermaine had said. Her usually pale cheeks were flushed with the heat; there was a sooty smudge on her forehead. She wielded the big knife with professional dexterity. She looked up and saw Bruce, her face lighting instantly and her lips parting.

'We're having a Hungarian goulash for lunch – bully beef, potatoes and onions.'

'As of now I am rating you acting second cook without pay.'

'You are too kind,' and she put her tongue out at him. It was a pink pointed little tongue like a cat's. Bruce felt the old familiar tightening of his legs and the dryness in his throat as he looked at it.

'Shermaine, the locomotive is damaged beyond repair. It is of no further use.' He spoke in English.

'It makes a passable kitchen,' she demurred.

'Be serious.' Bruce's anxiety made him irritable. 'We're stranded here until we think of something.'

'But, Bruce, you are the genius. I have complete faith in you. I'm sure you'll think of some truly beautiful idea.' Her face was solemn but she couldn't keep the banter out of her eyes. 'Why don't you go and ask General Moses to lend you his transportation?'

Bruce's eyes narrowed in thought and the black inverted curves of his eyebrows nearly touched above the bridge of his nose.

'The food better be good or I'll break you to third cook,' he warned, clambered down from the cab to the ground and hurried back along the train.

'Hendry, Sergeant Major, come here, please. I want to discuss something with you.'

They came to join him and he led the way up the ladder into one of the covered coaches. Hendry dropped on to the bunk and placed his feet on the washbasin.

'That was a quick one,' he grinned through the coppery stubble of his beard.

'You're the most uncouth, filthy-mouthed son of a bitch I have ever met, Hendry,' said Bruce coldly. 'When I get you back to Elisabethville I'm going to beat you to pulp before I hand you over to the military authority for murder.'

'My, my,' laughed Hendry. 'Big talker, hey? Curry, big, big talker.'

'Don't make me kill you now – don't do that, please. I still need you.'

'What's with you and that Frenchy, hey? You love it or something? You love it, or you just fancy a bit of that fat little arse? It can't be her titties – she ain't got much there, not even a handful each side.'

Bruce started for him, then changed his mind and swung round to stare out of the window. His voice was strangled when he spoke.

'I'll make a bargain with you, Hendry. Until we get out of this you keep off my back and I'll keep off yours. When we reach Msapa Junction the truce is off. You can do and say whatever you like and, if I don't kill you for it, I'll try my level best to see you hanged for murder.'

'I'm making no bargain with you or nobody, Curry. I play along until it suits me, and I won't give you no warning when it doesn't suit me to play along any more. And let me tell you now, Bucko, I don't need you and I don't need nobody. Not Haig or you, with your fancy too-good-to-kiss-my-arse talk; when the time comes I'm going to trim you down to size – just remember that, Curry. And don't say I didn't warn you.' Hendry was leaning forward, hands on his knees, body braced and his whole face twisting and contorted with the vehemence of his speech.

'Let's make it now, Hendry.' Bruce wheeled away from the window, crouching slightly, his hands stiffening into the flat hard blades of the judo fighter.

Sergeant Major Ruffararo stood up from the opposite bunk with surprising grace and speed for such a big man. He interposed his great body.

'You wanted to tell us something, boss?'

Slowly Bruce straightened out of his crouch, his hands relaxing. Irritably he brushed at the damp lock of dark hair that had fallen on to his forehead, as if to brush Wally Hendry out of his mind with the same movement.

'Yes,' controlling his voice with an effort, 'I wanted to discuss our next move.' He fished the cigarette pack from his top pocket and lit one, sucking the smoke down deep. Then he perched on the lid of the washbasin and studied the ash on the tip of the cigarette. When he spoke again his voice was normal.

'There is no hope of repairing this locomotive, so we have to find alternative transport out of here. Either we can walk two hundred miles back to Msapa Junction with our friends the Baluba ready to dispute our passage, or we can ride back in General Moses's trucks!' He paused to let it sink in.

'You going to pinch those trucks off him?' asked Ruffy. 'That's going to take some doing, boss.'

'No, Ruffy, I don't think we have any chance of getting them out from under his nose. What we will have to do is attack the town and wipe him out.'

'You're bloody crazy,' exclaimed Wally. 'You're raving bloody mad.'

Bruce ignored him. 'I estimate that Moses has about sixty men. With Kanaki and nine men on the bridge, Haig and de Surrier and six others gone, we have thirty-four men left. Correct, Sergeant Major?'

'That's right, boss.'

'Very well,' Bruce nodded. 'We'll have to leave at least ten men here to man that ambush in case Moses sends a patrol after us, or in case of an attack by the Baluba. It's not enough, I know, but we will just have to risk it.'

'Most of these civilians got arms with them, shotguns and sports rifles,' said Ruffy.

'Yes,' agreed Bruce. 'They should be able to look after themselves. So that leaves twenty-four men to carry out the attack, something like three to one.'

'Those *shufta* will be so full of liquor, half of them won't be able to stand up.'

'That's what I am banking on: drunkenness and surprise. We'll hit them and try and finish it before they know what's happened. I don't think they will have realized how badly we were hit; they probably expect us to be a hundred miles away by now.'

'When do you want to leave, boss?'

'We are about twelve miles from Port Reprieve – say, six hours' march in the dark. I want to attack in the early hours of tomorrow morning, but I'd like to be in position around midnight. We'll leave here at six o'clock, just before dark.'

'I'd better go and start sorting the boys out.'

'Okay, Ruffy. Issue an extra hundred rounds to each man and ten grenades. I'll want four extra haversacks of grenades also.' Bruce turned to Hendry and looked at him for the first time. 'Go with the sergeant major, Hendry, and give him a hand.'

'Jesus, this is going to be a ball,' grinned Wally in anticipation. 'With any luck I'll get me a sackful of ears.' He disappeared down the corridor behind Ruffy, and Bruce lay back on the seat and took off his helmet. He closed his eyes and once again he saw Boussier and his wife standing together in the truck as it rolled back down the hill, he saw the huddle of frightened women, and André standing bareheaded staring back at him with big brown gentle eyes. He groaned softly. 'Why is it always the good ones, the harmless, the weak?'

A tap on the door roused him and he sat up quickly.

'Yes?'

'Hello, Bruce.' Shermaine came in with a multiple-decked metal canteen in one hand and two mugs in the other. 'It's lunchtime.'

'Already!' Bruce checked his watch. 'Good Lord, it's after one.'

'Are you hungry?'

'Breakfast was a century ago.'

'Good,' she said, lowered the collapsible table and began serving the food.

'Smells good.'

'I am a chef Cordon Bleu. My bully beef goulash is demanded by the crowned heads of Europe.'

They ate in silence for both of them were hungry. Once they looked at each other and smiled but returned to the food.

'That was good,' sighed Bruce at last.

'Coffee, Bruce?'

'Please.'

As she poured it she asked, 'So, what happens now?'

'Do you mean what happens now we are alone?'

'You are forward, monsieur. I meant how do we get out of here?'

'I am adopting your suggestion: borrowing General Moses's transportation.'

'You make jokes, Bruce!'

'No,' he said, and explained briefly.

'It will be very dangerous, will it not? You may be hurt?'

'Only the good die young.'

'That is why I worry. Please do not get hurt – I am starting to think I would not like that.' Her face was very serious and pale. Bruce crossed quickly and stooped over her, lifting her to her feet.

'Shermaine, I—'

'No, Bruce. Don't talk. Don't say anything.' Her eyes were closed with thick black lashes interlaced, her chin lifted exposing the long smooth swell of her neck. He touched it with his lips and she made a soft noise in her throat so he could feel the skin vibrate. Her body flattened against his and her fingers closed in the hair at the back of his head.

'Oh, Bruce. My Bruce, please do not get hurt. Do not let them hurt you.'

Wanting now, urgently, his mouth hunted upwards and hers came to meet it, willing prey. Her lips were pink and not greased with make-up, they parted to the pressure of his tongue, he felt the tip of her nose cool upon his cheek and his hand moved up her back and closed round the nape of her neck, slender neck with silky down behind her ears.

'Oh, Bruce—' she said into his mouth. His other hand went down on to the proud, round, deeply divided thrust of her buttocks, he pulled her lower body against his and she gasped as she felt him – the arrogant maleness through cloth.

'No,' she gasped and tried to pull away, but he held her until she relaxed against him once more. She shook her head, 'Non, non,' but her mouth was open still and her tongue fluttered against his. Down came his hand from her neck and twitched her shirt tails loose from under her belt, then up again along her back, touching the deep lateral depression of her spine so that she shuddered, clinging to him. Stroking velvet skin stretched tight over rubber-hard flesh, finding the outline of her shoulder blades, tracing them upwards then back to the armpits, silky-haired armpits that maddened him with excitement, quickly past them to her breasts, small breasts with soft tips hardening to his touch.

Now she struggled in earnest, her fists beating on his shoulders and her mouth breaking from his, and he stopped himself, dropped the hand away to encircle her waist. Holding her loosely within his arms.

'That was not good, Bruce. You get naughty very quick.' Her cheeks flamed with colour and her blue eyes had darkened to royal, her lips still wet from his, and her voice was unsteady, as unsteady as his when he answered.

'I'm sorry, Shermaine. I don't know what happened then, I did not mean to frighten you.'

'You are very strong, Bruce. But you do not frighten me, only a little bit. Your eyes frighten me when they look at me but do not see.'

You really made a hash of that one, he rebuked himself. Bruce Curry, the gentle sophisticated lover. Bruce Curry, the heavyweight, catch-as-catch-can, two-fisted rape artist.

He felt shaky, his legs wobbly, and there was something seriously wrong with his breathing.

'You do not wear a brassière,' he said without thinking, and immediately regretted it, but she chuckled, soft and husky.

'Do you think I need to, Bruce?'

'No, I didn't mean that,' he protested quickly, remembering the saucy tilt of that small breast. He was silent then, marshalling his words, trying to control his breathing, fighting down the madness of desire.

She studied his eyes. 'You can see again now – perhaps I will let you kiss me.'

'Please,' he said and she came back to him.

Gently now, Bruce me boy.

The door of the compartment flew back with a crash and they jumped apart. Wally Hendry stood on the threshold.

'Well, well, well.' His shrewd little eyes took it all in. 'That's nice!'

Shermaine was hurriedly tucking in her shirt tail and trying to smooth her hair at the same time.

Wally grinned. 'Nothing like it after a meal, I always say. Gets the digestion going.'

'What do you want?' snapped Bruce.

'There's no doubt what you want,' said Wally. 'Looks like you're getting it too.' He let his eyes travel up from Shermaine's waist, slowly over her body to her face.

Bruce stepped out into the corridor, pushing Hendry back and slammed the door.

'What do you want?' he repeated.

'Ruffy wants you to check his arrangements, but I'll tell him you're busy. We can put the attack off until tomorrow night if you like.'

Bruce scowled at him. 'Tell him I'll be with him in two minutes.'

Wally leaned against the door. 'Okay, I'll tell him.'

'What are you waiting for?'

'Nothing, just nothing,' grinned Wally.

'Well, bugger off then,' snarled Bruce.

'Okay, okay, don't get your knickers in a knot, Bucko.'

He sauntered off down the corridor.

Shermaine was standing where Bruce had left her, but with her eyes bright with tears of anger.

'He is a pig, that one. A filthy, filthy pig.'

'He's not worth worrying about.' Bruce tried to take her in his arms again, but she shrugged him off.

'I hate him. He makes everything seem so cheap, so dirty.'

'Nothing between you and I could be cheap and dirty,' said Bruce, and instantly her fury abated.

'I know, my Bruce. But he can make it seem that way.' They kissed gently.

'I must go. They want me.' For a second she clung to him.

'Be careful. Promise me you'll be careful.'

'I promise,' said Bruce and she let him go.

– 16 –

They left before dark, but the clouds had come up during the afternoon and now they hung low over the forest, trapping the heat beneath them.

Bruce led, with Ruffy in the middle of the line and Hendry in the rear.

By the time they reached the level crossing the night was on them and it had started to rain, soft fat drops weeping like a woman exhausted with grief, warm rain in the darkness. And the darkness was complete. Once Bruce touched the top of his nose with his open palm, but he could not see his hand.

He used a staff to keep contact with the steel rail that ran beside him, tapping along it like a blind man, and at each step the gravel of the embankment crunched beneath his feet. The hand of the man behind him was on his shoulder, and he could sense the presence of the others that followed him like the body of a serpent, could hear the crunch of their steps and the muted squeak and rattle of their equipment. A man's voice was raised in protest and immediately quenched by Ruffy's deep rumble.

They crossed the road and the gradient changed beneath Bruce's feet so that he had to lean forward against it. They were starting up the Lufira hills.

I will rest them at the top, he thought, and from there we will be able to see the lights of the town.

The rain stopped abruptly, and the quietness after it was surprising. Now he could distinctly hear the breathing of the man behind him above the small sounds of their advance, and in the forest nearby a tree frog clinked as though steel pellets were being dropped into a crystal glass. It was a sound of great purity and beauty.

All Bruce's senses were enhanced to compensate for his lack of sight; his hearing; his sense of smell, so that he could catch the over-sweet perfume of a jungle-flower and the heaviness of decaying wet vegetation; his sense of touch, so that he could feel the raindrops on his face and the texture of his clothing against his body; then the other animal sense of danger told him with sickening, stomach-tripping certainty that there was something ahead of him in the darkness.

He stopped, and the man following him bumped into him throwing him off balance. All along the line there was a ripple of confusion and then silence. They all waited.

Bruce strained his hearing, half crouched with his rifle held ready. There was something there, he could almost feel it.

Please God, let them not have a machine-gun set up here, he thought; they could cut us into a shambles.

He turned cautiously and felt for the head of the man behind him, found it and drew it towards him until his mouth was an inch from the ear.

'Lie down very quietly. Tell the one behind you that he may pass it back.'

Bruce waited poised, listening and trying to see ahead into the utter blackness. He felt a gentle tap on his ankle from the gendarme at his feet. They were all down.

'All right, let's go take a look.' Bruce detached one of the grenades from his webbing belt. He drew the pin and dropped it into the breast pocket of his jacket. Then feeling for the crossties of the rails with each foot he started forward. Ten paces and he stopped again. Then he heard it, the tiny click of two pebbles just ahead of him. His throat closed so he could not breathe and his stomach was very heavy.

I'm right on top of them. My God, if they open up now—

Inch by inch he drew back the hand that held the grenade.

I'll have to lob short and get down fast. Five-second fuse – too long, they'll hear it and start shooting.

His hand was right back, he bent his legs and sank slowly on to his knees.

Here we go, he thought, and at that instant sheet lightning fluttered across the sky and Bruce could see. The hills were outlined black below the pale grey belly of the clouds, and the steel rails glinted in the sudden light. The forest was dark and high at each hand, and – a leopard, a big golden and black leopard, stood facing Bruce. In that brief second they stared at each other and then the night closed down again.

The leopard coughed explosively in the darkness, and Bruce tried desperately to bring his rifle up, but it was in his left hand and his other arm was held back ready to throw.

This time for sure, he thought, this time they lower the boom on you.

It was with a feeling of disbelief that he heard the leopard crash sideways into the undergrowth, and the scrambling rush of its run dwindle into the bush.

He subsided on to his backside, with the primed grenade in his hand, the hysterical laughter of relief coming up into his throat.

'You okay, boss?' Ruffy's voice lifted anxiously.

'It was a leopard,' answered Bruce, and was surprised at the squeakiness of his own voice.

There was a buzz of voices from the gendarmes and a rattle and clatter as they started to stand up. Someone laughed.

'That's enough noise,' snapped Bruce and climbed to his feet; he found the pin in his pocket and fitted it back into the grenade. He groped his way back, picked up the staff from where he had dropped it, and took his position at the head of the column again.

'Let's go,' he said.

His mouth was dry, his breathing too quick and he could feel the heat beneath the skin of his cheeks from the shock of the leopard.

I truly squirted myself full of adrenalin that time, Bruce grinned precariously in the dark, I'm as windy as hell. And before tonight is over I shall find fear again.

They moved on up the incline of the hills, a serpent of twenty-six men, and the tension was in all of them. Bruce could hear it in the footsteps behind him, feel it in the grip of the hand upon his shoulder and catch it in the occasional whiffs of body smell that came forward to him, the smell of nervous sweat like acid on metal.

Ahead of them the clouds that had crouched low upon the hills lifted slowly, and Bruce could see the silhouette of the crests. It was no longer utterly dark for there was a glow on the belly of the clouds now. A faint orange glow of reflected light that grew in strength, then faded and grew again. It puzzled Bruce for a while, and thinking about it gave his nerves a chance to settle. He plodded steadily on watching the fluctuations of the light. The ground tilted more sharply upwards beneath his feet and he leaned forward against it, slogging up the last half mile to the pass between the peaks, and at last came out on the top.

'Good God,' Bruce spoke aloud, for from here he could see the reason for that glow on the clouds. They were burning Port Reprieve. The flames were well established in the buildings along the wharf, and as Bruce watched one of the roofs collapsed slowly in upon itself in a storm of sparks leaving the walls naked and erect, the wooden sills of the windows burning fiercely. The railway buildings were also on fire, and there was fire in the residential area beyond the Union Minière offices and the hotel. Quickly Bruce looked towards St Augustine's. It was dark, no flames there, no light even, and he felt a small lift of relief.

'Perhaps they have overlooked it, perhaps they're too busy looting,' and as he looked back at Port Reprieve, his mouth hardened. 'The senseless wanton bastards!' His anger started as he watched the meaningless destruction of the town.

'What can they possibly hope to gain by this?' There were new fires nearer the hotel. Bruce turned to the man behind him.

'We will rest here, but there will be no smoking and no talking.'

He heard the order passed back along the line and the careful sounds of equipment being lowered and men settling gratefully down upon the gravel embankment. Bruce unslung the case that contained his binoculars. He focused them on the burning town.

It was bright with the light of fires and through the glasses he could almost discern the features of the men in the streets. They moved in packs, heavily armed and restless. Many carried bottles and already the gait of some of them was unsteady. Bruce tried to estimate their numbers but it was impossible, men kept disappearing into buildings and reappearing, groups met and mingled and dispersed.

He dropped his glasses on to his chest to rest his eyes, and heard movement beside him in the dark. He glanced sideways. It was Ruffy, his bulk exaggerated by the load he carried; his rifle across one shoulder, on the other a full case of ammunition, and round his neck half a dozen haversacks full of grenades.

'Looks like they're having fun, hey, boss?'

'Fifth of November,' agreed Bruce. 'Aren't you going to take a breather?'

'Why not?' Ruffy set down the ammunition case and lowered his great backside on to it. 'Can you see any of those folks we left behind?' he asked.

Bruce lifted the glasses again and searched the area beyond the station buildings. It was darker there but he made out the square shape of the truck standing among the moving shadows.

'The truck's still there,' he murmured, 'but I can't see—'

At that moment the thatched roof of one of the houses exploded upwards in a column of flame, lighting the railway yard, and the truck stood out sharply.

'Yes,' said Bruce, 'I can see them now.' They were littered untidily across the yard, still lying where they had died. Small and fragile, unwanted as broken toys.

'Dead?' asked Ruffy.

'Dead,' confirmed Bruce.

'The women?'

'It's hard to tell.' Bruce strained his eyes. 'I don't think so.'

'No.' Ruffy's voice was soft and very deep. 'They wouldn't waste the women. I'd guess they've got them up at the hotel, taking it in turn to give them the business. Four women only – they won't last till morning. Those bastards down there could shag an elephant to death.' He spat thoughtfully into the gravel at his feet. 'What you going to do, boss?'

Bruce did not answer for a minute; he swung the glasses slowly back across the town. The field gun was still standing where he had last seen it, its barrel pointing accusingly up towards him. The transports were parked before the Union Minière offices; he could see the brilliant yellow and red paint and the Shell sign on the tanker. I hope it's full, Bruce thought, we'll need plenty of gasoline to get us back to Elisabethville.

'Ruffy, you'd better tell your boys to keep their bullets away from that tanker, otherwise it'll be a long walk home.'

'I'll tell them,' grunted Ruffy. 'But you know these mad Arabs – once they start shooting they don't stop till they're out of bullets, and they not too fussy where those bullets go.'

'We'll split into two groups when we get to the bottom of the hill. You and I will take our lot through the edge of the swamp and cross to the far side of the town. Tell

Lieutenant Hendry to come here.' Bruce waited until Wally came forward to join them, and when the three of them crouched together he went on.

'Hendry, I want you to spread your men out at the top of the main street – there in the darkness on this side of the station. Ruffy and I are going to cross the edge of the swamp to the causeway and lay out on the far side. For God's sake keep your boys quiet until Ruffy and I hit them – all we need is for your lot to start pooping off before we are ready and we won't need those lorries, we'll need coffins for the rest of our journey. Do you understand me?'

'Okay, okay, I know what I'm doing,' muttered Wally.

'I hope so,' said Bruce, and then went on. 'We'll hit them at four o'clock tomorrow morning, just before first light. Ruffy and I will go into the town and bomb the hotel – that's where most of them will be sleeping. The grenades should force the survivors into the street and as soon as that happens you can open up – but not before. Wait until you get them in the open. Is that clear?'

'Jesus,' growled Hendry. 'Do you think I'm a bloody fool, do you think I can't understand English?'

'The crossfire from the two groups should wipe most of them out.' Bruce ignored Wally's outburst. 'But we mustn't give the remainder a chance to organize. Hit them hard and as soon as they take cover again you must follow them in – close with them and finish them off. If we can't get it over in five to ten minutes then we are going to be in trouble. They outnumber us three to one, so we have to exploit the element of surprise to the full.'

'Exploit the element of surprise to the full!' mimicked Wally. 'What for all the fancy talk – why not just murder the bastards?'

Bruce grinned lightly in the dark. 'All right, murder the bastards,' he agreed. 'But do it as quickly as bloody possible.' He stood up and inclined the luminous dial of his wristwatch to catch the light. 'It's half past ten now – we'll move down on them. Come with me, Hendry, and we'll sort them into two groups.'

Bruce and Wally moved back along the line and talked to each man in turn.

'You will go with Lieutenant Hendry.'

'You come with me.'

Making sure that the two English-speaking corporals were with Wally, they took ten minutes to divide them into two units and to redistribute the haversacks of grenades. Then they moved on down the slope, still in Indian file.

'This is where we leave you, Hendry,' whispered Bruce. 'Don't go jumping the gun – wait until you hear my grenades.'

'Yeah, okay – I know all about it.'

'Good luck,' said Bruce.

'Your bum in a barrel, Captain Curry,' rejoined Wally and moved away.

'Come on, Ruffy.' Bruce led his men off the embankment down into the swamp. Almost immediately the mud and slime was knee-deep and as they worked their way out to the right it rose to their waists and then to their armpits, sucking and gurgling sullenly as they stirred it with their passage, belching little evil-smelling gusts of swamp gas.

The mosquitoes closed round Bruce's face in a cloud so dense that he breathed them into his mouth and had to blink them out of his eyes. Sweat dribbled down from under his helmet and clung heavily in his eyebrows and the matted stems of the papyrus grass dragged at his feet. Their progress was tortuously slow and for fifteen minutes at a time Bruce lost sight of the lights of the village through the wall of papyrus; he steered by the glow of the fires and the occasional column of sparks.

It was an hour before they had half completed their circuit of Port Reprieve. Bruce stopped to rest, still waist-deep in swamp ooze and with his arms aching numb from holding his rifle above his head.

'I could use a smoke now, boss,' grunted Ruffy.

'Me too,' answered Bruce, and he wiped his face on the sleeve of his jacket. The mosquito bites on his forehead and round his eyes burnt like fire.

'What a way to make a living,' he whispered.

'You go on living and you'll be one of the lucky ones,' answered Ruffy. 'My guess is there'll be some dying before tomorrow.'

But the fear of death was submerged by physical discomfort. Bruce had almost forgotten that they were going into battle; right now he was more worried that the leeches which had worked their way through the openings in his anklets and were busily boring into his lower legs might find their way up to his crotch. There was a lot to be said in favour of a zip fly, he decided.

'Let's get out of this,' he whispered. 'Come on, Ruffy. Tell your boys to keep it quiet.'

He worked in closer to the shore and the level fell to their knees once more. Progress was more noisy now as their legs broke the surface with each step and the papyrus rustled and brushed against them.

It was almost two o'clock when they reached the causeway. Bruce left his men crouched in the papyrus while he made a stealthy reconnaissance along the side of the concrete bridge, keeping in its shadow, moving doubled up until he came to dry land on the edge of the village. There were no sentries posted and except for the crackle of the flames the town was quiet, sunk into a drunken stupor, satiated. Bruce went back to call his men up.

He spread them in pairs along the outskirts of the village. He had learned very early in this campaign not to let his men act singly; nothing drains an African of courage more than to be on his own, especially in the night when the ghosts are on the walk-about.

To each couple he gave minute instructions.

'When you hear the grenades you shoot at anybody in

the streets or at the windows. When the street is empty move in close beside that building there. Use your own grenades on every house and watch out for Lieutenant Hendry's men coming through from the other side. Do you understand?'

'It is understood.'

'Shoot carefully. Aim each shot – not like you did at the road bridge, and in the name of God do not hit the gasoline tanker. We need that to get us home.'

Now it was three o'clock, Bruce saw by the luminous figures on his wristwatch. Eight hours since they had left the train, and twenty-two hours since Bruce had last slept. But he was not tired, although his body ached and there was that gritty feeling under his eyelids, yet his mind was clear and bright as a flame.

He lay beside Ruffy under a low bush on the outskirts of Port Reprieve and the night wind drifted the smoke from the burning town down upon them, and Bruce was not tired. For I am going to another rendezvous with fear.

Fear is a woman, he thought, with all the myriad faces and voices of a woman. Because she is a woman and because I am a man I must keep going back to her. Only this time the appointment is one that I cannot avoid, this time I am not deliberately seeking her out.

I know she is evil, I know that after I have possessed her I will feel sick and shaken. I will say, 'That was the last time, never again.'

But just as certainly I know I will go back to her again, hating her, dreading her, but also needing her.

I have gone to find her on a mountain – on Dutoits Kloof Frontal, on Turret Towers, on the Wailing Wall, and the Devil's Tooth.

And she was there, dressed in a flowing robe of rock, a robe that fell sheer two thousand feet to the scree slope below. And she shrieked with the voice of the wind along the exposed face. Then her voice was soft, tinkling like cooling glass in the Berg ice underfoot, whispering like nylon rope running free, grating as the rotten rock moved in my hand.

I have followed her into the Jessie bush on the banks of the Sabi and the Luangwa, and she was there, waiting, wounded, in a robe of buffalo hide with the blood dripping from her mouth. And her smell was the sour-acid smell of my own sweat, and her taste was like rotten tomatoes in the back of my throat.

I have looked for her beyond the reef in the deep water with the demand valve of a scuba repeating my breathing with metallic hoarseness. And she was there with rows of white teeth in the semicircle of her mouth, a tall fin on her back, dressed this time in shagreen, and her touch was cold as the ocean, and her taste was salt and the taint of dying things.

I have looked for her on the highway with my foot pressed to the floorboards and she was there with her cold arm draped round my shoulders, her voice the whine of rubber on tarmac and the throaty hum of the motor.

With Colin Butler at the helm (a man who treated fear not as a lover, but with tolerant contempt as though she were his little sister) I went to find her in a small boat. She was dressed in green with plumes of spray and she wore a necklace of sharp black rock. And her voice was the roar of water breaking on water.

We met in darkness at the road bridge and her eyes glinted like bayonets. But that was an enforced meeting not of my choosing, as tonight will be.

I hate her, he thought, but she is a woman and I am a man.

Bruce lifted his arm and turned his wrist to catch the light of the fires.

'Fifteen minutes to four, Ruffy. Let's go and take a look.'

'That's a good idea, boss.' Ruffy grinned with a show of white teeth in the darkness.

'Are you afraid, Ruffy?' he asked suddenly, wanting to know, for his own heart beat like a war drum and there was no saliva in his mouth.

'Boss, some questions you don't ask a man.' Ruffy rose slowly into a crouch. 'Let's go take a look around.'

So they moved quickly together into the town, along the street, hugging the hedges and the buildings, trying to keep in shadow, their eyes moving everywhere, breathing quick and shallow, nerves screwed up tight until they reached the hotel.

There were no lights in the windows and it seemed deserted until Bruce made out the untidy mass of humanity strewn in sleep upon the front verandah.

'How many there, Ruffy?'

'Dunno – perhaps ten, fifteen.' Ruffy breathed an answer. 'Rest of them will be inside.'

'Where are the women – be careful of them.'

'They're dead long ago, you can believe me.'

'All right then, let's get round the back.' Bruce took a deep breath and then moved quickly across the twenty yards of open firelit street to the corner of the hotel. He stopped in the shadow and felt Ruffy close beside him. 'I want to take a look into the main lounge, my guess is that most of them will be in there,' he whispered.

'There's only four bedrooms,' agreed Ruffy. 'Say the officers upstairs and the rest in the lounge.'

Now Bruce moved quickly round the corner and stumbled over something soft. He felt it move against his foot.

'Ruffy!' he whispered urgently as he teetered off balance. He had trodden on a man, a man sleeping in the dust beside the wall. He could see the firelight on his bare torso and the glint of the bottle clutched in one outflung hand. The man sat up, muttering, and then began to cough, hacking painfully, swearing as he wiped his mouth with his free hand. Bruce regained his balance and swung his rifle up to use the bayonet, but Ruffy was quicker. He put one foot on the man's chest and trod him flat on to his back once more, then standing over him he used his bayoneted rifle the way a gardener uses a spade to lift potatoes, leaning his weight on it suddenly and the blade vanished into the man's throat.

The body stiffened convulsively, legs thrust out straight and arms rigid, there was a puffing of breath from the severed windpipe and then the slow melting relaxation of death. Still with his foot on the chest, Ruffy withdrew the bayonet and stepped over the corpse.

That was very close, thought Bruce, stifling the qualm of horror he felt at the execution. The man's eyes were fixed open in almost comic surprise, the bottle still in his hand, his chest bare, the front of his trousers unbuttoned and stiff with dried blood – not his blood, guessed Bruce angrily.

They moved on past the kitchens. Bruce looked in and saw that they were empty with the white enamel tiles reflecting the vague light and piles of used plates and pots cluttering the tables and the sink. Then they reached the bar-room and there was a hurricane lamp on the counter diffusing a yellow glow; the stench of liquor poured out through the half-open window, the shelves were bare of bottles and men were asleep upon the counter, men lay curled together upon the floor like a pack of dogs, broken glass and rifles and shattered furniture littered about them. Someone had vomited out of the window leaving a yellow streak down the whitewashed wall.

'Stand here,' breathed Bruce into Ruffy's ear. 'I will go round to the front where I can throw on to the verandah and also into the lounge. Wait until you hear my first grenade blow.'

Ruffy nodded and leaned his rifle against the wall; he took a grenade in each fist and pulled the pins.

Bruce slipped quickly round the corner and along the side wall. He reached the windows of the lounge. They were tightly closed and he peered in over the sill. A little of the light from the lamp in the bar-room came through the open doors and showed up the interior. Here again there were men covering the floor and piled upon the sofas along the far wall. Twenty of them at least, he estimated by the volume of their snoring, and he grinned without humour. My God, what a shambles it is going to be.

Then something at the foot of the stairs caught his eye and the grin on his face became fixed, baring his teeth and narrowing his eyes to slits. It was the mound of nude flesh formed by the bodies of the four women; they had been discarded once they had served their purpose, dragged to one side to clear the floor for sleeping space, lying upon each other in a jumble of naked arms and legs and cascading hair.

No mercy now, thought Bruce with hatred replacing his fear as he looked at the women and saw by the attitudes in which they lay that there was no life left in them. *No mercy now!*

He slung his rifle over his left shoulder and filled his hand with grenades, pulled the pins and moved quickly to the corner so that he could look down the length of the covered verandah. He rolled both grenades down among the sleeping figures, hearing clearly the click of the priming and the metallic rattle against the concrete floor. Quickly he ducked back to the lounge window, snatching two more grenades from his haversack and pulling the pins, he hurled them through the closed windows. The crash of breaking glass blended with the double thunder of the explosions on the verandah.

Someone shouted in the room, a cry of surprise and alarm, then the windows above Bruce blew outwards, showering him with broken glass and the noise half deafening him as he tossed two more grenades through the gaping hole of the window. They were screaming and groaning in the lounge. Ruffy's grenades roared in the bar-room bursting through the double doors, then Bruce's grenades snuffed out the sounds of life in the lounge with violent white flame and thunder. Bruce tossed in two more grenades and ran back to the corner of the verandah unslinging his rifle.

A man with his hands over his eyes and blood streaming through his fingers fell over the low verandah wall and crawled to his knees. Bruce shot him from so close that the shaft of gun flame joined the muzzle of his rifle and the man's chest, punching him over backwards, throwing him spreadeagled on to the earth.

He looked beyond and saw two more in the road, but before he could raise his rifle the fire from his own gendarmes found them, knocking them down amid spurts of dust.

Bruce hurdled the verandah wall. He shouted, a sound without form or meaning. Exulting, unafraid, eager to get into the building, to get amongst them. He stumbled over the dead men on the verandah. A burst of gunfire from down the street rushed past him, so close he could feel the wind on his face. Fire from his own men.

'You stupid bastards!' Shouting without anger, without fear, with only the need to shout, he burst into the lounge through the main doors. It was half dark but he could see through the darkness and the haze of plaster dust.

A man on the stairs, the bloom of gunfire and the sting of the bullet across Bruce's thigh, fire in return, without aiming from the hip, miss and the man gone up and round the head of the stairs, yelling as he ran.

A grenade in Bruce's right hand, throw it high, watch it hit the wall and bounce sideways round the angle of the stairs. The explosion shocking in the confined space and the flash of it lighting the building and outlining the body of the man as it blew him back into the lounge, lifting him clear of the banisters, shredded and broken by the blast, falling heavily into the room below.

Up the stairs three at a time and into the bedroom

passage, another man naked and bewildered staggering through a doorway still drunk or half asleep, chop him down with a single shot in the stomach, jump over him and throw a grenade through the glass skylight of the second bedroom, another through the third and kick open the door of the last room in the bellow and flash of the explosions.

A man was waiting for Bruce across the room with a pistol in his hand, and both of them fired simultaneously, the clang of the bullet glancing off the steel of Bruce's helmet, jerking his head back savagely, throwing him sideways against the wall, but he fired again, rapid fire, hitting with every bullet, so that the man seemed to dance, a jerky grotesque twitching jig, pinned against the far wall by the bullets.

On his knees now Bruce was stunned, ears singing like a million mad mosquitoes, hands clumsy and slow on the reload, back on his feet, legs rubbery but the loaded rifle in his hands making a man of him.

Out into the passage, another one right on top of him, a vast dark shape in the darkness – kill him! kill him!

'Don't shoot, boss!'

Ruffy, thank God, Ruffy.

'Are there any more?'

'All finished, boss – you cleaned them out good.'

'How many?' Bruce shouted above the singing in his ears.

'Forty or so. Jesus, what a mess! There's blood all over the place. Those grenades—'

'There must be more.'

'Yes, but not in here, boss. Let's go and give the boys outside a hand.'

They ran back down the passage, down the stairs, and the floor of the lounge was sodden and sticky, dead men everywhere; it smelt like an abattoir – blood and ripped bowels. One still on his hands and knees, creepy-crawling towards the door. Ruffy shot him twice, flattening him.

'Not the front door, boss. Our boys will get you for sure. Go out the window.'

Bruce dived through the window head first, rolled over behind the cover of the verandah wall and came to his knees in one movement. He felt strong and invulnerable. Ruffy was beside him.

'Here come our boys,' said Ruffy, and Bruce could see them coming down the street, running forward in short bursts, stopping to fire, to throw a grenade, then coming again.

'And there are Lieutenant Hendry's lot.' From the opposite direction but with the same dodging, checking run, Bruce could see Wally with them. He was holding his rifle across his hip when he fired, his whole body shaking with the juddering of the gun.

Like a bird rising in front of the beaters one of the *shufta* broke from the cover of the grocery store and ran into the street unarmed, his head down and his arms pumping in time with his legs. Bruce was close enough to see the panic in his face. He seemed to be moving in slow motion, and the flames lit him harshly, throwing a distorted shadow in front of him. When the bullets hit him he stayed on his feet, staggering in a circle, thrashing at the air with his hands as though he were beating off a swarm of bees, the bullets slapping loudly against his body and lifting little puffs of dust from his clothing. Beside Bruce, Ruffy aimed carefully and shot him in the head, ending it.

'There must be more,' protested Bruce. 'Where are they hiding?'

'In the offices, I'd say.'

And Bruce turned his attention quickly to the block of Union Minière offices. The windows were in darkness and as he stared he thought he saw movement. He glanced quickly back at Wally's men and saw that four of them had bunched up close behind Wally as they ran.

'Hendry, watch out!' he shouted with all his strength. 'On your right, from the offices!'

But it was too late, gunfire sparkled in the dark windows and the little group of running men disintegrated.

Bruce and Ruffy fired together, raking the windows, emptying their automatic rifles into them. As he reloaded Bruce glanced back at where Wally's men had been hit. With disbelief he saw that Wally was the only one still on his feet; crossing the road, sprinting through an area of bullet-churned earth towards them, he reached the verandah and fell over the low wall.

'Are you wounded?' Bruce asked.

'Not a touch – those bastards couldn't shoot their way out of a French letter,' Wally shouted defiantly, and his voice carried clearly in the sudden hush. He snatched the empty magazine off the bottom of his rifle, threw it aside and clipped on a fresh one. 'Move over,' he growled, 'let me get a crack at those bastards.' He lifted his rifle and rested the stock on top of the wall, knelt behind it, cuddled the butt into his shoulder and began firing short bursts into the windows of the office block.

'This is what I was afraid of.' Bruce lifted his voice above the clamour of the guns. 'Now we've got a pocket of resistance right in the centre of the town. There must be fifteen or twenty of them in there – it might take us days to winkle them out.' He cast a longing look at the canvas-covered trucks lined up outside the station yard. 'They can cover the lorries from here, and as soon as they guess what we're after, as soon as we try and move them, they'll knock out that tanker and destroy the trucks.'

The firelight flickered on the shiny yellow and red paint of the tanker. It looked so big and vulnerable standing there in the open. It needed just one bullet out of the many hundred that had already been fired to end its charmed existence.

We've got to rush them now, he decided. Beyond the office block the remains of Wally's group had taken cover and were keeping up a heated fire. Bruce's group straggled up to the hotel and found positions at the windows.

'Ruffy.' Bruce caught him by the shoulder. 'We'll take four men with us and go round the back of the offices. From that building there we've got only twenty yards or so of open ground to cover. Once we get up against the wall they won't be able to touch us and we can toss grenades in amongst them.'

'That twenty yards looks like twenty miles from here,' rumbled Ruffy, but picked up his sack of grenades and crawled back from the verandah wall.

'Go and pick four men to come with us,' ordered Bruce.

'Okay, boss. We'll wait for you in the kitchen.'

'Hendry. Listen to me.'

'Yeah. What is it?'

'When I reach that corner over there I'll give you a wave. We'll be ready to go then. I want you to give us all the cover you can – keep their heads down.'

'Okay,' agreed Wally and fired another short burst.

'Try not to hit us when we close in.'

Wally turned to look at Bruce and he grinned wickedly.

'Mistakes happen, you know. I can't promise anything. You'd look real grand in my sights.'

'Don't joke,' said Bruce.

'Who's joking?' grinned Wally and Bruce left him. He found Ruffy and four gendarmes waiting in the kitchen.

'Come on,' he said and led them out across the kitchen yard, down the sanitary lane with the steel doors for the buckets behind the outhouses and the smell of them thick and fetid, round the corner and across the road to the buildings beyond the office block. They stopped there and crowded together, as though to draw courage and comfort from each other. Bruce measured the distance with his eye.

'It's not far,' he announced.

'Depends on how you look at it,' grunted Ruffy.

'There are only two windows opening out on to this side.'

'Two's enough – how many do you want?'

'Remember, Ruffy, you can only die once.'

'Once is enough,' said Ruffy. 'Let's cut out the talking, boss. Too much talk gets you in the guts.'

Bruce moved across to the corner of the building out of the shadows. He waved towards the hotel and imagined that he saw an acknowledgement from the end of the verandah.

'All together,' he said, sucked in a deep breath, held it a second and then launched himself into the open. He felt small now, no longer brave and invulnerable, and his legs moved so slowly that he seemed to be standing still. The black windows gaped at him.

Now, he thought, now you die.

Where, he thought, not in the stomach, please God, not in the stomach.

And his legs moved stiffly under him, carrying him half way across.

Only ten more paces, he thought, one more river, just one more river to Jordan. But not in the stomach, please God, not in my stomach. And his flesh cringed in anticipation, his stomach drawn in hard as he ran.

Suddenly the black windows were brightly lit, bright white oblongs in the dark buildings, and the glass sprayed out of them like untidy spittle from an old man's mouth. Then they were dark again, dark with smoke billowing from them and the memory of the explosion echoing in his ears.

'A grenade!' Bruce was bewildered. 'Someone let off a grenade in there!'

He reached the back door without stopping and it burst open before his rush. He was into the room, shooting, coughing in the fumes, firing wildly at the small movements of dying men.

In the half darkness something long and white lay against

the far wall. A body, a white man's naked body. He crossed to it and looked down.

'André,' he said, 'it's André – he threw the grenade.' And he knelt beside him.

– 17 –

Curled naked upon the concrete floor, André was alive but dying as the haemorrhage within him leaked his life away. His mind was alive and he heard the crump, crump of Bruce's grenades, then the gunfire in the street, and the sound of running men. The shouts in the night and then the guns very close, they were in the room in which he lay.

He opened his eyes. There were men at each of the windows, crouched below the sills, and the room was thick with cordite fumes and the clamour of the guns as they fired out into the night.

André was cold, the coldness was all through him. Even his hands drawn up against his chest were cold and heavy. His stomach only was warm, warm and immensely bloated.

It was an effort to think, for his mind also was cold and the noise of the guns confused him.

He watched the men at the windows with a detached disinterest, and slowly his body lost its weight. He seemed to float clear of the floor and look down upon the room from the roof. His eyelids sagged and he dragged them up again, and struggled down towards his own body.

There was suddenly a rushing sound in the room and plaster sprayed from the wall above André's head, filling the air with pale floating dust. One of the men at the windows fell backwards, his weapon ringing loudly on the floor as it dropped from his hands; he flopped over twice and lay still, face down within arm's length of André.

Ponderously André's mind analysed the sights his eyes

were recording. Someone was firing on the building from outside. The man beside him was dead and from his head wound the blood spread slowly across the floor towards him. André closed his eyes again, he was very tired and very cold.

There was a lull in the sound of gunfire, one of those freak silences in the midst of battle. And in the lull André heard a voice far off, shouting. He could not hear the words but he recognized the voice and his eyelids flew open. There was an excitement in him, a new force, for it was Wally's voice he had heard.

He moved slightly, clenching his hands and his brain started to sing.

Wally has come back for me – he has come to save me. He rolled his head slowly, painfully, and the blood gurgled in his stomach.

I must help him, I must not let him endanger himself – these men are trying to kill him. I must stop them. I mustn't let them kill Wally.

And then he saw the grenades hanging on the belt of the man that lay beside him. He fastened his eyes on the round polished metal bulbs and he began to pray silently.

'Hail, Mary, full of grace, the Lord is with thee.'

He moved again, straightening his body.

'Blessed art thou among women, and blessed is the fruit of thy womb, Jesus.'

His hand crept out into the pool of blood, and the sound of the guns filled his head so he could not hear himself pray. Walking on its fingers, his hand crawled through the blood as slowly as a fly through a saucer of treacle.

'Blessed is the fruit of thy womb, Jesus. Oh, Jesus. Pray for me now, and at the hour. Full of grace.'

He touched the smooth, deeply segmented steel of the grenade.

'Us sinners – at the day, at the hour. This day – this day our daily bread.'

He fumbled at the clip, fingers stiff and cold.

'Hallowed be thy – Hallowed be thy—'

The clip clicked open and he held the grenade, curling his fingers round it.

'Hail, Mary, full of grace.'

He drew the grenade to him and held it with both hands against his chest. He lifted it to his mouth and took the pin between his teeth.

'Pray for us sinners,' he whispered, and pulled the pin.

'Now and at the hour of our death.'

And he tried to throw it. It rolled from his hand and bumped across the floor. The firing handle flew off and rattled against the wall. General Moses turned from the window and saw it – his lips opened and his spectacles glinted above the rose-pink cave of his mouth. The grenade lay at his feet. Then everything was gone in the flash and roar of the explosion.

Afterwards in the acrid swirl of fumes, in the patter of falling plaster, in the tinkle and crunch of broken glass, in the small scrabbling noises and the murmur and moan of dying men, André was still alive. The body of the man beside him had shielded his head and chest from the full force of the blast.

There was still enough life in him to recognize Bruce Curry's face close to his, though he could not feel the hands that touched him.

'André!' said Bruce. 'It's André – he threw the grenade!'

'Tell him—' whispered André and stopped.

'Yes, André—?' said Bruce.

'I didn't, this day and at the hour. I had to – not this time.' He could feel it going out in him like a candle in a high wind and he tried to cup his hands around it.

'What is it, André? What must I tell him?' Bruce's voice, but so far away.

'Because of him – this time – not of it, I didn't.' He

stopped again and gathered all of what was left. His lips quivered as he tried so hard to say it.

'Like a man!' he whispered and the candle went out.

'Yes,' said Bruce softly, holding him. 'This time like a man.'

He lowered André gently until his head touched the floor again; then he stood upright and looked down at the terribly mutilated body. He felt empty inside, a hollowness, the same feeling as after love.

He moved across to the desk near the far wall. Outside the gunfire dwindled like half-hearted applause, flared up again and then ceased. Around him Ruffy and the four gendarmes moved excitedly, inspecting the dead, exclaiming, laughing the awkward embarrassed laughter of men freshly released from mortal danger.

Loosening the chin straps of his helmet with slow steady fingers, Bruce stared across the room at André's body.

'Yes,' he whispered again. 'This time like a man. All the other times are wiped out, the score is levelled.'

His cigarettes were damp from the swamp, but he took one from the centre of the pack and straightened it with calm nerveless fingers. He found his lighter and flicked it open – then, without warning, his hands started to shake. The flame of the lighter fluttered and he had to hold it steady with both hands. There was blood on his hands, new sticky blood. He snapped the lighter closed and breathed in the smoke. It tasted bitter and the saliva flooded into his mouth. He swallowed it down, nausea in his stomach, and his breathing quickened.

It was not like this before, he remembered, even that night at the road bridge when they broke through on the flank and we met them with bayonets in the dark. Before it had no meaning, but now I can feel again. Once more I'm alive.

Suddenly he had to be alone; he stood up.

'Ruffy.'

'Yes, boss?'

'Clean up here. Get blankets from the hotel for de Surrier and the women, also those men down in the station yard.' It was someone else speaking; he could hear the voice as though it were a long way off.

'You okay, boss?'

'Yes.'

'Your head?'

Bruce lifted his hand and touched the long dent in his helmet.

'It's nothing,' he said.

'Your leg?'

'Just a touch, get on with it.'

'Okay, boss. What shall we do with these others?'

'Throw them in the river,' said Bruce and walked out into the street. Hendry and his gendarmes were still on the verandah of the hotel, but they had started on the corpses there, using their bayonets like butchers' knives, taking the ears, laughing also the strained nervous laughter.

Bruce crossed the street to the station yard. The dawn was coming, drawing out across the sky like a sheet of steel rolled from the mill, purple and lilac at first, then red as it spread above the forest.

The Ford Ranchero stood on the station platform where he had left it. He opened the door, slid in behind the wheel, and watched the dawn become day.

– 18 –

'Captain, the sergeant major asks you to come. There is something he wants to show you.'

Bruce lifted his head from where it was resting on the steering wheel. He had not heard the gendarme approach.

'I'll come,' he said, picked up his helmet and his rifle

from the seat beside him and followed the man back to the office block.

His gendarmes were loading a dead man into one of the trucks, swinging him by his arms and legs.

'Un, deux, trois,' and a shout of laughter as the limp body flew over the tailboard on to the gruesome pile already there.

Sergeant Jacque came out of the office dragging a man by his heels. The head bumped loosely down the steps and there was a wet brown drag mark left on the cement verandah.

'Like pork,' Jacque called cheerily. The corpse was that of a small grey-headed man, skinny, with the marks of spectacles on the bridge of his nose and a double row of decorations on his tunic. Bruce noted that one of them was the purple and white ribbon of the military cross – strange loot for the Congo. Jacque dropped the man's heels, drew his bayonet and stooped over the man. He took one of the ears that lay flat against the grizzled skull, pulled it forward and freed it with a single stroke of the knife. The opened flesh was pink with the dark hole of the eardrum in the centre.

Bruce walked on into the office and his nostrils flared at the abattoir stench.

'Have a look at this lot, boss.' Ruffy stood by the desk.

'Enough to buy you a ranch in Hyde Park,' grinned Hendry beside him. In his hand he held a pencil. Threaded on to it like a kebab were a dozen human ears.

'Yes,' said Bruce as he looked at the pile of industrial and gem diamonds on the blotter. 'I know about those. Better count them, Ruffy, then put them back in the bags.'

'You're not going to turn them in?' protested Hendry. 'Jesus, if we share this lot three ways – you, Ruffy and I – there's enough to make us all rich.'

'Or put us against a wall,' said Bruce grimly. 'What makes

you think the gentlemen in Elisabethville don't know about them?' He turned his attention back to Ruffy. 'Count them and pack them. You're in charge of them. Don't lose any.'

Bruce looked across the room at the blanket-wrapped bundle that was André de Surrier.

'Have you detailed a burial squad?'

'Yes, boss. Six of the boys are out back digging.'

'Good,' Bruce nodded. 'Hendry, come with me. We'll go and have a look at the trucks.'

Half an hour later Bruce closed the bonnet of the last vehicle. 'This is the only one that won't run. The carburettor's smashed. We'll take the tyres off it for spares.' He wiped his greasy hands on the sides of his trousers. 'Thank God, the tanker is untouched. We've got six hundred gallons there, more than enough for the return trip.'

'You going to take the Ford?' asked Hendry.

'Yes, it may come in useful.'

'And it will be more comfortable for you and your little French thing.' Heavy sarcasm in Hendry's voice.

'That's right,' Bruce answered evenly. 'Can you drive?'

'What you think? You think I'm a bloody fool?'

'Everyone is always trying to get at you, aren't they? You can't trust anyone, can you?' Bruce asked softly.

'You're so bloody right!' agreed Hendry.

Bruce changed the subject. 'André had a message for you before he died.'

'Old doll boy!'

'He threw that grenade. Did you know that?'

'Yeah. I knew it.'

'Don't you want to hear what he said?'

'Once a queer, always a queer, and the only good queer is a dead queer.'

'All right.' Bruce frowned. 'Get a couple of men to help you. Fill the trucks with gas. We've wasted enough time already.'

They buried their dead in a communal grave, packing them in quickly and covering them just as quickly. Then they stood embarrassed and silent round the mound.

'You going to say anything, boss?' Ruffy asked, and they all looked at Bruce.

'No.' Bruce turned away and started for the trucks.

What the hell can you say, he thought angrily. Death is not someone to make conversation with. All you can say is, 'These were men; weak and strong, evil and good, and a lot in between. But now they're dead – like pork.'

He looked back over his shoulder.

'All right, let's move out.'

The convoy ground slowly over the causeway. Bruce led in the Ford and the air blowing in through the shattered windscreen was too humid and steamy to give relief from the rising heat.

The sun stood high above the forest as they passed the turn-off to the mission.

Bruce looked along it, and he wanted to signal the convoy to continue while he went up to St Augustine's. He wanted to see Mike Haig and Father Ignatius, make sure that they were safe.

Then he put aside the temptation. If there is more horror up there at St Augustine's, if the *shufta* have found them and there are raped women and dead men there, then there is nothing I can do and I don't want to know about it.

It is better to believe that they are safely hidden in the jungle. It is better to believe that out of all this will remain something good.

He led the convoy resolutely past the turn-off and over the hills towards the level crossing.

Suddenly another idea came to him and he thought about it, turning it over with pleasure.

Four men came to Port Reprieve, men without hope, men abandoned by God.

And they learned that it was not too late, perhaps it is never too late.

For one of them found the strength to die like a man, although he had lived his whole life with weakness.

Another rediscovered the self-respect he had lost along the way, and with it the chance to start again.

The third found – he hesitated – yes, the third found love.

And the fourth? Bruce's smile faded as he thought of Wally Hendry. It was a neat little parable, except for Wally Hendry. What had he found? A dozen human ears threaded on a pencil?

– 19 –

'Can't you get up enough steam to move us back to the crossing – only a few miles.'

'I am desolate, m'sieur. She will not hold even a belch, to say nothing of a head of steam.' The engine driver spread his pudgy little hands in a gesture of helplessness. Bruce studied the rent in the boiler. The metal was torn open like the petals of a flower. He knew it had been a forlorn request.

'Very well. Thank you.' He turned to Ruffy. 'We'll have to carry everything back to the convoy. Another day wasted.'

'It's a long walk,' Ruffy agreed. 'Better get started.'

'How much food have we?'

'Not too much. We've been feeding a lot of extra mouths, and we sent a lot out to the mission.'

'How much?'

'About two more days.'

'That should get us to Elisabethville.'

'Boss, you want to carry everything to the lorries? Searchlights, ammunition, blankets – all of it?'

Bruce paused for a moment. 'I think so. We may need it.'

'It's going to take the rest of the day.'

'Yes,' agreed Bruce. Ruffy walked back along the train but Bruce called after him.

'Ruffy!'

'Boss?'

'Don't forget the beer.'

Ruffy's black moon of a face split laterally into a grin.

'You think we should take it?'

'Why not?' Bruce laughed.

'Man, you talked me right into it!'

And the night was almost on them before the last of the equipment had been carried back from the abandoned train to the convoy and loaded into the trucks.

Time is a slippery thing, even more so than wealth. No bank vault can hold it for you, this precious stuff which we spend in such prodigal fashion on the trivialities. By the time we have slept and eaten and moved from one place to the next there is such a small percentage left for the real business of living.

Bruce felt futile resentment as he always did when he thought about it. And if you discount the time spent at an office desk, then how much is there left? Half of one day a week, that's how much the average man lives! That's how far short of our potential is the actuality of existence.

Take it further than that: we are capable of using only a fraction of our physical and mental strength. Only under hypnosis are we able to exert more than a tenth of what is in us. So divide that half of one day a week by ten, and the rest is waste! Sickening waste!

'Ruffy, have you detailed sentries for tonight?' Bruce barked at him.

'Not yet. I was just—'

'Well, do it, and do it quickly.'

Ruffy looked at Bruce in speculation and through his anger Bruce felt a qualm of regret that he had selected that mountain of energy on which to vent his frustration.

'Where the hell is Hendry?' he snapped.

Without speaking Ruffy pointed to a group of men round one of the trucks at the rear of the convoy and Bruce left him.

Suddenly consumed with impatience Bruce fell upon his men. Shouting at them, scattering them to a dozen different tasks. He walked along the convoy making sure that his instructions were being carried out to the letter; checking the siting of the Brens and the searchlights, making sure that the single small cooking fire was screened from Baluba eyes, stopping to watch the refuelling of the trucks and the running maintenance he had ordered. Men avoided catching his eye and bent to their tasks with studied application. There were no raised voices or sounds of laughter in the camp.

Again Bruce had decided against a night journey. The temptation itched within him, but the exhaustion of those gendarmes who had not slept since the previous morning and the danger of travelling in the dark he could not ignore.

'We'll leave as soon as it's light tomorrow,' Bruce told Ruffy.

'Okay, boss,' Ruffy nodded, and then soothingly, 'you're tired. Food's nearly ready, then you get some sleep.'

Bruce glared at him, opening his mouth to snarl a retort, and then closed it again. He turned and strode out of the camp into the forest.

He found a fallen log, sat down and lit a cigarette. It was dark now and there were only a few stars among the rain clouds that blackened the sky. He could hear the faint sounds from the camp but there were no lights – the way he had ordered it.

The fact that his anger had no focal point inflamed it rather than quenched it. It ranged restlessly until at last it found a target – himself.

He recognized the brooding undirected depression that was descending upon him. It was a thing he had not experienced for a long time, nearly two years. Not since the wreck of his marriage and the loss of his children. Not since he had stifled all emotion and trained himself not to participate in the life around him.

But now his barrier was gone, there was no sheltered harbour from the storm surf and he would have to ride it out. Furl all canvas and rig a sea anchor.

The anger was gone now. At least anger had heat but this other thing was cold; icy waves of it broke over him, and he was small and insignificant in the grip of it.

His mind turned to his children and the loneliness howled round him like a winter wind from the south. He closed his eyes and pressed his fingers against the lids. Their faces formed in the eye of his mind.

Christine with pink fat legs under her frilly skirt, and the face of a thoughtful cherub below soft hair cropped like a page boy.

'I love you best of all,' said with much seriousness, holding his face with small hands only a little sticky with ice cream.

Simon, a miniature reproduction of Bruce even to the nose. Scabs on the knees and dirt on the face. No demonstrations of affection from him, but in its place something much better, a companionship far beyond his six years. Long discussions on everything from religion, 'Why didn't Jesus used to shave?' to politics, 'When are you going to be prime minister, Dad?'

And the loneliness was a tangible thing now, like the coils of a reptile squeezing his chest. Bruce ground out the cigarette beneath his heel and tried to find refuge in his hatred for the woman who had been his wife. The woman who had taken them from him.

But his hatred was a cold thing also, dead ash with a stale taste. For he knew that the blame was not all hers. It was another of his failures; perhaps if I had tried harder, perhaps if I had left some of the cruel things unsaid, perhaps – yes, it might have been, and perhaps and maybe. But it was not. It was over and finished and now I am alone. There is no worse condition; no state beyond loneliness. It is the waste land and the desolation.

Something moved near him in the night, a soft rustle of grass, a presence felt rather than seen. And Bruce stiffened. His right hand closed over his rifle. He brought it up slowly, his eyes straining into the darkness.

The movement again, closer now. A twig popped underfoot. Bruce slowly trained his rifle round to cover it, pressure on the trigger and his thumb on the safety. Stupid to have wandered away from the camp; asking for it, and now he had got it. Baluba tribesmen! He could see the figure now in the dimness of starlight, stealthily moving across his front. How many of them, he wondered. If I hit this one, there could be a dozen others with him. Have to take a chance. One quick burst and then run for it. A hundred yards to the camp, about an even chance. The figure was stationary now, standing listening. Bruce could see the outline of the head – no helmet, can't be one of us. He raised the rifle and pointed it. Too dark to see the sights, but at that range he couldn't miss. Bruce drew his breath softly, filling his lungs, ready to shoot and run.

'Bruce?' Shermaine's voice, frightened, almost a whisper. He threw up the rifle barrel. God, that was close. He had nearly killed her.

'Yes, I'm here.' His own voice was scratchy with the shock of realization.

'Oh, there you are.'

'What the hell are you doing out of the camp?' he demanded furiously as anger replaced his shock.

'I'm sorry, Bruce, I came to see if you were all right. You were gone such a long time.'

'Well, get back to the camp, and don't try any more tricks like that.'

There was a long silence, and then she spoke softly, unable to keep the hurt out of her tone.

'I brought you something to eat. I thought you'd be hungry. I'm sorry if I did wrong.'

She came to him, stooped and placed something on the ground in front of him. Then she turned and was gone.

'Shermaine.' He wanted her back, but the only reply was the fading rustle of the grass and then silence. He was alone again.

He picked up the plate of food.

You fool, he thought. You stupid, ignorant, thoughtless fool. You'll lose her, and you'll have deserved it. You deserve everything you've had, and more.

You never learn, do you, Curry? You never learn that there is a penalty for selfishness and for thoughtlessness.

He looked down at the plate in his hands. Bully beef and sliced onion, bread and cheese.

Yes, I have learned, he answered himself with sudden determination. I will not spoil this, this thing that is between this girl and me. That was the last time; now I am a man I will put away childish things, like temper and self-pity.

He ate the food, suddenly aware of his hunger. He ate quickly, wolfing it. Then he stood up and walked back to the camp.

A sentry challenged him on the perimeter and Bruce answered with alacrity. At night his gendarmes were very quick on the trigger; the challenge was an unusual courtesy.

'It is unwise to go alone into the forest in the darkness,' the sentry reprimanded him.

'Why?' Bruce felt his mood changing. The depression evaporated.

'It is unwise,' repeated the man vaguely.

'The spirits?' Bruce teased him delicately.

'An aunt of my sister's husband disappeared not a short throw of a spear from my hut. There was no trace, no shout, nothing. I was there. It is not a matter for doubt,' said the man with dignity.

'A lion perhaps?' Bruce prodded him.

'If you say so, then it is so. I know what I know. But I say only that there is no wisdom in defying the custom of the land.'

Suddenly touched by the man's concern for him, Bruce dropped a hand on to his shoulder and gripped it in the old expression of affection.

'I will remember. I did it without thinking.'

He walked into the camp. The incident had confirmed something he had vaguely suspected, but in which previously he had felt no interest. The men liked him. A hundred similar indications of this fact he had only half noted, not caring one way or the other. But now it gave him intense pleasure, fully compensating for the loneliness he had just experienced.

He walked past the little group of men round the cooking fire to where the Ford stood at the head of the convoy. Peering through the side window he could make out Shermaine's blanket-wrapped form on the back seat. He tapped on the glass and she sat up and rolled down the window.

'Yes?' she asked coolly.

'Thank you for the food.'

'It is nothing.' The slightest hint of warmth in her voice.

'Shermaine, sometimes I say things I do not mean. You startled me. I nearly shot you.'

'It was my fault. I should not have followed you.'

'I was rude,' he persisted.

'Yes.' She laughed now. That husky little chuckle. 'You were rude but with good reason. We shall forget it.' She placed her hand on his arm. 'You must rest, you haven't slept for two days.'

'Will you ride in the Ford with me tomorrow to show that I am forgiven?'

'Of course,' she nodded.

'Good night, Shermaine.'

'Good night, Bruce,'

No, Bruce decided as he spread his blankets beside the fire, I am not alone. Not any more.

– 20 –

'What about breakfast, boss?'

'They can eat on the road. Give them a tin of bully each – we've wasted enough time on this trip.'

The sky was paling and pinking above the forest. It was light enough to read the dial of his wristwatch. Twenty minutes to five.

'Get them moving, Ruffy. If we make Msapa Junction before dark we can drive through the night. Home for breakfast tomorrow.'

'Now you're talking, boss.' Ruffy clapped his helmet on to his head and went off to rouse the men who lay in the road beside the trucks.

Shermaine was asleep. Bruce leaned into the window of the Ford and studied her face. A wisp of hair lay over her mouth, rising and falling with her breathing. It tickled her nose and in her sleep it twitched like a rabbit.

Bruce felt an almost unbearable pang of tenderness towards her. With one finger he lifted the hair off her face. Then he smiled at himself.

If you can feel like this before breakfast, then you've got it in a bad way, he told himself.

Do you know something, he retorted. I like the feeling.

'Hey, you lazy wench!' He pulled the lobe of her ear. 'Time to wake up.'

It was almost half past five before the convoy got under way. It had taken that long to bully and cajole the sleep out of sixty men and get them into the lorries. This morning Bruce did not find the delay unbearable. He had managed to find time for four hours' sleep during the night. Four hours was not nearly enough to make up for the previous two days.

Now he felt light-headed, a certain unreal quality of gaiety overlaying his exhaustion, a carnival spirit. There was no longer the same urgency, for the road to Elisabethville was clear and not too long. Home for breakfast tomorrow!

'We'll be at the bridge in a little under an hour.' He glanced sideways at Shermaine.

'You've left a guard on it?'

'Ten men,' answered Bruce. 'We'll pick them up almost without stopping, and then the next stop, room 201, Grand Hotel Leopold II, Avenue du Kasai.' He grinned in anticipation. 'A bath so deep it will slop over on to the floor, so hot it will take five minutes to get into it. Clean clothes. A steak that thick, with French salad and a bottle of Liebfraumilch.'

'For breakfast!' protested Shermaine.

'For breakfast,' Bruce agreed happily. He was silent for a while, savouring the idea. The road ahead of him was tiger-striped with the shadows of the trees thrown by the low sun. The air that blew in through the missing windscreen was cool and clean-smelling. He felt good. The responsibility of command lay lightly on his shoulders this morning; a pretty girl beside him, a golden morning, the horror of the last few days half-forgotten – they might have been going on a picnic.

'What are you thinking?' he asked suddenly. She was very quiet beside him.

'I was wondering about the future,' she answered softly. 'There is no one I know in Elisabethville, and I do not wish to stay there.'

'Will you return to Brussels?' he asked. The question was without significance, for Bruce Curry had very definite plans for the immediate future, and these included Shermaine.

'Yes, I think so. There is nowhere else.'

'You have relatives there?'

'An aunt.'

'Are you close?'

Shermaine laughed, but there was bitterness in the husky chuckle. 'Oh, very close. She came to see me once at the orphanage. Once in all those years. She brought me a comic book of a religious nature and told me to clean my teeth and brush my hair a hundred strokes a day.'

'There is no one else?' asked Bruce.

'No.'

'Then why go back?'

'What else is there to do?' she asked. 'Where else is there to go?'

'There's a life to live, and the rest of the world to visit.'

'Is that what you are going to do?'

'That is exactly what I'm going to do, starting with a hot bath.'

Bruce could feel it between them. They both knew it was there, but it was too soon to talk about it. I have only kissed her once, but that was enough. So what will happen? Marriage? His mind shied away from that word with startling violence, then came hesitantly back to examine it. Stalking it as though it were a dangerous beast, ready to take flight again as soon as it showed its teeth.

For some people it is a good thing. It can stiffen the spineless; ease the lonely; give direction to the wanderers; spur those without ambition – and, of course, there was the final unassailable argument in its favour. Children.

But there are some who can only sicken and shrivel in the colourless cell of matrimony. With no space to fly, your wings must weaken with disuse; turned inwards, your eyes become short-sighted; when all your communication with the rest of the world is through the glass windows of the cell, then your contact is limited.

And I already have children. I have a daughter and I have a son.

Bruce turned his eyes from the road and studied the girl beside him. There is no fault I can find. She is beautiful in the delicate, almost fragile way that is so much better and longer-lived than blond hair and big bosoms. She is unspoilt; hardship has long been her travelling companion and from it she has learned kindness and humility.

She is mature, knowing the ways of this world; knowing death and fear, the evilness of men and their goodness. I do not believe she has ever lived in the fairy-tale cocoon that most young girls spin about themselves.

And yet she has not forgotten how to laugh.

Perhaps, he thought, perhaps. But it is too soon to talk about it.

'You are very grim.' Shermaine broke the silence, but the laughter shivered just below the surface of her voice. 'Again you are Bonaparte. And when you are grim your nose is too big and cruel. It is a nose of great brutality and it does not fit the rest of your face. I think that when they had finished you they had only one nose left in stock. "It is too big," they said, "but it is the only nose left, and when he smiles it will not look too bad." So they took a chance and stuck it on anyway.'

'Were you never taught that it is bad manners to poke fun at a man's weakness?' Bruce fingered his nose ruefully.

'Your nose is many things, but not weak. Never weak.' She laughed now and moved a little closer to him.

'You know you can attack me from behind your own perfect nose, and I cannot retaliate.'

'Never trust a man who makes pretty speeches so easily, because he surely makes them to every girl he meets.' She slid an inch further across the seat until they were almost touching. 'You waste your talents, mon capitaine. I am immune to your charm.'

'In just one minute I will stop this car and—'

'You cannot.' Shermaine jerked her head to indicate the two gendarmes in the seat behind them. 'What would they think, Bonaparte? It would be very bad for discipline.'

'Discipline or no discipline, in just one minute I will stop this car and spank you soundly before I kiss you.'

'One threat does not frighten me, but because of the other I will leave your poor nose.' She moved away a little and once more Bruce studied her face. Beneath the frank scrutiny she fidgeted and started to blush.

'Do you mind! Were you never taught that it is bad manners to stare?'

So now I am in love again, thought Bruce. This is only the third time, an average of once every ten years or so. It frightens me a little because there is always pain with it. The exquisite pain of loving and the agony of losing.

It starts in the loins and it is very deceptive because you think it is only the old thing, the tightness and tension that any well-rounded stern or cheeky pair of breasts will give you. Scratch it, you think, it's just a small itch. Spread a little of the warm salve on it and it will be gone in no time.

But suddenly it spreads, upwards and downwards, all through you. The pit of your stomach feels hot, then the flutters round the heart. It's dangerous now; once it gets this far it's incurable and you can scratch and scratch but all you do is inflame it.

Then the last stages, when it attacks the brain. No pain

there, that's the worst sign. A heightening of the senses; your eyes are sharper, your blood runs too fast, food tastes good, your mouth wants to shout and legs want to run. Then the delusions of grandeur: you are the cleverest, strongest, most masculine male in the universe, and you stand ten feet tall in your socks.

How tall are you now, Curry, he asked himself. About nine feet six and I weigh twenty stone, he answered, and almost laughed aloud.

And how does it end? It ends with words. Words can kill anything. It ends with cold words; words like fire that stick in the structure and take hold and lick it up, blackening and charring it, bringing it down in smoking ruins.

It ends in suspicion of things not done, and in the certainty of things done and remembered. It ends with selfishness and carelessness, and words, always words.

It ends with pain and greyness, and it leaves scar tissue and damage that will never heal.

Or it ends without fuss and fury. It just crumbles and blows away like dust on the wind. But there is still the agony of loss.

Both these endings I know well, for I have loved twice, and now I love again.

Perhaps this time it does not have to be that way. Perhaps this time it will last. Nothing is for ever, he thought. Nothing is for ever, not even life, and perhaps this time if I cherish it and tend it carefully it will last that long, as long as life.

'We are nearly at the bridge,' said Shermaine beside him, and Bruce started. The miles had dropped unseen behind them and now the forest was thickening. It crouched closer to the earth, greener and darker along the river.

Bruce slowed the Ford and the forest became dense bush around them, the road a tunnel through it. They came round one last bend in the track and out of the tunnel of green vegetation into the clearing where the road met the railway line and ran beside it on to the heavy timber platform of the bridge.

Bruce stopped the Ranchero, switched off the engine and they all sat silently, staring out at the solid jungle on the far bank with its screen of creepers and monkey-ropes hanging down, trailing the surface of the deep green swift-flowing river. They stared at the stumps of the bridge thrusting out from each bank towards each other like the arms of parted lovers; at the wide gap between with the timbers still smouldering and the smoke drifting away downstream over the green water.

'It's gone,' said Shermaine. 'It's been burnt.'

'Oh, no,' groaned Bruce. 'Oh, God, no!'

With an effort he pulled his eyes from the charred remains of the bridge and turned them on to the jungle about them, a hundred feet away, ringing them in. Hostile, silent. 'Don't get out of the car,' he snapped as Shermaine reached for the door handle. 'Roll your window up, quickly.'

She obeyed.

'They're waiting in there.' He pointed at the edge of the jungle.

Behind them the first of the convoy came round the bend into the clearing. Bruce jumped from the Ford and ran back towards the leading truck.

'Don't get out, stay inside,' he shouted and ran on down the line, repeating the instruction to each of them as he passed. When he reached Ruffy's cab he jumped on to the running board, jerked the door open, slipped in on to the seat and slammed the door.

'They've burnt the bridge.'

'What's happened to the boys we left to guard it?'

'I don't know but we'll find out. Pull up alongside the others so that I can talk to them.'

Through the half-open window he issued his orders to each of the drivers and within ten minutes all the vehicles had been manoeuvred into the tight defensive circle of the laager, a formation Bruce's ancestors had used a hundred years before.

'Ruffy, get out those tarpaulins and spread them over the top to form a roof. We don't want them dropping arrows in amongst us.'

Ruffy selected half a dozen gendarmes and they went to work, dragging out the heavy folded canvas.

'Hendry, put a couple of men under each truck. Set up the Brens in case they try to rush us.'

In the infectious urgency of defence, Wally did not make his usual retort, but gathered his men. They wriggled on their stomachs under the vehicles, rifles pointed out towards the silent jungle.

'I want the extinguishers here in the middle so we can get them in a hurry. They might use fire again.'

Two gendarmes ran to each of the cabs and unclipped the fire-extinguishers from the dashboards.

'What can I do?' Shermaine was standing beside Bruce.

'Keep quiet and stay out of the way,' said Bruce as he turned and hurried across to help Ruffy's gang with the tarpaulins.

It took them half an hour of desperate endeavour before they completed the fortifications to Bruce's satisfaction.

'That should hold them.' Bruce stood with Ruffy and Hendry in the centre of the laager and surveyed the green canvas roof above them and the closely packed vehicles around them. The Ford was parked beside the tanker, not included in the outer ring for its comparative size would have made it a weak point in the defence.

'It's going to be bloody hot and crowded in here,' grumbled Hendry.

'Yes, I know.' Bruce looked at him. 'Would you like to relieve the congestion by waiting outside?'

'Funny boy, big laugh,' answered Wally.

'What now, boss?' Ruffy put into words the question Bruce had been asking himself.

'You and I will go and take a look at the bridge,' he said.

'You'll look a rare old sight with an arrow sticking out of your jack,' grinned Wally. 'Boy, that's going to kill me!'

'Ruffy, get us half a dozen gas capes each. I doubt their arrows will go through them at a range of a hundred feet, and of course we'll wear helmets.'

'Okay, boss.'

It was like being in a sauna bath beneath the six layers of rubberized canvas. Bruce could feel the sweat squirting from his pores with each pace, and rivulets of it coursing down his back and flanks as he and Ruffy left the laager and walked up the road to the bridge.

Beside him Ruffy's bulk was so enhanced by the gas capes that he reminded Bruce of a prehistoric monster reaching the end of its gestation period.

'Warm enough, Ruffy?' he asked, feeling the need for humour. The ring of jungle made him nervous. Perhaps he had underestimated the carry of a Baluba arrow – despite the light reed shaft, they used iron heads, barbed viciously and ground to a needle point, and poison smeared thickly between the barbs.

'Man, look at me shiver,' grunted Ruffy and the sweat greased down his jowls and dripped from his chin.

Long before they reached the access to the bridge the stench of putrefaction crept out to meet them. In Bruce's mind every smell had its own colour, and this one was green, the same green as the sheen of putrefaction on rotting meat. The stench was so heavy he could almost feel it bearing down on them, choking in his throat and coating his tongue and the roof of his mouth with the oily over-sweetness.

'No doubt what that is!' Ruffy spat, trying to get the taste out of his mouth.

'Where are they?' gagged Bruce, starting to pant from the heat and the effort of breathing the fouled air.

They reached the bank and Bruce's question was answered as they looked down on to the narrow beach.

There were the black remains of a dozen cooking fires along the water's edge, and closer to the high bank were two crude structures of poles. For a moment their purpose puzzled Bruce and then he realized what they were. He had seen those crosspieces suspended between two uprights often before in hunting camps throughout Africa. They were paunching racks! At intervals along the crosspieces were the bark ropes that had been used to string up the game, heels first, with head and forelegs dangling and belly bulging forward so that at the long abdominal stroke of the knife the viscera would drop out easily.

But the game they had butchered on *these* racks were men, his men. He counted the hanging ropes. There were ten of them, so no one had escaped.

'Cover me, Ruffy. I'm going down to have a look.' It was a penance Bruce was imposing upon himself. They were his men, and he had left them there.

'Okay, boss.'

Bruce clambered down the well-defined path to the beach. Now the smell was almost unbearable and he found the source of it. Between the racks lay a dark shapeless mass. It moved with flies; its surface moved, trembled, crawled with flies. Suddenly, humming, they lifted in a cloud from the pile of human debris, and then settled once more upon it.

A single fly buzzed round Bruce's head and then settled on his hand. Metallic blue body, wings cocked back, it crouched on his skin and gleefully rubbed its front legs together. Bruce's throat and stomach convulsed as he began to retch. He struck at the fly and it darted away.

There were bones scattered round the cooking fires and a skull lay near his feet, split open to yield its contents.

Another spasm took Bruce and this time the vomit came

up into his mouth, acid and warm. He swallowed it, turned away and scrambled up the bank to where Ruffy waited. He stood there gasping, suppressing his nausea until at last he could speak.

'All right, that's all I wanted to know,' and he led the way back to the circle of vehicles.

Bruce sat on the bonnet of the Ranchero and sucked hard on his cigarette, trying to get the taste of death from his mouth.

'They probably swam downstream during the night and climbed the supports of the bridge. Kanaki and his boys wouldn't have known anything about it until they came over the sides.' He drew on the cigarette again and trickled the smoke out of his nostrils, fumigating the back of his throat and his nasal passages. 'I should have thought of that. I should have warned Kanaki of that.'

'You mean they ate all ten of them – Jesus!' even Wally Hendry was impressed. 'I'd like to have a look at that beach. It must be quite something.'

'Good!' Bruce's voice was suddenly harsh. 'I'll put you in charge of the burial squad. You can go down there and clean it up before we start work on the bridge.' And Wally did not argue.

'You want me to do it now?' he asked.

'No,' snapped Bruce. 'You and Ruffy are going to take two of the trucks back to Port Reprieve and fetch the materials we need to repair the bridge.'

They both looked at Bruce with rising delight.

'I never thought of that,' said Wally.

'There's plenty of roofing timber in the hotel and the office block,' grinned Ruffy.

'Nails,' said Wally as though he were making a major contribution. 'We'll need nails.'

Bruce cut through their comments. 'It's two o'clock

now. You can get back to Port Reprieve by nightfall, collect the material tomorrow morning and return here by the evening. Take those two trucks there – check to see they're full of gas and you'll need about fifteen men. Say, five gendarmes, in case of trouble, and ten of those civilians.'

'That should be enough,' agreed Ruffy.

'Bring a couple of dozen sheets of corrugated iron back with you. We'll use them to make a shield to protect us from arrows while we're working.'

'Yeah, that's a good idea.'

They settled the details, picked men to go back, loaded the trucks, worked them out of the laager, and Bruce watched them disappear down the road towards Port Reprieve. An ache started deep behind his eyes and suddenly he was very tired, drained of energy by too little sleep, by the heat and by the emotional pace of the last four days. He made one last circuit of the laager, checking the defences, chatting for a few minutes with his gendarmes and then he stumbled to the Ford, slid on to the front seat, laid his helmet and rifle aside, lowered his head on to his arms and was instantly asleep.

– 21 –

Shermaine woke him after dark with food unheated from the cans and a bottle of Ruffy's beer.

'I'm sorry, Bruce, we have no fire to cook upon. It is very unappetizing and the beer is warm.'

Bruce sat up and rubbed his eyes. Six hours' sleep had helped; they were less swollen and inflamed. The headache was still there.

'I'm not really hungry, thank you. It's this heat.'

'You must eat, Bruce. Try just a little,' and then she smiled. 'At least you are more gallant after having rested. It is "Thank you" now, instead of "Keep quiet and stay out of the way".'

Ruefully Bruce grimaced. 'You are one of those women with a built-in recording unit; every word remembered and used in evidence against a man later.' Then he touched her hand. 'I'm sorry.'

'I'm sorry,' she repeated. 'I like your apologies, mon capitaine. They are like the rest of you, completely masculine. There is nothing about you which is not male, sometimes almost overpoweringly so.' Impishly she watched his eyes; he knew she was talking about the little scene on the train that Wally Hendry had interrupted.

'Let's try this food,' he said, and then a little later, 'not bad – you are an excellent cook.'

'This time the credit must go to M. Heinz and his fifty-seven children. But one day I shall make for you one of my tournedos au Prince. It is my special.'

'Speciality,' Bruce corrected her automatically.

The murmur of voices within the laager was punctuated occasionally by a burst of laughter. There was a feeling of relaxation. The canvas roof and the wall of vehicles gave security to them all. Men lay in dark huddles of sleep or talked quietly in small groups.

Bruce scraped the metal plate and filled his mouth with the last of the food.

'Now I must check the defences again.'

'Oh, Bonaparte. It is always duty.' Shermaine sighed with resignation.

'I will not be long.'

'And I'll wait here for you.'

Bruce picked up his rifle and helmet, and was half-way out of the Ford when out in the jungle the drum started.

'Bruce!' whispered Shermaine and clutched his arm. The voices round them froze into a fearful silence, and the drum beat in the night. It had a depth and resonance that you could feel; the warm sluggish air quivered with it. Not fixed in space but filling it, beating monotonously, insistently, like the pulse of all creation.

'Bruce!' whispered Shermaine again; she was trembling and the fingers on his arm dug into his flesh with the strength of terror. It steadied his own leap of fear.

'Baby, baby,' he soothed her, taking her to his chest and holding her there. 'It's only the sound of two pieces of wood being knocked together by a naked savage. They can't touch us here, you know that.'

'Oh, Bruce, it's horrible – it's like bells, funeral bells.'

'That's silly talk.' Bruce held her at arm's length. 'Come with me. Help me calm down these others, they'll be terrified. You'll have to help me.'

And he pulled her gently across the seat out of the Ford, and with one arm round her waist walked her into the centre of the laager.

What will counteract the stupefying influence of the drum, the hypnotic beat of it, he asked himself. Noise, our own noise.

'Joseph, M'pophu—' he shouted cheerfully picking out the two best singers amongst his men. 'I regret the drumming is of a low standard, but the Baluba are monkeys with no understanding of music. Let us show them how a Bambala can sing.'

They stirred; he could feel the tension diminish.

'Come, Joseph—' He filled his lungs and shouted the opening chorus of one of the planting songs, purposely off-key, singing so badly that it must sting them.

Someone laughed, then Joseph's voice hesitantly starting the chorus, gathering strength. M'pophu coming in with the bass to give a solid foundation to the vibrant, sweet-ringing tenor. Half-beat to the drum, hands clapped in the dark; around him Bruce could feel the rhythmic swinging of bodies begin.

Shermaine was no longer trembling; he squeezed her waist and felt her body cling to him.

Now we need light, thought Bruce. A night lamp for my children who fear the darkness and the drum.

With Shermaine beside him he crossed the laager.

'Sergeant Jacque.'

'Captain?'

'You can start sweeping with the searchlights.'

'Oui, Captain.' The answer was less subdued. There were two spare batteries for each light, Bruce knew. Eight hours' life in each, so they would last tonight and tomorrow night.

From each side of the laager the beams leapt out, solid white shafts through the darkness; they played along the edge of the jungle and reflected back, lighting the interior of the laager sufficiently to make out the features of each man. Bruce looked at their faces. They're all right now, he decided, the ghosts have gone away.

'Bravo, Bonaparte,' said Shermaine, and Bruce became aware of the grins on the faces of his men as they saw him embracing her. He was about to drop his arm, then stopped himself. The hell with it, he decided, give them something else to think about. He led her back to the Ford.

'Tired?' he asked.

'A little,' she nodded.

'I'll fold down the seat for you. A blanket over the windows will give you privacy.'

'You'll stay close?' she asked quickly.

'I'll be right outside.' He unbuckled the webbing belt that carried his pistol. 'You'd better wear this from now on.'

Even at its minimum adjustment the belt was too large for her and the pistol hung down almost to her knee.

'The Maid of Orleans.' Bruce revenged himself. She pulled a face at him and crawled into the back of the station wagon.

A long while later she called softly above the singing and the throb of the drum.

'Bruce.'

'Yes?'

‘I wanted to make sure you were there. Good night.’
‘Good night, Shermaine.’

Bruce lay on a single blanket and sweated. The singing had long ago ceased but the drum went on and on, never faltering, throb-throb-throbbing out of the jungle. The searchlights swept regularly back and forth, at times lighting the laager clearly and at others leaving it in shadow. Bruce could hear around him the soft sounds of sleep, the sawing of breath, a muted cough, a gabbled sentence, the stirring of dreamers.

But Bruce could not sleep. He lay on his back with one hand under his head, smoking, staring up at the canvas. The events of the preceding four days ran through his mind: snatches of conversation, André dying. Boussier standing with his wife, the bursting of grenades, blood sticky on his hands, the smell of death, the violence and the horror.

He moved restlessly, flicked away his cigarette and covered his eyes with his hands as though to shut out the memories. But they went on flickering through his mind like the images of a gigantic movie projector, confused now, losing all meaning but retaining the horror.

He remembered the fly upon his arm, grinning at him, rubbing its legs together, gloating, repulsive. He rolled his head from side to side on the blanket.

I’m going mad, he thought, I must stop this.

He sat up quickly hugging his knees to his chest and the memories faded. But now he was sad, and alone. So terribly alone, so lost, so without purpose.

He sat alone on the blanket and he felt himself shrinking, becoming small and frightened.

I’m going to cry, he thought, I can feel it there heavy in my throat. And like a hurt child crawling into its mother’s lap, Bruce Curry groped his way over the tailboard of the station wagon to Shermaine.

'Shermaine!' he whispered, blindly, searching for her.

'Bruce, what is it?' She sat up quickly. She had not been sleeping either.

'Where are you?' There was panic in Bruce's voice.

'Here I am – what's the matter?'

And he found her; clumsily he caught her to him.

'Hold me, Shermaine, please hold me.'

'Darling.' She was anxious. 'What is it? Tell me, my darling.'

'Just hold me, Shermaine. Don't talk.' He clung to her, pressing his face into her neck. 'I need you so much – oh, God! How I need you!'

'Bruce.' She understood, and her fingers were at the nape of his neck, stroking, soothing.

'My Bruce,' she said and held him. Instinctively her body began to rock, gentling him as though he were her child.

Slowly his body relaxed, and he sighed against her – a gusty broken sound.

'My Bruce, my Bruce.' She lifted the thin cotton vest that was all she wore and, instinctively in the ageless ritual of comfort, she gave him her breasts. Holding his mouth to them with both her arms clasped around his neck, her head bowed protectively over his, her hair falling forward and covering them both.

With the hard length of his body against hers, with the soft tugging at her bosom, and in the knowledge that she was giving strength to the man she loved, she realized she had never known happiness before this moment. Then his body was no longer quiescent; she felt her own mood change, a new urgency.

'Oh yes, Bruce, yes!' Speaking up into his mouth, his hungry hunting mouth and he above her, no longer child, but full man again.

'So beautiful, so warm.' His voice was strangely husky, she shuddered with the intensity of her own need.

'Quickly, Bruce, oh, Bruce.' His cruel loving hands, seeking, finding.

'Oh, Bruce – quickly,' and she reached up for him with her hips.

'I'll hurt you.'

'No – yes, I want the pain.' She felt the resistance to him within her and cried out impatiently against it.

'Go through!' and then, 'Ah! It burns.'

'I'll stop.'

'*No, No!*'

'Darling. It's too much.'

'Yes – I can't – oh, Bruce. My heart – you've touched my heart.'

Her clenched fists drumming on his back. And in to press against the taut, reluctantly yielding springiness, away, then back, away, and back to touch the core of all existence, leave it, and come long gliding back to it, nuzzle it, feel it tilt, then come away, then back once more. Welling slowly upwards scalding, no longer to be contained, with pain almost – and gone, and gone, and gone.

'I'm falling. Oh, Bruce! Bruce! Bruce!'

Into the gulf together – gone, all gone. Nothing left, no time, no space, no bottom to the gulf.

Nothing and everything. Complete.

Out in the jungle the drum kept beating.

Afterwards, long afterwards, she slept with her head on his arm and her face against his chest. And he unsleeping listened to her sleep. The sound of it was soft, so gentle breathing soft that you could not hear it unless you listened very carefully – or unless you loved her, he thought.

Yes. I think I love this woman – but I must be certain. In fairness to her and to myself I must be entirely certain, for I cannot live through another time like the last, and because I love her I don't want her to take the terrible wounding of a bad marriage. Better, much better to leave it now, unless it has the strength to endure.

Bruce rolled his head slowly until his face was in her hair, and the girl nuzzled his chest in her sleep.

But it is so hard to tell, he thought. It is so hard to tell at the beginning. It is so easy to confuse pity or loneliness with love, but I cannot afford to do that now. So I must try to think clearly about my marriage to Joan. It will be difficult, but I must try.

Was it like this with Joan in the beginning? It was so long ago, seven years, that I do not know, he answered truthfully. All I have left from those days are the pictures of places and the small heaps of words that have struck where the wind and the pain could not blow them away.

A beach with the sea mist coming in across it, a whole tree of driftwood half buried in the sand and bleached white with the salt, a basket of strawberries bought along the road, so that when I kissed her I could taste the sweet tartness of the fruit on her lips.

I remember a tune that we sang together, 'The mission bells told me that I mustn't stay, South of the border, down Mexico way.' I have forgotten most of the words.

And I remember vaguely how her body was, and the shape of her breasts before the children were born.

But that is all I have left from the good times.

The other memories are clear, stinging, whiplash clear. Each ugly word, and the tone in which it was said. The sound of sobbing in the night, the way it dragged itself on for three long grey years after it was mortally wounded, and both of us using all our strength to keep it moving because of the children.

The children! Oh, God, I mustn't think about them now. It hurts too much. Without the children to complicate it, I must think about her for the last time; I must end this woman Joan. So now finally and for all to end this woman who made me cry. I do not hate her for the man with whom she went away. She deserved another try for happiness. But I hate her for my children and for making shabby the love that I could have given Shermaine as a new thing. Also, I pity her for her inability to find the happiness for which she hunts so fiercely. I pity her for her coldness of body and of mind, I pity her for her prettiness that is now almost gone (it goes round her eyes first, cracking like oil paint) and I pity her for her consuming selfishness which will lose her the love of her children.

My children – not hers! My children!

That is all, that is an end to Joan, and now I have Shermaine who is none of the things that Joan was. I also deserve another try.

'Shermaine,' he whispered and turned her head slightly to kiss her. 'Shermaine, wake up.'

She stirred and murmured against him.

'Wake up.' He took the lobe of her ear between his teeth and bit it gently. Her eyes opened.

'Bon matin, madame.' He smiled at her.

'Bonjour, monsieur,' she answered and closed her eyes to press her face once more against his chest.

'Wake up. I have something to tell you.'

'I am awake, but tell me first if I am still dreaming. I have a certainty that this cannot be reality.'

'You are not dreaming.'

She sighed softly, and held him closer.

'Now tell me the other thing.'

'I love you,' he said.

'No. Now I am dreaming.'

'In truth,' he said.

'No, do not wake me. I could not bear to wake now.'

'And you?' he asked.

'You know it—' she answered. 'I do not have to tell you.'

'It is almost morning,' he said. 'There is only a little time.'

'Then I will fill that little time with saying it—' He held her and listened to her whispering it to him.

No, he thought, now I am certain. I could not be that wrong. This is my woman.

– 22 –

The drum stopped with the dawn. And after it the silence was very heavy, and it was no relief.

They had grown accustomed to that broken rhythm and now in some strange way they missed it.

As Bruce moved around the laager he could sense the uneasiness in his men. There was a feeling of dread anticipation on them all. They moved with restraint, as though they did not want to draw attention to themselves. The laughter with which they acknowledged his jokes was nervous, quickly cut off, as though they had laughed in a cathedral. And their eyes kept darting back towards the ring of jungle.

Bruce found himself wishing for an attack. His own nerves were rubbed sensitive by contact with the fear all around him.

If only they would come, he told himself. If only they would show themselves and we could see men not phantoms.

But the jungle was silent. It seemed to wait, it watched them. They could feel the gaze of hidden eyes. Its malignant presence pressed closer as the heat built up.

Bruce walked across the laager to the south side, trying to move casually. He smiled at Sergeant Jacque, squatted beside him and peered from under the truck across open ground at the remains of the bridge.

'Trucks will be back soon,' he said. 'Won't take long to repair that.'

Jacque did not answer. There was a worried frown on his high intelligent forehead and his face was shiny with perspiration.

'It's the waiting, Captain. It softens the stomach.'

'They will be back soon,' repeated Bruce. If this one is worried, and he is the best of them, then the others must be almost in a jelly of dread.

Bruce looked at the face of the man on the other side of Jacque. Its expression shrieked with fear.

If they attack now, God knows how it will turn out. An African can think himself to death, they just lie down and die. They are getting to that stage now; if an attack comes they will either go berserk or curl up and wail with fear. You can never tell.

Be honest with yourself – you're not entirely happy either, are you? No, Bruce agreed, it's the waiting does it.

It came from the edge of the clearing on the far side of the laager. A high-pitched inhuman sound, angry, savage.

Bruce felt his heart trip and he spun round to face it. For a second the whole laager seemed to cringe from it.

It came again. Like a whip across aching nerves. Immediately it was lost in the roar of twenty rifles.

Bruce laughed. Threw his head back and let it come from the belly.

The gunfire stammered into silence and others were laughing also. The men who had fired grinned sheepishly and made a show of reloading.

It was not the first time that Bruce had been startled by the cry of a yellow hornbill. But now he recognized his laughter and the laughter of the men around him, a mild form of hysteria.

'Did you want the feathers for your hat?' someone shouted and the laughter swept round the laager.

The tension relaxed as the banter was tossed back and forth. Bruce stood up and brought his own laughter under control.

No harm done, he decided. For the price of fifty rounds of ammunition, a purchase of an hour's escape from tension. A good bargain.

He walked across to Shermaine. She was smiling also.

'How is the catering section?' He grinned at her. 'What miracle of the culinary art is there for lunch?'

'Bully beef.'

'And onions?'

'No, just bully beef. The onions are finished.'

Bruce stopped smiling.

'How much is left?' he asked.

'One case – enough to last till lunchtime tomorrow.'

It would take at least two days to complete the repairs to the bridge; another day's travel after that.

'Well,' he said, 'we should all have healthy appetites by the time we get home. You'll have to try and spread it out. Half rations from now on.'

He was so engrossed in the study of this new complication that he did not notice the faint hum from outside the laager.

'Captain,' called Jacques. 'Can you hear it?'

Bruce inclined his head and listened.

'The trucks!' His voice was loud with relief, and instantly there was an excited murmur round the laager.

The waiting was over.

They came growling out of the bush into the clearing. Heavily loaded, timber and sheet-iron protruding backwards from under the canopies, sitting low on their suspensions.

Ruffy leaned from the cab of the leading truck and shouted.

'Hello boss. Where shall we dump?'

'Take it up to the bridge. Hang on a second and I'll come with you.'

Bruce slipped out of the laager and crossed quickly to Ruffy's truck. He could feel his back tingling while he was in the open and he slammed the door behind him with relief.

'I don't relish stopping an arrow,' he said.

'You have any trouble while we were gone?'

'No,' Bruce told him. 'But they're here. They were drumming in the jungle all night.'

'Calling up their buddies,' grunted Ruffy and let out the clutch. 'We'll have some fun before we finish this bridge. Most probably take them a day or two to get brave, but in the end they'll have a go at us.'

'Pull over to the side of the bridge, Ruffy,' Bruce instructed and rolled down his window. 'I'll signal Hendry to pull in beside us. We'll off-load into the space between the two trucks and start building the corrugated iron shield there.'

While Hendry manoeuvred his truck alongside, Bruce forced himself to look down on the carnage of the beach.

'Crocodiles,' he exclaimed with relief. The paunching racks still stood as he had last seen them, but the reeking pile of human remains was gone. The smell and the flies, however, still lingered.

'During the night,' agreed Ruffy as he surveyed the long slither marks in the sand of the beach.

'Thank God for that.'

'Yeah, it wouldn't have made my boys too joyful having to clean up that lot.'

'We'll send someone down to tear out those racks. I don't want to look at them while we work.'

'No, they're not very pretty.' Ruffy ran his eyes over the two sets of gallows.

Bruce climbed down into the space between the trucks.

'Hendry.'

'That's my name.' Wally leaned out of the window.

'Sorry to disappoint you, but the crocs have done the chore for you.'

'I can see. I'm not blind.'

'Very well then. On the assumption that you are neither blind nor paralysed, how about getting your trucks unloaded?'

'Big deal,' muttered Hendry, but he climbed down and began shouting at the men under the canvas canopy.

'Get the lead out there, you lot. Start jumping about!'

'What were the thickest timbers you could find?' Bruce turned to Ruffy.

'Nine by threes, but we got plenty of them.'

'They'll do,' decided Bruce. 'We can lash a dozen of them together for each of the main supports.' Frowning with concentration, Bruce began the task of organizing the repairs.

'Hendry, I want the timber stacked by sizes. Put the sheet-iron over there.' He brushed the flies from his face. 'Ruffy, how many hammers have we got?'

'Ten, boss, and I found a couple of handsaws.'

'Good. What about nails and rope?'

'We got plenty. I got a barrel of six-inch and—'

Preoccupied, Bruce did not notice one of the coloured civilians leave the shelter of the trucks. He walked a dozen paces towards the bridge and stopped. Then unhurriedly he began to unbutton his trousers and Bruce looked up.

'What the hell are you doing?' he shouted and the man started guiltily. He did not understand the English words, but Bruce's tone was sufficiently clear.

'Monsieur,' he explained, 'I wish to—'

'Get back here!' roared Bruce. The man hesitated in confusion and then he began closing his fly.

'Hurry up – you bloody fool.'

Obediently the man hastened the closing of his trousers. Everyone had stopped work and they were all watching him. His face was dark with embarrassment and he fumbled clumsily.

'Leave that.' Bruce was frantic. 'Get back here.'

The first arrow rose lazily out of the undergrowth along the river in a silent parabola. Gathering speed in its descent, hissing softly, it dropped into the ground at the man's feet and stuck up jauntily. A thin reed, fletched with green leaves, it looked harmless as a child's plaything.

'Run,' screamed Bruce. The man stood and stared with detached disbelief at the arrow.

Bruce started forward to fetch him, but Ruffy's huge black hand closed on his arm and he was helpless in its grip. He struck out at Ruffy, struggling to free himself but he could not break that hold.

A swarm of them like locusts on the move, high arching, fluting softly, dropping all around the man as he started to run.

Bruce stopped struggling and watched. He heard the metal heads clanking on the bonnet of the truck, saw them falling wide of the man, some of the frail shafts snapping as they hit the ground.

Then between the shoulders, like a perfectly placed banderilla, one hit him. It flapped against his back as he ran and he twisted his arms behind him, vainly trying to reach it, his face twisted in horror and in pain.

'Hold him down,' shouted Bruce as the coloured man ran into the shelter. Two gendarmes jumped forward, took his arms and forced him face downwards on to the ground.

He was gabbling incoherently with horror as Bruce straddled his back and gripped the shaft. Only half the barbed head had buried itself – a penetration of less than an inch – but when Bruce pulled the shaft it snapped off in his hand leaving the steel twitching in the flesh.

'Knife,' shouted Bruce and someone thrust a bayonet into his hand.

'Watch those barbs, boss. Don't cut yourself on them.'

'Ruffy, get your boys ready to repel them if they rush us,' snapped Bruce and ripped away the shirt. For a moment he stared at the crudely hand-beaten iron arrowhead. The poison coated it thickly, packed in behind the barbs, looking like sticky black toffee.

'He's dead,' said Ruffy from where he leaned over the bonnet of the truck. 'He just ain't stopped breathing yet.'

The man screamed and twisted under Bruce as he made the first incision, cutting in deep beside the arrowhead with the point of the bayonet.

'Hendry, get those pliers out of the tool kit.'

'Here they are.'

Bruce gripped the arrow-head with the steel jaws and pulled. The flesh clung to it stubbornly, lifting in a pyramid. Bruce hacked at it with the bayonet, feeling it tear. It was like trying to get the hook out of the rubbery mouth of a cat-fish.

'You're wasting your time, boss!' grunted Ruffy with all the calm African acceptance of violent death. 'This boy's a goner. That's no horse! That's snake juice in him, fresh mixed. He's finished.'

'Are you sure, Ruffy?' Bruce looked up, 'Are you sure it's snake venom?'

'That's what they use. They mix it with kassava meal.'

'Hendry, where's the snake bite outfit?'

'It's in the medicine box back at the camp.'

Bruce tugged once more at the arrowhead and it came away, leaving a deep black hole between the man's shoulder blades.

'Everybody into the trucks, we've got to get him back. Every second is vital.'

'Look at his eyes,' grunted Ruffy. 'That injection stuff ain't going to help him much.'

The pupils had contracted to the size of match heads and he was shaking uncontrollably as the poison spread through his body.

'Get him into the truck.'

They lifted him into the cab and everybody scrambled aboard. Ruffy started the engine, slammed into reverse and the motor roared as he shot backwards over the intervening thirty yards to the laager.

'Get him out,' instructed Bruce. 'Bring him into the shelter.'

The man was blubbering through slack lips and he had started to sweat. Little rivulets of it coursed down his face and naked upper body. There was hardly any blood from the wound, just a trickle of brownish fluid. The poison must be a coagulant, Bruce decided.

'Bruce, are you all right?' Shermaine ran to meet him.

'Nothing wrong with me.' Bruce remembered to check his tongue this time. 'But one of them has been hit.'

'Can I help you?'

'No, I don't want you to watch.' And he turned from her. 'Hendry, where's that bloody snake bite outfit?' he shouted.

They had dragged the man into the laager and laid him on a blanket in the shade. Bruce went to him and knelt beside him. He took the scarlet tin that Hendry handed him and opened it.

'Ruffy, get those two trucks worked into the circle and make sure your boys are on their toes. With this success they may get brave sooner than you expected.'

Bruce fitted the hypodermic needle on to the syringe as he spoke.

'Hendry, get them to rig some sort of screen round us. You can use blankets.'

With his thumb he snapped the top off the ampoule and filled the syringe with the pale yellow serum.

'Hold him,' he said to the two gendarmes, lifted a pinch of skin close beside the wound and ran the needle under it. The man's skin felt like that of a frog, damp and clammy.

As he expelled the serum Bruce was trying to calculate the time that had elapsed since the arrow had hit. Possibly seven or eight minutes; mamba venom kills in fourteen minutes.

'Roll him over,' he said.

The man's head lolled sideways, his breathing was quick

and shallow and the saliva poured from the corners of his mouth, running down his cheeks.

'Get a load of that!' breathed Wally Hendry, and Bruce glanced up at his face. His expression was a glow of deep sensual pleasure and his breathing was as quick and shallow as that of the dying man.

'Go and help Ruffy,' snapped Bruce as his stomach heaved with disgust.

'Not on your Nelly. This I'm not going to miss.'

Bruce had no time to argue. He lifted the skin of the man's stomach and ran the needle in again. There was an explosive spitting sound as the bowels started to vent involuntarily.

'Jesus,' whispered Hendry.

'Get away,' snarled Bruce. 'Can't you let him die without gloating over it?'

Hopelessly he injected again, under the skin of the chest above the heart. As he emptied the syringe the man's body twisted violently in the first seizure and the needle snapped off under the skin.

'There he goes,' whispered Hendry, 'there he goes. Just look at him, man. That's really something.'

Bruce's hands were trembling and slowly a curtain descended across his mind.

'You filthy swine,' he screamed and hit Hendry across the face with his open hand, knocking him back against the side of the gasoline tanker. Then he went for his throat and found it with both hands. The windpipe was ropey and elastic under his thumbs.

'Is nothing sacred to you, you unclean animal?' he yelled into Hendry's face. 'Can't you let a man die without—'

Then Ruffy was there, effortlessly plucking Bruce's hands from the throat, interposing the bulk of his body, holding them away from each other.

'Let it stand, boss.'

'For that—' gasped Hendry as he massaged his throat. 'For that I'm going to make you pay.'

Bruce turned away, sick and ashamed, to the man on the blanket.

'Cover him up.' His voice was shaky. 'Put him in the back of one of the trucks. We'll bury him tomorrow.'

– 23 –

Before nightfall they had completed the corrugated iron screen. It was a simple four-walled structure with no roof to it. One end of it was detachable and all four walls were pierced at regular intervals with small loopholes for defence.

Long enough to accommodate a dozen men in comfort, high enough to reach above the heads of the tallest, and exactly the width of the bridge, it was not a thing of beauty.

'How you going to move it, boss?' Ruffy eyed the screen dubiously.

'I'll show you. We'll move it back to the camp now, so that in the morning we can commute to work in it.'

Bruce selected twelve men and they crowded through the open end into the shelter, and closed it behind them.

'Okay, Ruffy. Take the trucks away.'

Hendry and Ruffy reversed the two trucks back to the laager, leaving the shelter standing at the head of the bridge like a small Nissen hut. Inside it Bruce stationed his men at intervals along the walls.

'Use the bottom timber of the frame to lift on,' he shouted. 'Are you all ready? All right, lift!'

The shelter swayed and rose six inches above the ground. From the laager they could see only the boots of the men inside.

'All together,' ordered Bruce. 'Walk!'

Rocking and creaking over the uneven ground the structure moved ponderously back towards the laager. Below it the feet moved like those of a caterpillar.

The men in the laager started to cheer, and from inside the shelter they answered with whoops of laughter. It was fun. They were enjoying themselves enormously, completely distracted from the horror of poison arrows and the lurking phantoms in the jungle around them.

They reached the camp and lowered the shelter. Then one at a time the gendarmes slipped across the few feet of open ground into the safety of the laager to be met with laughter, and back-slapping and mutual congratulation.

'Well, it works, boss,' Ruffy greeted Bruce in the uproar.

'Yes.' Then he lifted his voice. 'That's enough. Quiet down all of you. Get back to your posts.'

The laughter subsided and the confusion became order again. Bruce walked to the centre of the laager and looked about him. There was complete quiet now. They were all watching him. I have read about this so often, he grinned inwardly, the heroic speech to the men on the eve of battle. Let's pray I don't make a hash of it.

'Are you hungry?' he asked loudly in French and received a chorus of hearty affirmatives.

'There is bully beef for dinner.' This time humorous groans.

'And bully beef for breakfast tomorrow,' he paused, 'and then it's finished.'

They were silent now.

'So you are going to be truly hungry by the time we cross this river. The sooner we repair the bridge the sooner you'll get your bellies filled again.'

I might as well rub it in, decided Bruce.

'You all saw what happened to the person who went into the open today, so I don't have to tell you to keep under cover. The sergeant major is making arrangements for sanitation – five-gallon drums. They won't be very comfortable, so you won't be tempted to sit too long.'

They laughed a little at that.

'Remember this. As long as you stay in the laager or the shelter they can't touch you. There is absolutely nothing to fear. They can beat their drums and wait as long as they like, but they can't harm us.'

A murmur of agreement.

'And the sooner we finish the bridge the sooner we will be on our way.'

Bruce looked round the circle of faces and was satisfied with what he saw. The completion of the shelter had given their morale a boost.

'All right, Sergeant Jacque. You can start sweeping with the searchlights as soon as it's dark.'

Bruce finished and went across to join Shermaine beside the Ford. He loosed the straps of his helmet and lifted it off his head. His hair was damp with perspiration and he ran his fingers through it.

'You are tired,' Shermaine said softly, examining the dark hollows under his eyes and the puckered marks of strain at the corners of his mouth.

'No. I'm all right,' he denied, but every muscle in his body ached with fatigue and nervous tension.

'Tonight you must sleep all night,' she ordered him. 'I will make the bed in the back of the car.'

Bruce looked at her quickly. 'With you?' he asked.

'Yes.'

'You do not mind that everyone should know?'

'I am not ashamed of us.' There was a fierceness in her tone.

'I know, but—'

'You said once that nothing between you and I could ever be dirty.'

'No, of course it couldn't be dirty. I just thought—'

'Well then, I love you and from now on we have only one bed between us.' She spoke with finality.

Yesterday she was a virgin, he thought with amazement, and now – well, now it's no holds barred. Once she is roused a woman is more reckless of consequences than any man. They are such wholesale creatures. But she's right, of course. She's my woman and she belongs in my bed. The hell with the rest of the world and what it thinks!

'Make the bed, wench.' He smiled at her tenderly.

Two hours after dark the drum started again. They lay together, holding close, and listened to it. It held no terror now, for they were warm and secure in the afterglow of passion. It was like lying and listening to the impotent fury of a rainstorm on the roof at night.

– 24 –

They went out to the bridge at sunrise, the shelter moving across the open ground like the carapace of a multi-legged metallic turtle. The men chattered and joked loudly inside, still elated by the novelty of it.

'All right, everybody. That's enough talking,' Bruce shouted them down. 'There's work to do now.'

And they began.

Within an hour the sun had turned the metal box into an oven. They stripped to the waist and the sweat dripped from them as they worked. They worked in a frenzy, gripped by a new urgency, oblivious of everything but the rough-sawed timber that drove white splinters into their skin at the touch. They worked in the confined heat, amidst the racket of hammers and in the piney smell of sawdust. The labour fell into its own pattern with only an occasional grunted order from Bruce or Ruffy to direct it.

By midday the four main trusses that would span the gap in the bridge had been made up. Bruce tested their rigidity by propping one at both ends and standing all his men on the middle of it. It gave an inch under their combined weight.

'What do you think, boss?' Ruffy asked without conviction.

'Four of them might just do it. We'll put in king-posts underneath,' Bruce answered.

'Man, I don't know. That tanker weights plenty.'

'It's no flyweight,' Bruce agreed. 'But we'll have to take the chance. We'll bring the Ford across first, then the trucks and the tanker last.'

Ruffy nodded and wiped his face on his forearm; the muscles below his armpits knotted as he moved and there was no flabbiness in the powerful bulge of his belly above his belt.

'Phew!' He blew his lips out. 'I got the feeling for a beer now. This thirst is really stalking me.'

'You've got some with you?' Bruce asked as he passed his thumbs across his eyebrows and squeezed the moisture from them so it ran down his cheeks.

'Two things I never travel without, my trousers and a stock of the brown and bubbly.' Ruffy picked up the small pack from the corner of the shelter and it clinked coyly. 'You hear that sound, boss?'

'I hear it, and it sounds like music,' grinned Bruce. 'All right, everybody.' He raised his voice. 'Take ten minutes.'

Ruffy opened the bottles and passed them out, issuing one to be shared between three gendarmes. 'These Arabs don't properly appreciate this stuff,' he explained to Bruce. 'It'd just be a waste.'

The liquor was lukewarm and gassy; it merely aggravated Bruce's thirst. He drained the bottle and tossed it out of the shelter.

'All right.' He stood up. 'Let's get these trusses into position.'

'That's the shortest ten minutes I ever lived,' commented Ruffy.

'Your watch is slow,' said Bruce.

Carrying the trusses within it, the shelter lumbered out on to the bridge. There was no laughter now, only laboured breathing and curses.

'Fix the ropes!' commanded Bruce. He tested the knots personally, then looked up at Ruffy and nodded.

'That'll do.'

'Come on, you mad bastards,' Ruffy growled. 'Lift it.'

The first truss rose to the perpendicular and swayed there like a grotesque maypole with the ropes hanging from its top.

'Two men on each rope,' ordered Bruce. 'Let it down gently.' He glanced round to ensure that they were all ready.

'Drop it over the edge, and I'll throw you bastards in after it,' warned Ruffy.

'Lower away!' shouted Bruce.

The truss leaned out over the gap towards the fire-blackened stump of bridge on the far side slowly at first, then faster as gravity took it.

'Hold it, damn you. Hold it!' roared Ruffy with the muscles in his shoulders humped out under the strain. They lay back against the ropes, but the weight of the truss dragged them forward as it fell.

It crashed down across the gap, lifted a cloud of dead wood ash as it struck, and lay there quivering.

'Man, I thought we'd lost that one for sure,' growled Ruffy, then turned savagely on his men.

'You bastards better be sharper with the next one – if you don't want to swim this river.'

They repeated the process with the second truss, and again they could not hold its falling length, but this time they were not so lucky. The end of the truss hit the far side, bounced and slid sideways.

'It's going! Pull, you bastards, pull!' shouted Ruffy.

The truss toppled slowly sideways and over the edge. It hit the river below them with a splash, disappeared under the surface, then bobbed up and floated away downstream until checked by the ropes.

Both Bruce and Ruffy fumed and swore during the lengthy exasperating business of dragging it back against the current and manhandling its awkward bulk back on to the bridge. Half a dozen times it slipped at the crucial moment and splashed back into the river.

Despite his other virtues, Ruffy's vocabulary of cursing words was limited and it added to his frustration that he had to keep repeating himself. Bruce did much better – he remembered things that he had heard and he made up a few.

When finally they had the dripping baulk of timber back on the bridge and were resting, Ruffy turned to Bruce with honest admiration.

'You swear pretty good,' he said. 'Never heard you before, but no doubt about it, you're good! What's that one about the cow again?'

Bruce repeated it for him a little self-consciously.

'You make that up yourself?' asked Ruffy.

'Spur of the moment,' laughed Bruce.

'That's 'bout the dirtiest I ever heard.' Ruffy could not conceal his envy. 'Man, you should write a book.'

'Let's get this bridge finished first,' said Bruce. 'Then I'll think about it.'

Now the truss was almost servile in its efforts to please. It dropped neatly across the gap and lay beside its twin.

'You curse something good enough, and it works every time,' Ruffy announced sagely. 'I think your one about the cow made all the difference, boss.'

With two trusses in position they had broken the back of the project. They carried the shelter out and set it on the trusses, straddling the gap. The third and fourth trusses were dragged into position and secured with ropes and nails before nightfall.

When the shelter waddled wearily back to the laager at dusk, the men within it were exhausted. Their hands were bleeding and bristled with wood splinters, but they were also mightily pleased with themselves.

'Sergeant Jacque, keep one of your searchlights trained on the bridge all night. We don't want our friends to come out and set fire to it again.'

'There are only a few hours' life left in each of the batteries.' Jacque kept his voice low.

'Use them one at a time then.' Bruce spoke without hesitation. 'We must have that bridge lit up all night.

'You think you could spare a beer for each of the boys that worked on the bridge today?'

'A whole one each!' Ruffy was shocked. 'I only got a couple cases left.'

Bruce fixed him with a stern eye and Ruffy grinned.

'Okay, boss. Guess they've earned it.'

Bruce transferred his attention to Wally Hendry who sat on the running-board of one of the trucks cleaning his nails with the point of his bayonet.

'Everything under control here, Hendry?' he asked coolly.

'Sure, what'd you think would happen? We'd have a visit from the archbishop? The sky'd fall in? Your French thing'd have twins or something?' He looked up from his nails at Bruce. 'When are you jokers going to get that bridge finished, instead of wandering around asking damn-fool questions?'

Bruce was too tired to feel annoyed. 'You've got the night watch, Hendry,' he said, 'from now until dawn.'

'Is that right, hey? And you? What're you going to do all night, or does that question make you blush?'

'I'm going to sleep, that's what I'm going to do. I haven't been lolling round camp all day.'

Hendry pegged the bayonet into the earth between his feet and snorted.

'Well, give her a little bit of sleep for me too, Bucko.'

Bruce left him and crossed to the Ford.

'Hello, Bruce. How did it go today? I missed you,' Shermaine greeted him, and her face lit up as she looked at him. It is a good feeling to be loved, and some of Bruce's fatigue lifted.

'About half finished, another day's work.' Then he smiled back at her. 'I won't lie and say I missed you – I've been too damn busy.'

'Your hands!' she said with quick concern and lifted them to examine them. 'They're in a terrible state.'

'Not very pretty, are they?'

'Let me get a needle from my case. I'll get the splinters out.'

From across the laager Wally Hendry caught Bruce's eye and with one hand made a suggestive sign below his waist. Then, at Bruce's frown of anger, he threw back his head and laughed with huge delight.

– 25 –

Bruce's stomach grumbled with hunger as he stood with Ruffy and Hendry beside the cooking fire. In the early morning light he could just make out the dark shape of the bridge at the end of the clearing. That drum was still beating in the jungle, but they hardly noticed it now. It was taken for granted like the mosquitoes. 'The batteries are finished,' grunted Ruffy. The feeble yellow beam of the searchlight reached out tiredly towards the bridge.

'Only just lasted the night,' agreed Bruce.

'Christ, I'm hungry,' complained Hendry. 'What could I do to a couple of fried eggs and a porterhouse steak.'

At the mention of food Bruce's mouth flooded with saliva. He shut his mind against the picture that Wally's words had evoked in his imagination.

'We won't be able to finish the bridge and get the trucks across today,' he said, and Ruffy agreed.

'There's a full day's work left on her, boss.'

'This is what we'll do then,' Bruce went on. 'I'll take the work party out to the bridge. Hendry, you will stay here in the laager and cover us the same as yesterday. And Ruffy, you take one of the trucks and a dozen of your boys. Go back ten miles or so to where the forest is open and they won't be able to creep up on you. Then cut us a mountain of firewood; thick logs that will burn all night. We will set a ring of watch fires round the camp tonight.'

'That makes sense,' Ruffy nodded. 'But what about the bridge?'

'We'll have to put a guard on it,' said Bruce, and the expressions on their faces changed as they thought about this.

'More pork chops for the boys in the bushes,' growled Hendry. 'You won't catch me sitting out on the bridge all night.'

'No one's asking you to,' snapped Bruce. 'All right, Ruffy. Go and fetch the wood, and plenty of it.'

Bruce completed the repairs to the bridge in the late afternoon. The most anxious period was in the middle of the day when he and four men had to leave the shelter and clamber down on to the supports a few feet above the surface of the river to set the king-posts in place. Here they were exposed at random range to arrows from the undergrowth along the banks. But no arrows came and they finished the job and climbed back to safety again with something of a sense of anticlimax.

They nailed the crossties over the trusses and then roped everything into a compact mass.

Bruce stood back and surveyed the fruit of two full days' labour.

'Functional,' he decided, speaking aloud. 'But we certainly aren't going to win any prizes for aesthetic beauty or engineering design.'

He picked up his jacket and thrust his arms into the sleeves; his sweaty upper body was cold now that the sun was almost down.

'Home, gentlemen,' he said, and his gendarmes scattered to their positions inside the shelter.

The metal shelter circled the laager, squatting every twenty or thirty paces like an old woman preparing to relieve herself. When it lifted and moved on it left a log fire behind it. The ring of fires was completed by dark and the shelter returned to the laager.

'Are you ready, Ruffy?' From inside the shelter Bruce called across to where Ruffy waited.

'All set, boss.'

Followed by six heavily armed gendarmes, Ruffy crossed quickly to join Bruce and they set off to begin their all-night vigil on the bridge.

Before midnight it was cold in the corrugated iron shelter, for the wind blew down the river and they were completely exposed to it, and there was no cloud cover to hold the day's warmth against the earth.

The men in the shelter huddled under their gas capes and waited. Bruce and Ruffy leaned together against the corrugated iron wall, their shoulders almost touching, and there was sufficient light from the stars to light the interior of the shelter and allow them to make out the guard rails of the bridge through the open ends.

'Moon will be up in an hour,' murmured Ruffy.

'Only a quarter of it, but it will give us a little more

light,' Bruce concurred, and peered down into the black hole between his feet where he had prised up one of the newly laid planks.

'How about taking a shine with the torch?' suggested Ruffy.

'No.' Bruce shook his head, and passed the flashlight into his other hand. 'Not until I hear them.'

'You might not hear them.'

'If they swim downstream and climb up the piles, which is what I expect, then we'll hear them all right. They'll be dripping water all over the place,' said Bruce.

'Kanaki and his boys didn't hear them,' Ruffy pointed out.

'Kanaki and his boys weren't listening for it,' said Bruce.

They were silent then for a while. One of the gendarmes started to snore softly and Ruffy shot out a huge booted foot that landed in the small of his back. The man cried out and scrambled to his knees, looking wildly about him.

'You have nice dreams?' Ruffy asked pleasantly.

'I wasn't sleeping,' the man protested. 'I was thinking.'

'Well, don't think so loudly,' Ruffy advised him. 'Sounds though you sawing through the bridge with a cross cut.'

Another half hour dragged itself by like a cripple.

'Fires are burning well,' commented Ruffy, and Bruce turned his head and glanced through the loophole in the corrugated iron behind him at the little garden of orange flame-flowers in the darkness.

'Yes, they should last till morning.'

Silence again, with only the singing of the mosquitoes and the rustle of the river as it flowed by the piles of the bridge. Shermaine has my pistol, Bruce remembered with a small trip in his pulse, I should have taken it back from her. He unclipped the bayonet from the muzzle of his rifle, tested the edge of the blade with his thumb, and slid it into the scabbard on his web-belt. Could easily lose the rifle if we start mixing it in the dark, he decided.

‘Christ, I’m hungry,’ grunted Ruffy beside him.

‘You’re too fat,’ said Bruce. ‘The diet will do you good.’ And they waited.

Bruce stared down into the hole in the floorboards. His eyes began weaving fantasies out of the darkness, he could see vague shapes that moved, like things seen below the surface of the sea. His stomach tightened and he fought the impulse to shine his flashlight into the hole. He closed his eyes to rest them. I will count slowly to ten, he decided, and then look again.

Ruffy’s hand closed on his upper arm; the pressure of his fingers transmitted alarm like a current of electricity. Bruce’s eyelids flew open.

‘Listen,’ breathed Ruffy.

Bruce heard it. The stealthy drip of water on water below them. Then something bumped the bridge, but so softly that he felt rather than heard the jar.

‘Yes,’ Bruce whispered back. He reached out and tapped the shoulder of the gendarme beside him and the man’s body stiffened at his touch.

With his breath scratching his dry throat, Bruce waited until he was sure the warning had been passed to all his men. Then he shifted the weight of his rifle from across his knees and aimed down into the hole.

He drew in a deep breath and switched on the flashlight. The beam shot down and he looked along it over his rifle barrel.

The square aperture in the floorboards formed a frame for the picture that flashed into his eyes. Black bodies, naked, glossy with wetness, weird patterns of tattoo marks, a face staring up at him, broad sloped forehead above startlingly white eyes and flat nose. The long gleaming blade of a panga. Clusters of humanity clinging to the wooden piles like ticks on the legs of a beast. Legs and arms and shiny trunks merged into a single organism, horrible as some slimy sea-creature.

Bruce fired into it. His rifle shuddered against his shoulder and the long orange spurts from its muzzle gave the picture a new flickering horror. The mass of bodies heaved, and struggled like a pack of rats trapped in a dry well. They dropped splashing into the river, swarmed up the timber piles, twisting and writhing as the bullets hit them, screaming, babbling over the sound of the rifle.

Bruce's weapon clicked empty and he groped for a new magazine. Ruffy and his gendarmes were hanging over the guard rails of the bridge, firing downwards, sweeping the piles below them with long bursts, the flashes lighting their faces and outlining their bodies against the sky.

'They're still coming!' roared Ruffy. 'Don't let them get over the side.'

Out of the hole at Bruce's feet thrust the head and naked upper body of a man. There was a panga in his hand; he slashed at Bruce's legs, his eyes glazed in the beam of the flashlight.

Bruce jumped back and the knife missed his knees by inches. The man wormed his way out of the hole towards Bruce. He was screaming shrilly, a high meaningless sound of fury.

Bruce lunged with the barrel of his empty rifle at the contorted black face. All his weight was behind that thrust and the muzzle went into the Baluba's eye. The foresight and four inches of the barrel disappeared into his head, stopping only when it hit bone. Colourless fluid from the burst eyeball gushed from round the protruding steel.

Tugging and twisting, Bruce tried to free the rifle, but the foresight had buried itself like the barb of a fish hook. The Baluba had dropped his panga and was clinging to the rifle barrel with both hands. He was wailing and rolling on his back upon the floorboards, his head jerking every time Bruce tried to pull the muzzle out of his head.

Beyond him the head and shoulders of another Baluba appeared through the aperture.

Bruce dropped his rifle and gathered up the fallen panga; he jumped over the writhing body of the first Baluba and lifted the heavy knife above his head with both hands.

The man was jammed in the hole, powerless to protect himself. He looked up at Bruce and his mouth fell open.

Two-handed, as though he were chopping wood, Bruce swung his whole body into the stroke. The shock jarred his shoulders and he felt blood splatter his legs. The untempered blade snapped off at the hilt and stayed imbedded in the Baluba's skull.

Panting heavily, Bruce straightened up and looked wildly about him. Baluba were swarming over the guard rail on one side of the bridge. The starlight glinted on their wet skins. One of his gendarmes was lying in a dark huddle, his head twisted back and his rifle still in his hands. Ruffy and the other gendarmes were still firing down over the far side.

'Ruffy!' shouted Bruce. 'Behind you! They're coming over!' and he dropped the handle of the panga and ran towards the body of the gendarme. He needed that rifle.

Before he could reach it the naked body of a Baluba rushed at him. Bruce ducked under the sweep of the panga and grappled with him. They fell locked together, the man's body slippery and sinuous against him, and the smell of him fetid as rancid butter.

Bruce found the pressure point below the elbow of his knife arm and dug in with his thumb. The Baluba yelled and his panga clattered on the floorboards. Bruce wrapped his arm round the man's neck while with his free hand he reached for his bayonet.

The Baluba was clawing for Bruce's eyes with his fingers, his nails scored the side of Bruce's nose, but Bruce had his bayonet out now. He placed the point against the man's chest and pressed it in. He felt the steel scrape against the bone of a rib and the man redoubled his struggles at the sting of it. Bruce twisted the blade, working it in with his wrist, forcing the man's head backwards with his other arm.

The point of the bayonet scraped over the bone and found the gap between. Like taking a virgin, suddenly the resistance to its entrance was gone and it slid home full length. The Baluba's body jerked mechanically and the bayonet twitched in Bruce's fist.

Bruce did not even wait for the man to die. He pulled the blade out against the sucking reluctance of tissue that clung to it and scrambled to his feet in time to see Ruffy pick another Baluba from his feet and hurl him bodily over the guard rail.

Bruce snatched the rifle from the gendarme's dead hands and stepped to the guard rail. They were coming over the side, those below shouting and pushing at the ones above.

Like shooting a row of sparrows from a fence with a shotgun, thought Bruce grimly, and with one long burst he cleared the rail. Then he leaned out and sprayed the piles below the bridge. The rifle was empty. He reloaded with a magazine from his pocket. But it was all over. They were dropping back into the river, the piles below the bridge were clear of men, their heads bobbed away downstream.

Bruce lowered his rifle and looked about him. Three of his gendarmes were killing the man that Bruce had wounded, standing over him and grunting as they thrust down with their bayonets. The man was still wailing.

Bruce looked away.

One horn of the crescent moon showed above the trees; it had a gauzy halo about it.

Bruce lit a cigarette and behind him those gruesome noises ceased.

'Are you okay, boss?'

'Yes, I'm fine. How about you, Ruffy?'

'I got me a terrible thirst now. Hope nobody trod on my pack.'

About four minutes from the first shot to the last, Bruce guessed. That's the way of war, seven hours of waiting and boredom, then four minutes of frantic endeavour. Not only of war either, he thought. The whole of life is like that.

Then he felt the trembling in his thighs and the first spasm of nausea as the reaction started.

'What's happening?' A shout floated across from the laager. Bruce recognized Hendry's voice. 'Is everything all right?'

'We've beaten them off,' Bruce shouted back. 'Everything under control. You can go to sleep again.'

And now I have got to sit down quickly, he told himself.

Except for the tattoos upon his cheeks and forehead the dead Baluba's features were little different from those of the Bambala and Bakuba men who made up the bulk of Bruce's command.

Bruce played the flashlight over the corpse. The arms and legs were thin but stringy with muscle, and the belly bulged out from years of malnutrition. It was an ugly body, gnarled and crabbed. With distaste Bruce moved the light back to the features. The bone of the skull formed harsh angular planes beneath the skin, the nose was flattened and the thick lips had about them a repellent brutality. They were drawn back slightly to reveal the teeth which had been filed to sharp points like those of a shark.

'This is the last one, boss. I'll toss him overboard.' Ruffy spoke in the darkness beside Bruce.

'Good.'

Ruffy heaved and grunted, the corpse splashed below them and Ruffy wiped his hands on the guard rail, then came to sit beside Bruce.

'Goddam apes.' Ruffy's voice was full of the bitter tribal antagonism of Africa. 'When we get shot of these U.N. people there'll be a bit of sorting out to do. They've got a few things to learn, these bloody Baluba.'

And so it goes, thought Bruce, Jew and Gentile, Catholic and Protestant, black and white, Bambala and Baluba.

He checked the time, another two hours to dawn. His nervous reaction from physical violence had abated now; the hand that held the cigarette no longer trembled.

'They won't come again,' said Ruffy. 'You can get some sleep now if you want. I'll keep an eye open, boss.'

'No, thanks. I'll wait with you.' His nerves had not settled down enough for sleep.

'How's it for a beer?'

'Thanks.'

Bruce sipped the beer and stared out at the watch fires round the laager. They had burned down to puddles of red ash but Bruce knew that Ruffy was right. The Baluba would not attack again that night.

'So how do you like freedom?'

'How's that, boss?' The question puzzled Ruffy and he turned to Bruce questioningly.

'How do you like it now the Belgians have gone?'

'It's pretty good, I reckon.'

'And if Tshombe has to give in to the Central Government?'

'Those mad Arabs!' snarled Ruffy. 'All they want is our copper. They're going to have to get up early in the morning to take it. We're in the saddle here.'

The great jousting tournament of the African continent. I'm in the saddle, try to unhorse me! As in all matters of survival it was not a question of ethics and political doctrine (except to the spectators in Whitehall, Moscow, Washington and Peking). There were big days coming, thought Bruce. My own country, when she blows, is going to make Algiers look like an old ladies' sewing circle.

– 26 –

The sun was up, throwing long shadows out into the clearing, and Bruce stood beside the Ford and looked across the bridge at the corrugated iron shelter on the far bank.

He relaxed for a second and let his mind run unhurriedly over his preparations for the crossing. Was there something left undone, some disposition which could make it more secure?

Hendry and a dozen men were in the shelter across the bridge, ready to meet any attack on that side.

Shermaine would take the Ford across first. Then the lorries would follow her. They would cross empty to minimize the danger of the bridge collapsing, or being weakened for the passage of the tanker. After each lorry had crossed, Hendry would shuttle its load and passengers over in the shelter and deposit them under the safety of the canvas canopy.

The last lorry would go over fully loaded. That was regrettable but unavoidable.

Finally Bruce himself would drive the tanker across. Not as an act of heroism, although it was the most dangerous business of the morning, but because he would trust no one else to do it, not even Ruffy. The five hundred gallons of fuel it contained was their safe-conduct home. Bruce had taken the precaution of filling all the gasoline tanks in the convoy in case of accidents, but they would need replenishing before they reached Msapa Junction.

He looked down at Shermaine in the driver's seat of the Ford.

'Keep it in low gear, take her over slowly but steadily. Whatever else you do, don't stop.'

She nodded. She was composed and she smiled at him. Bruce felt a stirring of pride as he looked at her, so small and lovely, but today she was doing man's work. He went on. 'As soon as you are over, I will send one of the trucks after you. Hendry will put six of his men into it and then come back for the others.'

'Oui, Monsieur Bonaparte.'

'You'll pay for that tonight,' he threatened her. 'Off you go.'

Shermaine let out the clutch and the Ford bounced over rough ground to the road, accelerated smoothly out on to the bridge.

Bruce held his breath, but there was only a slight check and sway as it crossed the repaired section.

'Thank God for that,' Bruce let out his breath and watched while Shermaine drew up alongside the shelter.

'Allez,' Bruce shouted at the coloured engine driver who was ready at the wheel of the first truck. The man smiled his cheerful chubby-faced smile, waved, and the truck rolled forward.

Watching anxiously as it went on to the bridge, Bruce saw the new timbers give perceptibly beneath the weight of the truck, and he heard them creak loudly in protest.

'Not so good,' he muttered.

'No—' agreed Ruffy. 'Boss, why don't you let someone else take the tanker over?'

'We've been over that already,' Bruce answered him without turning his head. Across the river Hendry was transferring his men from the shelter to the back of the truck. Then the shelter started its tedious way back towards them.

Bruce fretted impatiently during the four hours that it took to get four trucks across. The long business was the shuttling back and forth of the corrugated iron shelter, at least ten minutes for each trip.

Finally there was only the fifth truck and the tanker left on the north bank. Bruce started the engine of the tanker and put her into auxiliary low, then he blew a single blast on the horn. The driver of the truck ahead of him waved an acknowledgement and pulled forward.

The truck reached the bridge and went out into the middle. It was fully loaded, twenty men aboard. It came to the repaired section and slowed down, almost stopping.

'Go on! Keep it going, damn you,' Bruce shouted in impotent anger. The fool of a driver was forgetting his orders. He crawled forward and the bridge gave alarmingly under the full weight, the high canopied roof rocked crazily, and even above the rumble of his own engine Bruce could hear the protesting groan of the bridge timbers.

'The fool, oh, the bloody fool,' whispered Bruce to himself. Suddenly he felt very much alone and unprotected here on the north bank with the bridge being mutilated by the incompetence of the truck driver. He started the tanker moving.

Ahead of him the other driver had panicked. He was racing his engine, the rear wheels spun viciously, blue smoke of scorched tyres, and one of the floorboards tore loose. Then the truck lurched forward and roared up the south bank.

Bruce hesitated, applying the brakes and bringing the tanker to a standstill on the threshold of the bridge.

He thought quickly. The sensible thing would be to repair the damage to the bridge before chancing it with the weight of the tanker. But that would mean another day's delay. None of them had eaten since the previous morning. Was he justified in gambling against even odds, for that's what they were? A fifty-fifty chance, heads you get across, tails you dump the tanker in the middle of the river.

Then unexpectedly the decision was made for him.

From across the river a Bren gun started firing. Bruce jumped in his seat and looked up. Then a dozen other guns joined in and the tracer flew past the tanker. They were firing across towards him, close on each side of him. Bruce struggled to drag from his uncomprehending brain an explanation of this new development. Suddenly everything was moving too swiftly. Everything was confusion and chaos.

Movement in the rear-view mirror of the tanker caught his eye. He stared at it blankly. Then he twisted quickly in his seat and looked back.

'Christ!' he swore with fright.

From the edge of the jungle on both sides of the clearing Baluba were swarming into the open. Hundreds of them running towards him, the animal-skin kilts swirling about their legs, feather headdresses fluttering, sun bright on the long blades of their pangas. An arrow rang dully against the metal body of the tanker.

Bruce revved the engine, gripped the wheel hard with both hands and took the tanker out on to the bridge. Above the sound of the guns he could hear the shrill ululation, the excited squealing of two hundred Baluba. It sounded very close, and he snatched a quick look in the mirror. What he saw nearly made him lose his head and give the tanker full throttle. The nearest Baluba, screened from the guns on the south bank by the tanker's bulk, was only ten paces away. So close that Bruce could see the tattoo marks on his face and chest.

With an effort Bruce restrained his right foot from pressing down too hard, and instead he bore down on the repaired section of the bridge at a sedate twenty miles an hour. He tried to close his mind to the squealing behind him and the thunder of gunfire ahead of him.

The front wheels hit the new timbers, and above the other sounds he heard them groan loudly, and felt them sag under him.

The tanker rolled on and the rear wheels brought their weight to bear. The groan of wood became a cracking, rending sound. The tanker slowed as the bridge subsided, its wheels spun without purchase, it tilted sideways, no longer moving forward.

A sharp report, as one of the main trusses broke, and Bruce felt the tanker drop sharply at the rear; its nose pointed upwards and it started to slide back.

'Get out!' his brain shrieked at him. 'Get out, it's falling!' He reached for the door handle beside him, but at that moment the bridge collapsed completely. The tanker rolled off the edge.

Bruce was hurled across the cab with a force that stunned him, his legs wedged under the passenger seat and his arms tangled in the strap of his rifle. The tanker fell free and Bruce felt his stomach swoop up and press against his chest as though he rode a giant roller coaster.

The sickening drop lasted only an instant, and then the tanker hit the river. Immediately the sounds of gunfire and the screaming of Baluba were drowned out as the tanker disappeared below the surface. Through the windscreen Bruce saw now the cool cloudy green of water, as though he looked into the windows of an aquarium. With a gentle rocking motion the tanker sank down through the green water.

'Oh, my God, not this!' He spoke aloud as he struggled up from the floor of the cab. His ears were filled with the hiss and belch of escaping air bubbles; they rose in silver clouds past the windows.

The truck was still sinking, and Bruce felt the pain in his eardrums as the pressure built up inside the cab. He opened his mouth and swallowed convulsively, and his eardrums squeaked as the pressure equalized and the pain abated. Water was squirting in through the floor of the cab and jets of it spurted out of the instrument panel of the dashboard. The cab was flooding.

Bruce twisted the handle of the door beside him and hit it with his shoulder. It would not budge an inch. He flung all his weight against it, anchoring his feet on the dashboard and straining until he felt his eyeballs starting out of their sockets. It was jammed solid by the immense pressure of water on the outside.

'The windscreen,' he shouted aloud. 'Break the windscreen.' He groped for his rifle. The cab had flooded to his waist as he sat in the passenger's seat. He found the rifle and brought it dripping to his shoulder. He touched the muzzle to the windscreen and almost fired. But his good sense warned him.

Clearly he saw the danger of firing. The concussion in the confined cab would burst his eardrums, and the avalanche of broken glass that would be thrown into his face by the water pressure outside would certainly blind and maim him.

He lowered the rifle despondently. He felt his panic being slowly replaced by the cold certainty of defeat. He was trapped fifty feet below the surface of the river. There was no way out.

He thought of turning the rifle on himself, ending the inevitable, but he rejected the idea almost as soon as it had formed. Not that way, never that way!

He flogged his mind, driving it out of the cold lethargic clutch of certain death. There must be something. Think! Damn you, think!

The tanker was still rocking; it had not yet settled into the ooze of the river bottom. How long had he been under? About twenty seconds. Surely it should have hit the bottom long ago.

Unless! Bruce felt hope surge into new life within him. The tank! By God, that was it.

The great, almost empty tank behind him! The five-thousand-gallon tank which now contained only four hundred gallons of gasoline – it would have a displacement of nearly eighteen tons! It would float.

As if in confirmation of his hope, he felt his eardrums creak and pop. The pressure was falling! He was rising.

Bruce stared out at green water through the glass. The silver clouds of bubbles no longer streamed upwards; they seemed to hang outside the cab. The tanker had overcome the initial impetus that had driven it far below the surface, and now it was floating upwards at the same rate of ascent as its bubbles.

The dark green of deep water paled slowly to the colour of Chartreuse. And Bruce laughed. It was a gasping hysterical giggle and the sound of it shocked him. He cut it off abruptly.

The tanker bobbed out on to the surface, water streamed from the windscreen and through it Bruce caught a misty distorted glimpse of the south bank.

He twisted the door handle and this time the door burst open readily, water poured into the cab and Bruce floundered out against its rush.

With one quick glance he took in his position. The tanker had floated down twenty yards below the bridge, the guns on the south bank had fallen silent, and he could see no Baluba on the north bank. They must have disappeared back into the jungle.

Bruce plunged into the river and struck out for the south bank. Vaguely he heard the thin high shouts of encouragement from his gendarmes.

Within a dozen strokes he knew he was in difficulties. The drag of his boots and his sodden uniform was enormous. Treading water he tore off his steel helmet and let it sink. Then he tried to struggle out of his battle-jacket. It clung to his arms and chest and he disappeared under the surface four times before he finally got rid of it. He had breathed water into his lungs and his legs were tired and heavy.

The south bank was too far away. He would never make it. Coughing painfully he changed his objective and struck upstream against the current towards the bridge.

He felt himself settling lower in the water; he had to force his arms to lift and fall forward into each stroke.

Something plopped into the water close beside him. He paid no attention to it; suddenly a sense of disinterest had come over him, the first stage of drowning. He mistimed a breath and sucked in more water. The pain of it goaded him into a fresh burst of coughing. He hung in the water, gasping and hacking painfully.

Again something plopped close by, and this time he lifted his head. An arrow floated past him – then they began dropping steadily about him.

Baluba hidden in the thick bush above the beach were shooting at him; a gentle pattering rain of arrows splashed around his head. Bruce started swimming again, clawing his way frantically upstream. He swam until he could no longer lift his arms clear of the surface and the weight of his boots dragged his feet down.

Again he lifted his head. The bridge was close, not thirty feet away, but he knew that those thirty feet were as good as thirty miles. He could not make it.

The arrows that fell about him were no longer a source of terror. He thought of them only with mild irritation.

Why the hell can't they leave me alone? I don't want to play any more. I just want to relax. I'm so tired, so terribly tired.

He stopped moving and felt the water rise up coolly over his mouth and nose.

'Hold on, boss. I'm coming.' The shout penetrated through the grey fog of Bruce's drowning brain. He kicked and his head rose once more above the surface. He looked up at the bridge.

Stark naked, big belly swinging with each pace, thick legs flying, the great dangling bunch of his genitals bouncing merrily, black as a charging hippopotamus, Sergeant Major Ruffararo galloped out along the bridge.

He reached the fallen section and hauled himself up on to the guard rail. The arrows were falling around him, hissing down like angry insects. One glanced off his shoulder without penetrating and Ruffy shrugged at it, then launched himself up and out, falling in an ungainly heap of arms and legs to hit the water with a splash.

'Where the hell are you, boss?'

Bruce croaked a water-strangled reply and Ruffy came ploughing down towards him with clumsy overarm strokes.

He reached Bruce.

'Always playing around,' he grunted. 'Guess some guys never learn!' His fist closed on a handful of Bruce's hair.

Struggling unavailingly Bruce felt his head tucked firmly under Ruffy's arm and he was dragged through the water. Occasionally his face came out long enough to suck a breath but mostly he was under water. Consciousness receded and he felt himself going, going.

His head bumped against something hard but he was too weak to reach out his hand.

'Wake up, boss. You can have a sleep later.' Ruffy's voice bellowed in his ear. He opened his eyes and saw beside him the pile of the bridge.

'Come on. I can't carry you up here.'

Ruffy had worked round the side of the pile, shielding them from arrows, but the current was strong here, tugging at their bodies. Without the strength to prevent it Bruce's head rolled sideways and his face flopped forward into the water.

'Come on, wake up.' With a stinging slap Ruffy's open hand hit Bruce across the cheek. The shock roused him, he coughed and a mixture of water and vomit shot up his throat and out of his mouth and nose. Then he blenched painfully and retched again.

'How's it feel now?' Ruffy demanded.

Bruce lifted a hand from the water and wiped his mouth. He felt much better.

'Okay? Can you make it?'

Bruce nodded.

'Let's go then.'

With Ruffy dragging and pushing him, he worked his way up the pile. Water poured from his clothing as his body emerged, his hair was plastered across his forehead and he could feel each breath gurgle in his lungs.

'Listen boss. When we get to the top we'll be in the open again. There'll be more arrows – not time to sit around and chat. We're going over the rail fast and then run like hell, okay?'

Bruce nodded again. Above him were the floorboards of the bridge. With one hand he reached up and caught an upright of the guard rail, and he hung there without strength to pull himself the rest of the way.

'Hold it there,' grunted Ruffy and wriggled his shiny wet bulk up and over.

The arrows started falling again; one pegged into the wood six inches from Bruce's face and stood there quivering. Slowly Bruce's grip relaxed. I can't hold on, he thought, I'm going.

Then Ruffy's hand closed on his wrist, he felt himself dragged up, his legs dangled. He hung suspended by one arm and the water swirled smoothly past twenty feet below.

Slowly he was drawn upwards, his chest scraped over the guard rail, tearing his shirt, then he tumbled over it into an untidy heap on the bridge.

Vaguely he heard the guns firing on the south bank, the flit and thump of the arrows, and Ruffy's voice.

'Come on, boss. Get up.'

He felt himself being lifted and dragged along. With his legs boneless soft under him, he staggered beside Ruffy. Then there were no more arrows; the timbers of the bridge became solid earth under his feet. Voices and hands on him. He was being lifted, then lowered face down on to the wooden floor of a truck. The rhythmic pressure on his chest as someone started artificial respiration above him, the warm gush of water up his throat, and Shermaine's voice. He could not understand what she was saying, but just the sound of it was enough to make him realize he was safe. Darkly through the fog he became aware that her voice was the most important sound in his life.

He vomited again.

Hesitantly at first, and then swiftly, Bruce came back from the edge of oblivion.

'That's enough,' he mumbled and rolled out from under Sergeant Jacque who was administering the artificial respiration. The movement started a fresh paroxysm of coughing and he felt Shermaine's hands on his shoulders restraining him.

'Bruce, you must rest.'

'No.' He struggled into a sitting position. 'We've got to get out into the open,' he gasped.

'No hurry, boss. We've left all the Balubes on the other bank. There's a river between us.'

'How do you know?' Bruce challenged him.

'Well—'

'You don't!' Bruce told him flatly. 'There could easily be another few hundred on this side.' He coughed again painfully and then went on. 'We're leaving in five minutes, get them ready.'

'Okay.' Ruffy turned to leave.

'Ruffy!'

'Boss?' He turned back expectantly.

'Thank you.'

Ruffy grinned self-consciously. ''At's all right. I needed a wash anyway.'

'I'll buy you a drink when we get home.'

'I won't forget,' Ruffy warned him, and climbed down out of the truck. Bruce heard him shouting to his boys.

'I thought I'd lost you.' Shermaine's arm was still round his shoulders and Bruce looked at her for the first time.

'My sweet girl, you won't get rid of me that easily,' he assured her. He was feeling much better now.

'Bruce, I want to – I can't explain—' Unable to find the

words she leaned forward instead and kissed him, full on the mouth.

When they drew apart, Sergeant Jacque and the two gendarmes with him were grinning delightedly.

'There is nothing wrong with you now, Captain.'

'No, there isn't,' Bruce agreed. 'Make your preparations for departure.'

From the passenger seat of the Ford Bruce took one last look at the bridge.

The repaired section hung like a broken drawbridge into the water. Beyond it on the far bank were scattered a few dead Baluba, like celluloid dolls in the sunlight. Far downstream the gasoline tanker had been washed by the current against the beach. It lay on its side, half-submerged in the shallows and the white Shell insignia showed clearly.

And the river flowed on, green and inscrutable, with the jungle pressing close along its banks.

'Let's get away from here,' said Bruce.

Shermaine started the engine and the convoy of trucks followed them along the track through the belt of thick river bush and into the open forest again.

Bruce looked at his watch. The inside of the glass was dewed with moisture and he lifted it to his ear.

'Damn thing has stopped. What's your time?'

'Twenty minutes to one.'

'Half the day wasted,' Bruce grumbled.

'Will we reach Msapa Junction before dark?'

'No, we won't. For two good reasons. Firstly, it's too far, and secondly, we haven't enough gas.'

'What are you going to do?' Her voice was unruffled, already she had complete faith in him. I wonder how long it will last, he mused cynically. At first you're a god. You have not a single human weakness. They set a standard for you, and the standard is perfection. Then the first time you fall short of it, their whole world blows up.

'We'll think of something,' he assured her.

'I'm sure you will,' she agreed complacently and Bruce grinned. The big joke, of course, was that when she said it he also believed it. Damned if being in love doesn't make you feel one hell of a man.

He changed to English so as to exclude the two gendarmes in the back seat from the conversation.

'You are the best thing that has happened to me in thirty years.'

'Oh, Bruce.' She turned her face towards him and the expression of trusting love in it and the intensity of his own emotion struck Bruce like a physical blow.

I will keep this thing alive, he vowed. I must nourish it with care and protect it from the dangers of selfishness and familiarity.

'Oh, Bruce, I do love you so terribly much. This morning when – when I thought I had lost you, when I saw the tanker go over into the river—' She swallowed and now her eyes were full of tears. 'It was as though the light had gone – it was so dark, so dark and cold without you.'

Absorbed with him so that she had forgotten about the road, Shermaine let the Ford veer and the offside wheels pumped into the rough verge.

'Hey, watch it!' Bruce cautioned her. 'Dearly as I love you also, I have to admit that you're a lousy driver. Let me take her.'

'Do you feel up to it?'

'Yes, pull into the side.'

Slowly, held to the speed of the lumbering vehicles behind them, they drove on through the afternoon. Twice they passed deserted Baluba villages beside the road, the grass huts disintegrating and the small cultivated lands about them thickly overgrown.

'My God, I'm hungry. I've got a headache from it and my belly feels as though it's full of warm water,' complained Bruce.

'Don't think you're the only one. This is the strictest diet I've ever been on, must have lost two kilos! But I always lose in the wrong place, never on my bottom.'

'Good,' Bruce said. 'I like it just the way it is, never shed an ounce there.' He looked over his shoulder at the two gendarmes. 'Are you hungry?' he asked in French.

'Mon Dieu!' exclaimed the fat one. 'I will not be able to sleep tonight, if I must lie on an empty stomach.'

'Perhaps it will not be necessary.' Bruce let his eyes wander off the road into the surrounding bush. The character of the country had changed in the last hundred miles. 'This looks like game country. I've noticed plenty of spoor on the road. Keep your eyes open.'

The trees were tall and widely spaced with grass growing beneath them. Their branches did not interlock so that the sky showed through. At intervals there were open glades filled with green swamp grass and thickets of bamboo and ivory palms.

'We've got another half hour of daylight. We might run into something before then.'

In the rear-view mirror he watched the lumbering column of transports for a moment. They must be almost out of gasoline by now, hardly enough for another half hour's driving. There were compensations however; at least they were in open country now and only eighty miles from Msapa Junction.

He glanced at the petrol gauge – half the tank. The Ranchero still had sufficient to get through even if the trucks were almost dry.

Of course! That was the answer. Find a good camp, leave the convoy, and go on in the Ford to find help. Without the trucks to slow him down he could get through to Msapa Junction in two hours. There was a telegraph in the station office, even if the junction was still deserted.

'We'll stop on the other side of this stream,' said Bruce and slowed the Ford, changed into second gear and let it idle down the steep bank.

The stream was shallow. The water hardly reached the hubcaps as they bumped across the rocky bottom. Bruce gunned the Ford up the far bank into the forest again.

'There!' shouted one of the gendarmes from the back seat and Bruce followed the direction of his arm.

Standing with humped shoulders, close beside the road, bunched together with mournfully drooping horns, heads held low beneath the massive bosses, bodies very big and black, were two old buffalo bulls.

Bruce hit the brakes, skidding the Ranchero to a stop, reaching for his rifle at the same instant. He twisted the door handle, hit the door with his shoulder and tumbled out on to his feet.

With a snort and a toss of their ungainly heads the buffalo started to run.

Bruce picked the leader and aimed for the neck in front of the plunging black shoulder. Leaning forward against the recoil of the rifle he fired and heard the bullet strike with a meaty thump. The bull slowed, breaking his run. The stubby forelegs settled and he slid forward on his nose, rolling as he fell, dust and legs kicking.

Turning smoothly without taking the butt from his shoulder, swinging with the run of the second bull, Bruce fired again, and again the thump of bullet striking.

The buffalo stumbled, giving in the legs, then he steadied and galloped on like a grotesque rocking horse, patches of baldness grey on his flanks, big-bellied, running heavily.

Bruce shifted the bead of the foresight on to his shoulder and fired twice in quick succession, aiming low for the heart, hitting each time, the bull so close he could see the bullet wounds appear on the dark skin.

The gallop broke into a trot, with head swinging low, mouth open, legs beginning to fold. Aiming carefully for the head Bruce fired again. The bull bellowed – a sad lonely sound – and collapsed into the grass.

The lorries had stopped in a line behind the Ford, and now from each of them swarmed black men. Jabbering happily, racing each other, they streamed past Bruce to where the buffalo had fallen in the grass beside the road.

'Nice shooting, boss,' applauded Ruffy. 'I'm going to have me a piece of tripe the size of a blanket.'

'Let's make camp first.' Bruce's ears were still singing with gunfire. 'Get the lorries into a ring.'

'I'll see to it.'

Bruce walked up to the nearest buffalo and watched for a while as a dozen men strained to roll it on to its back and begin butchering it. There were clusters of grape-blue ticks in the folds of skin between the legs and body.

A good head, he noted mechanically, forty inches at least.

'Plenty of meat, Captain. Tonight we eat thick!' grinned one of his gendarmes as he bent over the huge body to begin flensing.

'Plenty,' agreed Bruce and turned back to the Ranchero. In the heat of the kill it was a good feeling: the rifle's kick and your stomach screwed up with excitement. But afterwards you felt a little bit dirtied; sad and guilty as you do after lying with a woman you do not love.

He climbed into the car and Shermaine sat away from him, withdrawn.

'They were so big and ugly – beautiful,' she said softly.

'We needed the meat. I didn't kill them for fun.' But he thought with a little shame, I have killed many others for fun.

'Yes,' she agreed. 'We needed the meat.'

He turned the car off the road and signalled to the truck drivers to pull in behind him.

– 27 –

Later it was all right again. The meat-rich smoke from a dozen cooking fires drifted across the camp. The dark tree tops silhouetted against a sky full of stars, the friendly glow of the fires, and laughter, men's voices raised, someone singing, the night noises of the bush – insects and frogs in the nearby stream – a plate piled high with grilled fillets and slabs of liver, a bottle of beer from Ruffy's hoard, the air at last cooler, a small breeze to keep the mosquitoes away, and Shermaine sitting beside him on the blankets.

Ruffy drifted across to them, in one hand a stick loaded with meat from which the juice dripped and in the other hand a bottle held by the throat.

'How's it for another beer, boss?'

'Enough.' Bruce held up his hand. 'I'm full to the back teeth.'

'You're getting old, that's for sure. Me and the boys going to finish them buffalo or burst trying.' He squatted on his great haunches and his tone changed. 'The trucks are flat, boss. Reckon there's not a bucketful of gas in the lot of them.'

'I want you to drain all the tanks, Ruffy, and pour it into the Ford.'

Ruffy nodded and bit a hunk of meat off the end of the stick.

'Then first thing tomorrow morning you and I will go on to Msapa in the Ranchero and leave everyone else here. Lieutenant Hendry will be in charge.'

'You talking about me?' Wally came from one of the fires.

'Yes, I'm going to leave you in charge here while Ruffy and I go on to Msapa Junction to fetch help.' Bruce did not look at Hendry and he had difficulty keeping the loathing out of his voice. 'Ruffy, fetch the map will you?'

They spread it on the earth and huddled round it. Ruffy held the flashlight.

'I'd say we are about here.' Bruce touched the tiny black vein of the road. 'About seventy, eighty miles to Msapa.' He ran his finger along it. 'It will take us about five hours there and back. However, if the telegraph isn't working we might have to go on until we meet a patrol or find some other way of getting a message back to Elisabethville.'

Almost parallel to the road and only two inches from it on the large-scale map ran the thick red line that marked the Northern Rhodesian border. Wally Hendry's slitty eyes narrowed even further as he looked at it.

'Why not leave Ruffy here, and I'll go with you.' Hendry looked up at Bruce.

'I want Ruffy with me to translate if we meet any Africans along the way.' Also, thought Bruce, I don't want to be left on the side of the road with a bullet in my head while you drive on to Elisabethville.

'Suits me,' grunted Hendry. He dropped his eyes to the map. About forty miles to the border. A hard day's walk.

Bruce changed to French and spoke swiftly. 'Ruffy, hide the diamonds behind the dashboard of your truck. That way we are certain they will send a rescue party, even if we have to go Elisabethville.'

'Talk English, Bucko,' growled Hendry, but Ruffy nodded and answered, also in French.

'I will leave Sergeant Jacque to guard them.'

'NO!' said Bruce. 'Tell no one.'

'Cut it out!' rasped Hendry. 'Anything you say I want to hear.'

'We'll leave at dawn tomorrow,' Bruce reverted to English.

'May I go with you?' Shermaine spoke for the first time.

'I don't see why not.' Bruce smiled quickly at her, but Ruffy coughed awkwardly.

'Reckon that's not such a good idea, boss.'

'Why?' Bruce turned on him with his temper starting to rise.

'Well, boss,' Ruffy hesitated, and then went on, 'you, me and the lady all shoving off towards Elisabethville might not look so good to the boys. They might get ideas, think we're not coming back or something.'

Bruce was silent, considering it.

'That's right,' Hendry cut in. 'You might just take it into your head to keep going. Let her stay, sort of guarantee for the rest of us.'

'I don't mind, Bruce. I didn't think about it that way. I'll stay.'

'She'll have forty good boys looking after her, she'll be all right,' Ruffy assured Bruce.

'All right then, that's settled. It won't be for long, Shermaine.'

'I'll go and see about draining the trucks.' Ruffy stood up. 'See you in the morning, boss.'

'I'm going to get some more of that meat.' Wally picked up the map carelessly. 'Try and get some sleep tonight, Curry. Not too much grumble and grunt.'

In his exasperation, Bruce did not notice that Hendry had taken the map.

– 28 –

It rained in the early hours before the dawn and Bruce lay in the back of the Ranchero and listened to it drum on the metal roof. It was a lulling sound and a good feeling to lie warmly listening to the rain with the woman you love in your arms.

He felt her waking against him, the change in her breathing and the first slow movements of her body.

There were buffalo steaks for breakfast, but no coffee. They ate swiftly and then Bruce called across to Ruffy.

'Okay, Ruffy?'

'Let's go, boss.' They climbed into the Ford and Ruffy filled most of the seat beside Bruce. His helmet perched on the back of his head, rifle sticking out through the space where the windscreen should have been, and two large feet planted securely on top of the case of beer on the floor.

Bruce twisted the key and the engine fired. He warmed it at a fast idle and turned to Hendry who leaned against the roof of the Ford and peered through the window.

'We'll be back this afternoon. Don't let anybody wander away from camp.'

'Okay.' Hendry breathed his morning breath full into Bruce's face.

'Keep them busy, otherwise they'll get bored and start fighting.'

Before he answered Hendry let his eyes search the interior of the Ford carefully and then he stood back.

'Okay,' he said again. 'On your way!'

Bruce looked beyond him to where Shermaine sat on the tailboard of a truck and smiled at her.

'Bon voyage!' she called and Bruce let out the clutch. They bumped out on to the road amid a chorus of cheerful farewells from the gendarmes round the cooking fires and Bruce settled down to drive. In the rear-view mirror he watched the camp disappear round the curve in the road. There were puddles of rainwater in the road, but above them the clouds had broken up and scattered across the sky.

'How's it for a beer, boss?'

'Instead of coffee?' asked Bruce.

'Nothing like it for the bowels,' grunted Ruffy and reached down to open the case.

Wally Hendry lifted his helmet and scratched his scalp. His short red hair felt stiff and wiry with dried sweat and there was a spot above his right ear that itched. He fingered it tenderly.

The Ranchero disappeared round a bend in the road, the trees screening it abruptly, and the hum of its motor faded.

Okay, so they haven't taken the diamonds with them. I had a bloody good look around. I guessed they'd leave them. The girl knows where they are like as not. Perhaps – no, she'd squeal like a stuck pig if I asked.

Hendry looked sideways at Shermaine; she was staring after the Ranchero.

Silly bitch! Getting all broody now that Curry's giving her the rod. Funny how these educated Johnnies like their women to have small tits – nice piece of arse though. Wouldn't mind a bit of that myself. Jesus, that would really get to Mr High Class Bloody Curry, me giving his pretty the business. Not a chance though. These niggers think he's a god or something. They'd tear me to pieces if I touched her. Forget about it! Let's get the diamonds and take off for the border.

Hendry settled his helmet back on to his head and strolled casually across to the truck that Ruffy had been driving the day before.

Got a map, compass, coupla spare clips of ammo – now all we need is the glass.

He climbed into the cab and opened the cubby hole.

Bet a pound to a pinch of dung that they've hidden them somewhere in this truck. They're not worried – think they've got me tied up here. Never occurred to them that old Uncle Wally might up and walk away. Thought I'd just sit here and wait for them to come back and fetch me –

take me in and hand me over to a bunch of nigger police aching to get their hands on a white man.

Well, I got news for you, Mr Fancy-talking Curry!

He rummaged in the cubbyhole and then slammed it shut.

Okay, they're not there. Let's try under the seats. The border is not guarded, might take me three or four days to get through to Fort Rosebery, but when I do I'll have me a pocket full of diamonds and there's a direct air service out to Ndola and the rest of the world. Then we start living!

There was nothing under the seats except a greasy dust-coated jack and wheel spanner. Hendry turned his attention to the floorboards.

Pity I'll have to leave that bastard Curry. I had plans for him. There's a guy who really gets to me. So goddam cocksure of himself. One of them. Makes you feel you're shit – fancy talk, pretty face, soft hands. Christ, I hate him.

Viciously he tore the rubber mats off the floor and the dust made him cough.

Been to university, makes him think he's something special. The bastard. I should have fixed him long ago – that night at the road bridge I nearly gave it to him in the dark. Nobody would have known, just a mistake. I shoulda done it then. I shoulda done it at Port Reprieve when he ran out across the road to the office block. Big bloody hero. Big lover. Bet he had everything he ever wanted, bet his Daddy gave him all the money he could use. And he looks at you like that, like you crawled out of rotting meat.

Hendry straightened up and gripped the steering wheel, his jaws chewing with the strength of his hatred. He stared out of the windscreen.

Shermaine Cartier walked past the front of the truck. She had a towel and a pink plastic toilet bag in her hand; the pistol swung against her leg as she moved.

Sergeant Jacque stood up from the cooking fire and

moved to intercept her. They talked, arguing, then Shermaine touched the pistol at her side and laughed. A worried frown creased Jacque's black face and he shook his head dubiously. Shermaine laughed again, turned from him and set off down the road towards the stream. Her hair, caught carelessly at her neck with a ribbon, hung down her back on to the rose-coloured shirt she wore and the heavy canvas holster emphasized the unconsciously provocative swing of her hips. She went out of sight down the steep bank of the stream.

Wally Hendry chuckled and then licked his lips with the quick-darting tip of his tongue.

'This is going to make it perfect,' he whispered. 'They couldn't have done things to suit me better if they'd spent a week working it out.'

Eagerly he turned back to his search for the diamonds. Leaning forward he thrust his hand up behind the dashboard of the truck and it brushed against the bunch of canvas bags that hung from the mass of concealed wires.

'Come to Uncle Wally.' He jerked them loose and, holding them in his lap, began checking their contents. The third bag he opened contained the gem stones.

'Lovely, lovely grub,' he whispered at the dull glint and sparkle in the depths of the bag. Then he closed the drawstring, stuffed the bag into the pocket of his battle-jacket and buttoned the flap. He dropped the bags of industrial diamonds on to the floor and kicked them under the seat, picked up his rifle and stepped down out of the truck.

Three or four gendarmes looked up curiously at him as he passed the cooking fires. Hendry rubbed his stomach and pulled a face.

'Too much meat last night!'

The gendarme who understood English laughed and translated into French. They all laughed and one of them called something in a dialect that Hendry did not understand. They watched him walk away among the trees.

As soon as he was out of sight of the camp Hendry started to run, circling back towards the stream.

'This is going to be a pleasure!' He laughed aloud.

– 29 –

Fifty yards below the drift where the road crossed the stream Shermaine found a shallow pool. There were reeds with fluffy heads around it and a small beach of white river sand, black boulders, polished round and glossy smooth, the water almost blood warm and so clear that she could see a shoal of fingerlings nibbling at the green algae that coated the boulders beneath the surface.

She stood barefooted in the sand and looked around carefully, but the reeds screened her, and she had asked Jacque not to let any of his men come down to the river while she was there.

She undressed, dropped her clothes across one of the black boulders and with a cake of soap in her hand waded out into the pool and lowered herself until she sat with the water up to her neck and the sand pleasantly rough under her naked behind.

She washed her hair first and then lay stretched out with the water moving gently over her, soft as the caress of silk. Growing bold the tiny fish darted in and nibbled at her skin, tickling, so that she gasped and splashed at them.

At last she ducked her head under the surface and, with the water streaming out of her hair into her eyes, she groped her way back to the bank.

As she stooped, still half blinded, for her towel Wally Hendry's hand closed over her mouth and his other arm circled her waist from behind.

'One squeak out of you and I'll wring your bloody neck.' He spoke hoarsely into her ear. She could smell his breath, warm and sour in her face. 'Just pretend I'm old Bruce – then both of us will enjoy it.' And he chuckled.

Sliding quickly over her hip his hand moved downwards and the shock of it galvanized her into frantic struggles. Holding her easily Hendry kept on chuckling.

She opened her mouth suddenly and one of his fingers went in between her teeth. She bit with all her strength and felt the skin break and tasted blood in her mouth.

'You bitch!' Hendry jerked his hand away and she opened her mouth to scream, but the hand swung back, clenched, into the side of her face, knocking her head across. The scream never reached her lips for he hit her again and she felt herself falling.

Stunned by the blows, lying in the sand, she could not believe it was happening, until she felt his weight upon her and his knee forced cruelly between hers.

Then she started to struggle again, trying to twist away from his mouth and the smell of his breath.

'No, no, no.' She repeated it over and over, her eyes shut tightly so she did not have to see that face above her, and her head rolling from side to side in the sand. He was so strong, so immensely powerful.

'No,' she said, and then, 'Ooah!' at the pain, the tearing stinging pain within, and the thrusting heaviness above.

And through the pounding, grunting, thrusting nightmare she could smell him and feel the sweat drip from him and splash into her upturned unprotected face.

It lasted forever, and then suddenly the weight was gone and she opened her eyes.

He stood over her, fumbling with his clothing, and there was a dullness in his expression. He wiped his mouth with the back of his hand and she saw the fingers were trembling. His voice when he spoke was tired and disinterested.

'I've had better.'

Swiftly Shermaine rolled over and reached for the pistol

that lay on top of her clothes. Hendry stepped forward with all his weight on her wrist and she felt the bones bend under his boot and she moaned. But through pain she whispered. 'You pig, you filthy pig,' and he hit her again, flat-handed across the face, knocking her on to her back once more.

He picked up the pistol and opened it, spilling the cartridges into the sand, then he unclipped the lanyard and threw the pistol far out into the reed bed.

'Tell Curry I say he can have my share of you,' he said and walked quickly away among the reeds.

The white sand coated her damp body like icing sugar. She sat up slowly holding her wrist, the side of her face inflamed and starting to swell where he had hit her.

She started to cry, shaking silently, and the tears squeezed out between her eyelids and matted her long dark lashes.

– 30 –

Ruffy held up the brown bottle and inspected it ruefully.

'Seems like one mouthful and it's empty.' He threw the bottle out of the side window. It hit a tree and burst with a small pop.

'We can always find our way back by following the empties,' smiled Bruce, once more marvelling at the man's capacity. But there was plenty of storage space. He watched Ruffy's stomach spread on to his lap as he reached down to the beer crate.

'How we doing, boss?'

Bruce glanced at the milometer.

'We've come eighty-seven miles,' and Ruffy nodded.

'Not bad going. Be there pretty soon now.'

They were silent. The wind blew in on to them through

the open front. The grass that grew between the tracks brushed the bottom of the chassis with a continuous rushing sound.

'Boss—' Ruffy spoke at last.

'Yes?'

'Lieutenant Hendry – those diamonds. You reckon we did a good thing leaving him there?'

'He's stranded in the middle of the bush. Even if he did find them they wouldn't do him much good.'

'Suppose that's right.' Ruffy lifted the beer bottle to his lips and when he lowered it he went on. 'Mind you, that's one guy you can never be sure of.' He tapped his head with a finger as thick and as black as a blood-sausage. 'Something wrong with him – he's one of the maddest Arabs I've found in a long time of looking.'

Bruce grunted grimly.

'You want to be careful there, boss,' observed Ruffy. 'Any time now he's going to try for you. I've seen it coming. He's working himself up to it. He's a mad Arab.'

'I'll watch him,' said Bruce.

'Yeah, you do that.'

Again they were silent in the steady swish of the wind and the drone of the motor.

'There's a railway.' Ruffy pointed to the blue-gravelled embankment through the trees.

'Nearly there,' said Bruce.

They came out into another open glade and beyond it the water tank of Msapa Junction stuck up above the forest.

'Here we are,' said Ruffy and drained the bottle in his hand.

'Just say a prayer that the telegraph lines are still up and that there's an operator on the Elisabethville end.'

Bruce slowed the Ford past the row of cottages. They were exactly as he remembered them, deserted and forlorn. The corners of his mouth were compressed into a hard angle as he looked at the two small mounds of earth beneath the casia flora trees. Ruffy looked at them also but neither of them spoke.

Bruce stopped the Ford outside the station building and they climbed out stiffly and walked together on to the verandah. The wooden flooring echoed dully under their boots as they made for the door of the office.

Bruce pushed the door open and looked in. The walls were painted a depressing utility green, loose paper was scattered on the floor, the drawers of the single desk hung open, and a thin grey skin of dust coated everything.

'There she is,' said Ruffy and pointed to the brass and varnished wood complexity of the telegraph on a table against the far wall.

'Looks all right,' said Bruce. 'As long as the lines haven't been cut.'

As if to reassure him, the telegraph began to clatter like a typewriter.

'Thank God for that,' sighed Bruce.

They walked across to the table.

'You know how to work this thing?' asked Ruffy.

'Sort of,' Bruce answered and set his rifle against the wall. He was relieved to see a Morse table stuck with adhesive tape to the wall above the apparatus. It was a long time since he had memorized it as a boy scout.

He laid his hand on the transmission key and studied the table. The call sign for Elisabethville was 'EE'.

He tapped it out clumsily and then waited. Almost immediately the set clattered back at him, much too fast to be intelligible and the roll of paper in the repeater was exhausted. Bruce took off his helmet and laboriously spelled out, 'Transmit slower.'

It was a long business with requests for repetition. 'Not understood' was made nearly every second signal, but finally Bruce got the operator to understand that he had an urgent message for Colonel Franklyn of President Tshombe's staff.

'Wait,' came back the laconic signal.

And they waited. They waited an hour, then two.

'That mad bastard's forgotten about us,' grumbled Ruffy and went to the Ford to fetch the beer crate. Bruce fidgeted restlessly on the unpadded chair beside the telegraph table. He reconsidered anxiously all his previous arguments for leaving Wally Hendry in charge of the camp, but once again decided that it was safe. He couldn't do much harm. Unless, unless, Shermaine! No, it was impossible. Not with forty loyal gendarmes to protect her.

He started to think about Shermaine and the future. There was a year's mercenary captain's pay accumulated in the Crédit Banque Suisse at Zurich. He made the conversion from francs to pounds – about two and a half thousand. Two years' operating capital, so they could have a holiday before he started working again. They could take a chalet up in the mountains, there should be good snow this time of the year.

Bruce grinned. Snow that crunched like sugar, and a twelve-inch-thick eiderdown on the bed at night.

Life had purpose and direction again.

'What you're laughing at, boss?' asked Ruffy.

'I was thinking about a bed.'

'Yeah? That's a good thing to think about. You start there, you're born there, you spend most of your life in it, you have plenty of fun in it, and if you're lucky you die there. How's it for a beer?'

The telegraph came to life at Bruce's elbow. He turned to it quickly.

'Curry – Franklyn,' it clattered. Bruce could imagine the wiry, red-faced little man at the other end. Ex-major in the third brigade of the Legion. A prime mover in the O.A.S., with a sizeable price still on his head from the De Gaulle assassination attempt.

'Franklyn – Curry,' Bruce tapped back. 'Train unserviceable. Motorized transport stranded without fuel. Port

Reprieve road. Map reference approx—' He read the numbers off the sheet on which he had noted them.

There was a long pause, then:

'Is U.M.C. property in your hands?' The question was delicately phrased.

'Affirmative,' Bruce assured him.

'Await air-drop at your position soonest. Out.'

'Message understood. Out.' Bruce straightened from the telegraph and sighed with relief.

'That's that, Ruffy. They'll drop gas to us from one of the Dakotas. Probably tomorrow morning.' He looked at his wristwatch. 'Twenty to one, let's get back.'

Bruce hummed softly, watching the double tracks ahead of him, guiding the Ford with a light touch on the wheel.

He was contented. It was all over. Tomorrow the fuel would drop from the Dakota under those yellow parachutes. (He must lay out the smudge signals this evening.) And ten hours later they would be back in Elisabethville.

A few words with Carl Engelbrecht would fix seats for Shermaine and himself on one of the outward-bound Daks. Then Switzerland, and the chalet with icicles hanging from the eaves. A long rest while he decided where to start again. Louisiana was under Roman-Dutch Law, or was it Code Napoléon? He might even have to rewrite his bar examinations, but the prospect pleased rather than dismayed him. It was fun again.

'Never seen you so happy,' grunted Ruffy.

'Never had so much cause,' Bruce agreed.

'She's a swell lady. Young still – you can teach her.'

Bruce felt his hackles rise, and then he thought better of it and laughed.

'You going to sign her up, boss?'

'I might.'

Ruffy nodded wisely. 'Man should have plenty wives – I got three. Need a couple more.'

'One I could only just handle.'

'One's difficult. Two's easier. Three, you can relax. Four, they're so busy with each other they don't give you no trouble at all.'

'I might try it.'

'Yeah, you do that.'

And ahead of them through the trees they saw the ring of trucks.

'We're home,' grunted Ruffy, then he stirred uncomfortably in his seat. 'Something going on.'

Men stood in small groups. There was something in their attitude: strain, apprehension. Two men ran up the road to meet them. Bruce could see their mouths working, but could not hear the words.

Dread, heavy and cold, pushed down on the pit of Bruce's gut.

Gabbled, incoherent, Sergeant Jacque was trying to tell him something as he ran beside the Ford.

'Tenente Hendry – the river – the madame – gone.' French words like driftwood in the torrent of dialect.

'Your girl,' translated Ruffy. 'Hendry's done her.'

'Dead?' The question dropped from Bruce's mouth.

'No. He's hurt her. He's – you know!'

'Where's she?'

'They've got her in the back of the truck.'

Bruce climbed heavily out of the car. Now they were silent, grouped together, not looking at him, faces impassive, waiting.

Bruce walked slowly to the truck. He felt cold and numb. His legs moved automatically beneath him. He drew back the canvas and pulled himself up into the interior. It was an effort to move forward, to focus his eyes in the gloom.

Wrapped in a blanket she lay small and still.

'Shermaine.' It stuck in his throat.

'Shermaine,' he said again and knelt beside her. A great

livid swelling distorted the side of her face. She did not turn her head to him, but lay staring up at the canvas roof.

He touched her face and the skin was cold, cold as the dread that gripped his stomach. The coldness of it shocked him so he jerked his hand away.

'Shermaine.' This time it was a sob. The eyes, her big haunted eyes, turned unseeing towards him and he felt the lift of escape from the certainty of her death.

'Oh, God,' he cried and took her to him, holding the unresisting frailty of her to his chest. He could feel the slow even thump of her heart beneath his hand. He drew back the blanket and there was no blood.

'Darling, are you hurt? Tell me, are you hurt?' She did not answer. She lay quietly in his arms, not seeing him.

'Shock,' he whispered. 'It's only shock,' and he opened her clothing. With tenderness he examined the smoothly pale body; the skin was clammy and damp, but there was no damage.

He wrapped her again and laid her gently back on to the floor.

He stood and the thing within him changed shape. Cold still, but now burning cold as dry ice.

Ruffy and Jacque were waiting for him beside the tailboard.

'Where is he?' asked Bruce softly.

'He is gone.'

'Where?'

'That way.' Jacque pointed towards the south-east. 'I followed the spoor a short distance.'

Bruce walked to the Ford and picked up his rifle from the floor. He opened the cubby hole and took two spare clips of ammunition from it.

Ruffy followed him. 'He's got the diamonds, boss.'

'Yes,' said Bruce and checked the load of his rifle. The diamonds were of no importance.

'Are you going after him, boss?'

Bruce did not answer. Instead he looked up at the sky. The sun was half way towards the horizon and there were clouds thickly massed around it.

'Ruffy, stay with her,' he said softly. 'Keep her warm.'

Ruffy nodded.

'Who is the best tracker we've got?'

'Jacque. Worked for a safari outfit before the war as a tracker boy.'

Bruce turned to Jacque. The thing was still icy cold inside him, with tentacles that spread out to every extremity of his body and his mind.

'When did this happen?'

'About an hour after you left,' answered Jacque.

Eight hours start. It was a long lead.

'Take the spoor,' said Bruce softly.

– 31 –

The earth was soft from the night's rain and the spoor deep trodden, the heels had bitten in under Hendry's weight, so they followed fast.

Watching Sergeant Jacque work, Bruce felt his anxiety abating, for although the footprints were so easy to follow in these early stages that it was no test of his ability, yet from the way he moved swiftly along – half-crouched and wholly absorbed, occasionally glancing ahead to pick up the run of the spoor, stooping now and then to touch the earth and determine its texture – Bruce could tell that this man knew his business.

Through the open forest with tufted grass below, holding steadily south by east, Hendry led them straight towards the Rhodesian border. And after the first two hours Bruce knew they had not gained upon him. Hendry was still eight hours ahead, and at the pace he was setting eight hours' start was something like thirty miles in distance.

Bruce looked over his shoulder at the sun where it lay wedged between two vast piles of cumulonimbus. There in the sky were the two elements which could defeat him.

Time. There were perhaps two more hours of daylight. With the onset of night they would be forced to halt.

Rain. The clouds were swollen and dark blue round the edges. As Bruce watched, the lightning lit them internally, and at a count of ten the thunder grumbled suddenly. If it rained again before morning there would be no spoor to follow.

'We must move faster,' said Bruce.

Sergeant Jacque straightened up and looked at Bruce as though he were a stranger. He had forgotten his existence.

'The earth hardens.' Jacque pointed at the spoor and Bruce saw that in the last half hour the soil had become gritty and compacted. Hendry's heels no longer broke the crust. 'It is unwise to run on such a lean trail.'

Again Bruce looked back at the menace of gathering clouds.

'We must take the chance,' he decided.

'As you wish,' grunted Jacque, and transferred his rifle to his other shoulder, hitched up his belt and settled the steel helmet more firmly on his head.

'Allez!'

They trotted on through the forest towards the south-east. Within a mile Bruce's body had settled into the automatic rhythm of his run, leaving his mind free.

He thought about Wally Hendry, saw again the little eyes and round them the puffy folded skin, and the mouth below, thin and merciless, the obscene ginger stubble of beard. He could almost smell him. His nostrils flared at the memory of the rank red-head's body odour. Unclean, he thought, unclean mind and unclean body.

His hatred of Wally Hendry was a tangible thing. He could feel it sitting heavily at the base of his throat, tingling in his fingertips and giving strength to his legs.

And yet there was something else. Suddenly Bruce grinned: a wolfish baring of his teeth. That tingling in his fingertips was not all hatred, a little of it was excitement.

What a complex thing is a man, he thought. He can never hold one emotion – always there are others to confuse it. Here I am hunting the thing that I most loathe and hate, and I am enjoying it. Completely unrelated to the hatred is the thrill of hunting the most dangerous and cunning game of all, man.

I have always enjoyed the chase, he thought. It has been bred into me, for my blood is that of the men who hunted and fought with Africa as the prize.

The hunting of this man will give me pleasure. If ever a man deserved to die, it is Wally Hendry. I am the plaintiff, the judge and the executioner.

Sergeant Jacque stopped so suddenly that Bruce ran into him and they nearly fell.

'What is it?' panted Bruce, coming back to reality.

'Look!'

The earth ahead of them was churned and broken.

'Zebra,' groaned Bruce, recognizing the round uncloven hoof prints. 'God damn it to hell – of all the filthy luck!'

'A big herd,' Jacque agreed. 'Spread out. Feeding.'

As far ahead as they could see through the forest the herd had wiped out Hendry's tracks.

'We'll have to cast forward.' Bruce's voice was agonized by his impatience. He turned to the nearest tree and hacked at it with his bayonet, blazing it to mark the end of the trail, swearing softly, venting his disappointment on the trunk.

'Only another hour to sunset,' he whispered. 'Please let us pick him up again before dark.'

Sergeant Jacque was already moving forward, following the approximate line of Hendry's travel, trying vainly to recognize a single footprint through the havoc created there by the passage of thousands of hooves. Bruce hurried to join him and then moved out on his flank. They zigzagged slowly ahead, almost meeting on the inward leg of each tack and then separating again to a distance of a hundred yards.

There it was! Bruce dropped to his knees to make sure. Just the outline of the toecap showing from under the spoor of an old zebra stallion. Bruce whistled, a windy sound through his dry lips, and Jacque came quickly. One quick look, then:

'Yes, he is holding more to the right now.' He raised his eyes and squinted ahead, marking a tree which was directly in line with the run of the spoor. They went forward.

'There's the herd.' Bruce pointed at the flicker of a grey body through the trees.

'They've got our wind.'

A zebra snorted and then there was a rumbling, a low blurred drumming of hooves as the herd ran. Through the trees Bruce caught glimpses of the animals on the near side of the herd. Too far off to show the stripes, looking like fat grey ponies as they galloped, ears up, black-maned heads nodding. Then they were gone and the sound of their flight dwindled.

'At least they haven't run along the spoor,' muttered Bruce, and then bitterly: 'Damn them, the stupid little donkeys! They've cost us an hour. A whole priceless hour.'

Desperately searching, wild with haste, they worked back and forth. The sun was below the trees; already the air was cooling in the short African dusk. Another fifteen minutes and it would be dark.

Then abruptly the forest ended and they came out on the edge of a vlei. Open as wheatland, pastured with green waist-high grass, hemmed in by the forest, it stretched ahead of them for nearly two miles. Dotted along it were clumps of ivory palms with each graceful stem ending in an untidy cluster of leaves. Troops of guinea-fowls were scratching and chirruping along the edge of the clearing, and near the far end a herd of buffalo formed a dark mass as they grazed beneath a canopy of white egrets.

In the forest beyond the clearing, rising perhaps three hundred feet out of it, stood a kopje of tumbled granite. The great slabs of rock with their sheer sides and square tops looked like a ruined castle. The low sun struck it and gave the rock an orange warmth.

But Bruce had no time to admire the scene; his eyes were on the earth, searching for the prints of Hendry's jungle boots.

Out on his left Sergeant Jacque whistled sharply and Bruce felt the leap of excitement in his chest. He ran across to the crouching gendarme.

'It has come away.' Jacque pointed at the spoor that was strung ahead of them like beads on a string, skirting the edge of the vlei, each depression filled with shadow and standing out clearly on the sandy grey earth.

'Too late,' groaned Bruce. 'Damn those bloody zebra.' The light was fading so swiftly it seemed as though it were a stage effect.

'Follow it.' Bruce's voice was sharp with helpless frustration. 'Follow it as long as you can.'

It was not a quarter of a mile farther on that Jacque rose out of his crouch and only the white of his teeth showed in the darkness as he spoke.

'We will lose it again if we go on.'

'All right.' Bruce unslung his rifle with weary resignation. He knew that Wally Hendry was at least forty miles ahead of them; more if he kept travelling after dark. The spoor was cold. If this had been an ordinary hunt he would long ago have broken off the chase.

He looked up at the sky. In the north the stars were fat and yellow, but above them and to the south it was black with cloud.

'Don't let it rain,' he whispered. 'Please God, don't let it rain.'

The night was long. Bruce slept once for perhaps two hours and then the strength of his hatred woke him. He lay flat upon his back and stared up at the sky. It was all dark with clouds; only occasionally they opened and let the stars shine briefly through.

'It must not rain. It must not rain.' He repeated it like a prayer, staring up at the dark sky, concentrating upon it as though by the force of his mind he could control the elements.

There were lions hunting in the forest. He heard the male roaring, moving up from the south, and once his two lionesses answered him. They killed a little before dawn and Bruce lay on the hard earth and listened to their jubilation over the kill. Then there was silence as they began to feed.

That I might have success as well, he thought. I do not often ask for favours, Lord, but grant me this one. I ask it not only for myself but for Shermaine and the others.

In his mind he saw again the two children lying where Hendry had shot them. The smear of mingled blood and chocolate across the boy's cheek.

He deserves to die, prayed Bruce, so please don't let it rain.

As long as the night had been, that quickly came the dawn. A grey dawn, gloomy with low cloud.

'Will it go?' Bruce asked for the twentieth time, and this time Jacque looked up from where he knelt beside the spoor.

'We can try now.'

They moved off slowly with Jacque leading, doubled over to peer short-sightedly at the earth and Bruce close behind him, bedevilled by his impatience and anxiety, lifting his head every dozen paces to the dirty grey roof of cloud.

The light strengthened and the circle of their vision opened from six feet to as many yards, to a hundred, so they could make out the tops of the ivory palms, shaggy against the grey cloud.

Jacque broke into a trot and ahead of them was the end of the clearing and the beginning of the forest. Two hundred yards beyond rose the massive pile of the kopje, in the early light looking more than ever like a castle, turreted and sheer. There was something formidable in its outline. It seemed to brood above them and Bruce looked away from it uneasily.

Cold and with enough weight behind it to sting, the first raindrop splashed against Bruce's cheek.

'Oh, no!' he protested, and stopped. Jacque straightened up from the spoor and he too looked at the sky.

'It is finished. In five minutes there will be nothing to follow.'

Another drop hit Bruce's upturned face and he blinked back the tears of anger and frustration that pricked the rims of his eyelids.

Faster now, tapping on his helmet, plopping on to his shoulders and face, the rain fell.

'Quickly,' cried Bruce. 'Follow as long as you can.'

Jacque opened his mouth to speak, but before a word came out he was flung backwards, punched over as though by an invisible fist, his helmet flying from his head as he fell and his rifle clattering on the earth.

Simultaneously Bruce felt the bullet pass him, disrupting the air, so the wind of it flattened his shirt against his chest, cracking viciously in his ears, leaving him dazedly looking down at Sergeant Jacque's body.

It lay with arms thrown wide, the jaw and the side of the head below the ear torn away; white bone and blood bubbling over it. The trunk twitched convulsively and the hands fluttered like trapped birds. Then flat-sounding through the rain he heard the report of the rifle.

The kopje, screamed Bruce's brain, *he's lying in the kopje!*

And Bruce moved, twisting sideways, starting to run.

– 32 –

Wally Hendry lay on his stomach on the flat top of the turret. His body was stiff and chilled from the cold of the night and the rock was harsh under him, but the discomfort hardly penetrated the fringe of his mind. He had built a low parapet with loose flakes of granite, and he had screened the front of it with the thick bushy stems of broom bush.

His rifle was propped on the parapet in front of him and at his elbow were the spare ammunition clips.

He had lain in this ambush for a long time now – since early the preceding afternoon. Now it was dawn and the darkness was drawing back; in a few minutes he would be able to see the whole of the clearing below him.

I coulda been across the river already, he thought, *coulda been fifty miles away*. He did not attempt to analyse the impulse that had made him lie here unmoving for almost twenty hours.

Man, I knew old Curry would have to come. I knew he would only bring one nigger tracker with him. These educated Johnnies got their own rules – man to man stuff, and he chuckled as he remembered the two minute figures that he had seen come out of the forest in the fading light of the previous evening.

The bastard spent the night down there in the clearing. Saw him light a match and have hisself a smoke in the night – well, I hope he enjoyed it, his last.

Wally peered anxiously out into the gradually gathering dawn.

They'll be moving now, coming up the clearing. Must get them before they reach the trees again. Below him the clearing showed as a paleness, a leprous blotch, on the dark forest.

The bastard! Without preliminaries Hendry's hatred

returned to him. *This time he don't get to make no fancy speeches. This time he don't get no chance to be hoity-toity.*

The light was stronger now. He could see the clumps of ivory palms against the pale brown grass of the clearing.

'Ha!' Hendry exclaimed.

There they were, like two little ants, dark specks moving up the middle of the clearing. The tip of Hendry's tongue slipped out between his lips and he flattened down behind his rifle.

Man, I've waited for this. Six months now I've thought about this, and when it's finished I'll go down and take his ears. He slipped the safety catch; it made a satisfying mechanical click.

Nigger's leading, that's Curry behind him. Have to wait till they turn, don't want the nigger to get it first. Curry first, then the nigger.

He picked them up in his sights, breathing quicker now, the thrill of it so intense that he had to swallow and it caught in his throat like dry bread.

A raindrop hit the back of his neck. It startled him. He looked up quickly at the sky and saw it coming.

'Goddam it,' he groaned, and looked back at the clearing. Curry and nigger were standing together, a single dark blob in the half-light. There was no chance of separating them. The rain fell faster, and suddenly Hendry was overwhelmed by the old familiar feeling of inferiority; of knowing that everything, even the elements, conspired against him; the knowledge that he could never win, not even this once.

They, God and the rest of the world.

The ones who had given him a drunk for a father.

A squalid cottage for a home and a mother with cancer of the throat.

The ones who had sent him to reform school, had fired him from two dozen jobs, had pushed him, laughed at him, gaoled him twice – They, all of them (and Bruce Curry who was their figurehead), they were going to win again. Not even this once, not even ever.

'Goddam it,' he cursed in hopeless, wordless anger against them all.

'Goddam it, goddam it to hell,' and he fired at the dark blob in his sights.

– 33 –

As he ran Bruce looked across a hundred yards of open ground to the edge of the forest.

He felt the wind of the next bullet as it cracked past him.

If he uses rapid fire he'll get me even at three hundred yards.

And Bruce jinked his run like a jack-rabbit. The blood roaring in his ears, fear driving his feet.

Then all around him the air burst asunder, buffeting him so he staggered; the vicious whip-whip-whip of bullets filled his head.

I can't make it.

Seventy yards to the shelter of the trees. Seventy yards of open meadowland, and above him the commanding mass of the kopje.

The next burst is for me – it must come, now!

And he flung himself to one side so violently that he nearly fell. Again the air was ripping to tatters close beside him.

I can't last! He must get me!

In his path was an ant-heap, a low pile of clay, a pimple on the open expanse of earth. Bruce dived for it, hitting the ground so hard that the wind was forced from his lungs out through his open mouth.

The next burst of gunfire kicked lumps of clay from the top of the ant-heap, showering Bruce's back.

He lay with his face pressed into the earth, wheezing

with the agony of empty lungs, flattening his body behind the tiny heap of clay.

Will it cover me? Is there enough of it?

And the next hail of bullets thumped into the ant-heap, throwing fountains of earth, but leaving Bruce untouched.

I'm safe. The realization came with a surge that washed away his fear.

But I'm helpless, answered his hatred. *Pinned to the earth for as long as Hendry wants to keep me here.*

The rain fell on his back. Soaking through his jacket, coldly caressing the nape of his neck and dribbling down over his jaws.

He rolled his head sideways, not daring to lift it an inch, and the rain beat on to the side of his face.

The rain! Falling faster. Thickening. Hanging from the clouds like the skirts of a woman's dress.

Curtains of rain. Greying out the edge of the forest, leaving no solid shapes in the mist of falling liquid mother-of-pearl.

Still gasping but with the pain slowly receding, Bruce lifted his head.

The kopje was a vague blue-green shape ahead of him, then it was gone, swallowed by the eddying columns of rain.

Bruce pushed himself up on to his knees and the pain in his chest made him dizzy.

Now! he thought. *Now, before it thins*, and he lumbered clumsily to his feet.

For a moment he stood clutching his chest, sucking for breath in the haze of water-filled air, and then he staggered towards the edge of the forest.

His feet steadied under him, his breathing eased, and he was into the trees.

They closed round him protectively. He leaned against the rough bark of one of them and wiped the rain from his face with the palm of his hand. The strength came back to him and with it his hatred and his excitement.

He unslung the rifle from his shoulder and stood away from the tree with his feet planted wide apart.

'Now, my friend,' he whispered, 'we fight on equal terms.' He pumped a round into the chamber of the FN and moved towards the kopje, stepping daintily, the weight of the rifle in his hands, his mind suddenly sharp and clear, vision enhanced, feeling his strength and the absence of fear like a song within him, a battle hymn.

He made out the loom of the kopje through the dripping rain-heavy trees and he circled out to the right. There is plenty of time, he thought. I can afford to case the joint thoroughly. He completed his circuit of the rock pile.

The kopje, he found, was the shape of a galleon sinking by the head. At one end the high double castles of the poop, from which the main deck canted steeply forward as though the prow were already under water. This slope was scattered with boulders and densely covered with dwarf scrub, an interwoven mass of shoulder-high branches and leaves.

Bruce squatted on his haunches with the rifle in his lap and looked up the ramp at the twin turrets of the kopje. The rain had slackened to a drizzle.

Hendry was on top. Bruce knew he would go to the highest point. Strange how height makes a man feel invulnerable, makes him think he is a god.

And since he had fired upon them he must be in the turret nearest the vlei, which was slightly the higher of the two, its summit crowned by a patch of stunted broom bush.

So now I know exactly where he is and I will wait half an hour. He may become impatient and move; if he does I will get a shot at him from here.

Bruce narrowed his eyes, judging the distance.

'About two hundred yards.'

He adjusted the rear-sight of the FN and then checked the load, felt in the side pocket of his jacket to make sure the two extra clips of ammunition were handy, and settled back comfortably to wait.

'Curry, you sonofabitch, where are you?' Hendry's shout floated down through the drizzling rain and Bruce stiffened. *I was right – he's on top of the left-hand turret.*

'Come on, Bucko. I've been waiting for you since yesterday afternoon.'

Bruce lifted the rifle and sighted experimentally at a dark patch on the wall of the rock. It would be difficult shooting in the rain, the rifle slippery with wet, the fine drizzle clinging to his eyebrows and dewing the sights of the rifle with little beads of moisture.

'Hey, Curry, how's your little French piece of pussy? Man, she's hot, that thing, isn't she?'

Bruce's hands tightened on the rifle.

'Did she tell you how I gave her the old business? Did she tell you how she loved it? You should have heard her panting like a steam engine. I'm telling you, Curry, she just couldn't get enough!'

Bruce felt himself start to tremble. He clenched his jaws, biting down until his teeth ached.

Steady, Bruce my boy, that's what he wants you to do.

The trees dripped steadily in the silence and a gust of wind stirred the scrub on the slope of the kopje. Bruce waited, straining his eyes for the first hint of movement on the left-hand turret.

'You yellow or something, Curry? You scared to come on up here? Is that what it is?'

Bruce shifted his position slightly, ready for a snap shot.

'Okay, Bucko. I can wait, I've got all day. I'll just sit here thinking about how I mucked your little bit of French. I'm telling you it was something to remember. Up and down, in and out, man it was something!'

Bruce came carefully up on to his feet behind the trunk of the tree and once more studied the layout of the kopje.

If I can move up the slope, keeping well over to the side, until I reach the right-hand turret, there's a ledge there that will take me to the top. I'll be twenty or thirty feet from him, and at that range it will all be over in a few seconds.

He drew a deep breath and left the shelter of the tree.

Wally Hendry spotted the movement in the forest below him; it was a flash of brown quickly gone, too fast to get a bead on it.

He wiped the rain off his face and wriggled a foot closer to the edge.

'Come on, Curry. Let's stop buggering about,' he shouted, and cuddled the butt of his rifle into his shoulder. The tip of his tongue kept darting out and touching his lips.

At the foot of the slope he saw a branch move slightly, stirring when there was no wind. He grinned and snuggled his hips down on to the rock. *Here he comes*, he gloated, *he's crawling up, under the scrub*.

'I know you're sitting down there. Okay, Curry, I can wait also.'

Half-way up the slope the top leaves of another bush swayed gently, parting and closing.

'Yes!' whispered Wally, 'Yes!' and he clicked off the safety catch of the rifle. His tongue came out and moved slowly from one corner of his mouth to the other.

I've got him, for sure! There – he'll have to cross that piece of open ground. A couple a yards, that's all. But it'll be enough.

He moved again, wriggling a few inches to one side, settling his aim into the gap between two large grey boulders; he pushed the rate-of-fire selector on to rapid and his forefinger rested lightly on the trigger.

'Hey, Curry, I'm getting bored. If you are not going to come up, how about singing to me or cracking a few jokes?'

Bruce Curry crouched behind a large grey boulder. In front of him were three yards of open ground and then the shelter of another rock. He was almost at the top of the slope and Hendry had not spotted him. Across the patch of open ground was good cover to the foot of the right-hand turret.

It would take him two seconds to cross and the chances were that Hendry would be watching the forest at the foot of the slope.

He gathered himself like a sprinter on the starting blocks.

'Go!' he whispered and dived into the opening, and into a hell storm of bullets. One struck his rifle, tearing it out of his hand with such force that his arm was paralysed to the shoulder, another stung his chest, and then he was across. He lay behind the far boulder, gasping with the shock, and listened to Hendry's voice roaring triumphantly.

'Fooled you, you stupid bastard! Been watching you all the way up from the bottom.'

Bruce held his left arm against his stomach; the use of it was returning as the numbness subsided, but with it came the ache. The top joint of his thumb had caught in the trigger guard and been torn off; now the blood welled out of the stump thickly and slowly, dark blood the colour of apple jelly. With his right hand he groped for his handkerchief.

'Hey, Curry, your rifle's lying there in the open. You might need it in a few minutes. Why don't you go out and fetch it?'

Bruce bound the handkerchief tightly round the stump of his thumb and the bleeding slowed. Then he looked at the rifle where it lay ten feet away. The foresight had been knocked off, and the same bullet that had amputated his thumb had smashed into the breech, buckled the loading handle and the slide. He knew that it was damaged beyond repair.

'Think I'll have me a little target practice,' shouted Hendry from above, and again there was a burst of automatic fire. Bruce's rifle disappeared in a cloud of dust and flying rock fragments and when it cleared the woodwork of the rifle was splintered and torn and there was further damage to the action.

Well, that's that, thought Bruce, *rifle's wrecked, Shermaine has the pistol, and I have only one good hand. This is going to be interesting.*

He unbuttoned the front of his jacket and examined the welt that the bullet had raised across his chest. It looked like a rope burn, painful and red, but not serious. He rebuttoned his jacket.

'Okay, Bruce Baby, the time for games is over. I'm coming down to get you.' Hendry's voice was harsh and loud, filled with confidence.

Bruce rallied under the goading of it. He looked round quickly. *Which way to go? Climb high so he must come up to get at you. Take the right-hand turret, work round the side of it and wait for him on the top.*

In haste now, spurred by the dread of being the hunted, he scrambled to his feet and dodged away up the slope, keeping his head down using the thick screen of rock and vegetation.

He reached the wall of the right-hand turret and followed it round, found the spiral ledge that he had seen from below and went on to it, up along it like a fly on a wall, completely exposed, keeping his back to the cliff of granite, shuffling sideways up the eighteen-inch ledge with the drop below him growing deeper with each step.

Now he was three hundred feet above the forest and could look out across the dark green land to another row of kopjes on the horizon. The rain had ceased but the cloud was unbroken, covering the sky.

The ledge widened, became a platform and Bruce hurried across it round the far shoulder and came to a dead end. The ledge had petered out and there was only the drop below. He had trapped himself on the side of the turret – the summit was unattainable. If Hendry descended to the forest floor and circled the kopje he would find Bruce completely at his mercy, for there was no cover on the narrow ledge. Hendry could have a little more target practice.

Bruce leaned against the rock and struggled to control his breathing. His throat was clogged with the thick saliva of exhaustion and fear. He felt tired and helpless, his thumb throbbed painfully and he lifted it to examine it once more. Despite the tourniquet it was bleeding slowly, a wine-red drop at a time.

Bleeding! Bruce swallowed the thick gluey stuff in his throat and looked back along the way he had come. On the grey rock the bright red splashes stood out clearly. He had laid a blood spoor for Hendry to follow.

All right then, perhaps it is best this way. At least I may be able to come to grips with him. If I wait behind this shoulder until he starts to cross the platform, there's a three hundred foot drop on one side, I may be able to rush him and throw him off.

Bruce leaned against the shoulder of granite, hidden from the platform, and tuned his ears to catch the first sound of Hendry's approach.

The clouds parted in the eastern sector of the sky and the sun shone through, slanting across the side of the kopje.

It will be better to die in the sun, thought Bruce, *a sacrifice to the Sun god thrown from the roof of the temple*, and he grinned without mirth, waiting with patience and with pain.

The minutes fell like drops into the pool of time, slowly measuring out the ration of life that had been allotted to him. The pulse in his ears counted also, and his breath that he drew and held and gently exhaled – how many more would there be?

I should pray, he thought, *but after this morning when I prayed that it should not rain, and the rains came and saved me, I will not presume again to tell the Old Man how to run things. Perhaps he knows best after all.*

Thy will be done, he thought instead, and suddenly his

nerves jerked tight as a line hit by a marlin. The sound he had heard was that of cloth brushing against rough rock.

He held his breath and listened, but all he could discern was the pulse in his ears and the wind in the trees of the forest below. The wind was a lonely sound.

Thy will be done, he repeated without breathing, and heard Hendry breathe close behind the shoulder of rock.

He stood away from the wall and waited. Then he saw Hendry's shadow thrown by the early morning sun along the ledge. A great distorted shadow on the grey rock.

Thy will be done. And he went round the shoulder fast, his good hand held like a blade and the weight of his body behind it.

Hendry was three feet away, the rifle at high port across his chest, standing close in against the cliff, the cup-shaped steel helmet pulled low over the slitty eyes and little beads of sweat clinging in the red-gold stubble of his beard. He tried to drop the muzzle of the rifle but Bruce was too close.

Bruce lunged with stiff fingers at his throat and he felt the crackle and give of cartilage. Then his weight carried him on and Hendry sprawled backwards on to the stone platform with Bruce on top of him.

The rifle slithered across the rock and dropped over the edge, and they lay chest to chest with legs locked together in a horrible parody of the love act. But in *this* act we do not procreate, we destroy!

Hendry's face was purple and swollen above his damaged throat, his mouth open as he struggled for air, and his breath smelt old and sour in Bruce's face.

With a twist towards the thumb Bruce freed his right wrist from Hendry's grip and, lifting it like an axe, brought it down across the bridge of Hendry's nose. Twin jets of blood spouted from the nostrils and gushed into his open mouth.

With a wet strangling sound in his throat Hendry's body

arched violently upwards and Bruce was thrown back against the side of the cliff with such force that for a second he lay there.

Wally was on his knees, facing Bruce, his eyes glazed and sightless, and the strangling rattling sound spraying from his throat in a pink cloud of blood. With both hands he was fumbling his pistol out of its canvas holster.

Bruce drew his knees up on to his chest, then straightened his legs in a mule kick. His feet landed together in the centre of Hendry's stomach, throwing him backwards off the platform. Hendry made that strangled bellow all the way to the bottom, but at the end it was cut off abruptly, and afterwards there was only the sound of the wind in the forest below.

For a long time, drained of strength and the power to think, Bruce sat on the ledge with his back against the rock.

Above him the clouds had rolled aside and half the sky was blue. He looked out across the land and the forest was lush and clean from the rain. *And I am still alive*. The realization warmed Bruce's mind as comfortably as the early sun was warming his body. He wanted to shout it out across the forest. *I am still alive!*

At last he stood up, crossed to the edge of the cliff and looked down at the tiny crumpled figure on the rocks below. Then he turned away and dragged his beaten body down the side of the turret.

It took him twenty minutes to find Wally Hendry in the chaos of broken rock and scrub below the turret. He lay on his side with his legs drawn up as though he slept. Bruce knelt beside him and drew his pistol from the olive-green canvas holster; then he unbuttoned the flap of Hendry's bulging breast pocket and took out the white canvas bag.

He stood up, opened the mouth of the bag and stirred the diamonds with his forefinger. Satisfied, he jerked the drawstring closed and dropped them into his own pocket.

In death he is even more repulsive than he was alive, thought Bruce without regret as he looked down at the corpse.

The flies were crawling into the bloody nostrils and clustering round the eyes.

Then he spoke aloud.

'So Mike Haig was right and I was wrong – you can destroy it.'

Without looking back he walked away. The tiredness left him.

– 34 –

Carl Engelbrecht came through the doorway from the cockpit into the main cabin of the Dakota.

'Are you two happy?' he asked above the deep drone of the engines, and then grinning with his big brown face, 'I can see you are!'

Bruce grinned back at him and tightened his arm around Shermaine's shoulders.

'Go away! Can't you see we're busy?'

'You've got lots of cheek for a hitch-hiker – bloody good mind to make you get out and walk,' he grumbled as he sat down beside them on the bench that ran the full length of the fuselage. 'I've brought you some coffee and sandwiches.'

'Good. Good. I'm starving.' Shermaine sat up and reached for the thermos flask and the greaseproof paper packet. The bruise on her cheek had faded to a shadow with yellow edges – it was almost ten days old. With his mouth full of chicken sandwich Bruce kicked one of the wooden cases that were roped securely to the floor of the aircraft.

'What have you got in these, Carl?'

'Dunno,' said Carl and poured coffee into the three plastic mugs. 'In this game you don't ask questions. You fly out, take your money, and let it go.' He drained his mug and stood up. 'Well, I'll leave you two alone now. We'll be in Nairobi in a couple of hours, so you can sleep or something!' He winked. 'You'll have to stay aboard while we refuel. But we'll be airborne again in an hour or so, and the day after tomorrow, God and the weather permitting, we'll set you down in Zurich.'

'Thanks, old cock.'

'Think nothing of it – all in the day's work.'

He went forward and disappeared into the cockpit, closing the door behind him.

Shermaine turned back to Bruce, studied him for a moment and then laughed.

'You look so different – now you look like a lawyer!'

Self-consciously Bruce tightened the knot of his Old Michaelhouse tie.

'I must admit it feels strange to wear a suit and tie again.' He looked down at the well-cut blue suit – the only one he had left – and then up again at Shermaine.

'And in a dress I hardly recognize you either.' She was wearing a lime-green cotton frock, cool and crisp looking, white high-heel shoes and just a little make-up to cover the bruise. A damn fine woman, Bruce decided with pleasure.

'How does your thumb feel?' she asked, and Bruce held up the stump with its neat little turban of adhesive tape.

'I had almost forgotten about it.'

Suddenly Shermaine's expression changed, and she pointed excitedly out of the perspex window behind Bruce's shoulder.

'Look, there's the sea!' It lay far below them, shaded from blue to pale green in the shallows, with a round of white beach and the wave formation moving across it like ripples on a pond.

'That's Lake Tanganyika.' Bruce laughed. 'We've left the Congo behind.'

'Forever?' she asked.

'Forever!' he assured her.

The aircraft banked slightly, throwing them closer together, as Carl picked out his landmarks and altered course towards the north-east.

Four thousand feet below them the dark insect that was their shadow flitted and hopped across the surface of the water.